THE LIEUTENANT'S SECRET LOVE

CHARLESTON BRIDES ~ BOOK 5

ELVA COBB MARTIN

Copyright © 2023 Elva Cobb Martin

All rights reserved. No portion of this book may be reproduced or transmitted in any form or by any means - photocopied, shared electronically, scanned, stored in a retrieval system, or other - without the express permission of the publisher. Exceptions will be made for brief quotations used in critical reviews or articles promoting this work.

The characters and events in this fictional work are the product of the author's imagination. Any resemblance to actual people, living or dead, is coincidental.

Unless noted otherwise, Scripture quotations are taken from the Holy Bible, Kings James Version.

ISBN-13: 978-1-942265-69-6

This book is dedicated to all those who have had shocking things happen in their lives and wonder if any part of them can ever work out for their good.

"And we know that all things work together for good to them that love God, to them who are called according to His purpose."

— *ROMANS 8:28* THE HOLY BIBLE, KING JAMES VERSION

ACKNOWLEDGMENTS

I am forever grateful for my prayer partners who pray regularly for my writing. These include Sandra Fowler, my two sisters, Sonya and Phyllis, my husband Dwayne, writing friends Libby Reed and Colleen Hall, my pastor Rev. Phil Sears and members at Freedom Center Assembly of God church we attend. In addition, we request and receive regular prayer for the writing from three ministry partners: Kenneth Copeland Ministries, Charles Capps Ministries, and Rick Renner Ministries.

I give a hearty thanks to my talented publisher, Misty Beller, and all her editorial assistants at Wild Heart Books for taking my efforts and polishing them into something much finer.

Most of all I thank my heavenly Father and Lord and Savior Jesus Christ and the Holy Spirit who continue to be with me, inspiring new stories, energizing, and keeping me on task.

The Barbary Coast

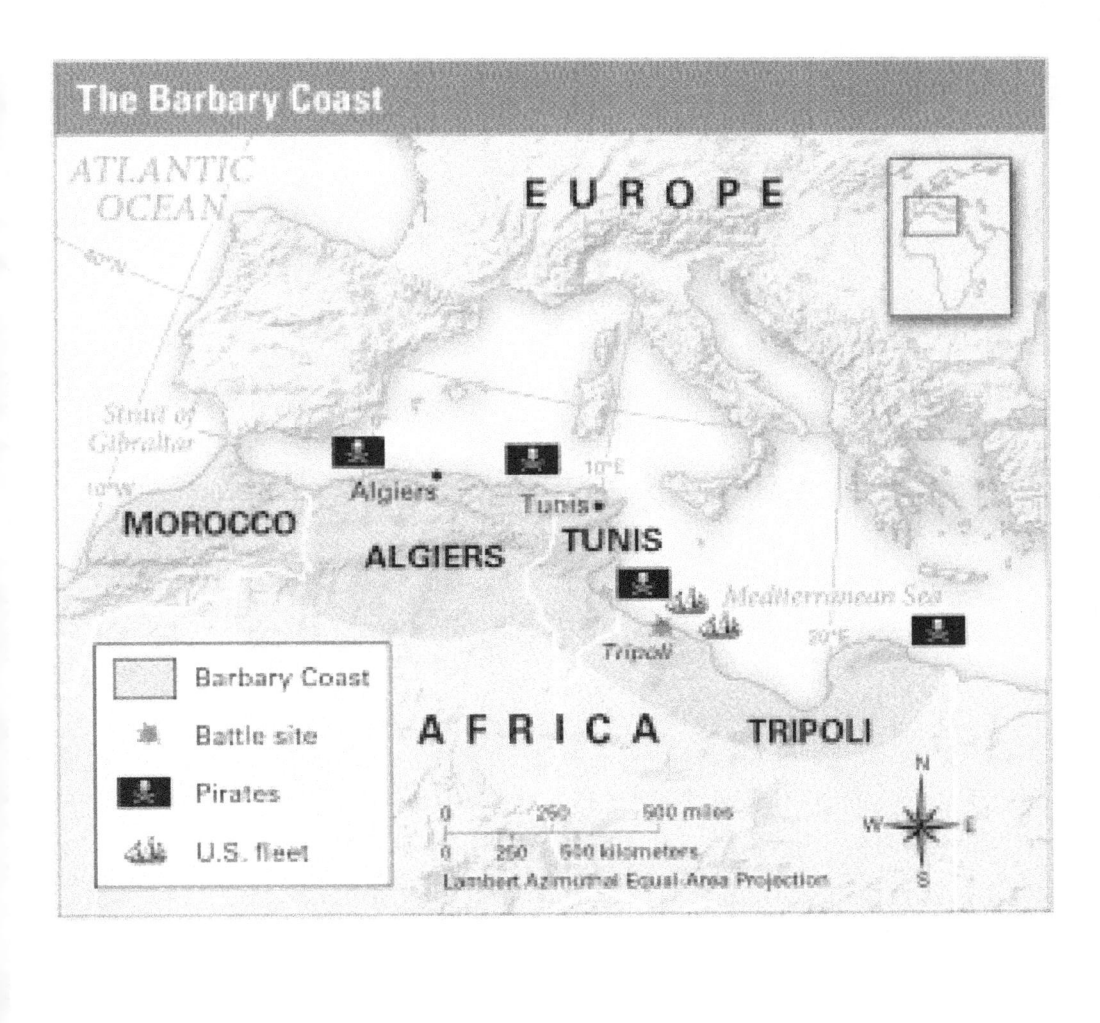

- Barbary Coast
- Battle site
- Pirates
- U.S. fleet

PROLOGUE

Charleston, 1784

The dark lines of the master's brow and his loud, drunken command shot tremors through Ezekiel as he stood in the doorway of the master's study. Cuddling the newborn wrapped in a blanket in his bony black arms, he lowered his head, and a long, heavy breath gushed from his lips.

"I said, take that baby and leave it far out in the woods to die. I'll not have another female in my house. This 'pose to be a *son*." Carter Seymour's harsh words echoed through the plantation house. He sat forward behind his desk and pointed his finger. "You hear me, boy? Don't think I'm too drunk to mean this." He slumped back in his chair where he'd spent the night as his wife struggled to give birth before she died.

"But, sirrah. She's a healthy one. A real blessing on this Good Friday." Ezekiel's large hands shook as he held the small bundle. He bent his gray head to look once more at the girl child with her curly blond wisp of hair, wrapped in a lacy white baby blanket with a *C* and *S* embroidered on one corner. "I'se real sorry about Miz Seymour. And look, this baby's got that crooked little finger just like her mama." He held up a little hand with its miniature fingers spread. The smallest finger on the left hand bent at the middle joint.

Seymour's eyes widened when he saw the peculiar trait of his wife's. "Take it out of my house. I never want to see it again," he thundered, and reached for his whiskey bottle. The child stiffened at the loud, angry words, and Ezekiel clasped her closer. The little one whimpered and pushed a tiny fist toward her rosebud mouth. Her face wrinkled, and she began to cry.

Turning, he stumbled out the door, shaken in mind and heart. He had no choice but to obey his master. His old heart hammered in his chest and made his legs heavy and slow.

Ezekiel passed down the long hall lined with servants who'd heard the master's command and the babe now weeping. The maids and footmen stared at him with rounded eyes and stunned faces.

He walked through to the kitchen where his wife Molly stood wringing her hands. Tears streamed down her face. She handed him a sugar tit she had dipped in milk. Ezekiel gave it to the baby, whose tiny mouth stopped in the middle of a mewling sound and latched onto the little ball of old linen with a spoonful of sandy sugar gathered in its center. He headed out the back entrance of the large house and swiped a tear that trickled down his cheek before it dripped from his chin onto the little one in his arms.

Leaving the plantation grounds, he trudged deep into the woods. Scents of pine, sweet cedar, and the damp, earthy smell of decomposing leaves flowed around him and the child. The morning sun moved higher in the sky with the promise of more heat to come. He pulled a handkerchief from his pocket and wiped the sweat from his brow.

The baby slept after the sugar tit ran out, but soon awakened and cried. He fell down on his knees next to a dirt road at the edge of the forest. "Lord Jesus, you knows I don't want this baby to die. I ain't no murderer. I needs your help. I'se in a terrible place on this Good Friday 'fore yo' Resurrection, Lord. Show me what to do."

The squeaking wheels of a wagon and clip-clop of horses' hooves approaching interrupted his prayer. Quickly, he placed the little bundle up against the trunk of a large oak that sheltered the roadway. The baby cried in earnest when his arms no longer held her. Ezekiel scrambled behind some bushes.

A surprised feminine voice rang out. "John, will thee stop the wagon? I'm sure I hear a baby crying."

Ezekiel peeked from his concealed spot. A bonneted woman in a plain gray dress with a white collar sat in the wagon holding a sleeping child in her arms. Another youngster rode on the wagon floor at her feet, clutching her skirt with one hand, sucking a thumb with the other.

"And it's not our Michael or Adam." The mother lifted her eyes and searched the shaded forest and wild growth encroaching on the roadway.

"Could be a baby goat, you know, caught in a vine or something," the man holding the reins replied.

"I believe it's a baby. Will thou please go search, husband?"

The man stopped the wagon and climbed down. He walked toward the large oak.

Ezekiel pushed back into the undergrowth, not daring to breathe.

"A baby, for sure, dear Sarah, and it looks like a newborn," the man called out. He bent and picked up the bundle with care and looked into the tiny porcelain-like face. The crying stopped. "And it's got violet eyes, the like of which I've never seen." The next moment heartrending cries again pierced the morning air. The husband hurried back to the wagon, shaking his head. "Who in tarnation would leave this tiny, helpless one out here in the woods?"

His wife laid her own sleeping child in the basket beside the toddler at her feet and reached for the infant. As it began to cry again, she rocked it in her arms. "I do believe it's a newborn and its probably hungry." She touched the snowy blanket and fingered the lace. "Its coverlet denotes it to be from rich folk." She opened her bodice and pressed the little one to her bosom, and suckling sounds and the gentle whisper of the wind in the trees replaced the cries of the child.

The toddler boy at her feet pulled himself up by grasping her skirt. He reached a pudgy hand out to pat the bundle with gentle care. "Babee? Babee not cry now?"

His mother smiled at him. "Baby happy now, dear Adam, and it looks as though thee may have a new sister or brother." The boy patted the small bundle again and laid his head on her knee. She called out to her husband. "Thee should see if thee can find anyone about."

The man looked up and down the road and walked a distance along the sides. "Hullo, is anyone out there?" He peered into the trees and called out several times.

Ezekiel shrank into the shadows.

The woman spoke from the wagon. "Will thou take us home, John White? Someone did not want this wee one, but God saw fit to have us come along in time to save it." She pulled back the blanket, and a joyous cry broke from her lips. "It's a girl. What a blessing for us to finally have a lassie after losing our Hannah. God has sent a replacement on this Good Friday, of all days. Shall we call her Hannah after our poor lost lamb the Lord has in His good care?"

The man smiled and nodded, swung back up into the wagon, and snapped the reins on the backs of the two horses. "Home, my four-footed friends, home."

The horses moved forward at a brisk pace, as if they understood the word.

Ezekiel stood from behind the bushes and wiped the tears from his cheeks. He raised his hands toward heaven. "Thank ye, Lord. Thank ye."

CHAPTER 1

Sixteen years later (1800)

Hannah White rode her mare, Bella, through the forest to the secret place she loved, a hidden pool with moss-covered banks where deer and her other animal friends came to drink. No human had ever appeared at her special spot, but many animals came. She could spend hours sitting and watching the parade of thirsty creatures. Besides deer, a raccoon and a fox often came by, as well as several kinds of birds. They would fill the nearby trees and move lower and lower in the branches, ever watchful of her, before hopping to the edge of the water to sip a drink.

She dismounted, laid her head against the shoulder of Bella for a loving moment and patted the mare, then tied the reins on a tree branch. She sat in her favorite spot on a rock, allowing a good view of the lake's colorful visitors.

As the sun climbed higher and the animals finished drinking, she undid her braided hair, wiped the perspiration from her brow, and slipped out of her boots and muslin dress. She gasped as she stepped into the cool, shadowed pool. The refreshing wetness wrapped around her feet and rose to her waist as she walked farther in, soaking her petticoat and chemise, which she didn't mind. She'd lie on the mossy hillside until they dried before returning home.

Today was a glorious summer day, but most happy because her older brother, Adam, would return from his two-year navy stint at sea, battling Barbary pirates attacking American merchant ships. How she'd missed her strong, cheerful, handsome sibling.

She emerged from the water and sat on a warm, moss-covered rock. After squeezing the excess moisture from her thick tresses, she lay on her back to dry her underclothing. Drowsiness pressed against her eyelids.

Her horse's neigh and the sound of hoof beats coming near roused her, and she sat up, her heart hammering, her mouth dry. No one ever came this far into the wood.

To her dismay, a horse and rider appeared in front of her before she could reach for her dress. And not an ordinary horse or person. The beautiful, glossy black stallion lowered his head and sniffed in her direction with pricked, fine-shaped ears. The young man in the saddle, dressed in a green silk waistcoat and breeches, grinned at her, and his eyes devoured her.

Heat flooded her cheeks at being seen in her undergarments. She jumped up and tried to move around the horse and rider to fetch her dress, but the man reined the animal to block her path.

"Sir, I beg of you. Let me pass."

"Why should I, you lovely forest nymph?" Pride and daring laced his voice.

She placed her hand on the velvet nose of the horse and whispered to him. The animal moved back, but the rider swung down from the saddle, grabbed her around the waist, and pulled her to him.

Hannah pushed him away. He fell back against his mount, and the horse snorted.

She slipped past them both and reached for her dress. But as she bent to retrieve it, he caught her from behind.

He turned her about and tried to kiss her.

She kicked his shins and scratched his cheek.

The young man cursed and twisted her arm behind her back. "Now I have you, little tigress, and you will not escape this time."

She cried out in pain.

He pressed her close and looked into her face. "What? Violet eyes? I've never seen such."

"Turn her loose, you scoundrel, or you'll see death like you've never seen before either." Her brother Adam's firm voice, with iron-like authority, made her heart fly.

Thank you, Lord.

Dressed in his smart, blue-and-white American naval uniform with its lieutenant insignia across his shoulders, Adam burst through the trees with a drawn pistol gripped in his wide, tanned hand.

Her attacker released his hold on her and faced the newcomer. The surprise blanketing his youthful face stiffened into haughtiness. He adjusted his silk waistcoat and frowned. "Who do you think you are, *sailor*?" He spit out the last word with derision. "Get off my property. I'm Saul Seymour, and this is Seymour Plantation land you're trespassing on."

"No, it's not. This spot belongs to my father, John White. He tenant farms for Drayton Plantation." Adam lowered his pistol and grinned at the young man, as if he were dealing with a misbehaving child.

Hannah slid her dress over her head, pulled on her boots, and hurried to stand beside her brother.

"We'll see about that, you squid." With one more furious glance at Adam, Saul Seymour turned on his heel and mounted his horse. He pressed his legs into the animal's sides and galloped away.

Hannah sighed. "Adam, I'm glad you came along when you did." She reached up and hugged his thick, corded neck. "And we're so glad to have you home. Mama and Papa will be most happy."

Adam pulled her arms from around his neck and looked into her face, frowning. "Are you all right, little sister? Did he harm you?"

"No, I'm fine." She gave him a big smile to relieve his worry. "You know, I think Saul Seymour is about my age, and probably spoiled and been given everything he's ever wanted. He's another of the Lord's many lost sheep."

"Now don't you go excusing the rascal, you tender-hearted one." Adam picked up his sailor's ditty bag where he'd dropped it and hefted it to his shoulder.

She mounted her horse, and they started toward home at a comfortable pace.

"Hannah, would you promise me not to come out alone anymore this far from the house?" The tone of Adam's question made her anything but comfortable.

～

Hannah looked down at him from her saddle with the wide, innocent violet eyes Adam knew well. It had probably never occurred to her to be afraid or worry when immersed in the wonderland of nature she loved.

"Why?" Her voice was both playful and serious.

"I don't think we've seen the last of Saul Seymour."

The frown stayed glued on his face despite his effort to relax it. Besides the shock of the scene he'd just walked up on, he couldn't stop thinking about how Hannah had grown up in his absence. He'd left her two years earlier as a thin waif of a girl, more bones than flesh and thick, unruly hair neither she nor their mother seemed able to keep managed for more than a few minutes.

The girl who'd just thrown her arms around his neck was a woman with curves in all the right places. Her hair had become the color of sweet sorghum syrup that glistened like gold when it caught a ray of sunshine blazing over the trees. She was, in fact, the beautiful young woman he'd dreaded her becoming—and local, unscrupulous men discovering. To make matters worse, his sister appeared unaware of her charms. How could he protect her when the long stints at sea took him away from their family's small farm? Especially when she was determined to be a free spirit traipsing over the countryside.

The two of them reached the yard of the cottage, with Hannah

THE LIEUTENANT'S SECRET LOVE

astride the mare and Adam walking alongside, shouldering his thick bag. A baby goat skipped from behind a shed to Hannah as soon as she dismounted. "Hello, there, Rupert. Are you glad I'm back?" She bent, picked the creature up, and hugged him and then set him back down. He playfully butted at her leg with the soft horn nubs barely visible on his head. She walked toward the stable, leading her mare.

A cry came from the kitchen window, and Adam's mother, Sarah, came running out to them. "Adam, my son. Thee made it home safe."

He dropped his sailor's sack and opened his arms to embrace her. "Thanks to yours and Papa's prayers, Mama."

Their freed house servants, Mammy and her thirteen-year-old daughter, stood on the porch looking on and smiling. He walked up and hugged Mammy, who'd helped raise him. She patted his muscled arm. "Lawsey me, Master John. You done got thick and hard. What kinda work they give you on them ships?"

"Way too much, Mammy, that's for sure." He grinned at Ada. "And you've grown at least a foot taller, young'un."

The girl's face crinkled into a smile.

The evening meal proved a blessed affair with his family that he'd looked forward to for months. Hannah and his younger brother, Michael, sat on either side of him at the wooden table. His mother and father took their usual seats across from them.

Papa led in the blessing. "Father God, we thank You for bringing our son Adam back safe. We ask you to bless this food now and keep us strong for our labors and Your kingdom work. Amen."

His father's strong English voice made Adam grin. John White certainly knew how to pay a brief prayer when folks were hungry. His mother had married him out of her faith and was discharged from the Quaker meeting as result. She attended her husband's Congregationalist church with her husband and children, and taught them righteous living to the best of her ability. Although Adam did not practice her Quaker faith, he dearly loved and honored his mother. As did Michael and Hannah.

Steamed cabbage, creamed corn, and baked chicken had never tasted so good to him. He ate two wedges of his mother's hot corn-

9

bread still in its iron skillet. How he'd missed his mother's cooking aboard ship.

After the meal, Michael, especially, wanted to hear about every port Adam's ship had sailed to and whatever adventures had come his way. He planned to join the navy after his eighteenth birthday, coming up in two months.

His father smoked a pipe and listened with few interruptions.

Mammy, her husband, Samson, and daughter, Ada—who made their home above the stables—sat in the kitchen doorway, their faces glowing at the invitation to hear Adam's stories too.

Hannah dropped on the braided rug at Adam's feet. Her bright eyes didn't leave his face as he related exciting—often frightening—adventures of his time at sea.

He took a deep breath. "It's been an interesting two years serving in the Marines on navy ships, and I've still got some time to serve that I look forward to. But I have decided one thing. I don't think I'll sign back up when my term ends."

His father sat forward. "You already know this, son? What do you have in mind for the future?"

"I have a dream of becoming a lawyer, Papa." There, he'd said it. Saying it gave it substance.

Hannah stared into his face. "I think it's great to have a dream, dear brother."

Michael shook his head. "I can't wait to make the navy my career."

His mother smiled, laid her sewing in the basket at her feet, and announced. "Now, children, thee may stay up as long as thou wantest to, but remember, it's still a workday tomorrow and the harvest won't wait."

His father grunted an assent, stood, and knocked the burned ashes from his pipe into the fireplace. The servants left by the back door.

∼

The next few weeks passed quickly for Adam as corn, wheat, and vegetables made it from the fields and garden into the barns or to the kitchen larder. He made the most of the three months' leave he had to help with the harvest. He also bought a pistol for Hannah and trained her how to use it. Another gift he found for her brought even more joy—a mixed mastiff puppy that should grow into a huge guard dog. The pup had sustained several injuries before being abandoned by its owner, but Hannah's gift for healing soon had him mended. She named the pup Hercules, and the two of them became instant friends and inseparable.

Despite his warnings, Hannah continued her visits to her wooded, happy places after she completed her day's work or at the crack of dawn before it began.

One day, she came back from a long jaunt with the half-grown puppy at her heels and confided to Adam. "I see no one, but I have the feeling at times I'm being watched."

He placed his hands on her small shoulders, and uneasiness creased his brow. "There, can you understand now why I'm asking you to please stop going so far out, dear sister?" He dropped his hands. "You're too pretty to be safe out there alone. How will I ever have peace about your safety when I have to go back to sea?"

She grinned. "All right, I promise to curtail my longer treks until Hercules grows up to help guard me. And I'll always ride Bella instead of walking. Will that make you happier?"

"Yes." He took a deep breath. "And I'll be praying daily for you, Hannah, to be wise and stay safe."

One morning after breakfast, three weeks before Adam's planned departure, two horses with riders pranced into the yard. His father opened the door and greeted the Seymour Plantation owner and his son, both dressed in silk waistcoats and polished black boots. When they dismounted and came up on the porch, he invited them into the sitting room, his face tight. His father had no dealings with the largest plantation owner in the parish. The Seymour Plantation was a neighbor to the Drayton estate, on which John White was a tenant farmer, but six hundred acres separated the two properties. They all sat in the simple, straight-backed chairs around the fireplace.

Hannah and their mother stayed in the adjoining kitchen with Mammy and her daughter. Michael was already at work in the south field with Samson.

After the usual pleasantries about weather and planting, Charles Seymour took charge of the conversation. His son had not said a single word, but he kept throwing glances at Adam.

"Now I guess you're wondering why we've come. Well, here it is." He gestured to his son, whose proud face brightened. "Saul here wants to take your daughter as his wife. I know they're both young, but she'll have everything she could want and one day will be mistress of Seymour Plantation. What do you say?"

Adam suppressed a snort, but his father's face turned pale.

Finally, Papa cleared his throat and spoke. "Sir, I cannot imagine why you've come here with such a request today. Hannah...will probably marry one day, but, as far I know, she doesn't even know your son." He cast a stiff glance at Saul as he spoke, and his voice was cold and exact.

Hannah stepped into the front room from the kitchen with their mother behind her. "Father, I've met Saul Seymour once." She eyed the young man. "And I have no desire whatsoever to marry him now or ever. I must decline."

Adam's heart swelled at Hannah's simple, confident response, but Saul smiled a strange smile at her, as if her words carried no weight.

Papa took a deep breath. "There, you have your answer, sir. Hannah will have the freedom to make her own choice of marriage partner when the time comes."

Charles Seymour frowned, and his already ruddy face went a shade darker red. "No, that's not the end of it, Mr. White." He stood and cracked his riding crop across his boot.

The loud, harsh sound caused Hannah to gasp and their mother to shudder. Adam clenched both his hands into fists.

"What do you mean, sir?" The slight tremor in his father's voice drew a quick glance from Adam. Seymour was nothing but a bully, maybe a wealthy one, but still a bully.

Adam stood. "You've heard my sister's response and my father's, sir. I don't think you and your son have any more business to conduct here."

Charles Seymour turned a hard, assessing eye on Adam. "Well, let's just see if I have." He walked to the window and tapped it with his riding crop. "Come see." He motioned to Adam and his father, and they stepped to the window. Seymour stood aside. Four riders on several sweating horses, stamping and neighing, entered the yard from the woods. Answering neighs sounded from the stable beyond the house.

His father's eyes widened, and Adam's nostrils flared as he peered at the scene. The riders milled about, armed with swords and muskets and carrying unlit torches—desperate men you could pay to do most anything, from the looks of their hard faces, their scraggly clothing, and their gaunt mounts.

A wicked smile creased Seymour's face but never met his hard eyes. "Yesterday I bought your tenant farm from Thomas Drayton. The girl comes with us, or we'll burn this place to the ground. The barns, too, and shoot the animals. You'll only escape with your lives."

Adam made a move to reach the musket hanging over the fireplace, but Charles pulled his pistol and barred his way. "I only have to give the men outside a thumbs up, and two of them will light their torches, and the others will begin shooting every animal on the place. You ready for that?"

CHAPTER 2

*H*annah cried out and fell at the man's feet. "No, please don't do any of that. I'll come." She burst into sobs, and young Hercules came to flop down beside her and whimper.

Adam gritted his teeth. He'd wrestle the gun away from the man and teach him a thing or two. And then he'd make short work of the son, if he were foolish enough to try and stop him. He balled his fists and stepped forward.

His mother had stood all this time quietly with her pale face perfectly still, not drawing back in fear. After lifting her hand toward Adam to stop him, she walked to a trunk in the corner. Rummaging down to the bottom, Sarah White brought out a baby blanket.

She turned to Charles Seymour and held the soft fabric up before him with the two embroidered initials, *C* and *S*, clearly in view. "Sir, doest thou recognize this baby blanket? Hannah is the baby girl we found wrapped in it sixteen years ago at the side of the road at the far back of your property. It was on Good Friday that year."

Charles Seymour's hard reddened face turned to chalk. He stumbled back into his chair.

Saul came to him. "Father, are you all right? Who cares how they found her as a baby? I want her." His petulant voice rose higher with the last phrase.

Charles brushed him away. "Girl, Hannah, show me your left hand." His voice came forth in a harsh whisper.

Hannah lifted her left hand with its bent little finger.

"Dear God. My dead wife's cursed finger. The daughter I abandoned is back to haunt me." Charles Seymour lowered his head into his hands.

Adam's breath caught in his lungs, and every muscle in his body tensed.

Hannah was not his blood sister?

Wiping the tears from her cheek, Hannah stared up at her mother, speechless. Had she heard right? Was the loving mother she'd always known *not her mother*? She wanted to stand and run to her and beg her to say it wasn't true, but her legs wouldn't work. Wave after wave of shock rocked her.

Then Adam was bending over her, reaching out his broad, warm hand. She took it and looked up into his face. His dark eyes held an expression she'd never seen before. Wonderment, tenderness? He lifted her to her feet.

Charles Seymour groaned and stood as well. He shook his head as if to clear it and then moved to the door as though his joints were the stiff ones of a much older man. He motioned for his son to follow.

Saul Seymour grabbed his father's arm. "Father, I don't know what this is all about, and I don't care. Why are we leaving without Hannah?"

"She's your half sister, son," his father roared and pushed out the door.

Saul followed, a thundercloud forming on his pale, oblong face. Curse words strung across the room behind him. "But that Abraham man in the Bible married his half sister."

Charles Seymour made no response. He plunged off the porch

and jerked the reins of Saul's horse from the hitching rail and cast them into his son's flushed face. They mounted their horses and headed away. The four other horsemen at the edge of the yard reined around and galloped behind them.

Hannah ran to her mother. "Mama, is it true? You're not my wonderful, precious mother? I don't think I can bear it. I certainly can't bear it if that...that man is my...?" She looked at her father and fresh moisture filled her eyes.

Sarah White put her arms around Hannah's shoulders. "There, there, child, thee will always be mine, and I will always be mother to thee, and John father to thee. But it's true. Thou are not our blood daughter."

Hannah broke away and ran up the narrow stairs to her room. She fell on her bed next to the window. Scalding tears rained down her cheeks and wet her pillow. Her breath came in gasping hitches until they subsided into hiccoughing sobs. No words came to her dazed mind to pray. But how she needed to pray.

Then her door opened, and a swishing skirt approached the bed, and her mother's sweet lavender scent flowed into the room.

Sarah White sat on the cot, and a soft hand touched Hannah's shoulder. "Thee is my precious daughter, child, that the Lord provided after we lost our other little one to the fever."

Hannah sat up and melted into her mother's embrace.

"Dear one, never have I been happier than the day we found thee and brought thee home. John and I will never forget that day. We believe God ordained it. And thee hast made all of us so happy all the years since."

Hannah lifted her head, swiped her damp cheeks with her sleeve, and sniffed. "You *found me*? Where?"

"On the side of the road crying thy precious heart out, and I'm glad you were, or we might never have heard and discovered thee."

"But that...man, Mr. Seymour...?" She could not ask the question.

"Yes, apparently, he is thy blood father, Hannah. The *C* and *S* on the blanket match his initials. I've often wondered about thy little crooked finger, but he said his first wife, I assume... thy birthing mother, had the same. Mayhap she died at thy birth, or thou would never have been abandoned. Who knows what went on in that home to prompt such an act?"

Hannah's eyes filled with fresh tears, and she held out her slender hand with its bent little finger. "But was that mother cursed? Am I also cursed by having this bent joint?"

Her mother grasped her extended hand. "No, no curse, my child. Jesus Christ became a curse for us on the tree. Dost thee not remember that scripture?" She took up both of Hannah's hands. "Besides, from the time thou was a child, I've felt thou hast healing in these hands, daughter. There's never been a sick or weak animal on the place thou hast not been able to help."

Hannah gulped back a sob. "But I don't want that man to be my father. Papa is my father."

Sarah White placed her firm hands on Hannah's shoulders. "Thee must have no fear. That man will probably never come here again. I'm so sorry thee had to learn of thy origin in such a shocking way. But I'm glad the truth is out. Thee canst go forward without fear now."

~

Downstairs, Adam couldn't relax and sit like his father, who had dropped into a chair as the sounds of the retreating horses grew faint. He paced across the living room like a caged animal, striking his fists together. "How hard for our Hannah to hear about her birth like this."

Glancing up the stairs, he could thank God his mother was doing her usual job of bringing peace. He no longer heard the gasping sobs that had torn forth from Hannah's throat when she fled from the room. That heartbreaking sound had poured hot lava through him, making him want to crush something...or kill someone. Taking a deep breath, he willed that murderous thought away. He was not on a navy vessel battling Barbary pirates pouring onto the deck with their scimitars. He was home with his family.

He rubbed his feverish brow, stopped pacing, and dropped into a chair beside his father. "I will never trust Saul Seymour to stay away from Hannah, even if he is her half brother. He's a complete rebel. We must do something, Papa. Before I have to leave again for duty. Have you any ideas?" His gravelly voice surprised even him.

Papa closed his eyes a moment, and his taunt face relaxed into its usual confident expression. "Yes, while you've been scurrying about like an angry tiger, son, I've been thinking. I agree we must do something, and I have an idea."

Adam took a deep breath. "Well, what is it?"

"I think it best we send Hannah to my sister in Charleston. Sophia has been a lonely widow now for five years and will welcome our Hannah, I'm sure of it. She'll be safe there for however long it takes, and can learn from her aunt all she knows about nursing the sick."

Adam jumped up. "A great idea. Hannah has always had a healing hand for whatever was ailing around the farm, even me and Michael with our scrapes and skinned knees. What an opportunity for her to learn how to minister to the ailing who come to Aunt Sophia for help." He faltered, frowning. "But isn't Aunt Sophia involved with more than ministering to the sick folk that come to her husband's old practice? Isn't she part of that high society the Rutledge family belongs to? Do you want to expose Hannah to that?"

His father hesitated. "Be that as it may, it's the best plan I can come up with, Adam."

Sarah White came down the stairs. "I heard thy idea, John, and I agree, though I'll miss our Hannah very much." She swept toward them and chose a chair. "Right now she just needs to recover from the shock she's had, then we can discuss it with her." She turned to Adam. "About the society goings on, have we not raised thy sister in the ways of the Lord and taught her how to make good choices?"

Adam lowered his head and released a heavy breath. "Yes, ma'am. That you have." His father rose and headed toward the back door. Adam followed him to the corn harvest in progress in the lower half of the tenant farm.

His heart throbbed with the shocking news that played over and over in his mind. Hannah, whom he'd guarded and loved since she was a toddler, was not his blood sister. He blinked his eyes. How could that idea fill him with a strange happiness or something like relief? Shouldn't he feel guilty for such feelings when she was so devastated? He shook off his disquieting thoughts and threw himself into the corn harvest alongside his papa.

~

*H*annah came down from her room for the mid-day meal and tried to keep up with the table talk, but finally, after a few bites, she laid her napkin aside and asked to be excused. She couldn't take all the eyes that kept turning her way, especially Adam's, that held some sort of question burning in their depths. She hurried out the front door to her animal friends outside. They always brought her peace and a sense of well-being. Her father's hunting dogs lifted their heads from their sleeping spots on the porch and stared at her, waiting for a pat.

The baby goat born a week earlier scampered up to her, and the flock of clucking bantams ran toward her as soon as she stepped off the porch. She threw corn from her pocket to the chickens, then bent to pick up the small black-and-white goat she'd named Rupert. She hugged him and kissed him on the top of his soft head. "Hello, little one." He nudged her cheek with his velvet muzzle. "What a beauty you are, my little friend."

She sat him down and headed toward the stable. The barking beagles followed her, but she shooed them away before entering the stable. A neigh welcomed her from the cool interior. The smell of hay and horses brought a familiar calmness to her.

She led Bella into the corridor and strapped the lovely English saddle on her back, Adam's birthday gift when she'd turned sixteen the past year. In a matter of minutes, she was astride the frisky filly and pacing along the borders of the lower fields of corn and oats.

The breeze lifted her hair, and she took deep breaths of the fresh air. But nothing so far—not even the clear sunlight baptizing her entire view of the farm with golden hues and the plethora of birdsong—lifted the weight that seemed stuck somewhere in her middle. Every time her mind wandered back to the shocking revelation of the morning, moisture gathered in her eyes.

True to her promise to Adam not to venture far from the home place, she finally reined Bella around and trotted home. She spent the rest of the day doing whatever her hand found to do, familiar things that took little thought. She assisted her mother and Mammy with cleaning and food preparation. Both her mother and the black woman who'd cared for her and her brothers from the time they were babies gave her gentle glances and asked little of her. Mammy surely knew what had taken place that morning, but she didn't ask a single question, for which Hannah was grateful.

After supper, as was their habit, all the family sat around the living area to talk—her father and brothers about the ongoing harvest, while she and her mother completed needlework. She couldn't help but feel the warm glances that her family cast her way, but she kept her eyes lowered, hoping she'd not burst into tears.

At the meal, her father had told her of their plan for her to go to Aunt Sophia's as soon as they could get a message to her and a response. But how could she leave the farm and all her animal friends? Who would help her mother and Mammy finish picking, preparing, and storing the vegetables for winter? Question after question bombarded her thoughts.

Her mind in too much turmoil for her to produce neat stitches, she laid aside her embroidery, walked out to the porch, and dropped into a rocker. Adam followed and took the chair next to hers.

"Hannah, I know you'll still fretting over what happened this morning. But can I tell you something?" He sat forward, his piercing gray eyes as serious as she'd ever seen them.

"Of course." Whatever was on his mind? Since he'd gone into the American navy two years earlier, she hardly knew him anymore. Was this to be something to surprise her or shock her about his sailing adventures?

"I'm sorry you had to hear about your birth like you did. But it doesn't change a thing as far as our family is concerned." He laid his hand on top of hers on the rocking chair arm and searched her face.

A breath caught in her throat at the affection shining in his gaze.

"You are still as much a part of us as you've always been. Nothing can change that. Do you understand?"

Moisture gathered in her eyes, and she lowered her head. "But everything's changed. You and I are not brother and sister anymore. And that terrible man is supposed to be my..." Her voice broke.

He squeezed her hand. "Trust me, Hannah, everything is going to be all right. Look up at me. Will you?"

She turned to him and tried to blink back tears, but one slipped down her cheek, and she swiped it away.

"A scripture in the book of Romans comes to mind. One of Mama's favorite texts. I know you remember it. It declares that all things work together for the good of those who love God, those called according to His purpose. Will you believe that promise now?" He gave her hand a last pat and removed his own.

"I'll try but..."

"One good thing about all this that I need to tell you is that I'm glad you're not my sister." He leaned back in his chair and grinned, making the dimple she loved to tease him about appear on his chin.

She gasped. "Glad?"

"Yes." He took a deep breath. "Now we can be the best of friends. And I think you're going to love being at Aunt Sophia's." His eyes twinkled. "Not to mention, you'll be so much closer when my ship docks in the harbor."

"You'll come to visit?"

"Nothing can keep me away every chance I get. And will you keep writing to me when I'm gone, telling me what you and Aunt Sophia are doing in the famed city of Charleston?"

She nodded.

He grinned, the old grin she knew well. "Just don't let any of those fancy Charleston gentlemen she will introduce you to make you forget your old brother and writing to him. Do you promise?"

A smile crept across her lips.

21

"There, I thought you had that somewhere, and we just needed to flush it out."

Hannah still cried herself to sleep that night, but she slept soundly and for the next several nights. During the daytime, a weight like a rock lodged in her chest. She went about her tasks with her usual diligence but with little joy, knowing that her simple life with her family and animal friends would soon change. Aunt Sophia had sent a message that she'd be delighted to have Hannah come to her in Charleston whenever she was ready. Her entire life hung on the precipice of immense alteration.

When she awoke on a Saturday morning, one week after she'd learned the shocking story of her birth, her first breath was like a drink of refreshing water. She felt as if some part of sorrow had lifted from her heart and a ray of gladness entered. What kind of cheerfulness was this, and from what source?

She rose and began her morning ritual—bathing, dressing, and plaiting her hair and pinning it up. As she looked in the mirror to survey her finished efforts, it settled on her like a feather from heaven. Her family and even Mammy were praying hard for her. That was the source of her peace. Maybe Adam was correct. Everything was going to be all right. Who couldn't get excited about going to stay in Charleston with all the sights and exciting things to do she'd often heard her Aunt Sophia describe? And most important, she'd be able to study nursing under her father's sister, who still carried on much of her deceased husband's medical practice. Besides, anything and anywhere would be a welcome change if it would keep her from ever having to see the Seymours again.

As she descended the stairs, galloping hooves sounded on their hard-pressed dirt drive. The beagles jumped off the porch, and their loud barking filled the morning. She stopped to stare out the window at the landing. Two horsemen rode into the yard. Her heart fell to her feet, and her stomach roiled.

Charles Seymour and another man she'd never seen before dismounted and headed toward the porch.

CHAPTER 3

*H*annah hurried back upstairs as sheer black fright gripped her. What now? Would Charles Seymour use some other threat against her family to force her to go with him? She stopped at the top of the staircase and pressed into the shadows to listen, her stomach clenched into a knot.

Male voices in the yard cursed at the barking dogs, and heavy steps sounded on the porch, then a sharp knock.

The chairs at the breakfast table screeched as her father and Adam stood. Her father's light stride moved to the door, and he opened it. "Mr. Seymour? What can we do for you?"

How could he sound so cordial? Why didn't he just slam the door in the man's face? Then her heart smote her. How many times had she, Adam, and Michael been taught never to hate or even give a harsh response to an enemy? Her mother's Quaker faith made no allowance for either.

"Mr. White, this is my factor, Henry Petrie. We have something to discuss with you. May we come in?"

"Certainly. Take a chair. You'll remember my son, Adam."

She peeped into the living room from her hidden spot. Mr.

Seymour, dressed in a gray waistcoat and breeches and polished black boots, whipped off his hat and held it, his face stiff, unsmiling. The other man, middle-aged like Mr. Seymour, had a droopy face and paunch at his waist. She took in a deep, shaky breath and thanked God that Saul Seymour did not accompany them.

The visitors took the offered chairs, and all the men sat. Charles pulled a document from his pocket. He handed it to her father. "I am giving you the deed to this tenant farm. My factor here will witness the deed I've already signed." His voice sounded clipped, not the harsh, commanding voice of the earlier visit.

Hannah drew back and her mouth fell open. Why was he giving her father the deed to the farm? She could imagine the surprised glances between Papa and Adam. What kind of trick was the man pulling? Her body stiffened, and the blood rushed to her head so fast she felt faint. A new, tempting ploy to get her to go with them?

Adam responded first, as if he read her thoughts. "Why are you doing this, Mr. Seymour?" His harsh, unimpressed tone fell like footfalls on gravel to Hannah's ears. "If you think it will change our minds about our Hannah going with you—"

"No, no. That's not in my mind at all. By this document, I'm not admitting she's my daughter, mind you, but I just want to discharge my duty to her, in case she is. When you accept this deed, you confirm that none of you, not even Hannah, will ever apply to me or my estate for any kind of consideration. There's a place for your father and for Hannah to sign. And my factor will witness this transaction."

Hannah struggled to breathe in her hiding place on the stairs. What kind of man was this person who was supposed to be her father? How could he think she or her family would ever apply to them for anything? She'd hoped never to see him or Saul Seymour again. And why would he *really* give away a farm? Could the man be feeling his first fiery singe of guilt? Not likely. He probably hoped this would put pressure on her to give in and accept Saul.

"Well, this is a complete surprise." Papa cleared his throat. "But I can't say it's unpleasant. Let me see the deed."

Silence reigned.

She peeped from her place. Her father and Adam read what appeared to be a legal document. Adam had studied law. He'd surely see the lie and trickery involved. How could anything good come from a man who had abandoned his own flesh and blood?

Hannah prayed. *Oh, Lord, help my father not be deceived into any false agreement with Charles Seymour.*

Seymour spoke again. "You may ask me or my factor any question. I tell you, this is a perfectly good legal document, and it will give you and your descendants this tenant farm, including the one hundred acres, this cottage, the outbuildings, and all the animals."

Hannah pressed her head against the wall behind her, feeling faint again. What did this mean? Surely, what he proposed could not be a bona fide gift. Not from a man like Charles Seymour.

Her father's next words made her tremble. "Adam, I can't see anything amiss in this document. What about you? You've studied law."

She waited to hear Adam throw the document back in Charles Seymour's face. Just what the man deserved.

"I'm very surprised, Papa, but I have to agree. This, apparently, is just what Mr. Seymour says it is. A deed, free and clear, for the farm and its land, buildings, and animals." Adam's voice matched their father's in surprise and agreement.

Another voice entered the conversation. The factor? "Of course it is, Mr. White. And I'm glad both of you've seen it for what it is. I, for one, would witness no document that was not legal or in the best interest of those to whom I would be responsible to if I witness their signature. Mr. Seymour is giving you this farm freely, with no cost to you. Only a promise to never apply to his estate for further remuneration regarding your daughter." He cleared his throat. "I should say...his lost daughter. What do you say?"

Lost? *Abandoned,* she wanted to scream.

Hannah passed the next two weeks in a dream-like state but completed her normal chores, helping with meal preparation, tending the vegetable garden, collecting the eggs, and caring for her animal friends. She'd signed the document when her father and Adam both encouraged her to do so, but she still felt uneasy about it. Who could trust a man who had abandoned his child? Adam agreed and both her parents and her brother still felt she should go to her aunt's in Charleston.

She stood for fittings for needed new clothes to take with her. Her mother and Mammy sewed several new outfits in the plain dress of her mother's Quaker faith.

Dressing plain, her mother had explained to her years earlier, meant choosing subdued colors—grays, tans, olive green, and dark gold, and rejecting fancy trims or superfluous ornament. Solid colors were the norm, but there was no prohibition of costly fabrics. Hannah was not Quaker—she'd followed her father's Congregationalist faith, as did Adam and Michael—but she respected her mother's faith and never complained about her simple, modest dresses. She really liked the gold and the green dresses they made for her out of muslin and the one evening frock out of silk that Adam had brought home from his travels. Her brothers and father whistled when she modeled the finished clothing.

The day arrived for her departure to Aunt Sophia's and Adam to his ship. Her parents had decided he would accompany her to her aunt's before reporting to his navy ship in the harbor.

Hannah stood before the wagon loaded with her trunk and bags, trying her best not to burst into sobs as her mother gave her a last hug. "Thee will do well in Charleston, my daughter. We've taught thee right from wrong, so we do not fret. We will pray daily for thee to learn everything you can from your aunt and fulfill God's plan for thy life, if it be nursing." Her mother's voice broke. She kissed Hannah on both cheeks and stepped back. Pulling a handkerchief from her sleeve, she dabbed at her eyes.

Her father gave her a warm clasp in his brawny arms but said nothing. His eyes, bright with moisture, gave away his deep feelings.

Hannah's pet goat pushed at her gold skirt, and she bent to pet the frisky Rupert, who then frolicked away with another goat. She blinked back tears. At least she was taking Hercules with her.

Michael hugged her and tweaked the bow to her bonnet, since it hid her braids. "You'll love discovering Charleston, dear sister. I'm next to be leaving the old farm, so don't feel strange." Her brother had confirmed to the family two days earlier he'd be joining the navy in three weeks when he turned eighteen.

Adam, smart in his blue-and-white uniform, smiled and moved to thump Michael on his shoulder. "You've been determined to get aboard a navy vessel, brother, ever since I joined. I sure hope you don't regret it. It's a lot more work than play. My sage advice is to pray you don't get assigned on the *Enterprise* under my command."

Michael gave his brother's arm a hard thumping in return, and they both laughed.

Mammy and Ida brought a basket of food and a waterskin and sat them in the wagon. Their dark eyes shone with well wishes. Her second mother hugged Hannah. "Now, chile, you don't go a-worrying none. I knows you going to do good at whatever you sets your hand to. Just remember, old Mammy is praying for you every day. You hear?"

Hannah nodded and swiped at a tear that escaped down her cheek.

Adam threw his sailor's bag into the back of the wagon and turned to her. "We'd better get started if we want to make it before dark." He grinned at her and emitted a deafening whistle for Hercules. His confident voice and good cheer lifted the heaviness in her heart. Hercules burst from around the corner of the house, barking. Adam lifted the half-grown pup and placed him in the wagon. He tied a rope to his collar, then to the wagon post, and commanded the hound to sit on his old blanket spread for him. The dog sat, wagging his tail as if delighted to be going on a trip.

Next, he assisted Hannah into the wagon. His strong, broad hand clasped hers as she climbed aboard, and his warm, approving glance of her in her new dress and bonnet did more to bolster her peace and wellbeing than she'd thought possible. Adam swung up beside her, gripped the reins handed to him from Samson, clicked his tongue, and they were off at a fast pace.

Hannah did not look back in case she might lose her fragile emotional control as the wagon rumbled away toward the main road. She patted Hercules, who had thrust his head onto her lap, and set her thoughts on Adam beside her. The warmth and energy emanating from him gave her confidence and a measure of peace. That Adam would be on his ship in the nearby harbor as she spent her first night at her aunt's townhouse pleased her. How did a girl survive who didn't have a good brother like Adam White?

She stole a glance at him driving the horses and humming as if he hadn't a care in the world. His muscular physique, dark curly hair, handsome, tanned face with its thin mustache, and his confident attitude must be attractive to women in the ports he visited. But he'd never shared about those experiences, if he'd had them. He'd been gone so long on his last stint, she hardly recognized him as the same brother who'd teased her growing up.

Halfway to Charleston, Adam pulled the two horses and wagon off the road under a shade tree with an inviting log lying on the ground which looked as if it could serve as a bench. A brook trickled nearby. He drove the horses forward to the edge of the creek, and they sucked in the gurgling water. Then he jumped from the wagon and helped Hannah down. She stretched in the sunshine. What a joy to have a respite from the road.

Adam loosened the rope from Hercules's collar and set him on the ground. Then he stooped to talk to the dog. "You may run in the field yonder, boy, but no farther away. Do you understand? Or we just might leave you behind."

What if the half-grown dog might truly get lost? But he was off and running before Hannah could speak.

Again, Adam seemed to read her mind. He straightened and

turned toward her. " Dear Hannah, have no fear. That pup will not leave you long. Otherwise, I'd never released him. Now, let's have a picnic."

He removed his topcoat and pulled the basket and skin of water from the wagon. They sat on the log and enjoyed Mammy's fried chicken legs, buttered bread, baked sweet potato, and a golden apple each from their orchard that Hannah had helped pick, polish, and store for the winter. Before they finished their repast, Hercules loped back and begged for his share.

When it was time to climb back into the wagon, instead of taking her hand, Adam circled her waist with his large hands and lifted her up to the seat. She gasped at how easily he sat her in place.

"Hey, you smell of lavender. Am I right?"

She nodded, still finding it hard to breathe since he'd lifted her as if she were a feather. And she grappled with his spicy manly scent she'd never noticed before. How little she really knew about this lieutenant brother of hers.

They entered Charleston when the sun had begun its descent toward the west. Adam turned to her. "Do you mind if we drive down by the dock? Just want to make sure they anchored the ship I report to there. I won't be stopping the wagon."

"Of course I don't." They still had plenty of light. "In fact, I'd love to see your navy vessel you spend so much time on."

He guided the wagon toward the harbor. The fresh scent of the sea flowed over Hannah and refreshed her from their long trip. As they drew nearer to the dock, myriad smells of food cooking and sounds flooded her senses—sheep bleated, chickens squawked, dogs barked. Amid it all, the raucous laughter and shouts of men and slaves working rang from ship to ship and across the wooden dock.

She leaned toward Adam. "Tell me the name of your ship again."

"The *USS Enterprise*. And there she is." He gestured toward a trim schooner flying a United States flag, anchored and bobbling with the tide at the end of the row of ships in Gadsden Harbor. She appeared shining and clean, from her crisp white rolled sails to her sparkling decks. A few sailors in blue-and-white uniforms, somewhat like Adam's, stood guard at various posts topside.

"Are you a naval officer or a marine, Adam? I've heard you speak both those terms."

He grinned at her. "Let me unconfuse you, young lady. I'm a marine, actually part of four marines, who've been assigned for duty on that navy ship. We are the captain's strong detachment for special help during battles and anything else he wants done."

Hercules pricked his ears and barked at the workers scurrying close by their wagon, loading and unloading goods from the gangplanks. She quieted him as Adam turned down a side road and toward her aunt's townhouse on Ladson Street.

He pulled the wagon up at the intricate black wrought-iron gate to Sophia's drive Hannah remembered from her family's annual visits. A servant in a stiff green livery bowed to Adam and opened the entrance. Soon they stood at the steps to the three-story house with its wrap-around porches on the first two levels. Servants poured forth to unload her possessions with Aunt Sophia right behind them, instructing them and calling out a welcome. She wore a lacy yellow mob cap over her gray hair, matching the lovely silk day dress that ballooned behind her as she hurried down the steps.

"My dear, dear Hannah and Adam. I'm so happy to see you both."

When Adam jumped down from the wagon, she gave him a hearty hug. After he reached up and set Hannah down before her, the woman pulled her into a warm embrace.

Hannah breathed in the clean, lemony scent of her aunt and marveled at the softness of the silk fabric her cheek pressed into.

"Now let me look at you, dear girl. It's been too long since you visited. I've seen Adam when he comes into port, and I've longed to see you more often, sweet girl." Aunt Sophie stepped back an arm's length from Hannah and examined her. Her light-blue eyes flashed with approval. "You've grown into a lovely young lady, as I knew you would. How old are you now?"

Warmth rose in Hannah's cheeks. "Sixteen."

Her aunt tilted Hannah's bonnet back. "And I see you still have those braids. You're old enough for a new hairstyle, my girl, especially now that you're in Charleston." Then the woman shooed the three servants—two men and one young woman—back into the house with Hannah's baggage and led her and Adam up the steps. A young black boy took possession of Hercules's lead, patted his head, and led him toward the stables. The pup seemed happy to lope along beside the whistling youth.

Hannah touched the thick braids circling her head. She'd always loved her hair in the simple up-sweep, especially when she had work to do. But she had no room in her heart for worry about a changed hairdo. Adam would leave on that ship in the harbor at first tide on the morrow.

They entered through the thick oak door held by a butler into a lovely hall. The servants chattered as they ascended the carpeted stairs with Hannah's trunk and baggage.

Aunt Sophia turned left into the spacious parlor with its black granite fireplace and large gold filigree candelabra Hannah remembered for its beauty and abundant light. The luxurious ceiling light had intrigued her the first time she saw it as a child. At the moment, it was unlit since the long windows lining two sides of the room, with their heavy drapery pulled wide, emitted plenty of afternoon radiance.

Sophia turned to Adam. "Nephew, how soon do you have to report to your ship? Do you have time for tea?"

Adam's tanned face spread into a smile, and the dimple in his chin deepened. "I will certainly take time for some of your tea, Aunt Sophia. It might be a long time before I have another opportunity."

Hannah's heart twinged. She never enjoyed saying goodbye to Adam when he left on his navy assignments. He and she sat on the satin sofa while their aunt walked to the fireplace and pulled a thick tassel hanging beside the granite column. Another young black woman appeared almost immediately with a laden tea tray. She set it on the low table before them, and before turning to leave, her bright, chocolate-colored eyes flew to Hannah. Hannah smiled at the girl.

Time passed much too quickly as she and her brother and aunt enjoyed an abundant tea of small ham sandwiches, biscuits, preserves, plump raisins, and chocolate cake. At the back of her mind, she kept telling herself she would not cry when Adam took his leave. Her aunt plied her and Adam with questions about their father and mother and the farm as the light from the windows faded. When a servant came to light the candles in the candelabra, Adam stood and reached for his bicorn he'd set on a nearby chair.

"Aunt Sophia, thank you for this wonderful tea send off." He smiled. "The memory of it will stay with me sailing on the wide blue Atlantic." He turned to glance at Hannah.

Despite her resolve, moisture gathered in her eyes.

He leaned over, lifted her chin, and looked into her face. "Now don't you go getting teary-eyed, Hannah. You know the Lord will keep me safe and I'll be back before you know it. Besides, you'll be so busy here, I bet you'll not even miss your old brother."

His words only made it worse, and Hannah turned her chin away from his grasp before a tear escaped down her cheek. She blotted it with her aunt's lacy napkin. "But you haven't even told us where you're going, Adam, and for how long." Hating the quiver in her voice, she cleared her throat.

Aunt Sophia stood and touched his forearm. "Yes, Adam, where is our president sending his navy this coming year?"

He pursed his lips. "Oh, I have an idea. But we never know until we report for roll call and Captain Sterett opens the secret box. Actually, he checks it after we're out to sea, and then we know our exact destination."

"Secret box?" Hannah stood, thankful her voice had returned to normal.

"Everything right now is under wraps, since rumor has it Tripoli might declare war on the United States."

Hannah's middle stiffened and her hands clenched. "War?"

Adam whistled and knocked his bicorn on his leg. "Now why did I have to say that and upset you ladies?"

"I'm not upset," Aunt Sophia assured him. "I think it's high time we declared war against those horrid Barbary pirates rather than pay all that tribute for the safe passage of our ships in the Mediterranean. Not to mention, free all our American crews they've taken captive into slavery and put a stop to their exorbitant ransom demands. I've read about it all in the *Carolina Gazette*."

Adam looked at his aunt with new respect blanketing his face. "I'm glad you're keeping up with things, Aunt Sophia. But all this is probably new to Hannah." He drew her to him. "Now, listen, young lady. I'll not have you worrying about me, you hear? I'm going to be fine. Just pray for me every day and write to me as often as you can. Is that a deal?"

Hannah took a deep, shaky breath, enjoying the closeness and strength that emanated from Adam's thick arms and chest. She must try to relieve his fears about her. After all, she was practically grown, wasn't she? She looked up into his handsome face. "I promise not to worry, and I'll write." She even managed to add a proper smile to that assurance.

He released her and shouldered his ditty bag.

Sophia came near. "You won't have time to worry, child. We've got a very busy season headed our way." She put her arm around Hannah's shoulders.

"That's my girl." Adam placed a quick kiss on Hannah's forehead, then strode out of the room and from the house. His boots echoed down the front steps, and each retreating sound left its mark on Hannah's heart.

With great effort, for the rest of the evening, she did her best to appear lighthearted and excited about coming to Charleston. Hannah busied herself with the help of the servant girl June, unpacking in her lovely room on the second floor. And she managed dinner and conversation with her aunt, who listed the seriously ill and the not so sick they would attend in her deceased husband's healing ministry. Hannah even responded with interest to her aunt's announcement about the fall Charleston soirée the two of them would attend in three weeks.

But when she laid her head on the fine lace pillow in the big, soft bed in her room that night, her fabricated peace fled. Whispered words gushed up from her heart.

"Mama, Papa, I miss you. Father God, will You please, please keep Adam safe on whatever his dangerous mission is?"

Turning her face into the pillow, she sobbed.

CHAPTER 4

Adam sat on his narrow cot in his small officer's quarters on the *USS Enterprise* sloop minutes before light-out bells would ring throughout the ship. He placed the law book he'd been studying back into his sailor bag and took a deep breath to dispel the tightness around his chest when he thought of Hannah. If only, during the long months at sea stretching before him, he could carry the mental picture of her smiling and promising to write. But the image seared on his mind was of her lovely face with tears ready to overflow. It did something to his peace, and he couldn't deny the strong protective feelings that churned in his heart.

But what protection could he provide Hannah while sailing far away at sea for months, even a year or more? He turned over in his mind for the hundredth time the fact that she was not his blood sister. How did the potent emotions he'd battled since learning of it fit into his or her future? He exhaled a hot breath and reached for the worn Bible he'd already unpacked from his seabag. What was the verse he'd given Hannah? *All things work together for the good...*

He'd have to trust God for her safety and his...and for both their futures. He blew out his lantern. Tomorrow's first bells at five and all the work he'd help supervise to sail on the morning tide would come soon enough. He lay back on his cot and slept.

The next day, with the ship well out to sea, Captain Sterett called Adam to his quarters after the mid-day meal. This being Adam's third assignment as lieutenant of the marine team on the *Enterprise*, he knew his superior well, and liked him. He tapped at the door and heard the word, "Come."

When he entered, he found the captain staring at the black box on his table a high-ranking Charleston naval officer had delivered to the ship minutes before they left the harbor that morning. Adam saluted his handsome, vibrant commander, only a few years older than himself.

Captain Sterett glanced up at him with a frown, returned the salute, and tapped the box. "Lieutenant White, a surprising note came with this, instructing me not to open it until we were at Latitude 18 degrees north and 76 degrees west."

Adam swallowed a gulp and his heartbeat increased. "But sir, that's—"

"The middle of the Caribbean." The captain's tight voice interrupted.

A ping of happiness shot through Adam. He'd be closer to Charleston...and Hannah...than he'd hoped. Maybe he'd be able to keep more of an eye out for her.

But his superior banged a fist on the table. He strode to his cabin's bank of windows and back, his brows drawn even closer and his lips in a tight line. "White, I don't need to tell you, I was hoping for a Mediterranean assignment. That's where the real action is these days. But chasing pirates in the West Indies? Can you look forward to that?"

Adam wiped the relieved expression from his face. He appreciated his superior trusting him enough to share his personal feelings he'd never share with the crew. This trust carried with it not only Adam's responsibility to protect the captain's life and carry out his commands, as all marines committed to do, but to encourage him if necessary. He hooked his hands behind his back and took a deep breath. "Sir, may I remind you, we took three extra crates on board with the black box. That's never happened before, to my knowledge. It stands to reason, this assignment could mean more than chasing pirates." Adam smiled as he spoke and welcomed a familiar shiver of anticipation starting up his back.

Sterett's brow eased. He expelled a breath, and a glimmer of his old smile and navy derring-do brightened his face. "Hey, you're right, I'd forgotten about the crates. They could mean some kind of special adventure." He grabbed his bicorn and set it firmly on his head. "Now, let's hit the deck and make sure every sailor is doing his part to keep this ship in top navy shape while we're on our way south."

~

Hannah awoke to sunshine pouring through her window and the sound of birdsong in the oak trees shading her aunt's townhouse. Gone was the heavy heart she'd battled the night before. She lifted her hands toward heaven and prayed aloud the Lord's prayer her mother had taught her before she'd learned to read. Seconds after she whispered her *amen*, a knock sounded at the door. She reached for her robe and called out, "Come in."

The pretty black servant who'd helped her unpack the evening before came striding in with a bucket of steaming water. She set it on Hannah's small table. "Miss, I thought you might like to bathe before breakfast. The meal will be in the small dining room in thirty minutes." The woman wore a blue muslin dress and matching cloth wrapped about her head. She looked at Hannah and her lips spread into a smile. Springy dark curls escaped around her oval face.

"Yes, I would like to very much. My name is Hannah. What is yours?"

"April." Again, the bright smile lit the soft bronze cheeks. "I sho liked the prayer I heard from the hall, and I'll be glad to assist you any way I can, miss."

"Thank you, April, but I believe I can manage. I should be

finished in twenty minutes if you want to come back to remove the water and show me the way to the dining room."

"Yes, miss. I'll be back." She left, her soft footsteps hardly making a sound, and neither did the door when she exited.

When the servant returned, Hannah sat facing the mirror on her dresser and struggling with her thick hair. Her fingers refused to plait with smoothness and her arms ached. The woman looked thoughtful as she came forward behind Hannah.

"Miss, I'd luv to help with your hair. Might I?"

Hannah looked at April in the mirror. Why not see if she had a hand with unruly hair? Her mother had always been available to help her at home, and she missed those deft hands. She handed the brush to April. "Have a try."

The young woman gave brisk brush strokes to Hannah's head until her hair shone. "Why, miss, yo hair is just about the color of the sugar cane syrup Miz Sophia imports from them islands."

A pang shot through Hannah's heart, and she clenched her eyes shut. Adam used to say it was the color of the sorghum syrup the family made each fall on the farm. Where would dear Adam be now?

April stopped her ministrations and stared at Hannah in the mirror, her own face stricken. "Oh, Miss, did I say something wrong or pull too hard?"

Hannah's eyes flew open, and she shook her head. "No, of course you didn't. I just had a thought, wondering where my...brother Adam might be right now and if he's safe. His ship was to sail at first tide this morning. He's in the navy."

"Oh, that tall, good-looking man that brung you yesterday? If he sailed at first tide, he's out to sea by now, for sure." She continued her work with Hannah's hair and soon had it pulled into neat coils instead of braids. "Now, you don't be worrying about him, are you? That same God I heard you pray to this morning will keep him safe, if you ask Him."

Hannah turned to stare into April's bright eyes. "Are you a believer, April?"

"I sho am and not ashamed to say so. My mammy raised me

right." She cocked her head. "Miss, I 'pologize for staring, but I ain't never seen violet eyes like yours. And lookie there, even as I'm watching, they's changing to lighter."

Hannah laughed. "My mother once said they turned more violet when I was upset and lightened when I got over it." She took a deep breath and pivoted her head to view April's handiwork in the mirror. "You've done a great job. Thank you. Now, what dress should I wear for my first day in Charleston?" She stood and pulled open her wardrobe. April came behind her and pointed to her green muslin with its white trim.

Hannah followed April to the small dining room where the servant left her. Breakfast smells of ham, eggs, and fresh bread made her mouth water.

Her aunt sat at the head of the long table and greeted her, looking much younger than her sixty years. "There you are, my dear girl." She patted the place setting to her right. "Come, sit near me. We've a lot to talk about, but first, let us give our thanks and ask God to bless our endeavors today."

Aunt Sophia prayed a most enlightening prayer to Hannah's ears, not the usual quick thanks her hungry father usually sent up at mealtime. When it ended, she glanced at her aunt with new respect and unfolded the snowy, lace-edged napkin over her lap. She took modest portions from the platters of steaming eggs and bacon a heavy-set black woman and a young man passed around the table. The woman's kind face lit when Hannah thanked her as she poured a cup of coffee for her and her aunt. Something about her brought April to mind. The two went back through the swinging doors.

"That dear servant is Mama Larnie, April's mother, and her son, July."

Hannah paused a spoon of eggs headed toward her lips. "July?"

Her aunt pressed her napkin to her lips and smiled. "Yes, Larnie has quite a few children, and she names them after the month in which they were born. The entire family is precious and my most loyal and trusted people."

When Hannah finished the meal, she folded her napkin and laid it beside her plate. She felt her aunt's gaze resting on her.

"Dear, did you sleep well? It would be normal to need some time to adjust to a change in your life like this."

She looked up in surprise.

Aunt Sophia's knowledgeable eyes seemed to see into Hannah's heart. Warmth rose in her cheeks. Did the kindhearted woman hear her sobs into her pillow last night?

She finally mustered an answer. "Yes, it is a...change, but I'm so grateful for your taking me in hand, Aunt Sophia, and I look forward to learning all I can about nursing and anything else you want to teach me." There, as she spoke the words, she meant them, and everything was going to be all right. Just as Adam had said.

Aunt Sophia patted Hannah's hand and stood. "Good, now let's start in the library with my dear husband's collection of commonplace books. Do you know about these type of books, Hannah?"

"Are they like the household books some families have? My mother has one handed down from her Quaker grandmother. It has cookery recipes, household hints, and remedies."

"Exactly. My precious husband was able to borrow several commonplace books during his years of practice, and being a doctor, particularly those with more medical knowledge and remedies. He had them hand copied, or he copied out segments that interested him."

They entered the library, and Hannah breathed in the pleasant smell of old books, leather, and lemon oil that must be what caused the shelves to shine as they did.

Aunt Sophia pulled out two worn, loosely bound volumes of handwritten notes from a shelf and placed them on a small table with two chairs. She pointed to the first one. "This is a compilation of remedies my dear Andrew made over the years from common books he borrowed to study." She lovingly touched the second bound manuscript. "This is where he recorded his experiences and opinions about remedies and newer procedures he learned, often by trial and error."

Hannah took a quick breath, and a shiver of anticipation traipsed through her middle. How wonderful to be allowed to study her deceased uncle's medical findings. Her parents had often commented about the man's medical practice—not only among the Charleston elite, but, apparently, he never turned down a needy person who showed up at his surgery door. She pulled out the chair her aunt gestured to and sat. "Aunt Sophia, I'm honored to be shown Uncle Andrew's work. I'm sure there is much I can learn."

"Good. I'm so glad you're interested, my dear. For a beginning schedule, let's consider your studying these each morning here in the library while I see about household duties. After the mid-day meal, I plan to show you nursing techniques and midwifery I've learned myself." She patted Hannah's shoulder. "But we will also have some days free to do other things I'm sure you'll enjoy, like the coming Fall Harvest Ball." She looked out the window and her voice turned wistful. "I've always wanted a daughter, Hannah." Her aunt looked back at her, smiling. "Can I pretend you're that for a while?"

Was that moisture Hannah saw in the pale blue eyes? "Oh, Aunt Sophia, I'd be happy to be in that role. Thank you for asking." She gave the woman a hug.

Her aunt left, and Hannah pulled the first bound manuscript toward her and sighed. She had two wonderful mother figures in her life now, but only one true father figure. An image of her papa's strong, kind face flowed into her mind, but alongside it, Charles Seymour's unhealthy, flushed, and proud countenance appeared too. Hopefully, she'd never have to see him again.

She opened the neatly handwritten volume. Her uncle had even placed an index in the beginning pages. Skimming down the list, one entry caught her eye, *Rosea Facial Coloring*.

Did *rosea* mean *red* or resemble flushing? She carefully turned the pages to the section and read the entry in her uncle's precise, neat hand. *Prolonged alcohol consumption can be associated with a continually flushed face, skin problems, yellowing of the eyes, and many other troubles that can even result in early death.* Was her natural father drinking his health away?

She put him from her mind and turned back to the front of the manuscript. Soon she found herself immersed in illnesses and the herbs for remedies that worked. She learned that wise plantation wives collected their own herbs and followed receipts they made in their own kitchens for their families and servants to have the remedy ready when sickness occurred. And they kept records and passed them down to their grown children.

For the next few weeks, Hannah studied the journals in the morning and accompanied Aunt Sophia around in her carriage to the sick or pregnant she ministered to in the afternoons. Sundays, they attended the morning service at her aunt's church on Meeting Street and rested in the afternoon, unless an emergency demanded their care.

Aunt Sophia's words returning from service the first weekend stayed in Hannah's mind. "If we ever have a genuine emergency on Sunday, or any other time, Hannah, it will probably be due to an accident or the birthing of a baby, one of those two."

Hannah looked forward to assisting at her first birthing with great anticipation and listened to everything her aunt shared about the work.

Sophia's thriving mid-wife ministry included a local lawyer's spouse, Joshua Becket's wife, Abigail. The woman counted on having her aunt's help when the time came.

The time came at four on a Thursday morning, but Hannah sprang from her bed when her aunt came for her, accompanied by a sleepy April who helped Hannah dress. A summer downpour pounded on the coach as she and Aunt Sophia headed to the lawyer's townhouse through the flooded cobblestone streets of Charleston. They munched on cheese and bread thrust into their hands by Mama Larnie for a fast breakfast. "Youse will need all the energy yous can get to help birth a baby," she'd exhorted in the hall.

Hannah ate several bites and willed her excited heart to a more normal beat on the way. Would she be able to help her aunt and prove she would make a good nurse? She whispered a prayer for her aunt and the mother, Mrs. Becket, to be able to birth a healthy child, and she asked the Lord for help herself, to know how to be the best assistant.

~

The *Enterprise* rose and dipped in the warm, startlingly blue waters of the West Indies. Adam stood on the poop deck and watched the glorious sunrise expand across the horizon in pink and golden clouds. The vessel had entered the Caribbean during the night. His loyal, right-hand marine team member and older friend, Scottish Josiah Campbell, leaned on the rail beside him.

The young midshipman, Samuel Cobb, approached and saluted. "Beggin' pardon, Lieutenant. Captain Sterett's compliments. Can you come to his cabin?" The boy of thirteen shifted from foot to foot, his gaze fixed on the deck.

Adam glanced at Josiah, then back to the boy. "Tell the Captain I will attend him right away as soon as I pick up my notebook from my cabin."

"Aye, aye." Cobb marched away.

Josiah's freckled face tightened into a mock-serious expression as the morning breeze ruffled his curly red hair. "Hoots, methinks the day of reckoning have come from the Lord, me lad. We will receive our orders from on high."

Adam shook his head at the man's turn of phrase and accent and hurried away.

When he entered the main cabin, he saluted the captain and helped pry open the black box on his desk. His superior officer pulled forth a large, folded black cloth. When they shook it out, Adam's intake of breath vied in volume with his commander's. A Jolly Roger pennant, its crossbones and skull etched in white across the thick black fabric of the flag, sprawled across the table.

"Whatever could this mean, Lieutenant?" His captain stared at Adam as if he had an answer. Then he pulled a single, official-looking document from the box and unfolded it. A thundercloud gathered on his brow as he perused the message. "What in the name of all sanity can this mean? A ship of the line used for this?" He tossed the letter to Adam while shaking his head and dropped into a chair.

Adam read fast, his heartbeat increasing with each sentence, and he blinked at the signature of the highest ranking naval officer in Charleston. "Sir, it would appear that they've sent us on a special mission, one that we could've never imagined."

Captain Sterett stared at him, his face tight as a drum. "Who can believe it? We are to lose our identity, Lieutenant White. Orders are to remove all visible naval identification both in armaments and dress and act independently of government restrictions, as *privateers*, no less." He ground out the last words and took a deep breath before continuing. "To seek out the pirate fleet hidden on one of these islands that is attacking our United States merchant ships. Then we are to report our findings to the naval base at Charleston for flotilla action." He exhaled a heavy breath and his lips thinned into a hard line.

Adam cleared his throat. "Do you mean they want us to...act as pirates, sir?"

CHAPTER 5

*H*annah and her aunt arrived at the elegant townhouse of Lawyer Joshua Becket and hurried upstairs to his wife, Abigail, in the advanced throes of labor, from the sound of her cries.

The housekeeper, whom they learned was Mrs. Pitt, greeted them from the foot of the bed. "Thank God you've come." She eyed Hannah.

"She is my assistant, ma'am. Take no thought about her. She's got a gift to nurse." Aunt Sophia deposited her midwife satchel on the trunk at the bottom of the bedstead and hurried to the head to encourage her patient.

Abigail Becket opened her clenched eyes once the current pain subsided. "Sophia, thank you so much for coming. I tried to wait some to not make you miss your entire night's sleep." Then her face crumpled in pain, and she groaned and threw her hand over her mouth. Sweat dotted her pale forehead.

Aunt Sophia patted her arm. "Never fear, dear one, you'll birth this child fine, and I don't think it's going to be long." She turned to the housekeeper. "Please fetch us a bowl of cool water, washcloths, extra linens, and a bucket of boiled water. Also, bring me a cup of butter and make a teapot of this." She opened her satchel and withdrew an herbal tea.

Hannah sat at the head and gently pressed a cool, wet cloth on Abigail's forehead. Aunt Sophia opened the drapes and a window, set up candles for good light, and the bed coverings for birthing. Blinking back sympathetic tears when her patient groaned and arched her back, Hannah gently brushed Abigail's hair back from her face and kept her pillow fluffed.

Mrs. Becket looked up at her with pain-darkened eyes. "My dear, you surely have healing in your hands. They so comfort me."

Hannah smiled and whispered a prayer for a healthy, quick delivery.

The housekeeper and a second servant returned with the items requested. Steam rose from the bucket they set at the foot of the bed, and the smell of herbal tea floated in the air.

Aunt Sophia dipped her fingers into the butter and gently examined Abigail. "Thank God we won't have to turn this little one. He's headed in the right direction, dear mother."

Between the pains, Hannah managed to get sips of the relaxing herbal tea of chamomile and valerian into Abigail.

Just before noon, the child slipped out of the birth canal into Aunt Sophia's waiting hands. Hannah rejoiced and worked hard not to burst into tears as she witnessed the miracle of birth. Abigail collapsed back on the pillows, exhaustion lining her gentle face.

"Sweet mother, you've a fine boy to be proud of," Aunt Sophia announced loudly over the child's cries. She tied and clipped the umbilical cord, then handed the wailing newborn to Hannah while she continued to work with Abigail. "There's nothing wrong with that young man's lungs."

Hannah blinked back tears of joy as she cradled the precious boy with his full head of black curly hair. She'd helped birth quite a few animals, but none compared to the advent of a human baby. A tiny fist found its way to the boy's mouth, and he stopped crying and looked up at Hannah with the dearest expression through his tears. She laid him on the bed beside his mother, quickly wiped him down with a warm, damp cloth, rubbed olive oil into his skin, then slipped a small gown over his head. He cooed at her ministrations. She took him back up and placed him into his mother's waiting arms.

Tears flowed down Abigail's cheeks. "My son. Joshua's son. Thank you, Lord Jesus, for this wonderful new life You've added to our household. She kissed the velvety forehead and held the child to her breast. He nursed with vigor.

Hannah beamed at mother and child and finally found her voice. "Do you have other children, Mrs. Becket?"

Yes, a daughter of my husband's, named Jade. She's eight and will love having her own baby brother. I can't wait to see her face."

A brisk knock sounded on the door. Aunt Sophia, finishing her ministrations to Abigail, called out, "You can come in now."

A handsome man with streaks of silver in this thick, dark hair entered with the housekeeper right behind him. Hannah backed away as he strode to the bedside and bent and kissed Abigail's cheek. "Dear one, will you forgive me for leaving the house? I couldn't bear to hear you suffer."

"Oh, but it was worth it, my love. Look at him, Joshua. You have a son. A healthy son, and he has your hair and your broad hands. See?" Abigail lifted a tiny hand of the nursing child and spread apart the miniature fingers. Joshua Becket touched the small palm with an expression of awe.

Aunt Sophia motioned to Hannah, and they gathered up what they'd brought and left the happy family enjoying their first moments with their newborn son.

On the way back to her aunt's house, Hannah took a deep satisfied breath. She'd passed her first test assisting, if Aunt Sophia's pat on her shoulder and warm smile meant anything. A memory of Adam's dark hair and strong, broad hands flashed across her mind. What would a son of his look like? Heat rose in her cheeks, and she turned her face away from her aunt's view.

The Harvest Ball loomed ahead the following week. Sophia bought lovely orange and beige fabrics and had her seamstress make up gowns for Hannah and herself, as she would accompany her niece. "I'm sorry that handsome brother of yours is off somewhere with the navy, or he could've escorted us."

Hannah looked forward to her first ball with anticipation and not a little anxiety. What did one do at a ball? How wonderful it would've been if Adam were going to be with her. He knew about everything.

The afternoon of the event, Hannah bathed and completed her bath with a rub of lavender oil. April helped her don the lovely pale-orange gown with its flowing empire waist and then designed a sophisticated hairdo for Hannah. How different she looked in the mirror. The peach color of the dress pulled out the golden highlights in her thick coils of hair and side curls. If only Adam could see her now. What would he think of his little sister?

"I think the gentlemens will all be wanting a spot on your dance card, miss."

"Oh, I'm not planning to have a dance card, April. I don't know how to dance. I'm just going to observe this first ball I've ever attended."

At Hampton Plantation, Hannah sat beside her aunt next to the green-potted plants banking the left side of the large ballroom. She knew no one but tried to keep an interested expression on her face as the ladies in bright gowns, their partners in silk waistcoats, swung by them in a rainbow of colors and sunny smiles.

Bits of conversation floated on the surrounding air. One bit that reached her ears caused heat to rise in her cheeks. A male voice asked his dance partner, "Do you know who the lovely orange butterfly sitting with Mrs. Rutledge is?" They swirled on by before the partner replied.

The next hour, she turned down four offers to dance. To her aunt's questioning look, she whispered, "I don't know how to dance."

Her aunt nodded and smiled. "That's now on my list to help you learn."

THE LIEUTENANT'S SECRET LOVE

Hannah fanned her face. Just how long did her aunt expect to stay? A few minutes later, someone broke away from the dancers and stopped before them. The rapid movement of Hannah's fan abruptly ceased as she glanced up into the face of Saul Seymour. Dressed in a black silk waistcoat and white trousers, he looked every bit the rich, young heir he was. Her heart sank to her feet, and her stomach roiled.

He bowed to her aunt and then to her. "Hannah, it took me a moment to recognize you. You look lovely. I have some folks for you to meet. Your two sisters, in fact." He moved aside and two women stepped up.

Hannah turned her stricken gaze to them. Her *sisters?*

"May I present Ruth Seymour?"

Ruth had black hair and large, dark eyes, but a gentle light shone from them. She held out her gloved hand, and Hannah shook it, trying to swallow her shock.

"I'm so pleased to meet you, Hannah...White?" The woman's brown eyes beamed with kindness. Dressed modestly in a well-cut gown of blue silk, she manifested simple elegance.

"Yes. And I'm...glad to meet you...Ruth."

The other younger woman stepped forward. With her blond hair swept much too high, she seemed about to totter. Her blue eyes reflected a brittleness instead of softness, and her low-cut gown barely covered a large bust. "And I'm Diana Seymour, the married daughter. We are delighted to have another sister. Believe me, we would've never allowed Father to do what he did if we'd known about it." Despite her words, her breathy voice lacked sincerity.

Ruth stiffened and frowned at her sister.

Hannah's tongue stuck to the roof of her mouth, and Saul's closeness and continued gawk made her tremble.

Aunt Sophia intervened with grace. "Thank you, ladies, for coming and making yourself known to Hannah. Unfortunately, we were just about to leave. We have an early morning tomorrow with our doctoring work." She stood and Hannah moved with her, forcing her shaky knees to stay firm.

Saul's eyes latched onto Hannah. "Oh, but couldn't you stay for one more dance, dear Hannah? I'm leaving tomorrow for England and the university."

Aunt Sophia took Hannah's arm. "Sorry, we do have to leave." She cast a glance at the Seymour sisters and smiled. "Perhaps you two can visit Hannah for tea one afternoon. We are usually at home on the second Thursdays."

With that, her aunt led her out of the ballroom and to the front door to request their carriage. How happy Hannah was to get away from her nemesis. But finding she had two sisters made her heart glow. She would look forward to getting to know them. But would she have to deal with Saul again? Was he really going away to a university in England? That idea made her glad. But then she thought of her work with her aunt. Even if he did go away, would she stay in Charleston and continue learning how to nurse? Would her parents mind her not coming home?

~

Adam stepped out on deck from his officer's quarters in his new privateer clothing of a green shirt and black trousers, a side arm stuck in his sash and a sword at his side, topped off with a plumed gray hat. The past two days, the crew and ship had made their change from the *USS Enterprise* to the privateer *Scorpion*. The new name blazoned across the side of the ship with fresh paint, and the crew now wore new pirate-like clothing instead of the American navy blues and whites.

Josiah walked up, saluted, and then covered a chuckle with his hand. "Sorry, sir. You've always made a splash in the towns with the lassies. I don't know how we'll keep 'em off you in this new garb."

Don't you go worrying, Josiah. We've got work to do to find the pirate fleet hiding on one of these islands. My guess is, we won't be stopping off at any ports to meet any ladies."

Captain Sterett walked up. Both Adam and Josiah saluted and tried to cover grins at their commander's new clothing of baggy brown trousers and a white ruffled shirt. He didn't crack a smile. "Adam, I've come up with an idea for getting on the island of the pirates we think we located last evening. It involves you and two of your marines. You and Josiah come to my cabin."

Adam and Josiah paid careful attention when the captain explained his plan. He suggested that the best way to get on the island and map out their defenses would be to pretend to join them. He looked long and hard at Adam. "And that's going to take some doing, even some pain for you."

"Me?" Adam's interest quickened, and so did his heartbeat. What kind of pain was the captain talking about?

"Yes. My idea is that the only way you can hope to join them is to show up as a deserter from the navy. And that means, you'll have to take the cat-o'-nine-tails flogging for a deserter to prove it to them. Are you up to it? Just you, as the leader, not your other two men."

Adam took a deep breath and leaned forward, a marine to the core. "If it's the only way, Captain, I'm your man."

He had cause to regret his easy capitulation the next day, strapped to the mainmast on the hot deck with the burley Italian bosun, Samson, swinging his cat-of-nine tails and the entire silent crew looking on. Did the man take particular pleasure in flogging an officer rather than an enlisted man? Adam passed out before the ordeal ended.

Drug back to the captain's cabin, he regained consciousness as Josiah washed his wounded back and then applied a salve under the captain's direction.

"I'm sorry you had to suffer this, Lieutenant." The captain's brusque voice had a trace of regret. Maybe.

"Sure you are, sir. Remind me every day while I'm healing."

Josiah snorted and kept applying the salve.

Ten days later, at sunset, Adam, Josiah, and David Barron, all dressed in dirty, ragged navy uniforms, rowed away from the *Scorpion* toward a destination barely visible on the horizon. Adam pressed the oars through the sea, very careful not to stress the freshly healed wounds on his back. They rowed the boat toward a deserted beach, disembarked, and made their way toward the noise of merriment coming from beyond the lush green overgrowth at the edge of the white sands.

A giant of a man, fully armed with guns and a sword, moved to confront them as they walked out of the trees. He pointed a large pistol at them. "Who goes there? Answer fast or I'll make you into shark bait." His dirty blue shirt and pantaloons hung on him almost in shreds. The lack of covering revealed the massive muscles on his chest, arms, and legs. Not a man to mess with.

Adam looked the enormous, scowling man in the face and responded in the way he'd planned. "We're navy deserters looking for seaman of any stripe to fall in with and any kind of work...on any side of the law. Can you take us to your leader?"

The pirate grunted and turned. They followed him into a thatched settlement and to a dilapidated building where light tumbled onto the dusty narrow track and sounds of revelry blasted into the night air.

They entered, and he led them through a drunken crowd of pirates and painted women who cast interested but bleary eyes at Adam. The man opened an inner door and strode up to a pile of cushions on a dais where a man and a woman sprawled, drinking and laughing. The man's blond hair and ginger beard surprised Adam. Could he be English? The woman glanced up at Adam and smiled.

The man pushed her away, still holding his goblet, and looked Adam up and down, then slid a glance toward Josiah and David. "What have we here, Dagon? You'd better not of disturbed me for no good reason."

"These say they navy deserters and wanna join us, Cap'n. But just tell me and I'll run 'em through." He unsheathed his sword so fast, the scabbard appeared to be oiled.

Adam stepped forward. "We are at your service, sir. My name is Adam White. May I know to whom I'm speaking?"

The man threw his head back and roared in laughter. "Do you

hear that, Dagon? He don't know he's standing in the presence of the last great pirate of the West Indies."

Adam hoped that the man would be just that. He was here to make sure it happened. "Say you're a deserter? What country? What rank?"

"America, sir. And I was a lieutenant, sir."

"More likely, you are a spy, sirrah." The man threw his goblet against the wall and nodded at Dagon.

The giant grabbed Adam and placed the tip of his sword under Adam's chin within inches of his jugular vein. When Josiah and David started to his aid, two other pirates jumped them from behind.

"Cut his shirt off his back, Dagon. If he's a deserter, he'll have the marks."

Adam braced his shoulders as the sword point ripped up the back of his shirt. Dagon grunted and spun him around.

"Well, sir. Seems you got the marks of the cat. Lucy, bring the man and his two friends some rum. Dagon move away." Adam breathed a sigh of relief and dared not glance at his two partners. They'd passed the first test. Would they make it through the others sure to come?

The young woman rose from the cushions, left the room, and soon returned with four goblets and a jug. She placed them on a table in the corner, and before moving away, she slid an interested glance toward Adam.

The pirate leader arose and invited them to join him. They sat, and Adam tried to pull the tattered parts of his shirt over his back.

The leader guffawed. "Lucy, you think you can find a shirt to fit this deserter?" He looked at Adam and his two partners. "Sure, we can use three good men like you. I'm Captain Butler." He threw out a tanned, calloused hand, and Adam shook it. Then the leader poured rum in all the goblets and took a deep swig. "That is if you're really here for the reason you said. If you're not, you won't live to brag about it."

Josiah and David stiffened, but Adam didn't move an eyelash as he took a sip from his cup. The man must see him strong, not worried. Even if he did feel his gut turn at the threat.

Dagon still glared at them from his new position guarding the door, distrust evident in every angle of his giant body.

Whatever they hoped to do, it must be fast and quiet. The longer they stayed on the island, the risk of discovery of their real mission would increase.

~

Over the next three days, mostly at two and three in the morning, when most every island dweller was in a dead-drunk sleep, Adam and his men located and drew a map of the island fortifications, the number of pirates, and the number of ships. On the third night, as soon as Adam and his men completed their map, they made their way by moonlight to the small beach and their hidden rowboat.

To their shock, Dagon confronted them. "What goes here, you black-hearted scoundrels?"

Before the man had time to unsheathe his sword, Adam lowered his head and went at him like a charging bull. He struck the man's middle and almost passed out. It was like hitting a brick wall, but the man staggered and fell back.

Josiah and David jumped on him and soon pummeled him into unconsciousness.

David shook his head to clear it, and the three of them pulled the boat from the bushes, pushed it into the tide, and jumped in.

Before daylight, they finished the long row back to the *Scorpion*, hidden in a deserted cove on the other side of the island. Captain Sterett and the crew cheered them as they rowed into sight. Adam praised God that they'd been able to complete their mission. On board, he couldn't keep a smile from his face as he changed into clean clothes.

After enjoying the morning meal, he posed questions to the captain on the quarterdeck. "Where are we headed now, sir?"

"Glad you asked, White. Remember our orders? We're headed to Charleston to report our findings for flotilla action against the hideout. He leaned over the rail and shouted, "Stand by to make sail! Hoist the stars and stripes! We're going home!"

The crew below cheered and hurried to their posts.

"Sir, do we change back into our navy uniforms and insignia of the *Enterprise*?"

"Yes, we're American navy again. Give the orders." The next afternoon, the lookout in the eagle's nest shouted, "A sail off port side. Coming fast."

Captain Sterett, standing with Adam on the quarterdeck, whipped out his eyeglass and scanned the approaching vessel, then handed it to Adam. "You see their pennant?"

"It's the Jolly Roger, sir. And it's a large frigate."

"It looks as though our streak of luck has run out and we will have to battle pirates. He shouted over the deck, "Prepare to confront!"

A flurry of activity spread over the deck, and the screeching sound of cannons being rolled to ports filled the arid air.

The approaching ship sent a warning shot over the bow of the *Enterprise*. "They hope to make us raise a white flag, but let's surprise them. Who's afraid of the big bad wolf?" Captain Sterett snapped his eyeglass shut and sent word to his gunner to aim for the mainmast and below the water level. Loud booms filled the air and smoke rose like a cloud.

The pirate frigate, no doubt taken by surprise that such a smaller vessel would dare fire on them, returned cannon shots, but they fell short.

Captain Sterett kept his cannons firing until the pirate ship's main mast exploded and fell onto the deck. Fire broke out and smoke rose in waves. Finally, a white pennant climbed above the ship, signaling surrender.

Adam and his four marines were the first to swing over onto its smoking deck when the *Enterprise* drew alongside the beleaguered vessel. They rounded up the pirates who'd survived, put chains about their wrists, and sent them as captives to their own vessel. Fire continued to spread and grow on the deck.

Josiah hurried toward Adam. "Sir, this ship is gonna go. We hit her below the waterline, and she's filling full o' water below. We gotta go fast."

"In a minute, my man." Adam ran to the hatch and shouted down the steps. "Hullo, is anyone down there?" Was that coughing he heard? He slid down the steps and scooted along the passageway. His boots sloshed in cold water. "Hullo, is anyone here? You must come, for this ship is sinking fast."

A woman's head appeared out of a door down the passage. "Yes, we're here, and we need help."

He hurried toward her. "Ma'am, we're part of the United States Navy on a secret mission, and we've taken this ship. You've got to evacuate right now."

She looked into his face, and her eyes lit up. "Praise the Lord for our own navy!"

Adam helped her pull the water-logged door wide. She pointed at a cot on which lay a young woman who appeared to be in a faint or knocked out by falling debris.

"I'm Mrs. Hancock, governess to that lamb. She fell in a swoon soon after the cannon blasts rocked the ship. Can you take her up?"

He lifted the slight form in his arms, and a sigh escaped the tender lips. Thick blond lashes partially opened over pale eyes, then clenched tight again. Her long, flaxen hair fell down beyond Adam's arms as he hurried up the passage, followed by the older woman.

Josiah helped the governess swing over to the *Enterprise*. Then he followed, urging Adam to come.

The girl groaned and reached her arms around Adam's neck as he held her with one arm around her small waist and swung over to the Scorpion's deck with the other.

The crew cheered him.

He dropped to the deck with a jolt, and the girl lifted her head. She made no move to lower her arms. Lovely sea-green eyes looked into his face, and soft full lips opened and formed words. "You saved my life, sir."

Before Adam guessed her intention, she pressed her mouth to his, blasting all his senses, then fell back into his arms.

The *Enterprise* crew broke out with whistles and stamping feet until Captain Sterett had the bosun blow his whistle for order.

Blood rushed to Adam's face, and he turned to take the young woman somewhere, anywhere, so she could fully recover. The best place, away from the leering crew, seemed to be his own quarters.

Mrs. Hancock followed him. When he laid the girl on his cot, the governess burst into tears, but they ended fast, like a quick summer shower. "Thank you, sir. What a nightmare we've been through since those blackguard pirates took our ship two weeks ago. It's been all I could do to keep their hands off her. But the promise of a big ransom finally convinced them. Her name is Juliet Nelson." She touched the girl's shoulder. "She's been very brave until your cannons started finding their mark."

"Where are you two from, Mrs. Hancock?"

"From Charleston, of course, but we were on our way to Jamaica to meet Juliet's English fiancé, Duke Charles Montagu."

The talk seemed to drain the rest of the woman's strength, and she dropped into the only chair in the room.

"Well, you see about the young lady, ma'am, and rest. I'll send food and tea after I check on our prisoners."

"Thank you, sir. I thank God for you and this ship."

∼

Two nights later, Adam tramped up on deck to honor his time at guard duty. He really didn't mind the quiet night hours aboard the ship, sailing slower than in the daylight. The helmsman and he were the only crew members awake, but many men snoring in hammocks hanging all about could be roused fast in any emergency.

The thought foremost in his mind was whether they'd make it home to Charleston by Christmas Eve, at least. There was a good chance they would. That thought lightened his step as he walked up to the poop deck and looked at the moonlight shimmering over the lapping Atlantic. Hannah flowed into his thoughts. How was she doing at her aunt's? There'd not been an opportunity to exchange letters in the weeks he'd been gone, not with his ship on a secret mission and no rallying with other American navy vessels to exchange mail bags.

A movement at the bottom of the steps caught his eye. To his amazement, Juliet Nelson flew up them and to his side, her skirts swishing and swinging. She wore a cloak pulled close about her head and person, but strands of her golden hair escaped around her pale face, giving her identity away. He had guessed her a little older than Hannah, probably a year or two.

He put on his sternest expression and lowered his voice, but authority still laced it. "Miss Nelson, you must not come alone on deck ever, especially during the night hours. I thought we'd made that plain to you and to Mrs. Hancock."

She dropped her chin, but only for a moment, then she flashed him a glorious smile.

He looked away.

"But I so want to talk to you and show you my gratitude for saving me and my governess. You know, it was a very brave thing you did, risking your own life staying on a sinking ship."

A quirky wind blew the cloak away from her head, and her hair glistened like gold in the moonlight. The same light of the moon cast a pearl-like glow on her lovely oval face.

Adam's breath snagged in his throat at her beauty, thus exposed. He couldn't turn his gaze from her.

She seemed to know the effect she was having on him and leaned close. "I so hope we'll make it home before Christmas. Do you think we will?" Her bright eyes searched his face.

The gardenia scent she wore flowed over him. A sudden, pressing desire to take her into his arms possessed him. Who would know, and who would care on this sleeping ship in the moonlight, somewhere between the West Indies and Charleston?

CHAPTER 6

A shock rolled through Adam at what he was thinking of doing, and he caught himself in time. The young woman had shown her disrespect for authority by coming on deck alone, especially at night. She was also engaged to be married and should not be toying with him or any other man. He cleared his throat and took her elbow in a firm grasp. "Miss Nelson, if the weather holds, we should be home before Christmas, but come with me. I'll escort you back to your cabin."

She groaned but permitted him to lead her back to her door.

He returned to his post and thanked God for helping him overcome an enticing temptation. He'd had quite enough adventure for now. Soon enough, he'd be home, among the reassuring security of family...and...Hannah.

*T*he Seymour sisters came to call on a Thursday afternoon when Hannah and her aunt were receiving. No one else had shown up on the nippy, wet, November day.

The butler brought the two into the parlor lit by a warm fire. Aunt

Sophia and Hannah greeted Ruth and Diana, and the guests settled on the rose settee, keeping their shawls pulled close until the warmth from the fire could knock off the chill from their carriage ride.

Hannah breathed her relief that Saul Seymour was not with them. He must've really gone to England to university.

Ruth, the older with her black hair and eyes, sat forward and pulled something from her reticule. A small framed picture. "We wanted to bring you a memento of our dear mother." She handed it to Hannah.

The painting revealed a pretty young woman with auburn hair set in coiffed curls. Happiness lit her eyes, and a lovely pearl necklace graced her slender neck.

"They made this right after she married our father. It's yours to keep."

"Oh, thank you, but..." Despite the Seymour girls' thoughtful gesture, a protest bubbled up in Hannah's throat as thoughts of her precious Quaker mother reared up in her mind. This was not her mother and never would be.

Aunt Sophia asked to see it, and Hannah gladly passed it to her. "How nice of you sisters to want to share something like this with a sibling you didn't know you had until recently." She smiled at Hannah as if she knew her hesitancy to accept it. Instead of handing it back to her, she laid it on the end table and asked the Seymours about their home life.

Ruth spent some time sharing about the plantation work she took a big part in. The woman had strength, and unless Hannah was mistaken, faith and wisdom to help oversee the plantation. All Diana could talk about, after giving a brief description of her three children, was the latest ball she'd attended in Savannah, and the dress she wore, and what others wore. She lived in Georgia's main seaport with her husband and children and seldom came to visit her Seymour relations, as her calendar, she declared, was always so full.

Over tea, Hannah shared briefly about her family and their busy farm life. Ruth smiled, but Diana sniffed and lifted her nose an inch higher. The sisters left soon after to get back to the Seymour townhouse before dark.

Hannah liked Ruth Seymour. Diana was a different story.

∼

The *Enterprise* pulled into the Charleston Harbor on Christmas Eve as the winter sunset baptized the city in glorious shades of pink, gold, and purple. Adam, the last to leave the ship before Captain Sterett, walked the few blocks to Aunt Sophia's townhouse. He congratulated himself on having been able to avoid Juliet Nelson and her governess's departure from the ship.

Carrying his sailor bag on his shoulder, he whistled a cheerful tune. He took deep breaths of the chilly city air, laced with the scent of fresh bread baking in a shop somewhere along the brightly lit cobblestoned streets. Joy to be back on land and in time to see his family for Christmas washed over him. He greeted the few hurrying passersby with a cheerful grin and nodded a greeting to occupants of carriages jangling past with bells on the horses' harness.

Holly, with red berries, lined the front fence and the banisters on the three levels at Sophia's house. He stamped up onto the first porch, and the elderly butler, Moses, swung open the door.

"Why, Mr. White, we's so happy you've made it home fo' Christmas. Yo' whole family's done come."

"Thank you, Moses. And Merry Christmas to you."

Adam dropped his bag in the hall and headed to the parlor. Someone on the pianoforte playing Christmas hymns spread cheer through the festive house, scented with the holiday smells of pine boughs, spices, and meat roasting over an open fire. He licked his lips. Sophia's cook, Mama Larnie—with his own mother's help, he was sure—would show out her cookery skills at tonight's dinner.

When he paused in the parlor doorway, the music stopped.

Hannah shot up from the piano and ran toward him. He gathered her in his arms, delighting in her sweet, clean scent. His father rose from the settee, and he gave him a hug—as did his mother, who entered from the hall in her white apron.

"Son, thou camest back safe. And in time for Christmas. We give God thanks." Mama pulled a handkerchief from her sleeve and dabbed at her eyes.

He glanced around the comfortable, inviting room. A large, highly decorated Christmas tree filled one corner, but where was Michael?

"Your brother is in the kitchen with Sophia, tasting the goodies the women are dishing up, Adam." His father patted his arm. "I assume that's who you're looking for, and he's got some interesting news for you."

Michael shared it at the dinner table. "Adam, the navy has assigned me to a new frigate, the *USS Philadelphia,* under Captain William Bainbridge."

Adam eyed his younger brother, noting the excitement in his voice and his more deeply tanned face. It was really an honor for a recruit like him to be assigned to such a large and important new navy vessel. He was looking for congratulations, but Adam couldn't resist a tease. "Is that all?"

Michael's face fell, but only for a moment, and he grinned, reminding Adam that he knew his brotherly antics well. "And that's not all, big marine man. The rumor mill has it we'll be sailing to the Mediterranean Coast after Thomas Jefferson takes office in February."

Comments flowed around the table about the new president and the fierce election battle he went through to win the nomination.

Adam's ship, while at sea on a secret mission, had received no newspapers. He listened as Aunt Sophia enlightened him. She read the *Charleston Gazette* as regularly as she read her Bible. He smiled at that thought but turned his full attention toward her after Mama Larnie finished serving the Christmas cake.

Aunt Sophia took one bite of the holiday cake with its fruit and nuts and then touched her red linen napkin to her lips. "Mr. Jefferson and Mr. Burr fought a bitter election, and it ended in an electoral tie between the two of them, so it had to go to the House of Representatives." She paused and took a sip of her tea and looked around the table. "Can any of you believe it took three votes in the House for them to finally declare Thomas Jefferson our next president?"

"It *is* hard to understand it took that many votes. I always thought Jefferson was the better choice," Adam's father added. He glanced at his two sons. "And you two navy men ought to be glad he won. I think he's got a vision for a strong United States Navy, unlike some of our other leaders." He rested his gaze on Adam. "Now, can you tell us what you and your ship have been doing the past three months, son? It was hard on your mother not getting a single letter. And it was the first thing Hannah asked when we arrived here for the holidays. She received nothing from you either."

Adam savored the last bite of his cake, wiped his mouth, and leaned back in his chair. He'd known the questions would come. "I can only tell you they assigned us on a secret mission."

Michael was all ears. "Well, is the secret over now, brother? Can you tell us anything about it?"

Adam thought of the map they've made of the pirate fleet's island fortifications that Captain Sterett had undoubtedly turned in to the Charleston Navy headquarters before he went to his own home for the holidays. The command center would plan a flotilla action against the pirates right after the first of the year. "No, it's not over yet, so my lips must stay sealed. Sorry."

Michael pressed him. "Can you at least tell us what part of the globe you were in? You're back too soon for it to have been very distant."

Adam expelled a deep breath. Perhaps it'd be all right to share that much. "The West Indies."

Hannah smiled. "Well, I for one am so happy it wasn't so distant and you could be with us for Christmas, dear brother."

Adam winked at her and her eyes twinkled.

Aunt Sophia laid her napkin next to her plate and stood. The others did the same and followed her to the parlor.

Adam sat beside Hannah on the window seat. "Tell me about

what you've been doing, Hannah. Have you learned a lot about nursing and doctoring?"

She turned her wide violet eyes on him. "Oh, yes, Adam. I've learned ever so much. Aunt Sophia is a wonderful teacher. So many here depend on her, and she's even called on to deliver babies. I love helping her."

"You been homesick at all, little sister? I was concerned about that when I deposited you here and then had to report for duty right away." He searched her face. How had she become even lovelier than he remembered?

Pink rose in Hannah's cheeks. "Maybe a little at first. I...missed Mama and Papa and..." She stopped and looked down at her hands folded in her lap.

Adam took one of her cool hands into his. "But you got over it, right? Believe it or not, when I first enlisted, your big, independent brother fought a bit of homesickness too."

She turned wondering eyes up to his. "You never told me that, Adam."

"Well, I didn't have a reason to until now." Holding her hand was doing something to his breathing, and he released it. And so did gazing into her almost-worshipful eyes.

He stood and walked over to the family gathered on the settees and chairs in front of the low-burning fire. He leaned up against the mantel and stared into the flickering logs, a plethora of emotions twisting through his mind. He could not deny a powerful attraction to Hannah that had only grown after his time away. But she was only a child, still, wasn't she? And she thought of him as what? Most likely, nothing but her big brother.

His mother came to stand beside him. "Dear Adam, art thou at peace, or is something bothering thou? Thou art happy to be with us? Yes?"

He turned and hugged her. "By all means. Getting here for Christmas was an answer to prayer. Yours and mine." He released her.

"So there is nothing bothering thee, my son, that made thine brow knit when you first came to stand here?"

Depend on it, his precious mother could read him like a book. "No, no, just a little tired, is all. You know aboard ship we retire about this time."

She smiled and patted his arm. "Yes, of course. I'd forgotten about a ship's early, strenuous hours. If thou'd like to go up now and make it a day, it will hurt none of our feelings, Adam. I believe Michael felt the same way when he first came home, but he's been here for a week and has recovered."

Adam retired, but not to perfect rest as he continued to mull over his increased attraction to Hannah. Where would it end? Her hating him? Or—and the thought made his heart beat double time in his chest—could she ever care for him as more than a brother? He finally rose, read his Bible, and committed the thing to God. Meanwhile, he'd just continue being her big brother and avoid too close a contact. That would be the best way.

He grimaced. Close contact? What a joke. He'd be off—only heaven knew where—with the navy in a few weeks, and there'd be no contact. Except the rare, long-in-transit letters they might exchange from land to sea. But that ought to help keep any untoward feelings at bay.

After Christmas, Adam's parents left for the farm, and Michael went with them. His brother already knew his orders, and he had a month off.

Adam had informed Captain Sterett he'd be at his Aunt Sophia's until after the holidays, awaiting his orders and to send them to her address.

It delighted Aunt Sophia that he'd be available to escort Hannah to the Heyward's New Year's soiree. Anticipation for it, the week after Christmas, filled his aunt's conversation and the entire house. She hired a dance instructor to show Adam and Hannah the favorite Charleston dances, and they spent several afternoons practicing. Despite Adam's lack of experience, it was no hardship, swirling Hannah around the parlor as she laughed and held onto him.

The night of the event, Hannah floated like a princess down the staircase in the lovely ivory gown Sophia'd had her seamstress make for her. The pale lavender flowers at the neckline and waist and the amethyst pendant necklace he'd given her for Christmas magnified her violet eyes. She took his breath away. How would he manage being near her all evening, holding her in the dances, without giving any hint of his feelings?

Although he'd hoped never to see Juliet Nelson again, she helped solve the problem.

They had no sooner entered the ballroom than she swished up to them in a magnificent yellow silk gown, set off by a priceless diamond-and-topaz necklace. Every eye in the room seemed turned toward her blonde loveliness, unique in the gathering. Even Hannah, beside him, emitted a soft gasp. Juliet's partner, a stiff, proper young man in a black waistcoat and white cravat, eyed Hannah, and a smile flashed across his face.

Juliet tapped Adam's arm with her lacy, golden fan. "Oh, dear Lieutenant White! How happy I am to see you, sir. What a poor officer you were not to see me off the ship. I looked everywhere for you when we disembarked."

Hannah dropped her reticule and Adam bent to retrieve it.

Juliet turned her eyes on Hannah, and a frown marred her perfect brow. "And who is this, may I ask?"

Adam acknowledged Juliet and her partner with a slight bow. "I'm sorry. This is Hannah White, my sister."

The frown disappeared and Juliet gave them both a glorious smile. "Hannah, I'm Juliet Nelson and this is Harry Hawthorne." She took a deep breath and leaned close to the man. "Dear Harry, will you please ask Mr. White's sister to dance? I have much to talk about with Lieutenant White. Remember, I told you how he rescued me. Before the New Year's fireworks, sir, I will get back with you, I promise." She patted the young man's sleeve but never took her eyes off Adam.

Harry bowed and extended his hand to Hannah. She looked

questioningly at Adam, and he nodded. She placed her gloved hand in Harry's, and they moved off to dance.

Adam had only one dance with Hannah. Whenever Juliet gave him a break, which was seldom, Hannah was off with other young men who clamored for a dance with her. He was happy her first New Year's soiree in Charleston was turning out to be a success.

Finally, at quarter to twelve, he deposited Juliet with Harry Hawthorn and went to look for Hannah. When he couldn't find her in the ballroom, he hastened out to the circular second-story porch for a breath of air and to escape any further contact with Juliet or other hopeful young women who kept appearing at his elbow. He leaned over the railing and looked down at the first-floor porch but saw no one. Most of the party would gather on the third-story porch to watch the fireworks, but surely, she'd not go there without him. Where could she be? He consulted his pocket piece. Five minutes to twelve.

A muffled sob came from the back side of the house.

He walked around the porch, and his heart dropped to his feet. Hannah stood in a shadowed corner with her head in her hands, her ivory gown glistening in the moonlight. He strode up to her and pulled her hands from her face. Tears ran down her cheeks.

"Hannah, dear, whatever has happened?"

She turned her face away from him.

He leaned closer to her. "Look at me. Did...any of the young men offend you...or take any kind of advantage?" Blood rushed to his head at the possibility. He should've been more vigilant. "You must tell me, and I'll make sure he's very sorry."

She lifted her wet face to his, shaking her head. "No, no, Adam. It was nothing like that."

"Then what was it? Why are you hiding here crying, dear Hannah?" His insides seemed to be tearing apart. He placed his hands on her shoulders.

The noise above them increased as the partygoers on the upper porch stamped their feet and shouted off the minutes until twelve for the fireworks to begin, then the mass shout, "It's eighteen hundred! A new century!"

The first deafening blast shot up and lit the night sky, exploding into an umbrella of multi-colors that descended like sheeting rain, baptizing them all.

Hannah jumped and pressed into his arms. Adam couldn't breathe. He placed his thumb under her chin and lifted her face to within inches of his. He got a question in before the next explosion filled the night sky. "Are you going to tell me what this is all about, dear Hannah?" Her soft, sweet closeness was making him as happy as he could remember ever being, and weak, as if he'd just fought off a horde of pirates trying to take the *Enterprise*.

Hannah's mumbled words came fast, her breath feathering against his neck. "Adam, I wanted to dance with you, not all those… others. And was that Juliet on the ship with you?"

Their eyes locked as they stood with their faces inches apart. It was too much. The fireworks shooting across the southern night began ricocheting inside of him. He bent and touched her lips with his own. It was like heaven. Her knees gave way, and he held her up, pressed against him.

A sob escaped her lips.

His heart pinged with regret. "Hannah, I'm sorry. Can you forgive me? I shouldn't have done that."

The fireworks ceased, and the voices above them faded as the watchers went back inside the house. She moved away from him and took a deep, shaky breath. "Adam, I'm so confused. But you…don't need to apologize. Can we go home now?"

~

*H*annah lay in her bed that night, her mind totally wrapped around that shocking, wonderful kiss, her first kiss. Was it wrong of her to have enjoyed it? But Adam really wasn't her brother, was he? The blood pounded in her head again when she thought of the magic moment his lips had pressed hers—

gentle, not demanding, but oh so sweet, a kiss as tender as a summer breeze in midwinter. Her lips still burned with that one touch.

And then he had apologized. He'd thought she cried afterward for regret. But far from it. She'd felt transported on a soft, wispy cloud, so delighted that such a feeling could exist, it had made her weep.

Another thought intruded, and the romantic memories flew away like so many wistful butterflies. Adam had never answered her question about the woman with whom he'd danced all night. What history did he have with the beautiful Juliet? And why had she been on the *Enterprise*?

CHAPTER 7

The next morning, Hannah startled awake and stared at the daylight streaming from her windows. It must be late. She threw the covers back, slid her feet into soft slippers, and donned her robe. Splashing water on her face from the bowl, she dried it, then pulled the bell rope. Something pushed her to hurry, and an irrational fear gnawed at the edge of her mind. She tugged her wardrobe open and selected a dress. A knock sounded at the door, and she called out, "Enter."

April came in, smiling, and headed toward the hearth. "You look rested after your late hours last night, miss. Yo' aunt say to let you sleep, so that's what I did." She bent to stoke the warm embers into flames and added two logs.

"What time is it, April? Do you know?"

"Why, it's ten o'clock, Miss White. But no need to worry. Yo' aunt done said today would be a quiet day. No big plans after the late hour at the ball last night."

Hannah took a deep breath as April helped her into her clothes, and her heart skipped a beat. Had Adam also slept late? Not likely, being the sailor he was. Today, they needed to have a talk. Remembering the kiss, color crept into her cheeks.

She finished her toilet and hurried downstairs. After a quick trip to the kitchen for a cup of Mama Larnie's tea, she went in search of Adam. Walking into the parlor, she found Aunt Sophia engrossed in her embroidery, but no brother in sight. Where could he be? "Good morning, Aunt Sophia. I'm looking for Adam. Did he go out somewhere?" Surely, he'd not gone off for a horseback ride without her. He knew she loved riding with him—the few chances she received.

"Oh, hello, Hannah." Her aunt laid her handiwork aside and smiled at her. "Yes, I'm afraid Adam has gone off somewhere—to that ship of his in the harbor, and heaven knows where they're sailing off to. His orders were hand-delivered early this morning."

A sense of intense desolation swept over Hannah. She sank onto the settee. "But he didn't even say goodbye."

Her aunt clucked her tongue. "Dear me, yes, he did. He wrote you a note. It's on the mantel."

Hannah jumped up, strode to the mantel, and reached for the note. He'd propped it against the vase of red camellias she'd placed there for New Year's.

"He was in such a hurry and decided it best not to waken you due to your late hours last night."

Her aunt's voice faded away as she perused Adam's neat, clipped handwriting.

Dear Hannah,

I'm so sorry there is no time to do this in person. My navy orders are explicit. I must report to the Enterprise *as soon as possible this morning. I'd loved to have been able to spend more time with you, especially to talk about last night. Except for your tears, it was one of the happiest times in my life. Hope it was for you. Don't forget to write and pray for our safe mission, wherever it is to be.*

Your loving brother,
Adam

Hannah's heart leaped with hope at his admitting the night

before was one of the happiest in his life, for surely he meant the kiss. But, then her insides twisted with dismay. He'd left thinking she'd cried because of it. She swallowed the massive lump of disappointment in her throat and pushed the note into her skirt pocket. How many long months would it be before she saw him again?

Aunt Sophia interrupted her unhappy thoughts. "I know you're disappointed, Hannah. But come, sit down and tell me about the Heyward's soiree."

She composed her face and returned to her seat on the sofa. After sharing about the lovely, well-decorated house, the many dances and partners, Hannah took a deep breath. "Aunt Sophia, I met a young woman there named Juliet Nelson. She seemed to know Adam. What do you know about her and her family?"

"The Nelsons? I know all about them. Her wealthy father and her mother died during a ship disaster on their way back from England several years ago. Juliet became the ward of an uncle until her eighteenth birthday...a while back. Let's see, she must be about twenty now and is engaged to be married."

"Engaged?"

"It was in the *Gazette* last year. She's to marry an English Duke Montagu, but they have not announced a date yet, to my knowledge." She lifted her brows. "Of course, most of us Americans don't care too much about these English titles now." Hannah thought for a moment. "Do you know if it is...a love match?"

"Love match?" Sophia shook her head. "I doubt it very much. It's probably a marriage arranged by her uncle who, I understand, believes we colonials should've never rebelled against the king of England. He probably hopes to move back to England with the bride and be welcomed by the peerage after she gains her new title." Her aunt smiled and added, "There is quite a fortune, I understand, that Juliet inherits from her parents when she marries, which just may also be what the duke needs to keep up his large estate."

Hannah walked back to her room to change into her riding habit. She would enjoy a ride, even if Adam could not be with her.

She rode the roan filly, Dancer, Sophia's groom had saddled for her, through the quiet city park. Hercules sniffed at everything around them and barked at shadows.

A vision of Adam holding Juliet Nelson while dancing, her blond head so close to his, intruded into her thoughts. The muscles in her stomach tightened, and something dark and cloudy settled over her heart. Could the lovely Juliet Nelson, a woman of means, be persuaded or tempted to marry anyone she didn't love, or who didn't love her, even to gain a title? Not likely. Did she show the same excited and coquettish ways toward her duke fiancé as she had with Adam?

Hannah's lips tightened, and she wished she could kick something, but not her obedient mount. Why hadn't Adam explained his relationship to Juliet? Why had she been aboard his navy vessel?

The bridle path brought Hannah through the trees to a sun-washed meadow. Hercules sped after a squirrel with delight. The bright sunlight did something to Hannah's heart, as if it blazed into her inner being and exposed the feelings she was battling. Her conscience struck her. Jealousy fueled the thoughts she'd been hosting.

She stopped, dismounted, and walked, leading Dancer. For the first time in her life, she knew what that destructive emotion felt like. She shook her head and prayed. *Father, forgive me for...being jealous and letting my thoughts run in this terrible rut. I hate feeling this way. What do I need to do?*

As she rode back toward the stable, Hercules ahead of the filly, a gentle nudge in her spirit brought peace. Adam, wonderful Adam, who had never evidenced a single contentious or deceptive bone in his body, would undoubtedly tell her how he knew Miss Nelson in his first letter. And if he didn't? Why, she'd ask him, as she'd done all her life about anything that bothered her.

*F*ully provisioned and with all necessary repairs made to the vessel, the *Enterprise* had set sail with the morning tide from the Norfolk shipyards, along with three other ships. Adam stood on the quarterdeck to discuss their new assignment to the Mediterranean with his marine detachment. He trusted these three men with his life, and they trusted him in the same way. And that might prove vital, given the task before them.

Adam's promotion to lieutenant a year earlier had brought him the privilege of selecting members of his team. Ginger-bearded Josiah Campbell, a staunch Presbyterian and oldest of the detachment, served as his right-hand man. Besides wisdom and prowess for battles, he kept Adam supplied with spirited quotes from the Bible and the Reverend John Knox. Barrel-chested David Barron, age twenty-five, had ample experience as a marine, unfailing courage, and a knack for following Adam's orders with precision. Sandy-haired, muscle-bound Joel Murray, the youngest at twenty, looked up to the other marine members and was always ready to jump into a fight. Adam smiled—for this was so even if no one invited Joel to assist.

"Men, Tripoli has declared war on the United States. Captain Sterett has received orders for the *Enterprise* to join Commodore Richard Dale's flotilla to the Mediterranean. We're to blockade Tripoli's harbor and protect our American merchant vessels whenever we encounter them. If we are separated from the other three ships in our flotilla as we are sailing across the Atlantic, we're to meet at Gibraltar. Questions?"

Josiah Campbell nodded. "Who are the other captains and ships in the fleet?"

"Good question. Commodore Dale's flagship is *The President*. The *Philadelphia* has Samuel Barron as captain, and the *Essex*, captained by William Bainbridge, make up the other ships in our flotilla. We're part of a fine fleet."

Joel Murray glanced at David Barron. "You kin to that Captain Barron of the *Essex*?"

"An uncle. He inspired me to join the navy with all his tales." David leaned on the rail and flexed his brawny arms. "Are we going to fight the Barbary pirates and rescue our American sailors they've taken into slavery, or just guard merchant ships, Lieutenant White?"

"Glad you asked that, Barron. President Jefferson has given explicit orders to Commodore Dale to blockade the Tripoli harbor, but he's not authorized us to attack Barbary ships outright except to protect an American vessel under fire from them."

All three of the marines' lips tightened. Their desire for armed action, though unspoken, gripped their tanned faces.

Josiah came up with a Bible verse. "And David inquired of the Lord, saying, Shall I pursue after this troop? Shall I overtake them? And He answered him, Pursue: for thou shalt surely overtake them and recover all." His voice sounded more like an Old Testament prophet's than an American sailor's.

Adam smiled. The man was uncanny. Many times, he had a relevant text or quote ready at decisive moments.

That evening, before eight bells and lights out, Adam read again Hannah's first letter that had finally reached him.

Dear Adam,

I know it takes a long time for letters to come to you, so by now you're probably headed to wherever your orders are taking you. Be assured, Aunt Sophia and I, and Mama and Papa, are praying for you and Michael every day to be safe. I was so looking forward to talking with you after the New Year's soiree, but it was not to be.

Can you tell me how Juliet Nelson came to be on your ship? Aunt Sophia told me she was engaged to an English duke.

This week, Aunt Sophia and I have been ministering to the sick in the small hospital in town. She is very concerned over the conditions there and the little care being given. I've learned how to cleanse and sew up wounds, use healing herbs, and speak comfort. Aunt Sophia is such a skilled nurse and teacher.

I've saved the big news for last. Yesterday morning, we found a precious newborn left in a basket on our doorstep with "Peter" pinned to his ragged blanket. Aunt Sophia is beside herself about this child. She loves infants and took right to the little fellow, as did I. Mama Larnie has a married daughter who can nurse Peter, and Aunt Sophie will pay her to take care of him. It seems the Charleston Orphan House will not accept a child under the age of three. So we will make sure he receives the best care here with us. Right now, the daughter is visiting with Mama Larnie, so Peter is with me. I hear him waking now, and I'm happy to sit with him. I think it amazing that the Lord has me caring for an abandoned infant, like I once was.

Your forever loving sister,
  Hannah

Adam reread the missive, especially the closing. *Your forever loving sister.* What more proof did he need that she thought of him only as her brother? She hadn't changed her mind, even after that first kiss he'd pressed on her lips that still manifested in his dreams.

∼

Hannah strode downstairs to breakfast. Would she get a response from her letter to Adam today? Her heart lightened at the thought. It'd been three months since her note to him. She'd planned to ask him about that kiss on New Year's but could not get up her nerve or think of what to write. But she did ask him about Juliet Nelson. The young woman was hosting a soiree next month. Hannah had been invited but had little desire to attend. She walked into the breakfast room. Aunt Sophia sat at the table with her place cleared and the breakfast items replaced with plantation books and lists.

She glanced up as Hannah served herself from the buffet. "Dear, today, let's review all the herbs and remedies we'd talked about so far. Once you get this, you can nurse almost anyone. I'm so proud of your progress."

"Of course, Aunt Sophia. And thank you."

After Hannah finished her light repast, she moved closer to her aunt and the lists she was perusing. Sipping her coffee, she peered at the fine writing, eager for knowledge, as always.

"Let's start with a review of the common herbs." Aunt Sophia handed a list to Hannah that included drawings of the various plants. "Be sure to ask me if you have questions."

Hannah read aloud. "*Aloe vera is used topically for wound healing and burns. Orally for constipation, ulcers, and breathing problems. Echinacea helps heal colds, coughs, fever. Garlic is also good for colds, coughs, arthritis, and may help the blood. Chamomile tea is for calming and sleep. So are valerian, spearmint leaves, lemongrass, blackberry leaves, orange blossoms, hawthorn berries, and rosebuds.*" She stopped reading and looked at her aunt. "Why are so many things listed for calming and sleep?"

"Because the sick most often need their fears calmed, which will help them get well faster, and sleep may be the best healer of all. Also, the list includes herbs that are obtainable in different seasons. They're not all available the year round. Now do you understand?"

"Yes, I do." Hannah continued to read the list aloud until she finished.

Aunt Sophia pulled the largest old plantation household book nearer to her and opened to its remedies page, one that Hannah had studied many mornings. "Let me quiz you on some common ailments and the proper treatments." She smiled at Hannah. "You don't mind, do you?"

"Not one bit. I love to learn how to help hurting people."

"Tell me, what are two fundamental rules for a sick room that my Andrew stressed?"

"Keep a window partially open for fresh air at all times, and cover chamber pots and keep them in a closet instead of under the bed." Hannah couldn't help smiling. She'd kept a window opened, at least part way, since she'd read her uncle's thoughts on it. And she now kept her bedpan inside her closet, covered with a thick cloth.

Hannah found it interesting that her aunt did not agree with some of the most common treatments of the day. So many of the remedies for diseases listed in the old books included induced bleeding, sweating, raising blisters on the body to drain supposed poisons, and purging patients—making them vomit.

"Aunt Sophia, you promised to tell me the story of President Washington's medical treatment and unexpected death that helped prove what you and Uncle Andrew suspected about bleeding patients."

"So I did. The fact that Andrew was a prominent doctor and involved in Charleston politics means that I still hear certain things through the medical grapevine. You know, Andrew's father even hosted the president on one of his visits to Charleston. President Washington ended up with a sore throat after a horseback ride in sleet and snow on December 11, 1799. Three days later, after the physicians attending him, bled him, applied mustard blisters, and purged him with calomel, he passed away. But I believe the bleeding most likely caused his death." Sophia shook her head with regret. "Within thirteen hours, the attending physicians drew two quarts and a half of blood from the president. They soon observed that he 'expired without a struggle,' as the newspaper quoted them." Her aunt's eyes darkened in anger. "The poor man had no strength to put up a fight after losing all that blood."

Hannah shivered. "How terrible, Aunt Sophia."

Her aunt sighed. "Now you know what supposed help they gave him."

"I remember Mama teaching us that the Bible says the life of the flesh is in the blood. So it makes sense to me that when you draw blood from the body, you're also drawing away life, so we never did it."

"Your mother taught you that?"

"Yes. Actually, that same scripture is found in the book of Leviticus. It prohibits eating blood, and that was what Mama used to explain why we did not eat the blood of animals or bleed for sickness."

"Your mother is a smart, fine woman, Hannah. I've always thought so."

Hannah smiled. "Thank you, Aunt Sophia."

Her aunt closed the books, stacked the herbal lists, then stood and fixed her gaze on Hannah. Her clear blue eyes danced. "I saw the invitation to Juliet Nelson's soiree next month, and I have just the escort for you, niece."

"But...I'm not sure I want to attend."

"Pshaw. Of course, you'll want to attend, dear one." Aunt Sophia laid her hand on Hannah's shoulder. "I should've said escort for both of us, as I plan to attend. Where else will I have the opportunity to tell Dr. Barnes about the deplorable conditions we've seen in the Charleston Hospital? He heads the board, and maybe we can spur him to make improvements." A frown creased her smooth brow. "Or he may forbid us to frequent the premises with our new-fangled ideas of cleanliness and comfort for the hurting. I'm not ignorant that there could be repercussions to my talking plainly to him."

Hannah blinked at her aunt. "Surely not. Why wouldn't he want all the help he can get for the hospital? We saw so few workers there and hardly any with much knowledge."

Her aunt sighed. "Unfortunately, I have an unhappy history with Dr. Thomas Barnes."

Hannah requested that Aunt Sophia expound on that, but no amount of pleading would produce an explanation. Aunt Sophia would rarely speak ill of a doctor unless a patient's safety was in jeopardy. Following her aunt from the room, she let the matter rest. Perhaps, if she attended the soiree, she'd learn more. But who was this perfect escort her aunt had secured?

CHAPTER 8

*A*dam stood on the deck of the *Enterprise* with Captain Sterett. They'd left the rest of the flotilla blockading the Tripoli harbor as they'd set sail for Malta two days earlier to procure much-needed water stores for the squadron.

"A sail. A sail!" The shout rang out from the morning watch high in the eagle's nest.

Captain Sterett whipped out his eyeglass and viewed the approaching ship. He gave a dangerous sort of smile, then thrust the scope to Adam. "The side says it's the *Tripoli*. It's got to be part of Bashaw Yusuf's navy, with all that crazy paint."

"I think you're right, sir." Adam handed the eye piece back.

The captain looked at the ship again through the scope. "It could actually be an American ship they've captured and repainted for their own use. Something about it reminds me of the *Betsy* that was taken a couple of years back. And they still hold every one of her American crew in dastardly slavery under the sultan." His face hardened. "We may be under orders not to chase any of their vessels, but that's not to say we can't check them out if they drop into our laps. "Right, Lieutenant?"

At the possibility of seeing action, Adam's heart jumped in his chest. "Aye, aye, sir."

Sterett leaned over the railing and shouted, "Prepare for battle!"

Adam flew down the quarterdeck steps, repeating the command. Scurrying and yelling erupted on the deck as the sailors ran to their posts. Guns screeched across the decking as the excited seaman pushed and mounted them into the gun ports.

The enemy ship made no move to flee their approaching vessel flying British colors instead of the American flag. Commodore Dale's orders permitted the use of any colors as deception during a confrontation. The sultan was at peace with England, but at war with America. Adam's breath came fast and hot as his team of marines took their position with him on deck, fully armed for hand-to-hand combat, if it came.

"Resistance to tyranny is obedience to God." Josiah Campbell quoted Reverend Knox with a wink as he strode to stand beside Adam.

When the two ships came within shouting distance, Captain Sterett hailed the captain of the *Tripoli* and asked him about the object of his journey.

"We're out to cruise after the Americans. But we've yet to find any to fight."

Some of the *Enterprise* sailors hidden from view beside the guns swore.

Captain Sterett slammed his fist on the railing and hissed an order for the British flag to be lowered and the American flag raised. As the US colors went up, he yelled to his gunners, "Fire!"

The guns produced a deafening roar. Along with the flying cannon balls, streaks of fire seemed to emerge from the iron cannon muzzles. The crashing sound of solid shot striking the *Tripoli* followed. At such close range, few shots missed their mark.

The surprised pirates returned fire only sporadically but drew ever closer to the *Enterprise*. "I know their plan," Adam shouted in the crashing conflict to his team. "They hope to get close enough to swarm over our sides with their scimitars and pistols. They prefer hand-to-hand, man-to-man battle." He drew his pistol, and his men followed suit.

And his prediction proved correct. Adam's small marine detachment repulsed the pirates attempting to swing aboard, dropping many to the deck before they had a chance to use their deadly scimitars that could take off a sailor's head in one fell swoop.

The *Tripoli* moved off and, seeming to surrender, lowered their flag. Adam shook his head as the *Enterprise* crew assembled on deck and gave three cheers as a mark of victory.

Within moments, the sound of gunfire drowned the cheers. Disregarding the rules of war, the pirates hoisted their Tripoli flag again and fired at the exposed Americans, who scrambled for shelter.

The battle resumed and two additional times the *Enterprise* brought the Tripolitans to surrender, only to see them raise their flag again and start bombarding their ship.

Captain Sterett bounded over to Adam and his team. "We will stop this treachery now." He leaned over the railing and shouted to his gun crew, "Sink the villains!" In the minutes that followed, the sustained American cannonade did not cease until the *Tripoli's* Admiral Rous called for mercy and truly surrendered.

Captain Sterett ordered his surgeon to minister to the wounded on the defeated vessel. Adam and his team helped investigate the ship. One marine discovered in the hold a sword with an American insignia, and also an American navy uniform. So the *Tripoli* had fought and overcome an American ship somewhere and undoubtedly taken its crew into slavery. It was the custom of the Barbary pirates when capturing American vessels to strip the crew of their clothing and wear it to mock their new slaves before sending them to their sultan's dungeon.

Later the next day, Adam wrote to Hannah about the victory.

Dear Hannah,

Yesterday our ship soundly defeated the Tripoli, *one of the sultan's ships. Most amazing of all, the* Enterprise *miraculously suffered not a single casualty, nor injury, and with only minor damage to our vessel.*

This has to be an answer to prayer. I know you and the family are praying. Keep it up.

Good news. We are headed home. We will sail from Gibraltar down the North Coast of Africa, then across the Atlantic to the West Indies, then north by northwest to Charleston. In case you're wondering about this route, it's the only way to keep the wind at our backs. Why? Because prevailing winds in the North Atlantic run west to east, but by the North coast of Africa, they switch and run east to west. It would take us much longer to sail straight from Gibraltar toward Charleston with the winds in our faces. There, your lesson about sailing for today. Hope to see Charleston soon, if good weather holds.

Your loving brother,
Adam

~

Sailing from the Caribbean toward Charleston, Adam stood on the windy poop deck in his night watch duty about two hours before dawn and scoured the darkened horizon. A quick flash of light made uneasiness grip his insides. Lightning? He took out his eyeglass and turned it southeast, directly into the wind.

There it was again—a glimmering flash at the horizon, so fast he wanted to discount it. But when he saw it a third time, he knew it was no illusion. Josiah Campbell strode up beside him and saluted. Adam handed him the eyepiece.

The man frowned. "It's an enormous blow coming. Something woke me up feeling uneasy, sir. This was why."

On the horizon, a slice of light formed between the ocean and the sky. Lightning slashed across it, and an eerie light flashed across waves to the ship. Adam took a deep breath. They had only a brief window to prepare.

"Go tell Captain Sterett. I'll alert the rest of the crew." Adam leaned over the railing and shouted, "All hands on deck! Storm coming!"

Josiah bounded down the steps, yelling the same thing.

As the crew clamored from their hammocks, Captain Sterett arrived on deck and shouted his orders. "Prepare a storm anchor! Lash everything down double tight! Rig all sails for storm! Batten down the hatches!"

Within minutes, the storm became visible to all hands, a beast that rumbled toward them, blowing wind and fire. Thick darkness denser than midnight soon settled over the ship. The cracking and streaking of lightning shed the only temporary light. Rain fell in heavy sheets and almost blinded one if facing into the wind.

Adam and his marine crew threw overboard all but the most vital supplies to lighten the ship, while Captain Sterett stood behind the helmsman, gripping the wheel with him to help steer the tossing ship. The crew tied ropes around their waists, and several lashed themselves to the masts, including Adam and his men, to keep from being washed overboard. They strained to remain on deck as the ship rose, turned, and dove into watery gullies, then shot back up the mountains of water.

Every barrel and rigging not tied or hammered down washed overboard. A deafening, cracking sound filled Adam's ears, and the mast he'd lashed himself to broke off midway. Before he could get free, it tumbled to the deck, its end crushing one of his legs. His groan and prayer for God's help rose against the pounding storm tossing the ship. Then the wind and rain abated, and he fell into a dark pit where he felt no pain.

"Lieutenant, you back with us?" The concerned voice of Josiah Campbell roused Adam. "I saw that mast land on you. We've pulled it off." The man leaned over him, frowning.

Adam groaned as he tried to sit up. Dawn spread across the sky, and the ship no longer tossed. The driving rain and wind had settled down like a wounded lion. "It's my right leg, Josiah. Can't move it."

"Lie still, sir. Don't you worry none. We'll get you to your cabin as soon as I can rouse our sleepy team members."

Someone harrumphed. "Don't pay any attention to him, sir. We're here and don't need any rousing." David Barron leaned toward Adam with Joel Murray right behind him.

Josiah grinned at them. "We do give thanks to God Almighty. We've made it through the hurricane, but sure hate to see you injured, sir."

When his team hoisted him, Adam again lost consciousness.

~

In late summer, a week and a half before Juliet's soiree, Hannah sat on the front porch of her aunt's house in a swing, studying the herb lists again. Two strongly built sailors in their blue-and-white navy uniforms, carrying a man on a stretcher, stopped at their front gate. Another carried a sailor's bag across his broad shoulders.

She stiffened and dropped her lists, then ran down the steps. Adam lay on the cot, his large frame overfilling it. A gasp rose in her throat, and moisture threatened in her eyes. How badly was he injured?

"Miss, the lieutenant said for us to bring him here." The man who spoke was tall and red-headed. He swung the heavy canvas seabag down from his shoulder. The other two men looked younger, and their bulging muscles made the cot and Adam's bulk it supported look lightweight. All the sailors' faces and arms bore the bronze glow of many seagoing adventures. Except Adam's. His pale countenance under a full beard caused her heart to fall to her feet.

"By all means, bring him in." She opened the gate and held it for them to come through. Her eyes flew over Adam, especially his right leg sheathed in bandages with bright bloodstains peeping through below his knee.

Adam's eyes met hers. With his broad hands she knew so well folded across his chest, he smiled at her. "Hello, Hannah. It's not as bad as it looks. I bet you and Aunt Sophia will have me up and running in no time." His voice wavered as if he were exhausted. The entourage moved past her and up the steps.

She couldn't hold the tears back any longer. Swiping them off her cheeks, she followed.

Aunt Sophia came through the front door and held it for the sailors to bring in the stretcher and ditty bag. "Well, Adam, thank God you've made it home." Even she sounded choked up on the last words.

The three men followed Aunt Sophia up the stairs and to Adam's bedroom. They gently deposited him on the bed and propped pillows behind his back. The older sailor swung the seabag from his shoulder to the floor next to the chifferobe. Its solid thump suggested heavy books and clothing stretched the canvas to its limits.

Hannah stood at the door, swallowed, and tried to compose her face.

Adam motioned to her. She came to stand by her aunt near the bed. "Aunt Sophia, I want you and Hannah to meet my fine marine team members. Josiah Campbell is the red-head, the burly one is David Barron, and the *youngster* is Joel Murray."

The younger man's face reddened, and he balled an enormous fist at Adam. "Sir, I'd hate to bump that ailing leg of yours, accidental like." All four chuckled.

Adam tilted his head toward Hannah and Aunt Sophia. "Gentlemen, this is my Aunt Sophia and my sister, Hannah." At the word *sister*, the two younger men eyed Hannah with fresh interest.

Josiah turned to Aunt Sophia. "Ma'am, we best be getting back now that we've got this troublesome patient off our hands." He smiled at Hannah. "Seems to me as though he's going to get all the care he can use. Meanwhile, the navy's done given him leave for however long it takes."

Aunt Sophia thanked them, and Hannah expressed her thanks as well. Joel and David gave her a warm grin as the three retreated from the room. Their heavy footsteps sounded down the stairs and then across the porch.

"Come here, Hannah." Adam held out his hand, and she came forward and took it.

His weak clasp shocked her.

"Hannah, I'm going to be fine, so don't you fret. Hear me?"

She nodded, and he released her hand.

Aunt Sophia bent to examine the bandaged leg, sniffed, then frowned. "Adam, we read about your ship taking that Barbary pirate ship in the Mediterranean. Why, you're all heroes, your captain awarded, and the crew given a bonus, but the write-up in the *Gazette* said you suffered no casualties or injuries."

Adam took a deep breath, and he lifted his head from the pillow. "Aunt, this didn't happen in the Mediterranean. It happened during a hurricane as we came home through the Caribbean. We almost lost the ship and all our lives, but God intervened." He tried to adjust his bandaged leg and groaned. "I was injured when the mast I was lashed to split and fell across my leg, but thank God, the ship didn't go down." A smile lit his pale face, and much of the heaviness lifted from the room. "I'm sure all the prayers you and Hannah and Mama and Papa prayed had much to do with us surviving." He dropped back on the pillow as if the story had taken his last energy. Two red spots appeared on his cheeks above his thick, dark beard.

Her aunt leaned closer. "You are in pain, my dear boy." She laid her hand across his forehead.

"Not too much unless I try to move the leg. The ship surgeon set the broken bone and told me it'd take six to eight weeks for complete healing. That was a week ago. But it started feeling warm yesterday, if that means anything."

Aunt Sophia clicked her tongue. "It means a lot, dear boy, and your forehead is hot with fever. Thank God you're here so we can take care of you. We are going to have to unwrap it and see if infection has set in."

Hannah bit her lip. The presence of blood on the bandages meant the bone had broken through the skin when the mast hit him. An infection in an injury like that could be deadly.

"Uh, can we get some grub first? I could not eat much of anything today."

"Hannah, go ask Mama Larnie to prepare some strong, cool broth for Adam, and a slice of her homemade bread. We'll get that in him before we go to work."

She flew from the room and down to the kitchen. Mama Larnie had a tray almost ready to go. She'd gotten the word of Adam's arrival. By now, Hannah was well acquainted with Sophia's healing broths.

She took the tray up to Adam and sat beside him as Aunt Sophia left to prepare water and linens. Adam's hand shook, trying to lift the spoon to his mouth, so Hannah took over spooning the cool, hearty broth to his lips. She basked in the warmth of his gray eyes resting on her face.

When he finished eating what he could, she sponged his face with cool water and brushed his hair back from his forehead. She laid her palm over his forehead again and found it too warm. She closed her eyes and whispered a prayer. When she opened them, he was staring at her.

"What healing hands you have, dear Hannah. I'm truly feeling better."

She tried not to look at his injured leg with its bloodstained wrappings and mustered a bright smile. He would need a lot of care for several weeks to pull through an infection and fully recover the use of his leg. Of course, she'd need to change her plan to attend Juliet Nelson's soiree. Her aunt would surely agree.

Aunt Sophia returned with supplies and Mama Larnie's son July. "July will be a help in nursing Adam. He can bathe him, assist him, and give him a shave when he's ready."

July nodded. "Yes'm. I'm happy to do everything I can for Mr. Adam."

Indeed, he proved a great boon in the following days, even helping Hannah tend to little Peter when she needed to fetch something for Adam. She'd never forget Adam's surprise and smile when she first brought the baby into his room.

He looked from her to the boy in her arms. "This must be little

Peter you told me about in your last letter." He winked at her. "Don't tell me you've gotten attached to him. His parents may yet show up and want him back."

She'd sat down with Peter on her knees. The boy turned his bright blue eyes on Adam, gave a happy squeal, and captivated her brother as he had her and Aunt Sophia. The two became fast friends, especially after Adam whittled a toy boat, smoothed it to satin, and presented it to the boy.

Aunt Sophia did not agree with calling off their attendance at the soiree. After a week and a half of careful ministrations, with July's help and herbs of Echinacea, garlic, and goldenseal, she declared Adam would be fine without the two of them for one evening. July would stay within call. Even Adam insisted they go.

On the night of the soiree, Hannah finished dressing in her fashionable empire waisted yellow dress with April's help. After the young woman also arranged an elegant hairdo for her, she thanked the maid and stood and gazed at herself in her chifferobe mirror. Her satin dress shimmered in the lantern light, as did her hair. April had added some perfumed sunflower oil that brought out the golden highlights in the soft curls framing her face. A pearl comb graced a chignon at the back of her head. Aunt Sophia had brought and insisted she wear a matching pearl necklace and earrings.

Hannah picked up her lacy wrap and walked over to baby Peter, who slept in his small bassinet. Brushing the blond curls from his forehead, she kissed his velvety cheek. He spread a small hand out, sighed, and continued to sleep. April picked up the basket and carried him away for his nighttime with her sister, who nursed him and returned him mornings.

Hannah sighed as she stepped from the room. How she wished Adam awaited in her aunt's parlor, not the man Aunt Sophia had asked to escort them to the soiree. She searched her mind for his name. Oh yes. Gideon Falconer, an exiled Englishman. Her aunt had reminded Hannah when she shared the man's name with Adam as they ministered to her brother that morning.

Grasping and lifting the front of her soft, flowing skirt, she descended the stairs. and swept into the parlor. Aunt Sophia sat conversing with a gentleman who stood near the mantel, leaning on it with his elbow. He was tall, maybe more so than Adam, and his thick shoulders bulged in his waistcoat. But his countenance looked more like stone or steel. Dressed in a dark-green coat and tan trousers, with his light brown hair cropped in the latest fashion, and tall, shining black boots reaching to his knees, he made quite the picture of virile male strength.

He cast Hannah an appreciative glance and smiled. Gentleness flowed over his countenance and emanated from his blue eyes, softening the stony look she'd first imagined.

"Here she is." Her aunt stood. "Hannah, please say hello to Gideon Falconer, my husband's nephew, who emigrated from England a while back. This is my niece, Hannah White."

"Hello." Hannah smiled and extended her hand.

The man strode forward, took her hand, and bowed. "Honored to make your acquaintance." He released her and turned to her aunt. "You have not exaggerated, dear Mrs. Rutledge." His voice was deep and warm. "And I'm delighted to escort both of you lovely ladies."

"You are too kind, sir." Hannah shot a questioning glance at her aunt.

In her pale, blue silk gown, Sophia practically glowed. "Shall we go, you two?"

Hannah hesitated. "Yes, but perhaps I should check quickly on Adam first."

But Aunt Sophia took Hannah's light wrap from her hands and drew it about her shoulders. "No need to fret about Adam, dear. He'll be fine." She smiled and turned toward the door.

~

*A*dam sat upstairs at his bedroom window. He could make it now from the bed to the chair waiting there with the help of July and the crutches Aunt Sophia had her carpenter make for him.

He looked up from his law book he was studying as three figures descended from the front porch and walked to the carriage.

Hannah took his breath away in a flowing, yellow satin dress. He frowned, watching the courtly newcomer help first his aunt, then Hannah into the carriage. The man had the bearing of an aristocrat. He pressed his lips together, and leaned his head on the back of the chair and closed his eyes. What he wouldn't give to be the one helping Hannah into the conveyance, dancing with her, holding her in his arms

Then his leg began to ache. He struggled back to his bed and dropped onto it with a groan.

Who was this Gideon Falconer?

CHAPTER 9

Gideon's hands exuded warmth and strength through several dances, but also gentleness. He guided her through the dance steps as if she were like the china doll Adam had once brought her from his travels. If she closed her eyes, she could imagine she was dancing with Adam. Dear Adam. He wouldn't be dancing again for quite some time.

"Hannah, are you tiring? I know my clumsy movements might tire anyone. Want to sit awhile?"

Heat rose in Hannah's face. Gideon must have noticed the few moments she closed her eyes. "Well, maybe sitting a bit would be nice." She looked up into his handsome face and smiled. "But it has nothing to do with your dancing. You dance very well, sir."

He led her out to the cooler veranda, with its lit lanterns. They sat beside a small wicker table under a sweet-smelling climbing rose, which twined over the balustrade and up one of the porch columns.

He stood with an apology. "Forgive me, I didn't think. Would you like some refreshment?"

"Some of that punch would be just right, I think. Thank you for asking."

The man was thoughtful to a fault. He strode away and soon returned with two cups, then sat beside her.

Hannah sipped the apple cider laced with mint and sighed. Just what she needed after the many dances, most of which had been with the man beside her. Although other young women appeared at his elbow at the end of each dance, he took little notice of them, other than being polite.

Upon their arrival at the soiree, the three of them, or rather Gideon, had made quite an entrance. Only quick glances turned on her and Aunt Sophia. Scarcely a woman of any age in the gathering proved impervious to the handsome, refined looks of the tall, well-built Gideon Falconer. All eyes had examined her escort before giving Hannah their approval.

She finished her cider and set the cup on the wicker table. "Tell me about your immigration to Charleston, Mr. Falconer."

"Please, call me Gideon."

"All right. Gideon, I'm all ears."

"My story is not a happy one and may not be so good for a young lady like yourself, Hannah."

She cocked her chin at him. "But please, still share it. Does Aunt Sophia know your story?"

He took a deep breath. "Yes, I'd say she knows most of it."

She smiled. "She'll tell me if you don't, but I'd rather hear it from you, sir."

"Very well, you asked for it." He drained his cup of cider and set it on the small table with so much care, even with his large hands, it might have been a family heirloom.

Hannah settled back and gave him her full attention.

"I grew up in Suffolk, England, an only child. My parents died of fever when I was ten years old, and an uncle took charge of the estate. By the time I was sixteen, he had gambled away all the profits and the land itself. We had raised sheep and sold wool, which was a profitable business as long as my parents lived, but not after my uncle took charge. At seventeen, penniless, and without a home, I signed on a ship that frequented our coast. I'm sorry to tell you, it was a slaver."

Hannah covered her mouth, but at his pained expression, nodded for him to continue.

"For three years, I regretted that decision and came to hate slavery. When I was able to return to England, I met a wonderful minister by the name of John Newton who had once served as a captain of a slave ship. He and his acquaintance, William Wilberforce, became great friends of mine." He glanced down at his firm hands clasped across his knees. "I came to know Jesus Christ as my Lord and Savior through Reverend Newton."

"That's wonderful, Gideon. I, too am a believer."

He nodded, looked around, then leaned closer. "I can tell you, there is a strong movement for abolition growing in England, and these two men are a big part. One day..." He stopped talking as another couple passed and then sat some distance away.

Hannah smiled and whispered, "My mother is of the Quaker faith, though I'm not. But Quakers have come out against slavery, and I agree. Our family freed our few slaves some time ago."

He sat up and looked at her with a new expression.

Aunt Sophia came out to the veranda. Dr. Barnes trailed behind her with a rather sheepish grin. Gideon stood and offered his chair, but Sophia waved his invitation down.

"I missed you two in the ballroom, so here you are."

"Aunt Sophia, Mr. Falconer—Gideon was just telling me how he came to Charleston." She looked at him. "Or at least, he was just getting ready to tell that part."

"Do tell her, Gideon, or she'll ferret it out of me later." Aunt Sophia motioned Dr. Barnes forward. "But first, please meet my friend Dr. Thomas Barnes. He's in charge of the Charleston Hospital. Doctor, this is Gideon Falconer, my husband's nephew who has recently emigrated from England. And you know my niece, Hannah White."

The two men nodded and shook hands. Dr. Barnes, handsome in a black silk waistcoat, white trousers, and spotless cravat, smiled at Hannah. "Of course, I could not forget your Hannah. You have quite an ally in her, I believe, for hospital improvements." His tone was not sarcastic. Indeed, he seemed much more friendly and relaxed than when Hannah had met him briefly on a recent visit to the hospital. In fact, he hardly seemed the same stiff man that had frowned at them when he walked into a patient's room to discover them tugging at a window sash, trying to get some fresh air into the sickroom.

Aunt Sophia smiled at the doctor, though she addressed Gideon. "Don't let us interrupt your continued story, nephew."

Dr. Barnes took Sophia's elbow, and pink rose in her aunt's cheeks. Hannah swallowed her surprise as they walked toward the garden with its lanterns on poles illuminating the shell-paved path. The soft light gleamed on the man's salt-and-pepper hair. Was this the same man with whom her aunt had said she had an unhappy history?

"Hannah?" Gideon's deep voice drew her attention from the two moving down the garden path. His chiseled profile was most handsome, she had to admit, and his blue eyes warmed as she met his glance. "Do you want to hear the rest of my story? It's fine, if not."

She shook her head. "Oh no, I want to hear it. Be assured. How did you end up immigrating to Charleston?"

He ducked his head, revealing the neat part in his thick, smooth brown hair. "I found a job as a gamekeeper on an estate after I became a Christian. I love the fields, the forests, the farmlands, and all of God's beautiful creatures. But I couldn't countenance arresting hungry people who sometimes came to hunt for food—such as rabbits, of which we had many—on the property."

She practically held her breath as this man opened his heart to her. Who would've thought they had so much in common? "And?"

A muscle worked in his neck. "Actually, I started helping desperate families on the brink of starvation find the rabbits, the quail, and whatever was more abundant in the forests and fields of my employer and which might not be missed. But when he discovered what I'd been doing, he became furious and went for the sheriff." He glanced at her. "Truthfully, I was wrong to do what I did, but the poor families were starving, and it seemed the only way I could help."

She stared at him. "Did the sheriff arrest you?"

He took a deep breath and shook his head. "He didn't have a chance. I fled the estate with the little savings I had and found a ship heading for Charleston. I knew my mother had a brother named Andrew Rutledge here, but I didn't know he'd passed." He sat forward in his chair. "Your wonderful Aunt Sophia has treated me royally. She helped me find a position on a plantation, Brighton Hall. I'm working there as a manager and factor."

Hannah smiled. "I'm glad you shared your story, Gideon. You and I have something in common. I love God's creation and also helping hurting people."

His tight face relaxed. "So you don't mind that your escort tonight is a fugitive, a wanted man in England?"

"No." She let out a small chuckle, almost disbelieving her own admission. "In fact, my escort has turned out to be a rather pleasant surprise."

Later that night, sipping a cup of hot chocolate in the kitchen before bedtime, Hannah's aunt asked her about what Gideon had shared of his story, and she gave a quick review.

When Hannah finished, Aunt Sophia gave a nod. "Just as I thought. He never tells that his father was a viscount. That makes Gideon a baron." She drained her cup. "Of course, here in America, we put little store by those peerage titles. Not since our glorious revolution. But Gideon is truly a remarkable man to have come through all he has and still be strong, but also gentle and without bitterness." She stood and smiled. "Someone once said blood will tell. Perhaps our Gideon is an example of that good heritage that refuses to be defeated."

As they went up the stairs together, her aunt shared a not-too-pleasant surprise with Hannah. Tomorrow Juliet Nelson would come to visit their patient.

To Hannah's hidden pleasure the next day, Adam proved no

happier than she when he learned Juliet was coming and insisted on being moved to a chair before her arrival. Right after the mid-day meal, Hannah and July settled him in his favorite place before the window.

The young woman arrived promptly at two o'clock, the usual time for visiting in Charleston. Hannah came down to the parlor alone to greet her. Aunt Sophia was out on a call.

Dressed in a lilac satin frock that flowed over her slender form from its empire waistline to her satin shoes, and with a matching ribbon in her high curled hair, Juliet was a portrait of blond beauty. What in the world would Hannah talk about with the sophisticated Charleston belle? They walked toward the stairs as Hannah turned things to say over in her mind. But it proved no problem. Juliet Nelson could talk nonstop about her own activities and her plans for the future.

She glided into the upstairs bedroom with its sitting alcove and right up to Adam's chair. Being careful of his extended, bandaged leg, she reached for his hand. "Dear Adam, I'm so sorry you've suffered a wound." He freed his hand, and she pulled a nearby chair closer and sat staring at him, her face lit up like a lantern.

Little Peter, in his bassinet on the other side of the room, gave one of his happy hollers.

Juliet Nelson's eyes almost popped out of her head. "What...whose baby...?" She stared first at Adam, then at Hannah.

Peter emitted another sound, not as joyful. Hannah went to him and picked him up. He twisted around in her arms to look at the brightly colored vision next to the window.

Hannah walked over with him. "This is Peter, a foundling that someone left on Aunt Sophia's doorstep a few months ago." Peter stuck the last three fingers of one hand in his mouth and lifted the other hand toward the shining, warm color of Juliet's gown.

Juliet's face turned gentle. "Why, I believe he wants to come to me. Do you think he would?"

Hannah swallowed the quick, negative answer that flew to her lips and moved closer. Juliet lifted her hands and Peter went to her. She placed him on her knee and rocked him. He laughed with glee and reached for the ribbon in her hair.

Hannah bent to push his damp hand away. "Don't let him spoil your coiffure, Juliet."

"I'm not one bit worried about being spoiled. What a lovely boy you are, Peter. I've a good mind to take you home with me." She bent and kissed the top of his blond curls.

Something like a knife pressed against Hannah's chest. Take him home with her?

Adam shook his head. "Oh no, we could never let this boy get away. Why, he's helping me recover fast."

He held out his wide hands and Peter came to him. He drew the child to his chest and nuzzled his cheek. Peter withdrew his wet fingers from his mouth and chortled, then reached for Adam's ear.

Juliet straightened her fine skirt and quizzed Hannah. "You mean someone actually left this precious child on your doorstep? I'm sure we have an orphanage here in Charleston. I've made several donations to it—the Charleston Orphan House is the name."

Hannah nodded. "Yes, but it does not take children under the age of three."

"How ridiculous. This is the first time I've heard of this." Juliet frowned and lifted her lovely blue eyes first to Adam, then to Hannah. "I believe most folks in Charleston know I became an orphan myself when only ten years old after my parents died in a mishap at sea. Of course, my uncle became my guardian, and the estate has provided well for me. But orphans are close to my heart. So what has happened to other foundlings?"

Aunt Sophia entered the room. "I can answer that, Juliet." She pulled a chair for herself and one for Hannah into the window area. "The board for orphans tries to find a foster home and a wet nurse to raise the child until they can admit it to the Charleston Orphan House at age three."

"Why do they insist the child be three?" Juliet's porcelain forehead wrinkled.

"They say the ratio of staff to children at the orphanage is such that there are no resources available to nurture the youngest and neediest of infants. The children need to be able to dress, wash, and feed themselves and respond to verbal commands with a minimum of mollycoddling and handholding." Sophia finished her response with the tightening of her lips.

"Well, I do say. This is unacceptable, to say the least." Juliet sat back in her chair, then she smiled at Adam. "You look very domesticated with that child in your lap, Adam. Pretty different from the strong marine I remember rescuing me when the pirate ship was burning and sinking."

Hannah and Aunt Sophia gave her their full attention, and she quickly told the story of her capture by pirates and later rescue by the *Enterprise* and Adam.

Peter reached toward Hannah, and she took the boy into her arms. She stood. "Please excuse us. It's almost time for his next feeding, and his wet nurse will be waiting downstairs."

Happy to leave the gathering, Hannah hurried down the stairs, hugging Peter close. Later, she released a soft sigh when Juliet's carriage pulled away from the front drive. Surely, her remark about taking Peter home meant nothing. How could it, coming from a Charleston butterfly soon to marry a duke and move to England?

~

Two weeks after the soiree, Sophia announced an emergency visit to a friend's rice plantation and invited Hannah to go with her. This was an associate of her late husband who had employed Gideon Falconer. The owner needed Sophia's advice on an ill slave.

Mr. Jude Thompson was a jovial, robust, middle-aged man who wore a silk waistcoat of light blue with black trousers and boots showing the evidence of an earlier muddy walk. His ginger-colored beard matched his straggly, curly hair that flowed to his shoulders.

They arrived just in time for lunch, and he invited them to a spread of baked fowl, steamed cabbage, and two kinds of squash with fresh-baked cornbread. A fragrant, cinnamon-rich apple pie completed the menu. Gideon Falconer shared the meal with them. Hannah enjoyed his straightforward conversation about the plantation and his work while her aunt questioned the plantation owner about the ailing slave.

After the delicious meal, Gideon invited Hannah for a horseback ride over the plantation. She looked at her aunt. "Yes, that would be great, Gideon. Hannah, you don't need to accompany me and Mr. Thompson to check on his sick servant. By all means go for a ride. The weather is perfect."

Hannah was happy to agree, and soon she rode alongside Gideon down the plantation road on the good mount he'd saddled for her. He pointed out the various outbuildings and then different fields of crops they passed. Tall, tasseled corn, alfalfa, and oats braved the hot summer air. Cattle and sheep which filled various meadows lifted their heads and stared at them when they passed.

Gideon turned in the saddle to look at her. "How about a shady rest about now?"

Hannah nodded. "That would be fine with me."

They stopped under the wide limbs of a large oak, which had a wooden bench beneath it. They dismounted, tied the horses' reins to a branch, and sat.

"I've told you my story, Hannah. Would you tell me yours? Sophia has hinted that you have quite a tale yourself." Gideon chewed on a piece of oat straw he'd swiped from a field they'd just passed.

Hannah took a deep breath, inhaling the scent of hay and Gideon's clean, manly smell, not unlike Adam's scent of the sea she'd always loved. The nearness of Gideon's muscular form raised a surprising alertness in her.

She told him about her abandonment at birth and being found by the Whites. "Adam, the wounded marine Aunt Sophia and I have been nursing, is my brother, and he is also *not* my brother."

Gideon's handsome face brightened with inquisitiveness. "Really? How does that work?"

"We grew up as brother and sister, but we're no blood kin, as I found out last year."

"Just last year?"

She shared a little about Saul and Charles Seymour and her shock of discovering Charles was her father. She held out her hand with the crooked, small finger. "This is part of what, we think, convinced him. His wife, supposedly my mother, had a bent finger just like it. Then there was the blanket I was wrapped in with his initials embroidered on the top. Apparently, in a drunken rage, he instructed his servant to abandon me in the woods when he discovered I was a third daughter and not the son he wanted."

Gideon's nostrils flared. "But your mother—how could she ever agree to such a dastardly deed?"

"She died in childbirth."

Gideon shook his head, then took her hand, with its bent little finger, into his large, callused grasp. "It's such a small hand and yet so beautiful." He drew it to his lips and kissed her palm.

Sucking in a quick breath, Hannah pulled away and stood, her heart threatening to beat out of her chest.

Gideon was quick to apologize. "I'm sorry if I frightened you. Not sure what possessed me to do that. Will you forgive me?"

Hannah nodded and moved to her horse. What was she frightened of? It was not the first time a man had kissed her hand. But it was the first time she'd felt the kiss down to her toes.

CHAPTER 10

Adam pushed his law books into the bottom of his ditty bag, then added his clothing. The long weeks of convalescence had given him much time to study. He now knew what he wanted to do with his life after the navy—pursue a law profession.

Hannah came into the room holding a sleeping Peter. She tucked him into his cradle and faced Adam. "I can't believe it's time for you to go back to the navy. Are you sure you're well enough?"

Adam looked at her and smiled. "Yes. See?" He stamped his healed leg, but not too hard. "I'm glad I got to see Mama and Papa yesterday. But, Hannah, I hope you're going to look more happy when I leave than they looked yesterday saying their goodbyes."

She gave him a tremulous smile and folded her arms. "You've always told me what has to be, must be, and we displease God if we fret. I'll pray for you every day, Adam." She blinked hard.

He stopped his packing and walked over to her. He lifted her chin and gazed into her violet eyes, dark with emotion. "Good, I don't see a single tear. That's my girl." He moved away fast, forcing back the strong desire to kiss her tender lips.

How long could he keep secret his love for her? The one thing he now knew for sure, since his convalescence and daily contact with

Hannah, was that his affection for her was no longer simply a brotherly one. It was the pure love a man has for a woman like she'd become and like he'd desire to marry one day. But did she have any idea? A sharp pain crossed his middle. And what place did Gideon Falconer have in her heart?

The man had become almost a weekly visitor, and he sometimes came upstairs to greet Adam. He could find no fault with the big-framed man whose faith and good will blazed from his eyes and echoed in his confident voice and words. It would be a relief if he could discern some reason to advise Hannah not to encourage him. But that was an unworthy idea. Unworthy of all he stood for.

He cast his troublesome thoughts aside, strode over to the bed, and placed a kiss on the sleeping child's cheek. Then he hoisted the seabag onto his shoulder, grabbed his hat and jacket, and headed for the stairs. Hannah followed without a sound.

Aunt Sophia waited at the front door. He lowered his bag and hugged her.

Hannah hung back but suddenly came forward and into his arms. A sob escaped her lips.

"Hey, I told you, no tears." But he delighted in holding her slight form, smelling of lavender.

"Please come back in one sound piece, Adam." She drew away.

"I second that, dear boy." Aunt Sophia pulled a handkerchief from her sleeve and dabbed at her eyes. "We've gotten mighty used to having you here, Adam, and we are going to miss you. But we are so proud of what you're doing for our country, you and that strong team of yours. They reminded me of David's mighty men in the Bible."

Adam grinned. "And I'll miss you two very much as well, not to mention this tranquil life. I must get back to the navy before I lose all my derring-do." He winked at Hannah. "You will write to me, right?"

She nodded.

He pressed his bicorn on his head, picked up his bag, and sailed out of the door.

*A*fter watching Adam's wagon trot up the street toward the harbor from the window upstairs, Hannah picked up Peter, awaking from his brief nap, and hugged him tight. At least she had him to keep her busy when not working with her aunt and the sick they ministered to. The boy placed a small hand on her streaming cheeks and began to cry himself. She grabbed a towel from the washstand and wiped her face, then his cheeks. "Dear Peter, we will be fine while he's gone. The Lord will help us and keep him safe." She looked around the room for the small boat Adam had carved for the boy, found it, then placed it in his pudgy hand. The child crooned his delight. If only she could be so easily diverted.

∼

*T*wo weeks later, Aunt Sophia came for her as she sat on the second-story balcony writing to Adam. Her aunt's stiff face sent a warning shock through Hannah, and she laid down her ink pen. Glancing back through her bedroom door, she listened. Peter still slept after his noon feeding.

"Hannah, we have some visitors below. Some very surprising guests. Prepare yourself for both good news...and not so good."

She closed her inkwell and stood. "Whatever do you mean, Aunt Sophia?"

Her aunt took a deep breath. "A young man and woman, Peter and Pearl Benson, are here. They say they are baby Peter's parents...and they've come for their son."

Hannah's heart jumped into her throat. "Do you...think they are his true parents?"

"My first impression is they are, but I need you to come and decide for yourself, hear their story." She laid her hand on Hannah's arm. "I know you've grown attached to the precious boy, as I have, but we must seek God's best will for him."

Hannah nodded, but her lips tightened as she followed her aunt downstairs. An unspoken prayer formed in her heart. *Lord, how can*

THE LIEUTENANT'S SECRET LOVE

You let this be true when I've come to love Peter like a child of my own? Other questions careened through her mind.

The quiet couple sat on the satin sofa, not relaxed, but perched on the edge. A package lay in the woman's lap, and the man held her hand. The moment Hannah looked at Pearl, she saw the resemblance—the sunny blond hair, the pert nose and quick smile of Baby Peter. But he had his father's startling blue eyes. The man's dark, clipped beard covered the lower part of his strong, tanned face, and curly brown hair escaped from his ponytail. Both of them stood, and her aunt introduced them.

When they'd all taken seats again, Pearl sat forward and told her story, her eyes burdened with sorrow and guilt. "When little Peter was born, his father was at sea, and I was indentured. My master threw me and Peter onto the street." Her face drooped with sadness and she lowered her eyes. "You see, we weren't married." She looked up and her brown eyes widened. "But we are now, to be sure, ma'am. It was the first thing we did last week when Peter Sr. came into port." She addressed Aunt Sophia, then glanced at Hannah.

Her husband smiled and squeezed her hand. "Yes, ma'am. That's exactly what we did. I love Pearl, and I know I'll love my son." He gazed into his wife's face. "And I've got a year's pay and bonus to get us set up in our own place and start a seamstress business for Pearl. We can make a good home for Peter now. I did not know what my dear one was going through while I was on the other side of the world, part of a merchant ship's crew."

So the man sailed on a vessel the US Navy and Adam were sent out to protect during their passage to and from ports of call carrying American trade goods.

Aunt Sophia spoke up. "Pearl, tell again about leaving Peter on our doorstep and how you lived."

Pearl sighed and tears overflowed and streamed down her cheeks. "I went to live with a widow friend who already had too many children for me to bring Peter. So I sewed two identical blankets for him. I'd heard about you continuing your husband's work helping folks and your kind heart, ma'am. You would take good care of my baby. I pinned a note on his shirt with his name, which is like his father's." She stopped and wiped her tears. "It was the hardest thing I've ever done in my life, but I had no choice." As if remembering, she picked up the package in her lap and thrust it toward Aunt Sophia. "Here's the identical blanket I made for my boy. Do you still have the one I'd wrapped him in when you found him?" Her hopeful eyes rested on Sophia, then on Hannah.

Aunt Sophia took the package. "Yes, I think we do." She handed the parcel to Hannah, stood, and walked out of the room.

Hannah unwrapped the baby blanket, and her breath caught in her throat. How could she forget the loving design, the perfect stitches, and the little boat motif embroidered on its edge? The careful work had surprised both her and her aunt when they'd found Peter in his pretty blanket—and which now lay in his bassinet. A long, unhappy sigh escaped her lips, but she held her peace until Sophia returned and laid the two blankets side by side. An identical match.

The couple's faces brightened until they shone like sunshine. Pearl leaned forward. "If that doesn't prove my story, I've one other thing. Little Peter has a small, coin-size red birthmark on his left thigh."

Aunt Sophia nodded. "Yes, he does. I'd almost forgotten that, but I did note it when we changed his clothing the first time." She glanced at Hannah. "Do you need any other proof?" She turned back to the couple. "My niece has had a lot of the care of Peter and is greatly attached to him."

Hannah stirred herself up to be hospitable and kind. "No, no more proof. I'm quite attached to Peter. But I can rejoice that he will no longer be an orphan." She gulped back a sob that rose in her throat.

"We also have a good wet nurse who nurses him daily. What can you do about feeding him?" Aunt Sophia raised the question.

Pearl looked at her husband. "We've thought about it, and we decided we should give little Peter time to adjust and not just take him off in one day. I'm sure he's attached to all of you. If you agree, we'd like to leave Peter here a while longer, even a week or so, with the wet nurse and his familiar surroundings, while we visit him daily. And it will give us time to finish setting up our household and my sewing business. When he's ready to come with us, we will see if he can begin weaning."

"Sounds like a workable plan." Aunt Sophia smiled.

Hannah found she could breathe again. The thought that they might walk out with Peter today had made her feel faint.

"We promise, we will not intrude in your day-to-day household, and we could come in the kitchen door too. And not only that, but once we take him home, you both will be welcome to visit at any time." She turned pleading eyes on Aunt Sophia.

"And we're glad you're willing to give the child time to accept you. He's healthy and might can begin weaning, or you could continue with our same wet nurse, if need be. Where is your home?"

"On Ladson Street, and it's only six blocks away. We walked here." She hesitated and leaned forward. "Can we see our son now?" The faces of both Pearl and Tom blazed with expectation.

"Of course." Hannah's aunt looked at her. "He should be waking up from his nap. Don't you think?"

She stood, silently praying for the strength to be gracious. "Yes, I'll bring him down."

Little Peter, who had never known a stranger, went straight to Pearl and then to his father. Both parents swiped at tears. The child reached for his father's thick, dark beard and sank his damp, little fingers into it. His father chuckled—a hearty, lusty sound which startled the boy, and he withdrew his hand. Then he chortled and grabbed the fluffy beard again.

The parents' joy over the boy was so palpable, it filled the room with a holy awe.

Aunt Sophia looked on, her eyes bright with moisture.

Hannah, comforted, swallowed the emotion in her throat and returned to her balcony and the letter to Adam.

*A*dam and his team flowed up the gangplank to a new ship, the *USS Vixen*. He had no idea why navy officials changed their assigned ship. Something must be in the works. Once aboard, a certain heaviness hung in the air, in the greetings from other officers and crew members, and in their facial expressions that held little welcome when they saluted. But it didn't take long for him to understand why.

His men headed to their normal stations as a captain's messenger, a young midshipman probably only fourteen or fifteen, marched up. He eyed the lieutenant's epaulet on Adam's uniform, swept his hat off, then gave a perfect, stiff salute. "Message for Marine Lieutenant Adam White."

Adam saluted back. "You've found me, young sir."

"Captain Holt sends his regards, and will you please meet him in his cabin?" The middy took a deep breath and met Adam's eyes.

"Assure the captain I will join him as soon as I deposit this seabag in my cabin."

"Aye, aye, sir." The young man clicked his heels together, then hurried away.

In less than ten minutes, Adam entered the captain's cabin with its strong tobacco smell. The man who stood to greet him, pulling a pipe from his mouth, appeared to be middle-aged or more. He had a ruddy complexion, thick jowls, salt-and-pepper hair, and mutton-chop sideburns that flowed from his ears to his thick mustache and trimmed beard. His navy uniform included several medals and appeared stretched to its limit across a large chest and bigger abdomen. Not even a hint of a smile rested on the man's face.

"Lieutenant White, have a seat," he boomed, and gestured to a chair.

Not even a handshake? The sun streaming through the cabin's large window did nothing to ease the chilly reception. Glancing around the room, Adam sat on the left side of the large oak table. The wall behind the captain contained two rows of books and several keepsakes from around the world, including a carved coconut shell, a ceramic tiger, and a tin Chinese soldier. To the left, a bedroom alcove revealed a large bed with plain canvas-colored linens. A map covered another wall. No pictures decorated the cabin, nor did curtains frame or shade the wide window.

The man eased back down in his worn leather tall-backed chair at the head, pushed the pipe back between his teeth, then blew out a trail of smoke. "I asked you here to set things straight from the beginning. Happen to know you won a reward, along with the captain and crew of the *Enterprise,* for taking the *Tripoli.* So first, let me assure you, there will be no heroes here. We all work hard to do our duty and expect no accolades. Second, I run a tight ship. Do you have any problem with either?"

"No, sir."

"Your team is new. All my other crew know my rules. I've written them up." He slid a manual toward Adam. "You best read them, memorize them, and teach them to your marines, sir, if you want them to stay out of trouble."

Adam took a deep breath, then regretted it, as his lungs rebelled against the strong tobacco smoke floating in the room. "Aye, aye, sir." He took the manual, surprised at its thickness. "Sir, are there certain rules that differ from other navy ships that I might should study first?"

Captain Holt scowled at him. "There's one hundred rules there, sir, and few of them, I daresay, are observed on other navy ships." He leaned back in his chair after placing his pipe on a small dish. "No, sir. I maintain a rigid ship at all times, and my officers can expect censure if they allow the most trifling thing under them to be executed with indifference." He looked Adam straight in the eye. "And I expect my officers to set the example of perfect obedience and careful transmission of duties." He picked up the pipe, inhaled, then blew smoke toward the floor, for which Adam was grateful.

"Blasphemy, profanity and all species of obscenity or immorality are peremptorily forbidden on the *Vixen.* Mayhap you've met with that one before? Well, here, it's strictly enforced. And there are several unique rules. Our crew are not to wear their best uniforms when cleaning the ship, and when washing the deck, they're to pull off their shoes and stockings and tuck up their trousers." He glanced at Adam. "I'll bet that's a couple you've not met on other navy vessels. And we deal with every infraction with the full penalty, no second chances."

Adam didn't blink, but he was getting the picture of an uncompromising disciplinarian who ignored the navy's lesser punishment for a first offense and escalating for additional offenses of the same nature.

"Read the manual, Lieutenant White. Memorize it. Teach your men, and any sailors you see breaking any rule whatsoever, I expect you to report. Is that understood?"

Adam took a deep breath, his nostrils flaring. "Aye, aye, sir."

The captain dumped his pipe, stood, and extended his hand.

Adam rose and took it. The man's hand was soft and small for a man of his size.

"I trust we'll get along fine, and I'll expect you at my dinner table daily and promptly each evening." He released Adam's hand and gave what might pass as a smile. "I'm glad to have you and your team on board." He walked around the table, and a sound that suggested a laugh erupted from his mouth. "If the other three with you are as tough as you seem to be, sir, I'm sure we'll hear no whispers of mutiny aboard the *Vixen*." He walked Adam to the door. "Tomorrow, we will find out our sailing orders sealed in my box. Hope it's the Mediterranean where we'll see some action."

Adam saluted and left, his lips tight. What a strange remark from the captain about a mutiny. One of a marine team's duties on a naval vessel was to protect the captain in case of a mutiny. Did the man make a joke about it, or was he hinting he might have mutiny brewing on board already?

CHAPTER 11

◦≫≈◦

One fall afternoon, Hannah sat in her bedroom window seat mending a loose hem when a servant came with the message that a Miss Seymour had come to call on her.

Hannah greeted Ruth Seymour in the small parlor and took a seat across from her. Her face was thinner and paler, as if she'd lost weight since Hannah had met her at the ball months earlier. Her lovely lavender dress and shawl, even with their good cut and design, seemed to hang on her without truly fitting her.

"Miss White. May I call you Hannah?"

"Certainly." Hannah smiled at her. "After all, we are supposed to be sisters, are we not?" Would she ever get used to that idea?

Pink suffused Ruth's face. "Yes, I believe we are." Her face softened. "I really meant to visit you again before now, but things have been so difficult at the plantation since...since Father has become ill."

"Your...father is ill?" Charles Seymour, the strong, arrogant man who'd descended on her parents' house, had seemed bigger than life and not about to give in or give up to anything that would hinder him or his desires. She still could not think of him as her father. No way.

"Yes, and between me and you, I truly believe it's the drink. The doctor warned him years ago it was poisoning him, and he has given most of it up, but the doctor says the damage has been done."

Hannah sighed. "I'm sorry to hear it." Not that she had any affection for the man, but she could be sorry for anyone who'd destroy his own health.

Ruth straightened her shoulders. "I'll get right to the point. Overseeing the plantation work and the servants fills my days almost to the breaking point. Saul is in England and has married, and he plans to stay there for quite some time. He may never return. The doctor says Father needs a nurse to help him during the day while I'm tied up with the plantation labor."

Hannah's eyes widened. Surely, Ruth was not thinking of asking her to...?

Ruth leaned close, her amber eyes pleading. "I know it's asking a lot, Hannah, but I've been told you've really become an excellent nurse...and the doctor says father doesn't have much time."

Hannah stood, her mind in turmoil. A chill ran up her spine and she found it difficult to breathe. Nurse the man who'd abandoned her as an innocent babe without so much as a backward glance?

Aunt Sophia walked into the room and greeted them both. Seemingly sensing the taut emotion, she looked from one to the other.

Ruth took a deep breath. "Mrs. Rutledge, I'm afraid I've just shocked Hannah by asking her to come nurse our ill father. But I've no other option. Let me see if I can explain it better."

Aunt Sophia sat and Hannah came to sit beside her with her hands gripped tight in her lap.

Ruth retold what she'd spoken to Hannah, then continued. "I can't explain it, but when my father is at his worse, he has nightmares, and he calls out your name, Hannah, and our mother's name. Then he mourns and cries. Can either of you understand what this could mean?"

Aunt Sophia's brows raised, and she clicked her tongue. "It could certainly be guilt surfacing in his dreams for abandoning his third daughter after losing his wife. But what of his second wife, Saul's mother? Does she still live?"

"No, she passed with the fever when Saul was only five, and Father never remarried. Saul has married in England and plans to stay there for the foreseeable future. So I'm now trying to take care of Father and the plantation." She looked down and twisted her hands in her lap, then glanced at Hannah. "Our sister, Diana, is no use whatsoever. She still lives in Savannah with her husband and three children and thinks of nothing but the latest ball and gossip." She turned to Sophia. "Have I asked too much? We can certainly pay well, and we have a strong young servant who takes care of father's bathing and shaving." Ruth searched Aunt Sophia's face, then Hannah's.

Aunt Sophia leaned forward. "And are we to understand your brother has refused to return and run the plantation, given his father's illness?"

"Yes. Even though the doctor has sent him word Father doesn't have much time, he's given us no hope that he'll come home." She dropped her head and sighed. "I'm afraid he's just waiting for Father to die so he can inherit everything."

Everything in Hannah strained to rush to put an end to any hope Ruth might have that she'd even consider coming to nurse her birth father. But she sought a way to soften her negative answer. She cleared her throat. "I really thank you, Ruth, for thinking so highly of my skills, but I'm still learning and need to continue working with Aunt Sophia. We've been given an almost open door at the Charleston Hospital to effect improvements."

She glanced at her aunt, who tilted her chin. Hannah knew that movement. She'd seen it several times when Dr. Barnes was considering a new plan of treatment for a patient at the hospital and Aunt Sophia didn't agree. A pain shot through Hannah's tight middle.

Aunt Sophia reached over and patted Hannah's hand, then smiled at their guest. "Miss Seymour, Ruth, could you give Hannah, give us, a few days to think about this? Pray about it? I love having Hannah work alongside me, and it's true, they have given us more favor to bring about minor changes in the hospital, and there's still a long way to go."

Hannah's heart jumped into her throat. *Think about it?* She didn't

113

want to think about it at all. Or pray about it. Her mind was made up. But her respect for her aunt kept her silent.

Ruth's face lightened, and she smiled. "Of course, that will be fine. Thank you, thank you so much, Mrs. Rutledge and Hannah." She peered at both their faces, smiled, and stood. "That's all anyone can expect. The Lord knows, I'm at my wit's end, or I'd never have come here this morning. Since you promised to pray, whatever you decide, I believe will be God's will."

Aunt Sophia walked her to the door. Hannah trailed behind, her heart, mind, and emotions in an upheaval.

As soon as Ruth left in her carriage, Hannah swallowed the bile in her throat and ran upstairs to her room and threw herself on her bed, gulping back sobs.

A knock sounded at her door, and her aunt peeked in, then entered.

Hannah sat up and swiped at the tears on her cheeks. "Aunt Sophia...how could you...?"

The woman came, sat on the edge of the bed, and placed her arms around Hannah's shoulders. "Dear, wonderful girl, I'm sorry to cause you this pain, but it was as if the Lord stopped me from letting you give a negative answer to Ruth Seymour today. Can you forgive me?"

"But Aunt Sophia, the man abandoned me, an innocent babe, in the woods and never even thought about me again until his precious son tried to force me into marriage. How can I possibly care about helping him?"

Aunt Sophia dropped her arms and sighed. "I asked if you could forgive me."

"Of course, I forgive you, Aunt Sophia."

"But I think I asked the wrong question, Hannah. Can you forgive your birth father?"

Hannah squeezed her eyes tight, forcing back the tears. Forgive him? Why should she?

Her aunt walked to the door and glanced back at her. "I don't have the wise words I believe your precious mother would have right now,

Hannah, but would you think about what she'd say in this situation?" She smiled. "You don't have to decide today. Take your time. When I'm in a quandary about a decision, I find reading the Bible and just simply calling out to God helps so much. I believe the Lord will aid you with this decision."

The next day, Sunday, Hannah attended service with her aunt in her Anglican church. Covering the urge to yawn, she followed Aunt Sophia into the building. She'd sat up late the night before thinking about her mother and what she'd probably say. How many times had her dear mama impressed on all her children the vital necessity of forgiving others who'd wronged them?

She sat beside her aunt in the Rutledge cushioned pew, surrounded by the peace she'd felt on earlier visits inside the lovely sanctuary with its high, decorated ceiling. Heavy oak pews and carved altar furniture glowed and filled the air with the scent of lemon oil. The inspiring organ music quieted her soul, and the golden sunshine flowing through the stained-glass windows suggested God's blessing on the gathered worshippers.

After the singing of hymns and prayer, the minister took his place at the lectern. His white robe and black neck tassel made him stand out in front of the large auditorium. He looked around at the faces upturned to him. "Today, I want to speak to you about forgiveness."

His hearty, anointed voice shook Hannah out of her drowsiness. Had she heard right? He was going to speak about forgiveness? Not daring to glance at her aunt, she clutched her reticule tight in her lap and listened as the man preached from Mark the eleventh chapter. "*And whenever you stand praying, if you have anything against anyone, forgive him, that your Father in heaven may also forgive you your trespasses. But if you do not forgive, neither will your Father in heaven forgive your trespasses.*" The words entered her soul and confronted her unforgiveness harbored in her heart against her birth father.

On the ride home in their carriage, Hannah expected her aunt to say *something* about the timely message, but not a word fell from her aunt's lips. When no remonstrance or advice came forth, Hannah relaxed and mulled over the words of the minister and those he'd read from the Bible.

In her room, after the mid-day meal, Hannah again thought of the scripture. A soft whisper came forth in her spirit. *Can you show your father my love? He really needs it.*

Charles Seymour needed to know about God's love, and he might not have much time. She could do that, couldn't she? Show him God's love? Or at least do whatever she could. God had prepared her for this task—her own godly upbringing in God's love, her training with Aunt Sophia, and even baby Peter leaving for his happy new home about the same time Adam went away on a long navy assignment.

Though both those leave takings nearly broke her heart, there was nothing hindering her now, no strong attachment or responsibility tempting her not to go to Seymour Plantation on this assignment. She could almost hear Adam's voice reminding her that all things worked together for the good of those who sought God's will. She would be available to do His will.

Later that day, riding Dancer in the cool park, everything seemed brighter and fuller of life—the brilliant November sunshine more like summer, the trees in their glorious colors, the squirrels skittering about getting ready for winter. She stopped at a favorite oak resplendent in its fall robe of deep orange and yellow, dismounted, and laid her head tenderly against the mare's warm shoulder. Dancer nudged her and gave a low nicker.

The chaffing weight Hannah had carried since learning of her abandonment by her birth father released from her mind. She took a deep, pleasant breath of horse and leather and knew she'd passed through a dark place in her heart.

The next day at breakfast, she told her aunt she'd decided to go to Seymour Plantation.

Her aunt patted her hand and assured her. Though she would miss Hannah's assistance, the work at the hospital would progress. "Dr. Barnes," she said, smiling, "is now more of a help than a hindrance."

"Aunt Sophia, you've never told me about your unhappy history with Dr. Barnes."

Her aunt's face softened, and a faraway look came into her eyes. "Yes, and I mean to. Thomas Barnes and my husband, Andrew, were college mates and best friends, and they competed in almost everything, including courting me. I was engaged to Tom but broke it off when I fell in love with Andrew."

"Oh my." Hannah covered her mouth. She never would've guessed.

"After I chose Andrew, Dr. Barnes became angry and said some things I now know he regretted. He even challenged Andrew to a duel, a challenge that my husband ignored. I just got furious at Tom Barnes and, sorry to say, I encouraged Andrew to avoid him after our marriage. It ended that friendship." She took a deep breath. "The young can be so sure of themselves, and headstrong, and often not very compassionate."

Hannah lowered her head. Was she like that herself? She hoped not. She lifted her eyes toward her aunt. "Is there a possibility your relationship with Dr. Barnes might develop into something more now?"

Aunt Sophia smiled. "Who knows? He's still an attractive man, but I'm too busy to think about such things right now. How about you and Gideon?" Her aunt stood and her smile widened.

Heat rose in Hannah's cheeks. She stood and took a deep breath. "Same here. I'm too busy to think about love, too." But she did think about it, just not relating to Gideon Falconer.

~

Hannah stood in her bedroom beside her aunt and reexamined the herbal items and notes spread across her bed to be packed in her nursing bag. It had taken her and Aunt Sophia several days to collect the herbs and clarify her notes. Golden seal, aloe, garlic, and Echinacea for wounds and infections, powdered mustard for poultices, licorice for cough, ginger root for stomach disorders, chamomile, valerian, and lavender for calming and sleep, and pounded rice for tea that could stop diarrhea.

Aunt Sophia nodded. "Yes, I think this will prepare you for many needs that might arise." She gave Hannah a warm hug. "By the way, would you like to take Dancer? I'm sure their groom would give her good care, and you'll have an excuse to get out and exercise her and get a rest from the sickroom."

"That would be wonderful. Thank you, Aunt Sophia."

A knock sounded at the door, and they both called out, "Enter."

April came in, her dark eyes dancing, holding two letters in her hand. She brought them to Hannah.

Her heart jumped in her throat when she recognized Adam's neat block printing on one. He'd once told her cursive was anathema on a ship, as sailing on the waves could muss a writer's document fast.

"Go read your letters, Hannah. I'm going downstairs for some preserves to pack in your bag. "Sometimes you can get a patient to eat a little sweet preserves on bread when they'll eat nothing else."

Hannah hurried to her window seat and opened Adam's missive, the first she'd had received since he'd left months earlier on his current assignment.

Dear Hannah,

My team and I are now at Gibraltar aboard a different ship, the USS Vixen. *We're part of a new flotilla of six frigates President Jefferson has sent to the Mediterranean under Commodore Edward Preble to blockade the ports of Barbary pirates threatening our merchant ships.*

I'd like to tell you it's been a pleasant sailing experience crossing the Atlantic to this rendezvous with our squadron. But our captain is a very strict disciplinarian, and there is a spirit of unrest and fear among the crew, so different from my last ship and crew with Captain Sterett.

I found out one most fortunate thing when we docked at Gibraltar. Only a handful of us could go ashore, as many of the crew were being punished for various infractions of the captain's rules. The good news is, our brother Michael's ship, the USS Philadelphia, *with its new captain, William Bainbridge, is part of our squadron. I spent some time with Michael ashore. He's turned into a pretty good sailor, if his sailing buddies were sincere in their remarks about him.*

There goes that bell for the first night watch. It's time for me to take my shift. I dare not be one minute late. So until I can find a moment to write again,

Your loving brother,
Adam

Hannah sighed. It took months for his letters to reach her. What might have happened to him since he wrote?

Her other letter came from Ruth Seymour in response to Hannah's note accepting the position of nursing Charles Seymour. The woman expressed her delight that Hannah had decided to come and assured that she had her room ready.

Hannah checked again to make sure she had packed her writing materials in her trunk. She'd write to Adam about going to Seymour Plantation after she'd spent a little time there.

July drove the wagon with her and her baggage to the plantation. Dancer, tied at back, trotted and kept up. For the two-hour ride, Hannah wore a thick woolen shawl, a warm bonnet, and a blanket across her knees to keep the cold December air at bay. The winter sun overhead beamed down with cheerfulness but little warmth. Thank God, the clouds showed no evidence of rain.

"Miss White, ma'am, you gonna leave Miz Sophia for good?"

"No, July. I'm going to nurse Mr. Seymour, who has become ill. I'll be back."

"If you need anyone, I'll be glad to be your helper. Miz Sophia done tole me I could."

"Thank you, July. You did an excellent job helping with my brother Adam. I will keep your offer in mind after I see what's needed."

The rhythmic clip-clop of the horses, the fresh, brisk air, and being cocooned under her wraps made Hannah's tension that had been building since they left Charleston fade. Her chin sank to her chest and rested on the bow of her bonnet.

July's exclamation roused her. "We's just about there, miss. And I says, it's quite a sight. Them Seymours must be proud of such a house like that yonder."

Hannah smiled and looked ahead at intricate wrought-iron gates standing open. Their carriage turned in and crunched across a shell-paved drive. A large plantation house with white columns sat beyond under a canopy of oaks, only a few leaves remaining on the wide limbs. She'd tried to imagine what kind of house Charles Seymour would possess. This one exceeded her expectation of the proud man.

July pulled the wagon to the front entrance hitching post and jumped down. Two servants hurried from around the side of the house. One offered to help Hannah down, but she pushed back her blanket and nimbly climbed down herself, holding her shawl in place. She stood a moment to fluff out her thick skirts and adjust the tie to her bonnet.

Ruth Seymour, a warm welcome spread across her face, came down the porch steps, followed by two female servants in bright head wraps. "I'm so happy to see you, Hannah." She gestured to the servants, and they took her bags from the wagon and stood awaiting their mistress's further direction.

"We have your room ready, Hannah, and even some hot water if you'd like to freshen up before going to see Father. He's been mighty quiet today since I told him you were coming."

Hannah's tension returned, and an icy knot formed in her stomach. Did Charles Seymour even want her presence in his house, much less her ministrations as a nurse?

Father God, show me what to do and say to help this man to health and to You.

CHAPTER 12

Ruth led Hannah to her father's room upstairs. The man lying in the bed caused her steps to falter. He seemed much smaller and less intimidating than she remembered from when he'd visited their farm. The hands that lay on the coverlet were still large and callused, but the arms were thin. Propped up on two pillows, his stony face was the only thing that seemed unchanged. His pale eyes sought hers, and a shock ran through her at the contact.

"Father, this is Hannah. You've met. She has graciously agreed to come as your nurse. You know how I must stay busy with the plantation and the servants since you've been ill."

"Yeah, you let me know often enough all you have to do, daughter." His voice exuded sarcasm.

Ruth's shoulders shrank and her lips tightened.

Hannah took a deep, shaky breath. It was the same man, all right.

Charles gestured to a shadowed corner, and a movement there caught Hannah's eye. An ebony man dressed in farm labor clothing emerged into the light. "There's Ekon. He's all I need to play nurse to me, Ruth. I told you that. So you can just send her right back from where she's come." He flicked his hand as if to dismiss them, his thin lips tight under his gray mustache.

Ruth's face fell a foot, and she folded her arms and looked at Hannah, helplessness blanketing her form.

Something pulsed down Hannah's spine. She stepped forward. "Mr. Seymour, I do not want to nurse you—the man who abandoned me as an innocent babe—any more than you might want me here, but I think I can be of some help." She moved a step closer and gazed at the large ulcer on his forehead and another on one arm. "For example, I have some herbal salve with me that can bring relief to those sores on your forehead and arm."

His steel-gray eyes widened at her words, and he touched the ulcer on his head.

Hannah continued. "Ruth has told me you have some trouble sleeping. I have herbs that help bring restful sleep."

He stared at her, then he did the one thing she never dreamed he'd do. He laughed. A loud guffaw of a sound that made the slave jump back into the shadows.

Hannah gasped, and beside her, Ruth trembled.

"Well, little lady, you've got my bloodline for sure, and I guess you can stay. Remind me of my first wife. A bold lady, that woman was, and she never backed down to me."

Ruth expelled a long breath and touched Hannah's arm. "Father, I'm glad that's settled. Now I want to take Hannah down for some tea. She's traveled some distance today." She turned to glance at Hannah. "She may be back before your bedtime with the sleeping help she mentioned."

"Yes, I'll be back, Mr. Seymour." Hannah gave him a brief smile, and they left the room.

Sitting in the lovely parlor partaking tea and sandwiches, Hannah asked the question sticking in her mind. "Does Ekon perform any other duties for your father other than bathing and shaving him.

"He helps dress him and empties the chamber pot, and does any other thing he asks him. But I really can't trust Ekon much." She sighed. "I've wondered if he brings him alcohol, and I've warned him he must never do so, but his first loyalty is to my father."

That evening after dinner, Hannah cleaned and dressed Charles's sores with goldenseal and aloe. He scowled the entire time but submitted. She left a cup of chamomile and valerian tea on his nightstand, then retired to her spacious room. Tired to the bone, she undressed, whispered a quick prayer, and climbed into the canopied bed under clean-smelling linens and thick quilts.

She knew nothing until the crowing of several roosters awakened her. That was a sound she'd missed since leaving her parents' farm for Aunt Sophia's. She arose, stirred the coals in the hearth till sparks ignited, then added wood chips and two logs. After bathing in the chilly water left the night before, she dressed, went downstairs, and found the kitchen by following the scent of freshly baked bread.

Ruth sat at the kitchen table. "Good morning, Hannah. Won't you join me?"

She sat and enjoyed a breakfast of eggs, cheese, fresh bread and butter, and hot tea.

"What does your father usually have for this meal?" Hannah asked Ruth.

"Not much of anything, I'm afraid. We have trouble getting him to eat. But there's his tray if you want to put something on it."

"I believe I do."

On the tray, she placed a pot of tea, apple slices, a cup and saucer, a table knife, and two slices of the fresh bread, buttered and wrapped to keep them warm. On the way to Charles's room, she stopped by her own room and pulled a jar of strawberry preserves from her trunk and placed it on the tray.

She knocked and entered when bid by a sleepy voice. A brisk fire warmed the area. Ruth had told her Ekon stayed with her father at night but left early in the morning after building up the fire. She set the tray down and walked to the large windows. Throwing back the drapes, she pushed one window up three inches. When she turned, Charles's stare from the bed struck her like an arrow. He'd sat up and pushed another pillow under his head.

"Good morning, sir. I've brought your breakfast, and I'm letting in some fresh air to help you get well."

"I don't eat breakfast, miss." But he looked over at the tray and sniffed. "What's that you've got? It's not porridge, is it? I can't stand it."

She brought the tray to him and uncovered the bread, the preserves, and the apple slices, then poured him a cup of tea.

"Strawberry preserves?" He picked up the table knife and dipped it in the preserves, then spread it on the warm bread and pushed it into his mouth. The man cleaned up every crumb, interspersed with sips of tea. He made quick work of the apple slices, then leaned back on his pillow to nap.

The sense of satisfaction that overtook Hannah was altogether unexpected.

After the mid-day meal, which he also partook well, she sliced a fresh apple for him again.

He eyed her hand with its small, bent finger. "If I didn't know better, I'd think my first wife was helping me." Then he guffawed and stuffed two apple slices into his mouth at a time.

She dressed his sores again, and he informed her he wanted to sleep. Her room being next to his, she left her door ajar in case he awakened and needed her.

Ekon came back at sundown. She heard the muffled voice of Charles with the black man's responses next door. Why not speak to the helper and try to enlist his cooperation?

After waiting a few minutes, she knocked and entered when bid. Walking straight over to Ekon, she introduced herself. "I'm Miss White and I'll be helping with Mr. Seymour. I'm next door. If for any reason you need me at night, you may knock on my door and I'll come. Do you understand?"

The man's eyes darkened and his face stiffened. "Massa Seymour, he say yesterday he don't need nobody but me."

Behind them in the bed, Charles cleared his throat. "That's changed, Ekon. We're gonna let her stay. So you just do whatever she asks, and we'll all get along fine. Now, you still going to shave and bathe me whenever I get ready." His steely stare swung to Hannah. "That, she's never gonna do."

THE LIEUTENANT'S SECRET LOVE

Heat spread over Hannah's cheeks, and she turned and left. But victory tasted sweet. He'd accepted her work as a nurse.

The December days, with Christmas approaching, moved fast. Ruth was doubly busy with preparations for her sister and family coming Christmas Eve. Hannah continued her ministrations to Charles, thankful that she would go home to her parents' house in the next parish for the holidays. Her mother had written that Gideon Falconer had offered to bring her home from the Seymours' two days before Christmas. Would she ever be happier to see her dear family?

She could report some progress with Charles in her nursing journal, thanks be to God. His sores continued to improve, and he now sat up in a chair for an hour each day. One day, he even thanked her for helping him. She underlined that in her notes. His first thanks. She would get beneath that arrogant shell of his one day. She just knew it. And when she did, she would share God's love for him as the Lord had commissioned her.

Four days before Christmas, terrible yells from Charles's room awakened Hannah from a deep slumber. She jumped up, slid her arms into her robe, and hurried next door. One lantern burned in the room. Ekon was bending over Charles, trying to shake his shoulders and awaken him. He moved away when she drew near.

She bent over Charles. Stark terror twisted his sweating face. "Mr. Seymour, wake up. You're having a bad dream." As she laid her hand on his forehead, he relaxed.

The cup of chamomile tea still sat, full, on his bedside table. But beneath the bed, something rolled and bumped against her slippered foot. She moved and an empty whiskey bottle settled against her toe. She picked it up and glanced at Ekon. He slunk back into his corner. Her lips thinned as she laid the bottle on the table.

Charles awoke and grabbed her hand. "I saw hell! I felt the flames. God forbid I ever end up there!"

His wild eyes and terrified words chilled her to the core. She moved to dampen a cloth in the bowl of water on his stand. Dabbing it across his fevered brow, she whispered, "You don't have to end up there, Mr. Seymour." But did he hear? He closed his eyes and soon

125

snored. She sat beside his bed for a time until his breathing became normal and his face cooled and relaxed from its mask of horror.

The next morning, she told Ruth about the whiskey and the nightmare.

Ruth's jaw tightened. "If we can just get through Christmas, I will seek someone else to bathe and shave Father. Ekon must go. He will not stop getting the whiskey. We'll find someone we can trust."

"I know just such a person, Ruth." She shared about July's offer to come and highly recommended him.

~

Adam stood on the poop deck beside Josiah Campbell and watched the last rays of the sun drape purple shadows across the Mediterranean and the Tripoli Harbor they helped blockade. They'd both just been relieved on their afternoon watch. He could not remember ever being so uptight or miserable in his navy career. He'd received a letter from Hannah that day and learned she was at Seymour Plantation. Even with Saul Seymour in England indefinitely, he could not feel at peace for her. Why did she go?

Ship life under Captain Holt was harsher than with any captain with whom he'd sailed. Holt's outbursts of temper at even minor offenses made life aboard the ship almost unbearable. Mast-heading—forcing a sailor to climb the mast and stay there for a long period—and floggings took place almost daily. And there was always someone in chains in the hold, further punished with a diet of only bread and water.

The crew was far from becoming the cohesive fighting force the Tripoli War demanded. It was all Adam could do to keep encouraging the unhappy men day after day without inciting the captain's anger against himself. Accidents could happen in such an atmosphere—serious mishaps that could result from a distracted, fragmented crew. He did a lot of praying.

That very morning, after a sarcastic outburst and humiliating tirade against a sailor over a minor infraction on the main deck, the captain actually drew his sword and hit the cringing young man over the head, wounding him. Seeing it happen from the poop deck, Adam heard Josiah mutter under his breath. "Methinks *he that is slow to anger is better than the mighty; and he that rules his spirit than he that taketh a city.*"

The next morning, the drums called the sailors to breakfast. As Adam and his men settled down to eat, a loud boom interrupted their meal. The sound erupted from below decks, and moments later, the warning sailors dread most rose in a terrified shout. "The magazine is on fire!" The storeroom entrance where the gunpowder was kept was in flames.

Adam and his team knocked their chairs over standing and bolting to deal with the emergency. Using wet blankets over their heads, they descended to the magazine area, groping amid wreckage in the choking smoke. They sought to protect the ship's main powder store. Every man aboard the *Vixen* knew that one spark in the gunpowder room would cause a chain reaction that could blow the wooden ship to kingdom come and kill them all.

Other sailors formed two lines and passed water hand-to-hand to douse the flames. An hour and a half later, Adam, his team, and the exhausted crew—coughing, blackened by smoke—took stock of their losses.

The fire was out, but it had taken a toll. Fourteen men were so badly burned that they despaired of their lives. And the ship had much damage to be repaired.

Upon investigation, Adam discovered the fire had apparently begun with a candle not completely extinguished, left by a distracted crew member. To Adam's dismay, Captain Holt sentenced that sailor to keelhauling—one of the worst punishments a crew member could receive. Every sailor trembled at the thought of being thrown overboard on one side of the ship and dragged underneath the ship to the other side.

But Adam, the other officers standing with him, finally convinced Captain Holt that the *Vixen,* so desperately in need of repairs, should return to Malta at once. He glared at them and ordered the terrified sailor thrown into the hold in chains.

Two weeks later, they were ready to return to their blockading assignment with their squadron, but Captain Holt, Adam, and the other officers of the squadron were called to a rendezvous with Commodore Preble. On his ship, the *USS Constitution*, the commodore and his staff interviewed all the *Vixen* officers individually, including Adam, about the fire incident and life aboard the ship. The result of that meeting shocked him. Captain Holt was relieved of his duties, and they made Adam commander of the *Vixen*.

~

*H*annah returned to Seymour Plantation after a wonderful holiday with her family and Gideon Falconer, whom her mother invited to join their Christmas celebration. July also came with her to help with Mr. Seymour. After getting settled back in her room, she took him to meet the man.

"It's high time you got back, young lady. And was it you who sent my man away?" Charles Seymour was out of sorts.

"No, sir. But I have someone I want you to meet. He is a great helper in the sick room." She motioned behind her, and July came into the room. His tall, strong presence filled a bit of space. He doffed his hat and nodded at Mr. Seymour but kept his eyes downward.

"Come here, boy."

July strode to the bed and looked the patient in the eyes.

Something clicked in the old man's face. "You got nerve. Can you pick me up and put me in that chair? You look burly enough to me." He motioned to the chair next to the window.

"Oh yes, massa." July dropped his hat on the floor, slid his powerful arms under Charles, lifted him, then walked over and gently set him in the chair.

"Tea, Miss Hannah. I want some of that special tea of yours nobody could find while you were gone." Charles still didn't smile, but Hannah did as she left to get the tea. So he did like her cinnamon and orange spice tea she and her aunt had made up. He'd never told her before.

Ruth came later and took July to settle in his room above the stables he'd use when not in the sick room. When he returned, he seemed pleased with his new job and home.

After retiring that night, Hannah prayed for the Seymour household and Adam's safety. Then the handsome, gentle face of Gideon Falconer crossed her mind. Memories of the hours he'd spent with her and her family over the Christmas holiday played like new music in her head. The man was special. It was true. Both her mama and her papa seemed to take to him. Hannah sighed as Adam's beloved face superseded Gideon's.

Adam had her heart, didn't he? But was anything possible between them, having grown up as brother and sister? Many more months stretched ahead before she'd see him again to explore any possibility. By then, would things with Gideon have progressed to the point of a decision?

The following day, after July had gone to his room above the stables, Hannah sat beside Charles's bed and dressed the sore on his forehead that seemed determined to fester again. Also, her birth father seemed weaker than when she'd left him to go home for Christmas. And dark circles made his eyes look sunken in his head.

He caught her hand and glared at her. "Tell me, girl, what did you mean when I had that nightmare before Christmas? I told you I saw hell fire, and you said I didn't have to go there." He dropped her hand. "You probably thought I didn't hear you, but I did, and I've thought about it ever since. I've had that dream several times."

Hannah looked squarely in his face. "Tell me something first, Mr. Seymour. Did anyone else treat you over the holidays?"

He scowled. "Yeah, your sister, Diana—and Ruth joined in with her—would give me no peace until they called in old Doc Murphy to bleed me. Right after Christmas, I had a hard breathing spell, and he said I had heart trouble and it'd help. I wanted to refuse but finally gave up with three of them pestering me."

Hannah's heart sank. She'd seen the telltale signs of his having been bled inside his arm. No wonder he was weaker. Diana had gone home, but she'd need to talk to Ruth about the life being in the blood.

"Now answer my question I gave you."

Hannah whispered a silent prayer for help. "You really want to know?"

He glared at her. "Why would I ask you if I didn't?"

"I'll be glad to share with you what I know, Mr. Seymour, but I need to get something from my room. I'll be right back."

When she returned, he eyed the brown leather-bound book with its gold etching she held in her hand, the Bible her parents had given her on her sixteenth birthday. "So you gonna preach to me, are you? Just like my first wife."

"Only if you really want to know why I said you need never go to that terrible place you dreamed about, sir." Hannah remained standing, unsure of his seriousness.

"Sit down," he commanded. "I'll listen, but I don't make any promises."

Hannah opened her Bible to the Book of John and read from the third chapter, verse sixteen, in awe that she was actually sharing the gospel with her birth father she once hated. "I can assure you on the authority of this verse that our Father God loves you, and He does not want you to go to the hell you've dreamed about, Mr. Seymour."

A skeptical frown creased his forehead. "I have to doubt that, girl. I've done many a thing that book says not to do. In fact, those ten commandments written in there? I've probably broken all of them sometime or other."

Hannah took a deep breath and shared other texts that came to mind—verses that explained how Jesus Christ came to earth and died on the cross so anyone could be forgiven for anything they'd done. She read aloud from the book of Romans how one could be saved by repenting of his sin and accepting Jesus Christ as his savior. But when she looked up, Charles had fallen asleep.

She returned to her room and prayed. *Father, open his heart and mind to receive Christ, and please, give him time to do so.*

The following day, the sun came out bright, and with it, the weather seemed warmer. While Charles slept, Hannah had Dancer saddled, and she donned a warm outfit and wrap and set out for a pleasant horseback ride she'd not had for weeks. Dancer was beside herself with excitement, also having missed the long gallops Hannah knew the horse loved. The mare soon broke into her fastest gallop, and they flew down the farm road, then over two large, fallow fields before the animal slowed to catch her breath.

They approached a wood, now sparse without leaves, which Hannah did not remember seeing before, but an obvious trail made up of small rocks and shells invited their exploration. She reined Dancer onto the path. Woodsy scents of pine, sweet cedar, and birch, laced with the damp, earthy smell of decomposing leaves, wrapped their rich scent around her. Hannah reveled in the peace and well-being of the moment.

But it didn't last long. Dancer began to limp. Hannah pulled back on the reins and dismounted. She examined each leg and hoof but found nothing that might cause a problem. Frowning, she looked around, then up at the sun and its lessening brightness between the bare tree limbs overhead as it began its western descent. Was she even still on the Seymour estate?

She turned the mare around, and fearing her weight would make the problem worse, she led Dancer back the way they had come. Hoof beats sounded behind her down the trail, and a flicker of apprehension coursed through her. She was a long way from home and alone.

Casting aside what she decided was childish fear, she stopped walking the mare and glanced down the path. To her pleasant surprise, Gideon Falconer emerged on his beautiful roan gelding. He had a hunting gun tied to his saddle and a bow and arrow. Dancer threw her head up and whinnied, and the other horse responded.

He rode up alongside her, keeping the gelding's head away from Dancer's, and gave her a warm grin. "Well, Hannah, how pleasant to see you on Brighton Hall property."

"Hello, Gideon, have I really left the Seymour estate?" Hannah looked around, then back to him. "I've missed riding the last several weeks, so I'm afraid Dancer and I didn't notice how far we were coming." She turned to pat the horse's warm neck. "I'm walking because Dancer has begun to limp."

"Really?" Gideon swung off his horse and tied the reins to a nearby branch. In two breaths, he was in front of Dancer, lifting her trim hooves. She didn't seem to mind.

"Oh, I see the problem." He pulled a dagger from his boot and popped out a small stone from between the inner folds of Dancer's hoof.

The horse nudged him as if to thank him and stamped her leg when he released it.

Gideon moved close to show the rock to Hannah. His scent of fresh woodlands and some kind of spice tickled her nose. The stone seemed tiny in his wide palm.

Hannah thanked him. "I checked her hooves but saw nothing. I'm so glad you came along, Gideon."

He threw the stone aside and moved closer. "I'm glad I came along too."

She glanced up in his face and startled when his gaze moved to her mouth. He lifted her chin with his thumb, then he kissed her, his lips barely brushing hers, searing them. She pushed him away.

He looked apologetic, but a grin also lit his handsome face. "Sorry, but that was too big a temptation to pass up." Then he peered into her eyes. "Is there anyone else for you, Hannah? I'm afraid I'm mesmerized. But all you have to do is tell me to back off and I will. It's just that you remind me of...a girl I was engaged to back in England."

Hannah folded her arms, still clutching Dancer's reins. "What happened to the engagement?" She did not understand the racing of her heart from the gentle kiss except that his touch reminded her of Adam. *Dear Adam.* Where was he now, and was he safe? She'd had no letter for some time.

"My threatened arrest and fleeing the sheriff's men and England is what happened. My dear Lydia could've never lived down my being arrested and sent to prison."

"Did she say so?"

"Well, no. I've never seen her since and don't dare even write a letter back to England to find out. That sheriff had it in for me and would be happy to send his agents even here and try to apprehend me. I've a pretty good idea Lydia's uppity mother has helped her forget me. The woman always disapproved of me, especially after my uncle lost my parents' fortune."

"Gideon, I'm surprised at you, not giving her a chance to say what her feelings were." She glanced up at the sun, now farther in its downward westerly track. "It's getting late. Do you think I can now mount and ride Dancer back to Seymour Plantation? Will she be all right?"

He lifted his head and smiled. "Yes, she'll be fine now, and I'm going to see you to the edge of that property, or my name isn't Gideon Falconer."

At the estate border, he stopped and guided his mount beside her. "You didn't answer my question back there, Hannah."

"Gideon, I really don't have time to talk any more today. Please forgive me, but I have to go." She clicked her tongue and tightened her knees around Dancer and galloped away.

When she cantered up the entrance to Seymour Plantation, a coach piled high with luggage stood in front of the imposing house. Goodness. Who could be coming to Seymour Plantation, and for a long stay, if the luggage meant anything? She reined Dancer to give the conveyance a wide berth and headed to the stables.

"Sweet Hannah, wait up. I'm home."

She froze in the saddle. That proud, demanding voice she could never forget brought a gasp from her lips and sent a sharp pain through her middle.

CHAPTER 13

*A*dam stood on the quarterdeck of the *Vixen* with Josiah, now his first mate, and talked about the progress they'd made. After they'd worked with the crew for a month, the men were on the way to becoming a united fighting force. For the past few weeks, they had sailed in turns with the Mediterranean squadron, blockading the Tripoli harbor to force the sultan to come to reason.

The lookout in the eagle's nest shouted, "Commodore Preble's ship is flagging a message!"

Adam shot out his eyeglass. The flagship signaled a rendezvous, calling all commanders of the squadron to the *USS Constitution* for a meeting. "Signal the crew to lower our longboat, Josiah. Something has happened."

"Aye, aye, sir." Josiah hurried away.

Half an hour later, Adam walked into the commodore's cabin and took a seat around the large table. Edward Preble's pale, stiff face alerted Adam the man had serious news. He glanced around at the other captains taking their places. One was missing. Captain William Bainbridge from the *USS Philadelphia,* his brother Michael's ship.

Preble stood, cleared his throat, and looked into their faces. "Men, I've just received appalling intelligence. We've lost the *Philadelphia* to

Tripoli." Shocked intakes of breath sounded across the room, like a flock of birds swooshing up to the ceiling.

Adam stiffened, his heart pounding, his own breath catching in his throat. Michael was on that ship. What would happen—what *had* happened—to his brother?

Preble continued, "The loss of this ship and the capture of the crew of three-hundred men is of the utmost alarming nature to the United States." His taut voice drained the air out of the room.

"How did it happen, sir?" Lieutenant Stephen Decatur's question pulsated across the table with several other voices, including Adam's, echoing it.

"The news we have at this time is that the ship gave up the chase of a Tripolitan cruiser trying to break our blockade and ended up running aground on rocks." Commodore Preble's countenance contorted into lines that aged him. "Our charts showed no reef in that area. But there was one."

"But weren't they able to get off the reef, sir, with the change of tide, or at least defend the ship?" Decatur asked his second question. Every eye locked on Preble's glum face.

"No, with her hull stuck and broken on the rocks and her ability to fire her guns impaired, the *Philadelphia* was a sitting duck. I'm sure they tried everything they knew, but we're told after the enemy gunboats shot down her masts, Bainbridge had no choice but to strike her colors and surrender, rather than lose all their lives. The enemy took the ship and all her crew captive."

Adam sucked in a painful breath. Michael in captivity, in slavery, with the enemy. *If he still lived.* Adam lowered his head and lifted a silent prayer. *Lord, help him, save his life, deliver him.*

Another captain asked the next question burning in the forefront of Adam's mind, and probably of those around the table. "Sir, did they have time to scuttle the frigate before surrendering it?"

Preble's frown deepened, and he dropped into his chair. "That we don't know, but we pray they did. The *Philadelphia* was one of our latest warships and highly armed. All of you know what scuttling entails and the time it'd take to dampen the stores of their barrels of gunpowder, dismantle and throw all the cannons and stored weapons overboard, and even drill holes in the bottom to make the ship unsailable. We pray they had time. We certainly must hope and pray Captain Bainbridge destroyed his American signaling code book." Preble's eyes turned to flint. "If that has fallen into enemy hands...it will place the entire American navy at monumental risk." He shook his head, his lips a hard line. "And there's one other scenario that is the substance of nightmares. What if the Barbary pirates repair the ship and use it against us?"

Affirmative, concerned, angry voices echoed around the table.

When the captains rose to leave, Lieutenant Stephen Decatur strode over to the commodore, his low comment audible from where Adam still sat. "Sir, let me handpick some men and sail into the Tripoli harbor. We'll set the ship on fire to make sure the enemy can never use it against us."

Adam laid his hands on the table, rising. "Sir, I'd be most eager to join such a mission."

Decatur smiled at him. "You'd be one of the first I'd pick, White."

Preble looked at both of them. "It's much too risky. What if I lost another ship and both of you?"

Adam rowed back to the *Vixen*, his heart heavy. He'd heard what happened to other crews the Barbary nations took captive. The enemy confiscated their uniforms, beat them, and forced them into hard manual labor for the sultans' building projects, and with little food to sustain them. Many American sailors still languished in slavery years after their capture because of the outrageous ransom the sultans demanded.

He spent the night in prayer for Michael and the crew of the *Philadelphia*. Peace came into his heart that Michael had survived the battle and capture of the ship. Where there was life, there was hope.

∽

*H*annah found her ministrations to Charles Seymour much more difficult with Saul Seymour in the house. The day he'd called after her when she rode toward the stables, she'd ignored him. But that was increasingly difficult from day to day, living in the same house with him and his pregnant English wife.

The only thing that made his presence bearable was that Saul spent days away in Charleston every week. Most of the time, he'd leave happy and confident but return sad and angry.

However, Hannah immediately liked Amelia Seymour. The petite woman, in the late stages of pregnancy, had an impressive gentleness and quiet acceptance about her. Saul often demeaned her at the table, but she never reacted or tried to defend herself.

One of his favorite taunts infuriated Hannah, if not his wife. "There's little Amelia. *Lady* Amelia. Don't forget her title, now. Her blueblood relatives in England will be angry, won't they, my dear little wife?" Then he'd reach over and pat her cheek as if to remind her and all watching that he owned her and thought nothing of her title.

Ruth would glare at him and Hannah would seethe. Amelia made no comment. She just turned her cheek out of his reach.

How did such a sweet person like Amelia get involved with someone like Saul Seymour, much less marry him?

In Amelia's hesitant conversations about her family and life, the story that emerged hinted Saul had not deceived her, but he had deceived her parents. They'd insisted she accept the rich, young American's suit. She had turned twenty-five with no other prospects.

One evening, on Hannah's way to her room, Saul's loud, angry voice bled into the hall. Not wanting to eavesdrop, but concerned for Amelia, to whom Saul obviously ranted, Hannah slowed her steps.

"I will not ask you again, dear little wife. Hand me the ruby necklace. I don't have time to reason with you."

"But Saul, it belonged to my grandmother. It's the last piece I have of hers. Please don't take it." Tears laced the woman's gentle voice.

A thud sounded, and at a cry from Amelia, Hannah put her hand over her mouth and fell back against the wall. Had the man struck his pregnant wife?

The door flew open, and Saul emerged, stuffing something into his waistcoat pocket. When he saw Hannah, the anger on his face subsided, and he grinned. "Listening at doors, Hannah? I'm disappointed in you." He walked over and patted her cheek. "But more of a beauty than ever."

It was all she could do not to slap his smirking face.

He sailed past her, clumped down the stairs, and banged out the front door.

Hannah couldn't help but see Amelia through the open doorway, holding her head and sobbing. She took a deep breath and went in.

"Amelia, I'm so sorry. Are you injured?" She touched the shaking shoulder, and the woman lifted her tear-stained face to her. Redness grew over Amelia's left eye and cheek.

Hannah took a deep breath to keep in angry words about Saul. She placed her arm around Amelia. "Come, sit down in your chair. Let me put a cool cloth on that injury. Are you...all right everywhere else?"

Amelia patted her extended abdomen. "Yes, thank God he didn't hit me here. I gave him the necklace."

Hannah's eyes widened. Would Saul Seymour dare threaten to do *that*?

For the next thirty minutes, the mother-to-be opened her heart to Hannah. A picture of an only child growing up in the cool-hearted aristocracy of England came forth. Her parents' concern over the lack of suitors. Saul coming to visit from the university with charm and evident wealth. What no one knew was that he was almost penniless, having gambled away the fortune his father had sent with him to the university. When he discovered the considerable dowry Amelia's father had settled on her, he courted her with every charm and promise of a wonderful life as a Charleston plantation owner's wife. He assured her parents that his father was on his deathbed and he, Saul, would soon inherit all.

Amelia sighed and looked into Hannah's face after relating her story. "The reason we came here now was that Saul eventually gambled away my entire dowry, and he came home to... await his father's death. Until then, he asks for another piece of my jewelry almost weekly to finance his gambling."

Hannah shook her head and patted Amelia's hand. "I'm so sorry, Amelia."

After helping the heartbroken mother as well as she could and bringing a calming tea to her, Hannah walked to Charles's room carrying his night-time tea. He lay in his bed awake, his large hands folded over his chest, staring at the ceiling. Had he overheard the horrid incident between his son and pregnant wife? Saul's voice had been loud enough.

"Here's your night tea, sir." She sat the cup on the small table beside his bed and noted an angry flush on his cheeks. She laid her palm on his forehead but felt no fever. "Is there anything else I can do for you, Mr. Seymour?"

He shook his head.

Saul came back three days later, sullen and unhappy. Now Hannah understood his moods. He had undoubtedly lost money in gambling this time, instead of winning. She avoided him as much as possible. But she also wanted to keep encouraging Amelia and spent some time with her after Saul left on his next weekly jaunt to Charleston.

"Will you be my midwife, Hannah? Is that part of your training?" Amelia looked across at Hannah as they sat on the second-floor balcony, stitching baby clothing. Hannah loved helping make the small garments.

She smiled. "It is, but let's plan to have my Aunt Sophia come too. She's great at birthing babies and has much more experience."

"I'll be happy to have you both."

"Happy to have who, my love?" Saul Seymour came out on the balcony. Apparently, he'd won at his gambling this week. He was all smiles and charm.

Amelia frowned, then reset her face into a placid expression.

"Hannah and her Aunt Sophia are going to be my midwives when the time comes."

"Glad you've got that settled, little mother. Don't count on me being anywhere around when the birthing happens. No place for a gentleman."

Amelia's face fell, but she kept her chin down and examined the little garment coming forth in her hands.

Saul winked at Hannah, then left.

That evening, as she started up the stairs to check on Charles, she passed July descending.

"Miz Hannah, Mister Seymour, he done told me to take the night off tonight."

"Well, enjoy yourself, July. You've been a good, faithful helper. I don't know what I'd do without you."

As she reached the dimly lit landing and started around the corner, a door to an empty room on her left opened, and Saul swung out into her path. He grabbed her arm and pulled her inside the shadowed room, then kicked the door shut. He wrapped his arms around her, arms a lot stronger than she remembered from her encounter with him two years earlier. The scent of alcohol fanned forth on his breath, and the musty smell of the unused room blanketed her. The only light came from around the edges of the drawn, heavy drapes.

She drew herself up into a stiff board. "Saul Seymour, turn me loose right now, or I'll scream and have the entire house roused." She spat the words into his leering face so close to hers.

"No, you won't. I've waited a long time for that black boy of yours to be absent. He can't come to help you, and my father ain't able, bless his heart." He bent closer. "And that big brother of yours? I heard you tell Amelia he's halfway across the world. So forget about him."

He tried to kiss her. She forced her head away from his thick lips. They landed on her neck.

He took a deep sniff of her. "You smell mighty good, Hannah. I've always known you'd be mine one day." He pulled her toward a bed in the corner as she fought against him.

With the curtains drawn, the windows bolted, would anyone hear her if she screamed? Panic rioted within her, but she remembered one trick Adam had taught her. She twisted and thrust him in the groin with her knee, then opened her mouth and screamed.

He growled in pain but didn't let go. Instead, he bent her arm behind her back until she groaned. "You want to play rough? I can handle that."

The door flew open, and Ruth, her face pale, stiff, and angry, stood outlined in the dim light from the hall.

With a curse, Saul released Hannah.

"Saul Seymour, I order you from this house. I can't stop you from going to the townhouse, but I command you to leave this plantation." Her voice was more authoritative than Hannah had ever heard it.

Hannah strode to stand beside her.

"You can't command me, Ruth." Saul's tone, full of venom, lashed back at her. "This house, the whole plantation, is coming to me. Haven't you heard? After the old man goes, you'll only be able to stay here yourself by my good mercies."

Ruth motioned for Hannah to follow to their father's room.

Despite the late hour, Charles Seymour sat up in his bed, his eyes hard. Had he heard her scream?

Ruth walked to his bedside. "Father, Saul has attacked Hannah. I've ordered him to leave the house, move to the townhouse. Will you back me up?"

Charles's eyes moved to Hannah, then he motioned her forward.

She came to stand beside Ruth.

"Is this true, girl?" His eyes glinted like gun metal in lantern light.

"Yes, sir, it is...I'm sorry to say."

"Ruth, send Saul to me, and you two go about your business."

Hannah went to her room, shut the door, and leaned against it.

A few minutes later, a fervent knock sounded at her door. She opened it, and Amelia all but fell into her arms. Only her extended stomach separated them.

"Hannah, Charles has ordered Saul to leave the house. Please, please ask Mr. Seymour to let me stay. You know my time is not far away. I can't...stand the thought of leaving with him." She swallowed and swiped a tear. "I'm not only afraid for myself, but...for the baby."

Hannah's backbone turned rock hard. She led the woman to a chair. "Sit right here, Amelia. I'll see what I can do."

She met Ruth in the hall coming from Charles's room and told her about Amelia. "Of course, she must stay here. I'll clear it with Father. Tell her to stay with you until Saul is out of the house. He was cursing and throwing things in a bag in their room when I passed by. I've sent word for the buggy to be brought to the front entrance, and one of our stablemen will drive him to the townhouse tonight."

Hannah returned to her room and comforted Amelia until the carriage rolled away from the front entrance. Then she hurried downstairs and fixed two cups of calming tea, one for Mr. Seymour and one for Amelia.

She knocked, then entered Charles's room when bid. When she placed the cup and saucer on his bedside table, he touched her hand. She'd never seen such pain in his eyes.

"I told you I've broken every command in that book of yours. One of them was not raising my son right." He swiped a hand across his eyes. "I gave him everything he ever wanted, taught him to drink and even how to gamble. Tonight I saw the mess I've made." His voice trembled with regret. He looked into her face. "Can your God forgive that, girl?"

Hannah stood speechless for a moment, then the words she needed came. "Yes, Mr. Seymour, God can forgive any sin when we repent."

He turned his face to the wall. "I wish I could believe that."

～

A month later, as Hannah dressed for breakfast, she glanced out her window. A servant in the Seymour townhouse green livery galloped down the plantation road to the entrance. He jumped off the lathered horse and ran up on the porch and banged on the door. Ruth called out that she was coming. Then a strange silence filled the house.

Hannah left her room and started down the stairs.

Ruth, coming up, met her with a face turned to chalk. "Saul died in a duel early this morning."

Hannah gasped. Was his father well enough to get such news? What about Amelia, her baby due almost any day?

"Come with me, Hannah. Father must be told first."

After Ruth imparted the dreadful tidings, Charles shook his head and sighed—a long, mournful sound. A soft knock sounded at the door. His pain-filled eyes pivoted from Ruth to Hannah, then he called out, "Enter."

Amelia came in, almost waddling in her last stages of pregnancy. She looked at all their faces, and then her breath caught in her throat. "What has happened? It's something to do with Saul, isn't it?"

Hannah went to her. "Dear, come and sit down first." She pulled a chair from the window space, and Amelia moved slowly toward it, then sat, her eyes still pleading toward Ruth.

Charles exhaled a heavy breath. "She must know." He lifted a hand toward his daughter-in-law. "Your husband, my son Saul, was killed in a duel early this morning. I couldn't be sorrier to have to tell you."

She gasped, and her hand flew to her mouth, then sobs erupted from deep in her chest. The sorrowful sound filled the room.

Hannah, tears filling her eyes, went to her and laid a comforting hand on her thin, shaking shoulder. "Amelia, think of the little one. You must. However hard it is..."

The sobs dissolved into gulps and sniffs. Ruth swiped at her own wet cheek and came over to hand Amelia a handkerchief.

Charles leaned his head back on his pillow and closed his eyes. "Now, can all of you leave me to my grief and regrets?" He opened his eyes and looked directly at Hannah. "Take care of the little mother, girl. She's carrying the last descendent bearing the Seymour name we'll ever have."

Saul's funeral, held in the family cemetery, proved short and hurried, as rain threatened overhead. Hannah thought she'd never seen such a sad farewell service. Hannah, July, Ruth, the minister, and a handful of Seymour servants were all who attended. Amelia, not feeling well, had begged to stay in her room. Charles watched the proceedings from his window.

Within an hour after the funeral, Amelia's labor began, and Hannah sent July to fetch Aunt Sophia.

Her aunt's presence in the Seymour house brought instant peace. Hannah reveled in the wisdom and good will that rolled from the woman's lips. Even Mr. Seymour responded and rallied from his sadness, and asked for food. Amelia proved a strong woman through many hard hours of labor. Hannah assisted Sophia. A perfect little boy with a head full of dark Seymour hair appeared before sunset, an answer to Hannah's fervent, silent prayers all the long day.

When Ruth proudly carried the child to let her father see him, Charles Seymour took one look at the baby and smiled at Ruth and Hannah, who had tagged along. "He's a fine boy. Looks just like Saul looked the day he was born." He spoke to Ruth. "Send a servant for my lawyer in town, that Mr. Becket. "I'm going to change my will." Then he glanced at Hannah. "I aim to do a very different job raising this one, girl. You think you might can show me how from your book?"

Hannah cocked her chin. "Well, Mr. Seymour, that sounds like a good helpful plan. And I'm sure his mother will have something to say about the little man's raising. Why don't you ask her in a week or two when she's up and about?"

That night, though exhausted, Hannah wanted to write to Adam about all that had happened, but her head fell on her desk. She prepared for bed. Her letter could wait until tomorrow.

In the early dawn, heartrending cries from the newborn ripped Hannah from her sleep. An icy chill swept over her. Something was terribly wrong.

CHAPTER 14

⚜

*A*dam walked back to his cabin to read the letter from Hannah he'd received in the mail packet from the American schooner that had caught up with his ship. Though the missive would be several months old, his heart increased its beat as he sliced open the wax seal with his knife. Any word from Hannah always made his day. But the first sentence caused his heart to drop to his toes.

Dear Adam,

The days were going well here with few surprises until Saul shocked us all by showing up from England with his wife. But I've made fast friends with Amelia Seymour. She's pregnant with their first child, and my heart goes out to her for the unkind treatment she receives from Saul. An English education and marriage to someone as precious as his wife has not changed Saul for the good, but I am not afraid of him. July is here with me. He's grown into a powerful man and would be a great defense if Saul ever tried anything. One good thing is that Saul is often absent from the plantation. He spends several days a week in Charleston, living in the townhouse doing whatever his heart desires, which I suspect is gambling. But enough of that.

Charles Seymour (I'm still not comfortable calling him Father) and I have had some interesting conversations. I believe the Lord is truly dealing with his heart. Pray that he'll come to know the Lord Jesus as we do.

I find relief from my day to day diligent nursing efforts for Charles and frustration over Saul's treatment of his wife by taking horseback treks over the plantation. Aunt Sophia insisted I bring Dancer, and I'm so glad I did. A couple of weeks ago, I rode so much farther than I imagined and ended up in a pleasant woodland which turned out to be part of the plantation that employs Gideon Falconer as manager and factor. When Dancer started going lame, I was ever so glad to see Gideon ride up and help me. He discovered and removed the stone from the mare's hoof in about two heartbeats, and she was fine. He even insisted on riding back to the Seymour Plantation border with me. He's a fine man and a firm believer. You met him before you left on your navy assignment. I would love for you two to become good friends. Meanwhile, he and I are already friends. I feel safe with him.

It is time for my evening call on Charles with his night-time tea to help him get good rest.

So, my dear brother, be safe, and I look forward to your next home-coming. Will it be in the spring or summer?

Your loving sister,
Hannah

Adam folded the letter and placed it in a compartment of his officer's desk with his other letters. He walked up to the quarterdeck and tried to overcome his black thoughts of Saul being in the same house with Hannah. He prayed for her safety. Then the words she had penned about Falconer rose to taunt him. Was she falling in love with the man? That thought gripped his insides like a vise. Then a peace settled upon him. If Gideon Falconer was the one who could make Hannah happy, he'd be glad for her. Wouldn't he?

The next day, a summons to rendezvous at Syracuse came from Commodore Preble. Adam set sail for that harbor that had almost become a naval base for the US Mediterranean Squadron. The ancient city of Syracuse, rich in Greek and Roman history on the coast of Sicily, Italy, was no favorite of Adam's. A place of wealth and affluence a century earlier, gloom, poverty, and filth now filled its dilapidated streets. The one time he'd disembarked and headed to a new pub built for the American and English sailors, a parade of beggars had trailed him and Josiah.

Thankfully, he would only need to row to Preble's frigate in the harbor. He stepped into the longboat with a lifting heart. He hoped, *he prayed*, Preble had decided to do something about the *Philadelphia*. He was itching to see if there was anything they could do for Michael and the captured crew or stop the enemy from using the frigate against the United States.

"Come right in, Lieutenant White." Preble's voice held confidence it had not held a few months before when he had dropped the bombshell on the squadron about the *Philadelphia's* capture.

Adam saluted his leader, but why did only Stephen Decatur and the captain of the new *USS Syren* join him in taking a seat around the table? He greeted them and sat.

Preble stood tall and confident. "Sirs, we've decided to board and burn the *Philadelphia* so our enemy can never use it against the United States."

"Aye, aye, Commodore."

Adam's heart jumped into his throat, and he echoed Stephen Decatur's sentiments, as did the other captain. Would he be able to do anything to help Michael? Common sense told him it wasn't likely. Michael would be on shore in a Barbary prison. They would board the *Philadelphia* anchored in the Tripoli harbor in stealth and pray they didn't alert the shore sentries.

Preble turned to Decatur. "Lieutenant, your plan sounds as though it might work, especially since we now have in our possession the Tripolitan merchant ship, the *Mastico*, which you captured in so timely a manner."

Decatur, his color heightened, smiled and tapped his fist on the table. "Thank you, sir, and thanks to my diligent crew that worked hard to capture that vessel."

Adam liked the way the man refused to take all the glory for himself but was quick to point out his crew's assistance.

The commodore picked up a paper before him on the table and read. "I am authorizing you, Captain Stephen Decatur, with seventy-five handpicked men, to enter the Tripoli Harbor at night, board the frigate *Philadelphia*, burn her, and make good your retreat. The raiding party will ignite combustibles in the gunroom, berth deck, and cockpit storerooms." He stopped and looked soberly at the three men. "After the ship is well on fire, point two of the eighteen-pounders down the main hatch and blow her bottom out."

The man glanced back at his notes. "To avert all suspicion, you will sail the refitted merchant ship, the *Mastico*, now renamed the *Intrepid*, into the harbor." He turned to the newest captain. "The USS *Syren* will trail five miles behind to be your backup, Decatur. We will repaint her and outfit her also to look like a local Tripolitan merchant vessel." He paused and laid his paper down on the table. "Questions?"

The only question in Adam's head was one even the commodore could not answer. On this most dangerous mission they'd yet to undertake, would they be successful?

～

On Friday, February 3, Adam and his specially selected crew members set sail from Syracuse with Decatur and his hand-picked men aboard the *Intrepid*, flying a British flag. Designed for a crew of two dozen, the little ship now housed seventy-five armed men with berths for a third of those aboard. Decatur shared his small cabin with Adam, the pilot, and the ship's surgeon. Crew members bedded down in the rat-infested hold. Heavy seas, spoiled food, and fear that their ship might founder weighed heavy on the morale of the men.

To make matters worse, a winter gale struck. For five days, Adam, Stephen Decatur, and the crew suffered miserably battling the elements in the small, crowded vessel. Adam sent up quite a few prayers and stood determined with Decatur to maintain an appearance of absolute confidence and resolve to keep the crew from descending into a state of despair.

When the gale finally abated on February 12, Adam commiserated with Decatur upon discovering the storm had separated the *Intrepid* and the *Syren* far from each other and east of Tripoli. Decatur's knowledgeable pilot navigated back toward Tripoli by identifying features of the North African Coast. Hopefully, the *Syren's* pilot could do the same.

Other things went wrong on the way toward Tripoli. Fearing the ship was making the trip too fast and might arrive in the harbor before nightfall, Decatur ordered his men to toss overboard a drag line rigged with ladders, spars, buckets, and lumber. No doubt their leader hoped to slow the ship down without shortening the sails, which might be suspicious to a Tripolitan sentinel on shore. So Adam and the men did as commanded, and after tense moments, he breathed a sigh of relief as the *Intrepid* slowed while appearing to be sailing full speed ahead toward the Tripoli Harbor.

Most of the crew lay concealed and in complete silence as the little ship sailed closer to the harbor in the falling darkness. Adam, Decatur, the pilot, and only three crew members stood on the deck wearing the clothing of Maltese merchants. The British flag, as they'd hoped, seemed to fool the sentries onshore.

Decatur stopped his pacing near Adam on the small deck. "White, this expedition, which I am happy to lead, is bittersweet to me." His voice continued low for Adam's ears only. "The shipwrights of my home city, Philadelphia, used money raised by the citizens to build this ship we come to destroy." He paused and gazed ahead at the distant harbor. "My father became its first captain."

Adam searched for something to respond, but the wind dropped and Decatur whipped his eyeglass from his side and searched the moonlit waves behind them. The *Syren* should be somewhere behind them.

Decatur frowned. "They're too far back, White, and with the wind what it is, they'll never make it. Our plan calls for a ten o'clock attack, and it's going to take every minute we have to work our way over to the *Philadelphia*." He shut the telescope, and his lips thinned into a grim line. "The *Syren* won't be able to back us up."

Would Decatur abort the mission? Sweat slid down Adam's back. To be so close and have to give it up? Bile filled his mouth.

A moment later, a new confidence spread across Decatur's countenance. He turned to Adam. "We'll proceed with our plan, despite the absence of our partner ship. The fewer the number, the greater the honor."

Adam whispered a prayer of thanks and another for protection and success.

As darkness fell, the light of a crescent moon revealed the *Philadelphia*. Adam's throat dried to sawdust. The large vessel looked forbidding, with its Tripoli flag and guards stationed about her deck. Would they be able to board it, overcome the guards, burn it, and escape to safety? And Michael, had he survived the capture and weeks of slavery? Where was he now? Was he in pain and hopeless in chains?

He looked closer at the captured ship as they drew nearer. The sight had to be as heartrending to the few men on deck as it was to him. Her foremast remained a stump. Stripped of sails, she could go nowhere in her own power. Yet her sheer scale seemed awesome in a harbor where small local vessels sailed the waves.

As the ten o'clock hour approached, the little *Intrepid* came within hailing distance of the *Philadelphia*. As planned, Adam stood on deck with only Decatur and the pilot, Salvador Catalano, a Sicilian hired by Preble for his knowledge of the harbor and fluency in the common tongue of Mediterranean sailors.

A Tripolitan spoke from the tall frigate in a foreign language. He ordered their small vessel to keep away.

Though he stood at the helm, Decatur remained silent as Salvador Catalano answered. He told the planned story that the violent storm had stripped his merchant vessel of its anchors, and they only wanted a safe place to tether their little ship for the night. In the morning, they would secure new anchors ashore.

Adam, who'd been holding his breath, sucked in air when the

guards aboard the frigate appeared to accept the explanation. Both ships dispatched boats carrying lines to fasten them to each other. With the cables bound fast, the *Intrepid* drew near the side of the *Philadelphia*. Adam whispered a fervent prayer for protection and the success of the mission.

Suddenly, a sharp-eyed Tripolitan guard, who must have spotted something amiss, shouted out across the water, "Americanos!" But he was too late.

As the ships touched in the blanketing darkness, Stephen Decatur yelled a one-word order, "Board!" He, himself, leaped for the main chains of the frigate to climb the dozen feet to the deck of the tall ship. Adam came right behind him, and the rest of the hidden crew shot up from their hiding places and followed. They hung on the sides of the ship like a cluster of bees and scrambled up on deck.

His blood pounding in his ears and every muscle in his body taut, Adam dropped to the deck beside Decatur with his sword unsheathed. Four heavily armed Barbary sentries in their red fez hats, open shirts, and pantaloons rushed toward them, swinging deadly scimitars. Adam made quick work of the first one, then did the same of the second, who had moved toward Decatur, already battling two large warriors. Taken by surprise, none of the pirates were the deadly threat they'd hoped to be. One after another, the Muslim guards fell before Adam and Decatur's men.

Not a gunshot was fired. Decatur had ordered that only blades—swords, pikes, and knives—be used to avoid alerting the fortress guns a few hundred yards away.

In less than ten minutes, the savage, deadly fight was over, the guards overcome and silenced without attracting the attention of sentries on shore. With a quick counting around the boarding team, Adam noted they'd not lost a single man and had only one who'd suffered a minor wound. The man wrapped his neck kerchief around his wrist and stood ready for the next command.

Decatur gave the order to destroy the *Philadelphia*. The meticulous plan for burning the frigate began. Adam knew exactly what to do. He divided the men into squads, assigned to set fire to different sections of the frigate. Squad leaders carried a single lantern, and each man a three-inch length of spermaceti candle soaked in turpentine. The *Intrepid* crew left behind passed combustibles up to the frigate's deck. The squads took them below to plant in the storeroom, the gunroom, cockpit, and berth deck. Their hasty boots clattered down the various hatches.

Adam and his three-man team thumped down the extra hatches to the lower storeroom. The musty smell of a ship anchored too long in a harbor filled his nose. The minute his boots touched the lower passageway, the hair stood up on Adam's neck. He sucked in a breath and listened. A definite banging echoed somewhere down the way.

In a matter of seconds, he stood at the chained door of the storeroom, sword in hand, his squad behind him. Could there be more pirates guarding the stockroom, just waiting to emerge and destroy them? He leaned his ear to the door. Was that English he heard? "Who's in there? We're coming in and we're armed. Stand back!" He hacked the chain off the door and kicked it open. Their lantern spilled light into the dark room.

Adam almost dropped his sword, and his heart jumped into his throat. To his utter amazement, his brother Michael and another sailor stared at him with wide eyes, their bearded faces pale, their mouths open. And English spilled forth from their lips. "Praise God, praise God!" Their gruff voices came from deep within.

Gulping down an enormous lump almost choking him, Adam grabbed Michael in a bear hug. Tears streamed down his brother's face, and holding him, Adam's shock ignited into anger over Michael's thin body. He'd lost weight, but he was alive, and somehow on this ship. *Thank You, Father God.*

Wiping the wetness from his own face, Adam looked into Michael's eyes. "How did you come to be...?"

Michael swiped his mouth with the back of his hand. "Our captors garrisoned us here to make repairs. Both of us are good carpenters. They want to use the frigate against our navy."

Adam pulled the two from the room, then his squad entered with their combustibles.

"We're here to make sure they don't do that, brother."

Michael touched Adam's arm. "Thank God, what an answer to prayer. Show me what I can do to help."

"Me, too," the other sailor offered.

"You two have done enough, staying alive. Just keep close to my squad. It's all planned out." Adam watched his men preparing to set fire to the storeroom with its crates and burlap bundles of supplies that originally outfitted the *Philadelphia*.

Above, they heard the heavy tread of Stephen Decatur walking along the spar deck from forward to aft, pausing at each hatchway. Then he came to their hatchway and shouted, "Fire!"

Adam nodded, and each of his men lit his candle at the lantern and ignited the combustibles, then rushed from the room. All of them raced up the passage and hatches to the upper deck, the stench of the turpentine, whale oil, and burning burlap following them.

Smoke and flames roared across the deck as every man scooted down the side of the *Philadelphia* to the *Intrepid*. The smell of burning oak and combustibles filled the night air.

Once aboard the smaller vessel, Adam assisted the men struggling to free and drive the *Intrepid* away from the burning frigate. His eyes stung from the smoke and his breath came in spurts. The crew, working frantically to push the *Intrepid* away from the burning *Philadelphia* made no progress. In moments, the flames could spread to their vessel. He ordered long oars to be brought up to be used as poles to fend the vessel off. But the fire sucked in air from every direction and repeatedly drew the *Intrepid* back toward the frigate amid the sailors' grunts of physical exertion and disappointment.

Adam's mouth dried to sawdust as he did everything he knew to assist with the hopeless efforts. He lifted a fervent prayer. *Dear God, I know you didn't help me rescue Michael and finish our mission for all of us to die along with this burning ship.*

The sentries on shore, now fully alert, began yelling and shooting at them. Sweat ran down Adam's back and beaded his forehead. In moments, cannon from the fortress could blow them to bits.

Decatur pushed his way through the straining men to Adam's

side, his face a blackened mask of alarm such as Adam had never seen, but the man's eyes glowed. Did he have an idea to get them free of the burning wreck before the flames roaring across the night sky spread to the *Intrepid*?

Make is so, Lord Jesus.

CHAPTER 15

Hannah threw the bedclothes aside and pushed her feet to the floor. Amelia's infant should be fed, happy, and sleeping next to his mother's side. Not taking time to throw water on her face, she grabbed her robe and hurried down the hall runner barefoot. Ruth arrived at Amelia's door at the same time, and they both entered.

Aunt Sophia stood beside Amelia's bed, lifting the child from his mother's bedside. Tears streamed down her aunt's cheeks. The cries of the baby subsided into snuffling as she cradled him in her arms.

Hannah gasped and moisture filled her eyes as she looked at the cold, still form of Amelia Seymour. Her face, now in death, held the sweetest peace.

Sophia spoke, rocking the child in her arms. "I've never been so surprised to find this terrible loss after this precious woman made it so well through the birthing." She turned to look into Ruth's and Hannah's faces. "Do either of you know of any deep stress she might have been going through or hiding? It's as if she just gave up once she knew the child had made his way safely into the world."

The two of them looked at each other, and Ruth took a deep

breath. "Yes, Sophia. My brother Saul broke Amelia's tender heart, probably from the day they married."

Sophia sighed, then looked down at the newborn, now sucking his fist. "From the sound of this young man's lusty lungs, I don't think there's a thing wrong with him, except he's hungry."

Ruth moved forward, and her face, though wet with tears, shone with tenderness. "Give him to me. I will love him as my own child. And I know of a good wet nurse I can employ."

Sophia handed the precious bundle to her, and she clutched the child to her heart and left the sad room. Her crooning voice consoling the child as she walked down the hall brought some comfort to Hannah.

~

The morning of Amelia's funeral dawned with meager light from the February sun, as if nature grieved too. Gray clouds hung low over the bare trees of the Seymour family cemetery, enclosed with its wrought-iron fence. Hannah, with Gideon Falconer by her side, followed the small entourage made up of the minister, Ruth, Aunt Sophia, and Amelia's servant girl to the burial site. The only sound came from the soft weeping of Amelia's maid and the rustling of the long black skirts of the women as they brushed against the grass path. Charles Seymour watched from his high bedroom window in the plantation house.

A big "S" fashioned in wrought iron on the gate amid curlicues and lilies boasted the family initial. The smell of the newly tuned earth mingled with the fragrant spray of yellow Carolina Jessamine Hannah carried and which grew on the far fence of the graveyard. Ruth carried two stems of deep red camellias from the plantation garden hedge.

They walked past carved headstones of marble and granite in white, gray, and black hues. Moss grew at the base of the older ones, as well as ivy. Hannah glanced at the names and dates, but her attention settled to the newly dug grave ahead, beside Saul Seymour's recent grave. Two male servants with their shovels bided their time just outside the fence.

The gray-headed, robed minister stood at the head of the grave with his prayer book in his hand. Gideon held Hannah's elbow as she looked down at the pine box that held Amelia's body.

The minister read the twenty-third Psalm, his voice strong and sympathetic. Thunder rumbled in the eastern sky, and he looked up and closed his prayer book.

Hannah shivered in the cold air, and moisture gathered in her eyes as she remembered the sweet face and gentle spirit of Amelia and the precious child who would never know his mother. She glanced up at Ruth, who dabbed a handkerchief at her eyes. Aunt Sophia looked as sad as Hannah had ever seen her. Was this the first time a young mother she'd attended had passed like this? Her aunt would probably tell her later. Gideon touched her hand, and she looked into his handsome, gentle face. Thank goodness he'd come.

The minister led in a prayer. Ruth dropped her camellia stems onto the oak box, then bent and clutched a handful of the damp earth and cast it into the grave.

Hannah released her yellow Carolina Jessamine spray onto the top of the coffin.

The minister spoke to Ruth, then nodded at the others at the site and strode away, looking up at the gathering clouds. His horse-drawn coach rumbled down the plantation drive at a brisk pace.

Ruth motioned to the two servants to come with their shovels, and they climbed over the fence and started to cover the coffin with damp earth.

That she did not need to see. Hannah turned and walked back to the plantation house with Gideon's hand on her elbow. Sophia followed and Ruth soon joined them. Gentle rain began to fall as they entered the house. Once all had gathered in the parlor, the housekeeper served sandwiches, hot scones, and tea before the warm fireplace.

Later, on the porch after the rain had ceased, Hannah said goodbye to Gideon. A servant brought up his horse.

"Please let me know if there's anything I can do for you, Hannah. Will you be staying or going back with Sophia today? You know I plan to visit, wherever you are." A grin lit his face.

She sucked in a deep breath and sighed. Charles Seymour seemed better, actually much improved since she first came months ago to nurse him. And July deserved credit. The two men got on well. "I don't know yet, but I think I will go back to Sophia's soon. I've missed our work there."

As she walked back into the house and up the stairs, Gideon's last comment echoed in her mind. Did she really want him to visit more often? Was it fair to let him fill the void left by Adam's long stints at sea when there might be no real future with her in it? She sighed and shook her head, unable to decide.

~

In the following days, Hannah monitored Charles's improvement, especially notable when Ruth brought the baby to see him. Her sister did this sometimes twice a day after seeing the beneficial effect the visits had on her father. He liked the name Ruth agreed to for his grandson, Saul Charles Seymour. He called the boy Charlie and expressed his delight when holding him.

A month later, when spring blossoms brightened the landscape, Hannah told Ruth she would leave at the end of the week. Thankful for her father's improvement, Ruth was fine with her decision—especially since Charles had asked July to stay and he'd agreed to do so if Sophia Rutledge released him. Charles could now take brief walks about the room, but not the stairs yet.

There was one thing Hannah wanted to make sure of before leaving. She'd had several talks with her birth father about spiritual matters, but had she shared enough?

She spent time in prayer, asking the Lord about the situation and what, if anything else, she should say to Mr. Seymour. As she prayed, she felt the old resistance to calling him *Father*. He was not her father and never would be. John White was her father.

The morning before she was scheduled to leave, Charles called for her. He was sitting up in his chair at his window. Sight of the open Bible on his lap, one from his library she'd brought months earlier to his room, caused her steps to falter. The hefty, leather-bound, illustrated holy book had no doubt cost a pretty penny. Whose had it been in earlier days?

He glanced up at her. "Come sit right here, dear daughter Hannah. I've got a question for you."

She remembered well the day he stopped calling her *girl* and used her given name. Now he'd added the term *daughter*. Did he wish to hear her call him *Father*? He'd wish in vain.

Suddenly, she yearned to see John White and her precious mother. And dear Adam. Her heart skipped a beat as Adam's strong, confident face flashed across her mind, but it would be months before he'd return from his navy assignment. Every day, she lifted him and Michael up in prayer for protection and victory in the Tripolitan war. She often dreamed of Adam and, as frequently, reminded herself he was her brother who would only think of her as his sister. At those times, she would try to think positive things about Gideon Falconer. Besides being handsome, he was a Christian, a gentleman, kind, and knowledgeable. But he never appeared in her dreams.

She took a chair across from Charles in his window sitting area. Seriousness tightened his elderly face, which no longer boasted the red flush from alcohol overindulgence. "What do you think this really means right here in the book of John?" He pointed to a text in the volume open across his knees.

"Read it to me."

"*For God so loved the world that he gave his only begotten son, that whosoever believes in him, should not perish, but have everlasting life.*"

Hannah's heart sang. She whispered a prayer for guidance. "It means exactly what it says. "Father God sent Jesus Christ, his son, into the world, to save every human being from perishing who will believe he is the son of God and accept him."

He rubbed his gray stubby chin, not yet having had his shave by

July. "How do I do that? I've done a lot of bad things during my lifetime, some of which hurt you, my baby daughter I abandoned."

The words stung Hannah, hearing them from his lips. Yes, it had hurt when she learned of it, and the old ache churned across her middle. But the soft voice she knew so well whispered in her heart. *Have you forgiven him?* She tried to ignore the voice. Her mother's teachings came to her rescue for his question. "Jesus died on the cross for all the bad things any of us have done, but we have to pray, repent for the wrong things, ask God's forgiveness, and accept Jesus as our Savior from those sins." She took a deep breath, and another way of expressing it came to her.

"It's like Jesus' death on the cross has already paid for all the sins in the accounts of all men. But we have to repent and receive Him as our Savior to get His forgiveness and righteousness deposited into our account."

"Can He forgive me for all I've done? You only know some things."

"He knows them all, Mr. Seymour, and He can forgive them all."

He leaned forward. His pale blue eyes pierced hers. "Can you forgive me for abandoning you, Hannah? I'm really sorry. But I have to know before I can go any further."

She drew back. Her breath seemed to have solidified in her throat. Finally, she broke the brittle silence. "I...hadn't forgiven you, but I do so right now, Mr. Seymour."

His face relaxed. "Thank you, daughter. Now I can pray and ask God to forgive me. I believe He can forgive all I've done." His voice was thick, then he lowered his head, and his lips moved in a prayer. Lifting a thin, veined hand, he swiped at his cheek.

Tears sprang to Hannah's eyes. The man was sincere. A gentle whisper flowed into her heart. *Call him by his proper title. He's one of mine.*

When Charles finished praying and looked up, she reached out and touched his hand gripping the Bible. "I'm so happy you've done this...Father." A tear slipped down her cheek.

He looked startled, then a smile spread across his face. "You're a good girl, daughter."

She had room in her heart for two fathers.

That afternoon, she made time to write Adam and share all that had happened at the Seymour plantation. It took several pages. She closed her missive by sharing her decision to return to her aunt's townhouse.

~

Upon her move back to Charleston, Hannah fell right back in with Aunt Sophia's work at the Charleston Hospital. Going there daily, making the rounds with her aunt, made her realize how much she'd missed it.

One rather important change emerged in their routine. Dr. Thomas Barnes, more often than not, showed up before they left for the day. It took Hannah only to the second time he dropped by to understand something was happening between her aunt and the doctor. The way he looked at Aunt Sophia, as if he hung on every word, meant something, and how could she miss the way her aunt's face brightened when he appeared?

One afternoon, two weeks after her return, he stood before them in the hospital corridor, and his intelligent eyes flashed from Aunt Sophia to her.

Hannah smiled. "Dr. Barnes, I haven't told you, but I'm happy to see the appreciable changes that have taken place in the hospital since I left."

"And what might those changes be, young woman?" His brown eyes sparkled.

"The open windows for fresh air, the greater cleanliness, and...the chamber pots covered, to mention a few."

He chuckled. "Your dear aunt would give me no peace until those things became reality. Now I have to wonder what's next."

Aunt Sophia laughed. "You'll hear soon enough. But would you like to come for dinner tomorrow evening, Tom?"

"Definitely. What time?"

"Eight o'clock."

He came to dinner at least twice a week. Hannah found their happiness contagious, but it also left her yearning. Would she ever find such a relationship? What if Adam could never think of her as anything but as his little sister he needed to watch out for?

Gideon Falconer continued to show his interest. She appreciated his company, but it was Adam she longed to see. She'd heard nothing from him for some time. If he thought of her more than a sister, wouldn't he have written more often?

Gideon rode into Charleston almost every Sunday afternoon to see her as spring progressed into a long, hot summer. Still, she'd not heard from Adam. Why hadn't he written? Was he all right? Was he wounded—or had he not survived the dangerous missions on which she knew the navy sent him? Had their family just not received their notification of loss?

That terrible thought plagued her at times, dried up her appetite to eat, and snuffed out her desire to do anything. Then she'd spend time praying Scripture promises over Adam, such as Psalm 91, until peace came and she could go on with her life. She kept these thoughts to herself, not liking the idea of even sharing them with Aunt Sophia, who was happier than she remembered her ever being.

One warm afternoon, she and her aunt returned from visiting two new patients, mothers-to-be, and an envelope lay on the hall credenza for her. She recognized Adam's handwriting, grabbed it, and hurried to her room. Plopping on her bed, she tore the missive open.

Dear Hannah,

Forgive me, but this is the first good chance I'd had to write a letter. I just received your last letter telling me all that happened at the Seymour Plantation and your planned return to your aunt's. I wish I could've been there to help you through all that occurred. Charles Seymour's change of heart is an answer to our prayers.

A lot has happened since I last wrote, but I will try not to bore you with too much navy detail. President Jefferson sent our Mediterranean Squadron, led by Commodore Edward Preble, to block the Tripoli Harbor. You probably heard they declared war on the United States. One of our newest frigates, The USS Philadelphia, *Michael's assigned ship, ended up grounded on a hidden reef and was captured by the enemy. I feared for him and all the crew when I heard about it being taken. The Barbary states have hundreds of our sailors enslaved, and reports have come out of their terrible treatment and the demands for exorbitant ransom.*

I thank God Commodore Preble invited me to be part of a special expedition to sail into the Tripoli Harbor and burn the Philadelphia *so the enemy could not use it against us. Captain Stephen Decatur led this dangerous mission, and I've never known a more intelligent and brave officer. It was my distinct pleasure to be assigned to aid him. To cut the story short, by God's grace, we did exactly what the navy commissioned us to do, but almost perished when we couldn't get our little ship that had been tethered to the burning hulk loose. Decatur came up with an idea which freed us before the flames could consume us.*

I've saved the best two pieces of news for last. First, a genuine miracle. Our brother, Michael, turned up in the hold of the Philadelphia, *and we rescued him before burning the ship. They had garrisoned him and one other American on the ship to help repair it.*

Second, the U.S. Navy has given our special team that destroyed the Philadelphia *an award and extended leave. I'll be home not too long after you receive this letter, the Lord willing and the sea and wind amenable for sailing.*

Your loving brother,
Adam

Hannah squealed with delight. She thanked God for the good news, jumped from the bed, and ran downstairs to tell Aunt Sophia.

Her aunt sat on the sofa knitting. Hannah read Adam's letter to her.

Her aunt laid aside her needlework and lifted her hands high. "Praise the Lord! So thankful Adam made it safely through that dangerous mission and, thank God, he could rescue Michael." She smiled at Hannah. "It sounds as though he may even be here in time to take you to the St. Cecilia Ball next month. Our invitation has arrived." She picked back up her knitting. "Of course, I have an escort, and you can come with us if Adam doesn't get back in time."

Hannah tilted her chin. "Aunt Sophia, don't play coy with me. Would your escort be Dr. Barnes?"

Her aunt's smile broadened. "You guessed it." She stopped knitting for a moment. "Hannah, I know you're seeing Gideon Falconer almost every week. Are you...interested in him, or is it Adam? He's really not your blood brother, you know."

Heat flooded Hannah's cheeks, and she dropped beside her aunt on the settee, twisting her hands in her lap. Finally, someone to talk to about her feelings and questions. "Aunt Sophia...I've always loved Adam, and now...maybe more than a brother." There, she'd said it. Saying it gave it weight, lifted it from her dreams and hopes. "But is it all right? Since he's my known brother? I'm confused about it." Moisture gathered in her eyes.

Sophia laid her knitting aside and reached out and pressed Hannah's hand. "Just as I've guessed. These old eyes have been around a long time and miss little." She reached for her worn Bible nearby. "A text is coming to me I think we should look at. Have you ever read Song of Solomon?"

"Yes, some time ago. It's like a...love song, I think."

"It's regarded as one of the greatest wedding songs ever written. Some of our clergy want to say it's only a picture of the love that exists between Christ and the church." She smiled. "That may be so, but I think it's also an illustration of God's sanction for the love and intimacy between a husband and wife." She flipped pages, then ran her finger down a column. "Here is the passage that came to mind. *You have ravished my heart, my sister, my bride.* Did you notice the writer called his beloved his sister? I don't think he meant his blood sister, but that his love for her was like, but greater than that for, a sister." She closed the book. "Maybe that might help you, Hannah. Adam could love you as a sister, but he could also love you more than that. Do you have any idea?"

Hannah remembered Adam's gentle kiss on New Year's Eve two years earlier, followed by his apology. Was she putting more meaning to it than Adam meant it to have? And then there was Juliet Nelson, who had spent time on his ship. That name still rankled Hannah. "I don't know, Aunt Sophia." She swallowed to relieve her dry throat.

Her aunt looked at her with understanding eyes. "Are you also attracted to Gideon Falconer?"

Hannah sighed. "Somehow I am. He's such a fine Christian man, and his happy-go-lucky attitude keeps me from getting...depressed. You know he has a fiancée in England. He told me he assumes she's backed out since he fled the country to escape being arrested for helping hungry people poach on the estate where he was gamekeeper."

Her aunt chuckled. "I can't imagine a woman backing out from an engagement with Gideon Falconer. He's such a handsome man and a perfect gentleman." She squeezed Hannah's hand. "I'll be praying for the Lord to reveal His will for you, for Adam, and for Gideon."

The next Sunday afternoon, Gideon drove up in a carriage and asked Hannah to go for a drive in the park. The idea pleased her. He helped her up into her seat, and his manly scent that reminded her of Adam flowed over her. The now-grown pup, Hercules, who'd been so happy when she returned to her aunt's, jumped aboard and lay at her feet. He flapped his tail on the buggy floor and gave her a doggy smile with his mouth panting and his warm brown eyes searching her face as if begging to stay.

She patted his large blond head. "All right, Hercules, I guess you can go." Opening her parasol, she enjoyed the shade and the fresh breeze that lifted the ribbons on her bonnet and ruffled the lace on her sleeves.

Gideon shook the reins across the two bay horses' backs and commanded, "Let's go, boys."

The horses' hooves, clicking on the cobblestones as they headed to the city park, sounded pleasant. Birds flew among the trees and chattered as though happy to be alive. Her world seemed bright and expectant.

She told Gideon about Adam's letter.

"So he's coming home soon? That's just my luck."

Hannah cast a glance at him. "Your luck?"

He smiled at her, then turned his attention to driving the carriage as they made their way into the park. "I have an idea Adam might could be more than a brother to you, Hannah. Am I right?"

She moistened her lips but found she was at a loss for words.

"He's a fine man, and if that's the case, I will wish you both the best." He glanced at her and tilted his chin. "He's not been around much this past year, but now he's coming home, and a hero. Will you let me in on what might happen between you two?"

Hannah's cheeks warmed. Disappointment edged Gideon's usually cheerful voice. She stole a look into his eyes, but they were clear, untroubled. "You're too fine a person, Gideon, for me not to be honest about my feelings. I don't know what the future might hold, but I will always value your friendship. Is that a fair answer?"

He pressed his lips together, then his old smile creased his square, tanned jaw. "Of course it is. A poet, I think by the name of John Lyly, once wrote, *All is fair in love and war*."

"What does that mean?"

He chuckled. "That's what everyone has wondered since the man penned it. But I think it means you won't have to apologize to me if you decide Adam is the one for you." He pulled the carriage under a shade tree and shouted, "Whoa!" The two horses stopped and tossed their sweating necks, happy for a rest. He turned to face her. "There's also a scripture that assures us all things work together for good to them who love God, so I don't have to fret."

Adam's text.

She gave him a smile. "Does anything ever ruffle your feathers, Gideon?" She'd never seen him in any attitude except peaceful, confident, as if everything were fine with him.

"Oh yes. There are a couple of things that'd keep me riled if I let 'em."

She moved her parasol to see him better. "What are they?"

He wove the reins together in his broad hands. "Slavery and mistreatment of the poor."

Hannah nodded. "Yes, I remember your sharing about this when we first met. I feel the same. Is there anything we can do about the slavery issue, Gideon? My parents freed the slave family we owned years ago. As I shared earlier, my mother's Quaker faith teaches against slavery."

"One day, everyone will have to take their stand on the issue. Abolition is alive and strong in England, mainly because of my friends John Newton and William Wilberforce. In fact, according to my contacts, Wilberforce has a bill before the British Parliament now that will end all international slave trade in the British Empire. I pray daily for it to pass. It doesn't free those now enslaved, but it will stop any more slave importing, buying, or selling in all the British colonies worldwide. I see nothing on the horizon like that here. One doesn't even speak of it in the United States. I believe one day the issue will greatly divide this new country."

Gideon's firm voice sent a chill up Hannah's back and shadows across her heart. Mammy, Samson, and Ida were dear to her and her family. Sadness and worry threatened to overrun her mind at the plight of other slaves and what it might take to free them all. Then she remembered Adam was coming home, and her world settled back into hope and serenity.

That night before sleep took her, she thought of Adam as she'd last seen him. He'd walked jauntily down her aunt's steps with his navy seabag slung across his shoulder and whistled while she sat in the swing swallowing back sobs. Now a warm glow flowed through her. Soon, soon, he'd come back up those same steps.

Niggling thoughts intervened and tried to steal her rest. What if the navy decided they needed to send Adam on another assignment? What if before he even returned, a storm tossed his ship like last time, and...? She sat up, fluffed her pillow, then lay back down and prayed every promise she could think of for God's care and help for him, and sleep finally came.

CHAPTER 16

Standing on the quarterdeck with the early-morning breeze off the sea lifting his gold-braided collar, Adam rejoiced as the *Vixen's* pilot guided the sloop toward the busy Charleston Harbor. It was great to be sailing home. He only wished Michael could've been with him, but the navy had assigned him to Preble's ship after his rescue. If Adam knew anything about navy protocol, and he did, officials would question his brother and the other sailor about what happened on the *Philadelphia* before and after its capture. Everything had to be recorded. Stephen Decatur would also submit his full report on the burning of the frigate.

He took a deep breath and enjoyed the dawn colors of pinks, blues, and yellows streaking across the eastern horizon. Hannah's sweet face appeared in his mind's eye. Her last letter, which he'd only recently received, told of the happenings at Seymour Plantation and her decision to return to her aunt's Charleston townhouse and their work in the hospital. Would Hannah and Aunt Sophia be up at this time of day? He smiled. He'd awaken them if he had to. Had his little sister changed in all the past months, grown even more beautiful?

Josiah Campbell strode up the quarterdeck steps and stood beside him. "*Lo, God hath given thee all that sail with thee, Acts 27:24.*"

Adam smiled at his first mate. "Yes, we thank the Lord God for this safe journey without the loss of a single life, especially during the dangerous mission to burn the *Philadelphia*."

Josiah turned his ginger-bearded face into the breeze. "I'm still wishing I'd been able to go with you on that mission."

Adam gave the man's firm shoulder a friendly thump. "But you were the only one I knew I could trust to sail the *Vixen*, Josiah. And what you did was as important as anything the rest of us did."

"Don't seem that way."

"But you're getting the same bonus and extended leave, so the U.S. Navy thinks so. Where will you go, my man?"

"I'm going to the upcountry where my sister lives with her husband and kids." He looked back at Adam, his bright blue eyes shining. "I may just decide to stay there, help them farm. Might buy myself a few acres. Don't think I'll reenlist in the marines. What about you? Are you signing back up?"

Adam took a deep breath and leaned against the rail. "Interesting you asked that, friend. I might not reenlist either. I've got a hankering to see if I can get into a law firm as a clerk and learn all I can."

"Lawyering, is it? I might've known with those big law books you always lug around with you." He leaned on the railing beside Adam. "But I'll miss you, sir. We've been shipmates now these four years." He cast his heavy-lidded eyes at Adam, then out to sea.

Adam chuckled. "You'll miss all the work I assign you? Not likely." Then he cleared his throat and turned serious. "I'll miss you, too, Josiah, and your words of wisdom we've often heard. You've been a trusted marine partner and, lately, a good first mate. I wish you the best in that upcountry farming." Adam ducked his head and came back up with a grin. "And if you're determined to become a landlubber, old seadog, let me ask you, is there not a woman anywhere you have an interest in?"

Josiah pulled off his hat and ran his fingers through his red hair. "Well, now that you've asked, there is a young lassie up there what might be ken to see me. We've exchanged a few letters."

Adam chuckled. "You don't say? You've kept that a secret, my man."

The ship slid into its berth at the Gadsden Wharf, and they both strode away to see about their port duties.

Adam oversaw the increased activity on the top deck as sailors, like busy bees, set the rigging and sails for mooring, pulled down hammocks and stashed them, cleaned the decks, and collected personal possessions. With every man looking forward to going ashore and home, the duties progressed in a fast but orderly manner.

Checking off the work when accomplished, Adam couldn't help smiling when he thought of Josiah's secret romance. He, too, carried a secret love in his heart. What would he find ashore when he saw Hannah again after his long absence? Had she fallen in love with Gideon Falconer? Did he have a chance at all to overcome her brotherly image of him and win her heart?

He walked from the harbor on the cobbled street toward Aunt Sophia's townhouse with his sailor bag slung over his shoulder. The early September morning, heralded by birds amid the treetops turning on their beautiful fall colors, lifted Adam's heart. Somewhere in the city, a baker baked fresh bread, and the scent made his mouth water. How wonderful it'd be to actually have some real bread instead of navy hardtack. He began to whistle.

~

Hannah awoke when a sunbeam fell across her face from the part in the window drapes. A delicious sensation of expectation made her sit up, push back the light blanket, and search for her slippers. Something good would happen today. She rose, slipped on her robe, then lifted her hands and spoke a scriptural greeting she'd often heard her mother announce to the Lord and the new day. "*Glory to God in the highest and peace on earth, good will toward men.*"

She moved to the window, pushed the thick green drapes back, and lifted the sash. Fresh air flowed in, and she took a deep breath.

As she glanced down to the street through the colorful maple tree branches reaching to her window, her breath caught in her lungs. A sailor, a familiar figure, strode toward the house from the harbor. Adam! His whistle reached her ears. His long stride and easy carriage of a packed sailor bag slung across his shoulder sent a thrill through her.

She slammed the sash down and ran to her mirror. Her auburn hair tumbled about her shoulders. Hurriedly, she pinned two combs at the sides to give it some sort of neatness. She threw off her old, faded housecoat and pulled from the chifferobe her newest one, a birthday gift from her aunt, a jade-colored silk robe. She slipped it on, then hesitated.

What would Aunt Sophia say if she saw her greeting Adam when not fully dressed? The front gate squeaked and heavy footfalls landed on the front steps. Her heart hammered so hard, she found it hard to breathe. Well, she couldn't, she *wouldn't,* take time to dress. For better or for worse, she flew down the stairs and waited for Adam in the front hall, gripping her hands in front of her.

The butler opened the door. "Good mo'ning, Lieutenant. So good to see yo' back from yo' ship."

"Thank you, Moses. Great to be back and all in one piece this time."

Adam's deep voice thrilled Hannah's heart. She didn't realize, until that moment, how much she'd missed hearing him speak. His presence filled the entrance hall. He dropped the seabag to the floor, and his eyes found her. "Hannah, come here, little sister." A broad grin lit his face, and he held out his muscular arms.

She flew into them, and he hugged her close to his hard chest. His wonderful scent of the sea and the cardamom-cinnamon spice she recognized delighted her. She drew back, and heat climbed into her cheeks. *Little sister.* Was that all he thought of her? She must cast every other idea from her mind and dreams.

Aunt Sophia emerged from the breakfast room, followed by several servants. "Dear Adam, how wonderful you're home and safe in answer to our prayers." She came to get a hug. "What stories you've probably got to tell this time. I've read about you and the navy squadron President Jefferson sent to the Mediterranean to battle the Tripoli pirates. And I want to hear firsthand the story of your brave team burning the *Philadelphia*. Our Charleston *Gazette* got hold of the news just recently, but better late than never."

Hannah stood watching the exchange until her aunt's gaze fell on her. "Hannah, dear, hurry upstairs and dress, then join us for breakfast." She turned to Adam. "You are hungry, are you not, young man?"

Hannah turned, lifted the skirts of her robe, and fled up the stairs. Behind her, Adam's strong, clear voice pleased her ears. "Starving, Aunt Sophia, hungry for some of your good cooking."

Hannah ate some of her breakfast but delighted more in watching Adam partake with hungry male gusto. Scrambled eggs, slices of ham, grits, and tomatoes disappeared from his plate in short order, and Mama Larnie brought more. In between mouthfuls, he answered Aunt Sophia's questions about his exciting experience burning the *Philadelphia,* giving all the glory to one Stephen Decatur. But he gave God the glory for having Michael there to be rescued.

At last, he swiped his mouth with the linen napkin and smiled at Hannah. "Sister, I'm heading home to see mother and father soon as I finish. Are you coming with me?

Hannah's heart leaped into her throat. She glanced at her aunt. Would she mind not having her help at the hospital for a few days? "Aunt Sophia, would you mind if..."

"Hannah, dear," her aunt interrupted her, "by all means, go, and I think you might want to call April upstairs to help you pack fast. This man sounds as though he's eager to get home." She turned to throw up her hand as Hannah stood. "But remember to be back for the St. Cecilia's Ball next Friday. We don't want that lovely gown to go to waste." She turned to Adam. "Can we count on you to escort Hannah, please?"

Adam cocked his bearded chin. "St. Cecilia's Ball? Are you sure we Whites are welcome at such an uppity affair?"

Aunt Sophia laughed. "If you're not, I'm not. Be assured, I have invitations for Hannah and her escort."

"Very well. If you say so, Aunt Sophia." He turned his gray eyes up to Hannah, and her heart turned over at the warmth of his gaze. "I'm game if Hannah is."

She nodded, then fled from the room and up the stairs to pack for home.

The drive back to the farm proved a wonderful experience, one Hannah knew she'd never forget. Adam opened up and shared his heart about possibly not re-enlisting and looking for a law firm clerk position to prepare for a law profession. What a relief it would be, not to carry concern over his safety every day.

She loved the way his startling pale eyes lit up as he talked of the future. And the way he looked at her made a tingle shoot through the pit of her stomach. Sitting beside his powerful form disturbed her in every way. A vitality he radiated drew her like a magnet. She did not understand any of it but found herself soaking in his presence. Did she have the same look on her face she'd noticed on her aunt's when Dr. Barnes conversed with her?

Then a pain gripped her insides. All these plans of Adam's— would she, *could she,* ever be a part of them? Did he want her to be? What would her parents think if they knew her feelings for him?

The three-hour carriage ride home seemed but a short time in duration. By the time they drove up in the cottage front yard, her heart beat in tune with Adam's exciting hope for his life outside the marines. She pushed down, way down, any worry about whether she could be a part. She would find a way. When he lifted her down from the buggy, he held her a moment longer than necessary, and his quick intake of breath matched her own. A quiver surged through her. They stood staring at one another for several seconds, then he released his hands from her waist.

When her family burst from the house, Hannah stirred herself to step back. Hugs passed all around.

Her precious mother in her plain dress, Quaker bonnet, and welcoming smile reached her brother first. "Adam, dear son. God has answered our prayers and brought thee home safe." Her mama's sweet voice rose above the others. When Adam released his mother, she dabbed her eyes with a handkerchief she pulled from her sleeve, then opened her arms toward Hannah. The tight hug and sweet, clean lavender scent of her mother made moisture gather in Hannah's eyes. Her father stepped near, grasped her, and kissed her cheek.

Mammy, who had stood back watching the family reunion, came forward and hugged Hannah and Adam. Ada and Samson followed and greeted them, wide smiles framing their shining faces.

While Adam answered his parents' questions about Michael and when he might be home, Hannah's pet goat came around the corner of the barn and made a beeline for her. No longer young, a full-grown Rupert trotted up to her and gently butted her skirts, emitting a soft goat sound deep in his throat. She patted his head. Good thing he was dehorned or her skirts might have suffered.

Hannah followed her family into the sitting room and listened, entranced, as Adam shared his adventures in the Mediterranean. Hearing it from his lips was so much more exciting than reading it in his letters. He was bigger than life, sitting among them. He was Adam, the brother she grew up worshipping. She loved the way his gray eyes flashed and his easy chuckles that peppered the sharing of his escapades. Would this wonderful man ever care for her in any way other than as a sister he needed to protect? She clenched her jaw to kill the sob in her throat. A sudden tiredness settled on her like a blanket.

At supper that evening, her mother and Mammy outdid themselves by serving Adam's favorite dishes. Back-eyed peas, fried chicken and gravy, steamed squash and carrots from the garden, as well as creamed potatoes and biscuits. Again, Hannah delighted in watching him eat and almost forgot to eat herself until her mother reminded her. She could only force a few mouthfuls in, and she turned down the chocolate cake. What was wrong with her appetite?

"How long canst thou stay, son? And thou, Hannah?" Her mother's voice held a quiver, and Adam reached over and patted her hand.

"We have an entire week before we need to start back, Mama. Aunt Sophia has managed to get us an invitation to a Charleston event next Friday." He glanced at Hannah. "I understand she has supplied your daughter with a special gown for the occasion."

Her mother's eyes lowered, and her lip trembled. Then she sat up straighter and smiled at both of them. "That's wonderful. I'm sure Sophia has the best of hearts, and I expect she's looking on thou, Hannah, like the daughter she never had." She glanced at her husband. "She's your sister, John. Doest thou agree with that assessment?"

"Yes, I'm glad Hannah can bring Sophia a little joy. She's probably had little of it since Andrew passed."

Hannah rose and came to place her hands on her mama's shoulders. "I appreciate Aunt Sophia, Mama, but she can never take your place in my heart, any more than...than Mrs. Seymour, my birth mother, could. If she had lived."

Her mama put her warm hand on top of Hannah's and patted it. "There, now, thou hast brought up the Seymours." She laid her napkin aside, stood, and looked at her husband and son. "Wilt thou come into the sitting room? We want to hear thy story, Hannah, about nursing Mr. Seymour. Thou wrote brief letters, but I am sure there's more." She took Hannah's hand, and Adam and her father followed them.

Mammy quietly cleared the table, then sat in the kitchen doorway to listen. Mama smiled and nodded at her. The freed black woman was part of the family.

The next hour, Hannah shared all she could recall of Charles Seymour, Saul and his death by dueling, his wife's birth of their son, then her untimely death. The air lightened in the room when she told of Charles's change of heart and how much he doted on the child. As she finished her story, she ended up feeling drained, even dizzy. She shook her head to clear it and tried to cover it with a smile. Under Adam's steady scrutiny, she couldn't think.

"Well, that's quite a tale, and we all rejoice about the old man's change of heart." Adam's face appeared framed in a fog.

Her father and mother agreed with vigorous nods and murmurs.

Adam reached out to touch Hannah's shoulder, his eyes full of concern. "But, little sister, you look tired, and probably need to call it a day."

Mama stood. "Oh my, yes. Thee art right, Adam. Come, Hannah, thy old room is ready."

Hannah rose, but her head began to spin and everything went black.

CHAPTER 17

Dimly aware of brawny arms lifting her as if she were a featherweight, Hannah breathed in a familiar scent as her face pressed against a firm shoulder. When released, and the bed enveloped her like a soft cloud, she identified the spicy smell. Adam. The brother to whom she wanted to express her love...but was afraid to do so. A sob escaped her lips, and tears she could not control streamed down her face. She was swimming through a fog of feelings, her heart frozen in limbo.

Adam's concerned voice asking her mama what could be wrong with her were the last words she heard before falling into an exhausted darkness.

The following morning, she opened her eyes in her bed, in her nightgown, with her hair loosened from its braids she'd worn on the buggy ride home.

Her mother sat beside her, and a smile lit her dear face. "Thee doest feel better, daughter? Yes? Thou gavest us quite a scare last evening."

Hannah took a deep breath, moistened her lips, and sat up. Her mother, possibly with Ida's or Mammy's help, had removed her clothing and prepared her for bed. Why did she not remember it?

And her face felt tight and her lips salty. Then she remembered it was Adam who had brought her in his arms to her room when everything went black after she shared her story the night before. Again, tears gathered in her eyes, and her mother leaned forward, her face concerned.

"Dear child, thee must tell me what botherest thee. Hast something happened that thee art afraid to tell us? Art thee worried about something?"

She clenched her eyes shut to stop the tears and swallowed the lump in her throat. She was afraid to tell her mother how she felt about Adam. What would her mother, with her simple, gentle faith, think about it? She looked into her eyes and saw only love.

Her mother took a deep breath. "If thee won't tell me, then I must guess. This is not an illness, it is a heavy heart, my daughter."

How could her mama know that?

Mama smiled and patted her arm. "With some plain old exhaustion mixed in, I expect. Thou and Adam had much to share last night." She looked away, then turned her gentle, beloved face back to Hannah. "This is about Adam, isn't it, dear one?"

Hannah's heart lurched. And her hand flew to her mouth.

"Thee doesn't need to worry. He's not spoken to me, although he might. But I have eyes to see, precious daughter. I've known for a long time thee hast practically worshipped him, as a little sister might care for a handsome big brother. I watched thee tonight, sitting beside him at the table, and thee ate like a sparrow. Then later, when he shared his exploits, thee hung on his every word. It is about Adam. Am I right?"

Hannah nodded and sucked in a breath. The struggle within her tied her middle into a knot.

"But now thee art both grown. And have been separated and had a lot of things happening in thy lives. Doth Adam seem less a big brother now, and more of an attractive man to thee?"

Hannah nodded again and pressed her fingers against her eyelids. Where did her mother get such discerning? Clearing her throat, she finally responded. "He's like someone I've known, but not well anymore, and I want to...know him better." She searched the loving face in front of her for any sign of distress or surprise and found none.

Mama smiled. "That's perfectly normal, daughter. Adam is not your blood brother. It may be God has a plan for thee and him together. I don't know. But time will tell. Be at peace. All is well. Whatever is the Lord's will, your father and I will be happy."

Smothering a sob, Hannah fell into her mother's arms, her heart and mind slipping into alignment. Relief enveloped and flowed through her like warmth from the hearth on a winter morning.

Her mother left, then returned with her breakfast. After eating with renewed appetite, Hannah fell into restoring slumber.

~

Adam paced in the parlor below, then approached his mother when she returned from taking up breakfast. He'd not seen her when he had dined earlier with his father. "Is Hannah going to be all right?"

Mama smiled and patted his arm. "Of course. She's going to be fine. I think she may have gotten over-tired, and then trying to tell us all about her Seymour experiences proved too much. We relive the stories we share. She'll probably sleep a little more this morning and be good as new."

Adam's tight shoulders relaxed. "Good." For a moment, he thought of speaking to his mother about his feelings for Hannah, but no. His sister was still young and probably only thought of him as her big brother. If that changed, then he'd speak.

He grabbed his hat and hurried out the back door to the barn to catch up with his father and Samson preparing to harvest the oats in the south field.

Could Hannah be thinking of Gideon Falconer as a proper suitor? She'd commented on him in her letters. How much time had they spent together while he was away for the past many months? Good thing he'd not spoken to his mother about his feelings for Hannah. They could be hopeless altogether.

At supper, Adam kidded Hannah when she appeared at her regular place at the table. Her cheeks glowed with color, and the shining complexion he adored looked refreshed. He leaned toward her, smiling. "It's high time you got up and started helping your mama and Mammy put the vegetables away for winter, girl."

"Oh, and what, may I ask, have you done to help anyone?" she quipped.

Father defended him. "He's been a big help to me and Samson harvesting the south field. We've got an abundance of oats for the winter and even some to sell. Soon we'll dig the potatoes and will need you ladies to help sort, dust off, and prepare for storing."

The next day, Adam tweaked Hannah's shiny plait hanging down her back as she sat alongside his mother, Mammy, and Ida, shelling bushels of dried peas and butter beans for storing in jars. She threw butter bean shells at him as he slipped away.

The rest of the week passed in a flurry of activity and happy family times, harvesting and storing dried field corn, hard winter squash, potatoes, and peppers.

The last day they worked, Adam assisted his father and Samson in butchering a pig and rubbing down the hams and bacon with layers of salt to make it keep for winter. They wrapped and strung up the meat on hooks in the cool stone larder attached to the house.

When he drove the wagon and his sister back to Aunt Sophia's, Hannah seemed withdrawn at first, but soon he had her relaxing and talking freely. He teased her about Gideon Falconer, but Hannah refused to take his bait. Did that mean the man was or wasn't a serious suitor?

When they pulled into Sophia's drive, another buggy sat under a tree. A new, expensive one, with a fringed top to protect the driver and passengers from the sun. The horse, a lovely Arabian, neighed, and Adam's horses responded. He glanced at Hannah. "You recognize that pretty contraption?" Surely, Gideon Falconer would never drive such a feminine carriage.

She shook her head.

A male servant hurried up the steps from the basement of the townhouse and greeted them. Adam handed the reins to him and helped Hannah down from her seat, then escorted her up the steps to the main entrance.

The door between decorated glass panels opened, and Juliet Nelson emerged with Aunt Sophia just behind her.

A bright smile lit Juliet's face. "Oh, good. Adam, I came to see you. So glad you've arrived before I left." She glanced at Hannah, her smile fading. "Hello." Then she stepped forward and hooked her arm through Adam's. "Please, come with me for a walk in the garden. I have to talk to you about something."

He blinked at Hannah and then Aunt Sophia and raised his brows. Aunt Sophia shrugged, but her face remained expressionless. Juliet gave him little choice.

He cocked his head, then pasted on a smile. "Well, ladies, I guess I'm due for a walk in the garden. Will you two excuse us?"

Hannah stood at her top-floor bedroom window and watched Adam and Juliet walking below in the garden. The woman still had his arm in her grasp. Why didn't he brush her off? Or was he enjoying this little cozy, private chat?

Juliet was talking with excitement and gestures, and every so often, she would stop walking and look into Adam's face. He didn't seem overly happy—Hannah would give him that much. But what was it all about? She was about to turn away from the window when Juliet threw herself into Adam's arms and hugged his neck. And the man smiled. Hannah bit her lower lip and strode from the window. So there was something still going on with Miss Juliet Nelson. *Brother Adam, do I know you at all?*

Hannah sent word she would have her dinner in her room and go to bed early. Tomorrow was a big day. The St. Cecilia Ball that evening would take some preparation time. She refused to worry if

Juliet would do as she'd done at the last ball and expect Adam to dance every dance with her. Somehow, Hannah would outwit her this time.

The next afternoon, Hannah enjoyed a long, warm bath scented with dried rose petals her aunt suggested she use, then April helped her dress in her undergarments. For the next hour, the talented maid worked Hannah's auburn tresses into a lovely upswept hairdo with loose curls framing her face. She placed combs with pale yellow silk rosebuds pasted on them in her hair. Hannah's breath caught in her throat as April buttoned up the lacy, pale yellow silk gown with its fashionable empire waist, scooped neckline, and short puffed sleeves. The dress was the loveliest Hannah had ever worn. She stared at the pearl necklace and earrings her aunt had loaned her as April placed them on her and smiled at her in the mirror. Then she pulled on her long white gloves and glided out of the room, her heart doing a double beat.

When she descended the stairs toward Adam, his eyes widened, and a low whistle escaped his lips.

She smiled. He looked the most handsome she'd ever seen him in his black satin waistcoat with a white lace cravat blossoming under his chin. His dark, cropped hair glistened like coal.

Her aunt came down the hall draped in a silver silk ball gown and matching wrap that made her gray hair glisten. Small diamonds twinkled at her ears. She smiled and clapped her hands when she saw Hannah. "Yes, it's the perfect color and gown for you, dear girl. You'll delight everyone—if you don't make them jealous." Then she turned to Adam. "And you'll be the most handsome man at the ball, I'm sure. Now you two, go and have a grand time. I will follow a little later. My dear Doctor Tom has a case at the hospital that may hold him up a bit. But we'll get there."

Dear Doctor Tom? Her aunt's words snagged Hannah's attention. Had their relationship changed, grown closer, while she and Adam had been away? She couldn't help smiling.

Adam helped Hannah into the carriage and swung up himself, avoiding disarranging her gown as he pressed in beside her. Their driver clicked his tongue, and the two bays—brushed to a shine, and in their polished rigging—took off at a good clip down the cobbled street. They arched their necks and stepped high as if they knew this trip was something special. She cast a sideways glance at Adam. Her heart melted when he turned and took her hand in his.

"I know who the most lovely woman will be at the ball tonight." He squeezed her hand.

Her cheeks warmed, and she smiled at him. He most certainly would be the best-looking man.

The clear evening with its sliver of moon above delighted her, and the fall coolness made her glad she'd brought her soft, lacy wrap. She breathed in the salty, coastal air and thanked God for Adam being home safe beside her, for this lovely evening ahead of them, and for the beautiful dress her aunt had bought for her.

As they turned the corner from Queen's Street to Meeting Street, the blazing entrance to the Greek-style hall hosting St. Cecilia's Ball came into sight. Muted candlelight tumbled down the marble steps from the two-storied, white-columned building. Other carriages drew up and deposited their occupants in their formal evening wear—lovely pastel gowns for the ladies and black and white attire for the men. Their driver pulled the carriage into line.

Adam escorted her through the black wrought-iron gate with a golden Irish harp fashioned in its overhead arch, then up the steps to the ornate oak door standing open. Two footmen in green livery bowed a welcome to them. They followed the other guests into a flamboyant ballroom lit by hundreds of candles and flanked by green plants, with an orchestra on a dais at the far end. To their right, a long, loaded table, attended by servants in white coats and gloves, displayed a punch bowl surrounded by gleaming crystal glasses and platters of delicacies.

Hannah looked around at the milling couples and held onto Adam's arm. "Oh, there you two are." Juliet Nelson broke away from a group and swirled toward them in a white, flowing gown soft and fleecy as a cloud. She wore a sparkling diadem in her blond hair. A short but distinguished man, probably in his thirties, followed her.

As they approached, his eyes rested first on Adam, then on Hannah.

Juliet stopped in front of them and waited for her escort to draw up beside her. "Adam, Hannah, please meet my fiancé from England, Charles Montagu, Duke of Cumberland."

A sincere smile lit the man's pale face. He nodded toward Adam, then took Hannah's gloved hand and bowed over it. "My pleasure, I'm sure."

Juliet gestured toward Adam. "Charles, dear, this is the brave sailor with his US Navy crew who rescued me from the pirates. I owe him my life."

Her partner's brows rose, and he looked more closely at Adam. "Thank you, sir, for rescuing my precious southern rose, Juliet." A grin lifted the corners of his mouth. "And I'm sure the pirates thanked you, too."

Adam chuckled.

Juliet's lips turned into a pout, but then she tilted her head at her fiancé and smiled. He winked at her.

Hannah liked the man. Duke or not, no one could fault his easy humor.

"Pray, do excuse us." Juliet took her fiancé's arm and pulled him toward the other guests entering the ballroom.

Hannah expelled a relieved breath. Miss Juliet Nelson would undoubtedly dance most of the dances with her duke.

The orchestra began a lovely melody, and Adam took her hand in his. "May I have this dance, Miss White?"

She moved toward the group dance forming in the middle of the floor. *Yes, she wanted to say. And every other dance tonight.*

Moving to the music with Adam as her partner was like a foretaste of heaven. If only it would never end. He was an excellent dancer. His clean, manly scent enveloped her, and his brawny arms as he twirled her in the movements made her world feel secure. But he seemed a little quiet, not his usual happy-go-lucky self. Glancing at his profile as they turned in the dance, she noted the tension in his square jaw. Was he worried about something?

They danced several rounds with only a brief break to greet her aunt and Dr. Thomas Barnes when they arrived, before the couple disappeared into the crowd.

Adam led her to the table holding the punch bowl. The servant in white livery handed them each a crystal glass of amber liquid. After the first swallow, Hannah shook her head. The potent punch had a wallop to it.

Adam grinned. "Did you know sailors in the East India Company borrowed the Sanskrit Indian word for *five*, the word "*punch*, and brought the idea to England in the sixteen-hundreds? Why five? Because they originally made the first true punches with five ingredients—alcohol, sugar, lemon, water, and tea or spices."

Hannah shook her head at Adam's knowledge. Was there anything he didn't know about? He asked the servant for apple cider, and the man bowed and provided it for them.

Finally, heated from the dancing and the many candles lighting the ballroom, Hannah begged for a cool respite.

To her surprise, Adam led her back out the entrance of the hall and a few steps away, to an adjoining park. An engraved sign at the entrance read, *Washington Square Park.*

Soft lamplight lit the cobbled stone path under trickles of gray Spanish moss hanging from ancient oaks decked in their colorful fall leaves. She took a deep breath of the cool night air with its woodsy scents of moss and decomposing leaves and laced with the briny breeze from the Charleston Harbor. Inviting benches lined the path to a monument honoring former President George Washington.

Adam whipped out his handkerchief and wiped a bench, then offered her a seat. She sank onto it and sighed. But Adam didn't sit. He paced in front of her, lightly popping a balled fist into his other hand, a frown creasing his handsome countenance.

Her heart plummeted to her feet, and she sat forward. "Adam, what's wrong?"

He turned his face toward her. Tension tightened his brow and thinned his lips. "I don't know how to tell you this, Hannah." His hoarse voice, as did his clenched fists. What could make this mighty marine who'd faced many battles stand before her as if he were...unsure, nervous, anxious?

Panic whirled inside her and snatched her breath. What in the world was he trying to tell her? Horrid thoughts assaulted her mind and congealed into one she loathed to even think possible. Had he *married* some woman in one of the ports he'd visited and kept it secret from the family? She knew women flocked to him. Like Juliet.

He stopped and stared down into her face. "First, tell me and tell me the truth, Hannah. Do you care for...Gideon Falconer?"

She sighed with some relief. "Of course, I care for him. He's a nice man." She sat back and looked up at him, shushing the pang of hurt that he'd emphasized she tell him the truth. Hadn't she always told him the truth? "But I'm not in love with him, if that's what you mean, dear brother."

He paced a few feet from her, then back, and cleared his throat. He glanced back at her. "Hannah, will you always think of me only as a brother? We're really not...blood kin." His voice was firm but also calm.

Hannah's eyes widened, and her heart jumped into her throat. "Adam, what are you saying?"

He took her hand, pulled her to her feet, and drew her into his arms. "I'm saying that I love you, Hannah, as a man loves a woman he wants to marry. Is this any kind of possibility for us?"

Joy blossomed in her with such a powerful force, she couldn't breathe. Moisture gathered in her eyes. He stood so close, she could feel the heat from his body and revel in his clean, male scent. Her pounding heart hindered her words. She gasped and swallowed. All she could manage to speak came out in a whisper. "Yes, Adam. I love you too."

His lips drew close to hers, and his warm breath feathered her cheek. His large hand lifted her chin. He brushed a gentle kiss across her forehead, then he touched her lips with his own, sending the pit of her stomach into a wild swirl. Crushing her to him, he deepened the kiss, and she responded with every fiber of her being. Ecstasy spiraled through her, and she lifted her arms to encircle his neck. For many moments, she visited a wonderful, new world of love she had never dreamed possible.

Adam lifted his head and drew back. Delight glowed across his tanned, chiseled countenance.

Her knees buckled, but he held her firmly, then gently sat her back on the bench. He sat beside her and took both her shaking hands into his.

"Dear, beautiful Hannah. You've made me the happiest man in Charleston. Will you marry me? That is, if our parents agree."

Hannah laid her spinning head against his firm shoulder, her lips still burning with fire. She moistened them to speak. "Yes, I most certainly will, Adam. And I think Mama and Papa will agree."

"You do?"

"I believe so." She touched his warm cheek where his beard ended and smiled. "After all, we're not blood kin."

He grinned. "Yes, thank God. Who'd ever dream I'd be glad to learn your real father abandoned you? I've been happy about our not being blood kin since the day I heard it."

Hannah's emotions settled a bit, and a question floated up in her mind. "Adam, if you don't mind my asking, what did Juliet Nelson tell you in the garden the day we arrived back at Aunt Sophia's?"

The man who had just kissed her passionately and proposed marriage frowned and looked away. A shadow passed over Hannah's heart. She drew her shawl closer against the cooling night air. Why was this a hard question?

CHAPTER 18

*A*dam finally responded. "It's nothing to get upset about, Hannah, please believe me, but I gave her my word not to mention it until she did so herself. I'm sorry. I believe she will take care of this soon, and no further secrecy will be necessary." His sincere eyes and voice calmed her.

They stood and walked back to the hall, and Adam called for the carriage. All the way home, Hannah tried to recapture the ecstasy and wonder she'd felt in Adam's arms. But it eluded her best effort until he took her into his arms and kissed her good night before entering her aunt's house. He kissed her lips, then her forehead, cheeks, and the tip of her nose, leaving her breathless. His kiss trumped every other thought or worry.

"One thing, my wonderful love—let's agree not to mention what's happened between us tonight until we can talk to Mama and Papa." He whispered this against her ear, then kissed it.

She trembled at his touch. "Yes, that's the best plan." With effort, she pulled away from his warmth, and he let her go, holding to her hand till the last moment.

Hurrying up the stairs to her room, she undressed and dropped into bed at midnight. Before sleep came, she found herself again in the wonderful place she'd visited when Adam kissed her. Joy filled her again. Adam loved her. They would be married. Nothing else mattered.

The following morning, Hannah found Adam in the breakfast room with her aunt. He stood and nodded to her, his eyes bright and happy, then he lowered his gaze and sat. She walked to the buffet, took a plate, and filled it with ham, grits, scrambled eggs, steamed apple slices, and a biscuit, then sat beside her aunt, who poured her a cup of coffee. It was all she could do not to respond to Adam's warm glances that made her heart beat double time as he enjoyed a bountiful breakfast.

Sophia stared at Adam, then at her, and a meditative smile spread across her lips. Had their aunt guessed their secret? "Adam says you two will go back home today for a visit."

Hannah nodded and lifted a forkful of eggs to her mouth.

"Well, that was quick." Sophia turned to Adam. "Is the harvest still to be finished? And when do you have to report back to the navy?"

"There's always something else to harvest on the farm, and I don't have to report back to the ship until the first of the year." He took another large bite of a ham biscuit, chewed, and swallowed. "But Aunt Sophia, I've decided I will not sign back up. My stint actually ends in January. What I'd really love to do is sign on as a clerk at some firm here in Charleston and pursue a law profession." He winked at Hannah.

Hannah's heart swelled. He was indeed including her in his future plans. How wonderful if he could pursue the law he'd always loved. He'd always packed at least two large law books in his ditty bag.

Sophia's eyes lit up. "What a wonderful idea, Adam. I have the perfect law firm for you to check out. Joshua Becket's. He's your man. I know him and will introduce you when you're ready." She glanced at Hannah. "You remember we delivered their first son, and now she's expecting again."

Hannah's heart rejoiced. She remembered Abigail Becket well. And her husband seemed a nice person. Exciting thoughts flooded her mind. This would mean they would need to live in Charleston after they married. She could even continue to help Sophia at the hospital.

~

Traveling home, Adam directed the horses with one hand while holding Hannah's with his other. They reached the farm about noon. He leapt down and came around to swing Hannah down. He fought an actual battle not to crush her in his arms and kiss her when her lovely face came into proximity to his. Her eyes widened as he set her down and stepped back.

Their mother came running from the house. "Thee are back so soon? I am glad. And just in time for the mid-day meal." She hugged Adam, then Hannah. She cast a long look at both of them before turning and leading the way into the house.

Adam strode into the dining room, where their father was already seated at the table. "Hello, son. Is anything wrong? We didn't expect you two back this quick. Is Sophia all right?"

Adam strode to stand before their father. He pulled Hannah to his side. "She's fine and nothing's wrong, Papa." He glanced at their mother, who was turning toward the kitchen to bring the food. "Wait, Mama, I've—we've got something to tell you both."

Their mother came back to stand near them. A smile started on her lips.

Adam placed his arm around Hannah's waist. "Hannah and I love each other, and I've asked her to marry me, and she's accepted."

Hannah nodded at their parents and leaned closer to Adam. Seemingly overcome with emotion, she appeared unable to speak.

Their father banged the table with his hand, stood, and came around it to place his arms around them both.

Mama came, too, pulling the ever-ready handkerchief from her sleeve. Tears formed in her eyes and slipped down her cheeks. She wiped them away and smiled. "That day your father placed newborn Hannah into my arms to nurse, Adam, you played at my feet as a toddler. You took to the tiny new baby right away. And from that first day, I knew you accepted the babe and would be her guardian." She sniffed and gave them both a big hug.

Papa cleared his throat. "Well, son, I can't think of a better man to release our dear Hannah to." He moved away and made a swipe at his eyes.

Mammy stood in the kitchen door with the edge of her apron held against her eyes. She came forward. "Come here, you two. "Ain't I raised you both? And ain't I happy to hear this? We's gonna have a wonderful family without losing Hannah to anyone else like I'se been regretting to even think 'bout." She pulled them both into her widespread, ample arms and hugged them.

They sat down at a bountiful table from the harvest—corn, butter beans, squash, okra, and fried chicken. Cherry pie topped off the meal, served with cups of hot tea.

As soon as dinner ended and Mammy and Mama had the table cleared, they all sat back down to discuss the wedding and Adam's future.

Adam held Hannah's hand, which he squeezed as he talked. He shared his decision not to re-enlist come the new year, and to find a clerk position in a law firm.

"I'm not due to report back to the navy until January." He turned to look deep into Hannah's eyes. "I would love to marry Hannah next month if she'll have me that soon. That'll give us some time together before I have to report. When we tell Aunt Sophia, I think she'll jump right on it and offer to host the wedding at her house or at her church, which would help my marine detachment who live closer to the harbor than our farm, attend." He looked at their parents, then at Hannah. "What do you think about these ideas?"

Hannah sat up straight and blinked. "You almost make me feel dizzy, Adam, to think we might be married within a month. I'm in perfect agreement with all you've said. I'm also sure Aunt Sophia will want to help. The woman is a skilled organizer." She turned to their mother and touched her hand on the table, then glanced at their father. "But Papa, Mama, what do you think?"

Papa cleared his throat. "I'm sure Sophia will want to have a huge part in this."

Mama smiled and nodded. "Adam, it sounds as though thee has done some real thoughtful planning. I think Sophia will be a great help. If she agrees, we can get it done, so I don't see any reason it couldn't take place next month."

***

After arriving back at Aunt Sophia's, Hannah, with Adam at her side, shared their news of the coming marriage and their hope to have the wedding within a month.

Their aunt laughed and expressed no surprise. "Listen, you two lovebirds. I wasn't born yesterday. These old eyes can see love blossoming, and I've seen it with you two for some time." She smiled. "Of course, that good-looking Gideon kinda threw an acorn in the mix for a while. But I always knew you'd win out, Adam, if you'd make it home in time."

Adam and Hannah shared a moment of laughter.

Aunt Sophia's eyes brightened like diamonds. "And the small chapel at our church would be a lovely place to hold the wedding. I feel sure my pastor will be happy to marry you two." She smiled at Adam. "He knows Hannah. She has been attending service with me." She took a deep breath. "And Adam, I've got an appointment for you this afternoon if you can make it, to talk to Joshua Becket."

Hannah's mind whirled at the fast moves of her aunt. If anyone could plan a wedding to take place in a month, *and* help Adam obtain a law clerk position after the navy released him, Sophia White Rutledge could.

After dinner, Hannah sat enraptured in the parlor, hearing Adam tell how the meeting with Becket went.

"I really like the man, and we became fast friends. We discussed much about the law and my hopes of becoming a lawyer. I think I could learn a lot from him."

Aunt Sophia was not one to beat around the bush. "Does he have an opening for a clerk's position?"

Adam grinned. "He said my coming was an answer to prayer, as his business has increased...and to get back to him as soon as the navy releases me."

Hannah clapped her hands and Aunt Sophia joined in.

The following day, as Hannah stood on a stool being measured for her wedding gown, April came to announce a surprise visitor—Juliet Nelson. Apologizing to the seamstress, Hannah let April help her back into her simple muslin day dress.

She walked down to the parlor and found her aunt and Adam also in attendance. Juliet sat in the elegant Queen Anne's chair, in a lovely blue frock that set off her startling azure eyes that seemed to shine more than usual. A matching feathered bonnet and intricate paisley shawl made her look more like a sophisticated English lady than a young colonial woman. She smiled at Hannah. "Hello, Hannah. May I offer my congratulations to you and Adam on your coming nuptials? And it seems you'll even be married before I am. My wedding will not be until December—and in England at the duke's family home."

Hannah acknowledged the remarks, smiled at Juliet, and took a seat beside Adam on the sofa. Had she come over just to offer her congratulations? Or to underscore the news that she would have a fine English wedding at the duke's castle?

"I know you wonder why I'm here. And I won't take a lot of your time. I'm sure you must be very busy planning the wedding." She took a deep breath and glanced around at all three of them. "And this will be no surprise to Adam. I shared this with him earlier but asked him not to announce it until I did. It's simply that I have put into place all the documentation for the donation and future support of my Charleston townhouse to be used as a home for foundlings. Your little Peter gave me this idea. And I would like to ask you, Sophia, your friend Dr. Barnes and you, Hannah, if you will accept my invitation to be on the board of directors for the planning and running of the home. Will you? I've already talked to Dr. Barnes, and he has agreed. I gave him all the documentation for the donation."

Hannah's hand flew to her mouth.

Sophia cleared her throat and her face lit up. "That's wonderful and generous of you, Juliet. I will be most happy to serve." She turned to Hannah. "What about you?"

Hannah swallowed and wet her dry lips. "Yes, if I can be of any help." She glanced at Adam, who smiled and nodded. So this was what Juliet had whispered to him that day in the garden. Heat blossomed in her cheeks at the unpleasant thoughts she'd hosted.

Juliet smiled. "That's good. To be honest, if his parents had not come for him, I might have adopted little Peter. Therefore, I'm calling the foundling home *Peter's House*. I was so sorry to learn that our Charleston Orphanage would only take children after age three. So, hopefully, the foundling home will fill this gap." She sighed and stood with a rustle of her skirts.

Sophia moved toward her and touched her hand. "Thank you, Juliet. This is wonderful. Your gift should make a substantial difference for the little needy ones. And we pray your wedding and move to England will be all you wish it to be."

Juliet cast a last glance at Adam, and Hannah did not miss its twinge of sadness. At the door, the future duchess turned and said to the three of them, "I'll have a noble title, and what will Charles gain? He'll have me, hopefully a future heir, and my fortune to keep his estate out of bankruptcy." Her breath came rapidly, and her lower lip trembled.

A wave of compassion swept over Hannah.

But Juliet tossed her blond curls and smiled as if all were well and swished out the door to her fancy waiting carriage.

~

The Wedding

*H*annah awoke on the morning of November tenth and threw back the covers. Adam had chosen the day for their marriage because it was the birthday of the Marine Corps in the year 1775.

Her mother, father, Michael, Mammy, and Ida had arrived at her aunt's the day before and would all be downstairs at breakfast. Mammy and Ida had made fast friends with Sophia's cook, who was happy to have help with the extra food and wedding refreshments. Even now, the smell of bacon frying in the kitchen below increased Hannah's appetite. And there would be Mammy's biscuits and gravy, scrambled eggs, and her mother's blackberry jam she'd promised to bring.

A knock sounded at the door and Hannah called, "Enter."

April came in with a bucket of steaming water for Hannah's bath.

She looked at the lovely cream wedding gown hanging ready on her chifferobe door, and her breath caught in her throat. Was she really going to marry Adam this afternoon?

She finished her bath and donned a yellow morning dress, one of the new gowns her aunt had bought for her. April fixed her hair with a yellow ribbon, promising a much more sophisticated hairdo for the wedding later.

As Hannah left her room to go down to breakfast, she stopped to gaze out the upstairs window over the front entrance. Her heart dropped to her feet. A naval officer in full dress uniform walked up to the porch, his handsome face and stiff shoulders under his golden epaulets a study in tension and importance. What could the navy want with Adam, today of all days? Or was the officer here for Michael, who was now also home on leave?

She sailed down the stairs and into the dining room and looked around for Adam. He stood at the end of the table talking to their father as Mammy and other servants lined the buffet with steaming dishes of food. Their mother and Aunt Sophia sat at the table chatting. The kitchen door swung open to reveal a glimpse of Michael sampling the dishes.

Adam's lips lit up in a smile as fresh as a morning sunrise, and he strode toward her. "Good morning, Sunshine, in that yellow frock."

The next moment, the butler entered, bowed, and announced, "Lieutenant Stephen Decatur to see Lieutenant Adam White."

Adam's expression changed to mute surprise, and a tense silence filled the room. He took Hannah's hands in his own and assured her, "I'll be right back, my love." He turned and followed the servant into the hall.

Hannah stared after him, a knot tightening in her stomach. *Dear Lord, please don't let the navy want Adam to report back to his ship.*

CHAPTER 19

Adam walked into the parlor and greeted his navy friend and superior, Lieutenant Stephen Decatur, who stood near the fireplace. The man strode forward, holding his hat under his arm and with a gloved hand outstretched.

Adam clasped it and shook it with vigor. "This is quite a surprise, sir, but I'm glad to see you. I hope."

Decatur tilted his smooth chin. "I heard that word, *hope*. And rightly so. But I'm not here to call you back to your ship, my good friend. Rest on that point." He chuckled. "Not on your wedding day, for sure. The navy and the marines have a heart, believe it or not."

Adam relaxed. "Sir, that's good to hear."

"I know you're busy, so I won't hold you up. I came to Charleston on some navy business but learned about your wedding at headquarters. I plan to attend this afternoon."

Adam grinned his pleasure. "That's wonderful. I feel special, sir."

"You are that, my man, after all we've been through. I could always count on you in whatever adventure I went after, especially burning the *Philadelphia*." The man's blue eyes shone and he grinned. "I have a wedding gift I'd like to offer you, if you can use it. I have a small sloop of my own, the *White Dove*, docked here in Charleston for when I come to visit headquarters. Would you like to use it for a wedding trip somewhere? I'm offering it with my pilot and two sailors in my employ. What do you say?"

Adam sucked in a deep breath. Amazing. He'd planned to take Hannah to Savannah for a honeymoon and travel the long way by coach. But how much more wonderful to travel by boat.

"Sir, I say thank you from my heart. I'd love to sail my new bride to Savannah on your sloop." Then he remembered his manners. "Sir, have you had breakfast? We're just sitting down to quite a spread. I know my family would love for you to join us."

"Don't joke with me, sailor. We navy men not on leave had breakfast *early* this morning. But thanks for the offer. I dock my sloop at the far end of Gadsden Wharf." He set his hat back atop his shining dark hair. "I'll alert my men that you'll be coming. The *White Dove* is ready to go. Right after the wedding, or first thing in the morning? Whatever you say."

Sailing off with Hannah this very afternoon? How delighted she'd be. Adam's heart beat double time. "Yes, we'll come aboard after the wedding today."

He walked Decatur to the door, watched his carriage move away, then reentered the dining room. Every face turned toward him with a tight, questioning look.

He threw up his hands. "No crisis, but a special wedding gift from Lieutenant Decatur."

His aunt and mother said in unison, "What kind of wedding gift?" They looked at each other and smiled.

Adam took his seat beside Hannah and reached for her hand. "My wonderful wife-to-be, the man has offered his private sloop to us for our honeymoon trip. What do you say?"

~

*H*annah took a deep, happy breath, and the tension of her shoulders relaxed. "Oh Adam, that would be..." Her voice broke, and she blinked. Determined to have no tears on her wedding day, not even happy ones, she finally added, "...wonderful."

~

At two o'clock, Hannah, in her lovely creamy satin wedding dress and flowing silk veil, marched down the aisle at the Anglican chapel on the arm of her father, John. She walked through sunlight streaming from the stained-glass windows. As she proceeded past the pews, her mother, Aunt Sophia, Dr. Barnes, Mammy, and Ida turned their smiling faces toward her from one side of the small auditorium. On the other side, Lieutenant Decatur, David Barron, Joel Murray, and her brother Michael, all in their navy or marine uniforms, pivoted around to look at her. And of all things, Charles Seymour and Ruth, holding little Charlie, smiled at her from another pew.

Adam, so handsome in his marine dress uniform, stood at the front with his best man and friend, Josiah Campbell, and the minister. She met Adam's happy eyes and no longer thought of anyone else in the room.

Adam held his arm around her waist through the ceremony, and she was grateful for his gentle squeezes when it was time for her to respond as they confirmed their vows. Her heart so overflowed with joy, she felt lightheaded.

As soon as the minister declared them man and wife and Adam kissed her, their mother, Aunt Sophia, Mammy, and Ida came to hug them both.

Charles Seymour walked up with his cane, handed Adam a small leather pouch, then shook his hand. He looked into Hannah's face and reached out an arm to hug her. She blinked back moisture.

Hannah rejoiced on the carriage ride back to her aunt's house with Adam's arm around her.

He kissed her ear and whispered, "Sweetheart, I would love to set sail for Savannah as soon as possible. Do you think Mammy would pack the wedding food for us to take with us? Would anybody be upset if we don't stay around?"

She smiled and laid her head on his shoulder. "I've already asked Mammy to do so, and no one will mind if we leave sooner than later." She touched his cheek. "And I've asked Mama and Aunt Sophia to keep everyone happy." She sat up and looked into Adam's face. "What did Charles Seymour hand you?"

"Glad you asked. I'd about forgotten." He reached inside his waistcoat pocket and pulled out the pouch. He opened it and whistled at the gold coins that filled it.

Hannah's eyes widened. "What a wonderful wedding present."

"Who would've thought the man had such a generous heart? You must've really nursed him well, little sister." He planted a kiss on her cheek.

"Oh no, his heart change came from Someone else who does the best work on hearts." She met his eyes, then lifted her lips for his kiss.

At Aunt Sophia's house, Adam helped her down from the carriage, and she lifted her skirts and hurried into the house and up to her room. April followed and helped her change into traveling clothing.

Within the hour, she and Adam came down the stairs, ready to depart, as servants carried their baggage and packed food to the carriage. Their mother and father, Aunt Sophia, and Adam's marine buddies stood on the porch to see them off.

Josiah Campbell opened a sack of rice and passed it around for everyone to take a handful. She and Adam flew across the porch and down the steps under a shower of the white pellets. She could hardly breathe in her excitement. To sail off into the sunset with her beloved was better than anything she could've ever dreamed.

July drove them to the harbor and helped load their baggage and basket of food onto Decatur's *White Dove*. He stood back on the dock and waved. "Now yo' two, don't forget to come back home to us."

In moments, the sturdy sloop moved away from the dock and the Charleston Harbor.

Adam took her to the poop deck out of sight of the pilot, and they stood there for some time and watched the sunset across the Atlantic, baptizing them, the ship, and the ocean in myriad colors of red, pink, orange, and lavender.

"I've stood on many decks like this all over the world and dreamed of your being beside me, Hannah."

Her heart was so full, she couldn't speak. She moved into his arms and warmth surrounded her.

He lifted her chin and kissed her lips, softly at first, then again. This time, the kiss was more startling and telling. Rainbows danced around her as they parted. Every fiber in her being recognized and responded to the look of love glowing on his strong countenance.

She took a deep breath and felt as if she were floating in the changing, golden light of the sunset. Everything she'd ever imagined about falling in love she now knew was true. Giddy, euphoric happiness—so real, she could almost touch it with her fingers. Surely, love of this sort must be a wonderful gift from a loving God.

"What did you say, my love?"

Had she spoken her thoughts aloud? Well, why not? "I was thinking about how I love you, Adam, and am so blessed to have you as my husband. This kind of love must be a wonderful gift from a loving God."

"Yes, it is." He drew her back close, into the crook of his arm.

She nestled there, his heart beating against her cheek.

"I've kept my love for you secret a long time, Hannah." His voice was low, passionate.

"Why?"

"Because you were young, and I couldn't figure out how you felt about me. Then there was Gideon Falconer you started mentioning in your letters."

She smiled with her face against his shoulder. Had he been jealous of the former gamekeeper? "Gideon is a fine person...but not the man I love."

He squeezed her tighter and moved his chin to rest on top of her head. "There's one other thing I want to ask you. You've been through many upsetting things, from being abandoned as a newborn to being asked to nurse the father who committed the terrible act. But do you remember the Scripture promise I reminded you of several times? Do you believe all things have worked together for your good?"

She lifted her head and looked into his eyes. "Oh yes, Adam. I doubted at times, but today I can give a firm *yes* and *amen*. Everything that happened to me has worked out for this great good, for this love we now share."

"I just wanted to make sure." Once again, he claimed her lips and kissed her until her knees gave way.

The End

Did you enjoy this book? We hope so!
Would you take a quick minute to leave a review where you purchased the book?
It doesn't have to be long. Just a sentence or two telling what you liked about the story!

∽

Receive a FREE ebook and get updates when new Wild Heart books release: https://wildheartbooks.org/newsletter

VOCABULARY APPENDIX

1) **Charleston Orphan House**

Charleston Orphan House, the first public orphanage in the United States, was an orphanage in Charleston, South Carolina from 1790 to 1951. Records of the Commissioners of the Charleston Orphan House are held at the Charleston County Public Library. Location: Calhoun Street, Charleston, South Carolina. Demolished: 1956

"This institution housed, fed, educated, and reared thousands of children in its time, but it did not accept children under three years of age. The ratio of staff to children at the Charleston Orphan House was such that there were no resources available to nurture the youngest and neediest of infants. To be admitted to the Orphan House, children needed to be able to dress, wash, and feed themselves, and they were required to respond to verbal commands with a minimum of mollycoddling and hand-holding." (excerpt from article)

2) **Famous American Quote: "Millions for Defense, but not one cent for tribute"**

This quote, sometimes attributed to and used by President Jefferson during the Barbary Wars, actually originated in 1797-98 during diplomatic negotiations with France to avoid an outright war with them. The then U.S. President Adams sent three diplomats to

VOCABULARY APPENDIX

France for these meetings. Two South Carolinians, Robert Goodloe Harper and Charles Pinckney were part of the delegation.

The French diplomat, Talleyrand, kept the American mission waiting for weeks, then sent a demand to them for a bribe of $250,000 for himself, and a $12 million loan for France to avoid war. Bribery was standard diplomatic fare at the time, but the amount was deemed exorbitant. C.C. Pinckney or Robert Goodloe Harper is said to have expressed dismay by stating either, "No, no, not a sixpence!" or "Millions for defense, but not one cent for tribute." This second quote was later often used in relation to the Barbary Wars and the exorbitant bribe demands sent to the United States to avoid having our merchant ships in the Mediterranean plundered, their crews captured. Robert Harper is best remembered for the phrase.

3) Brief History of the Navy

After the Revolutionary War, a heavily indebted United States disbanded the Continental Navy and sold its last remaining warship in August, 1785. (This is hard to believe, but true.)

Troubles soon began in the Mediterranean as the Muslin Barbary states (Algiers, Tripoli, Tunis, Morocco) challenged our new nation. Our ships were no longer under the protection of the British warships, and our merchant ships were being captured and the crews thrown into slavery. A long debate went on in Congress whether we needed a navy or just continue paying the exorbitant tribute for protection and ransom for the enslaved Americans! On January 2, 1794, by a narrow margin of 46-44 the House of Representatives voted to authorize building a navy and it passed as the Naval Act of 1794. But it included a clause that would bring an abrupt halt to the construction of ships if the United States reached a peace agreement with Algiers. *By 1800, Congress was paying twenty percent of our national revenue to Muslin Barbary pirates.*

Thomas Jefferson took office in 1801, and he announced there would be NO MORE tribute paid. He sent a small squadron of frigates into the Mediterranean and took on the Barbary pirates in a war that is barely remembered, but which, in many ways, we are still

VOCABULARY APPENDIX

fighting. He changed George Washington's and John Adam's policies to take on this collection of Muslim nations. Heroes like William Eaton, Edward Preble, Stephen Decatur, and Marine lieutenant Presley O'Bannon blazoned across history as they led to our victories and ultimate respect as a nation to be reckoned with on the high seas. It was during these battles with the Muslim Barbary pirates (1800-1805) in which the U.S. Marine Corps assisted and became the essential military force it is today—remembered in the words of the Marine hymn, "from the halls of Montezuma to the shores of Tripoli."

Today, the United States Navy is a powerhouse. The fleet comprises **roughly 430 ships** in active service or reserve. The vessels run the gamut from the massive Nimitz-class aircraft carrier, which stretches over 1,000 feet, to the Los Angeles-class submarine that slithers 900 feet below the ocean surface.

How did the Navy get its name? First attested in English in the early 14th century, the word "navy" came via Old French navie, "fleet of ships", from the Latin navigium, "a vessel, a ship, bark, boat", from navis, "ship."

4) Brief History of the Marines

On November 10, 1775, the Second Continental Congress meeting in Philadelphia passed a resolution stating that "two Battalions of Marines be raised" for service as landing forces with the Continental Navy, so November 10 is the birthday of the Marines. Serving on land and sea, the marines have distinguished themselves in many important operations, including the Tripoli Wars, the War of 1812, the Mexican War, and every other war our nation has fought. Their motto: Semper Fidelis means "Always Faithful." Their core values are Honor, Courage, and Commitment.

Note: I've tried to showcase in this novel the emergence of our mighty Navy and Marines during the Tripoli Wars. I loved learning about these two wonderful branches of our military.

5) USS Navy Ships Prefix

The names of commissioned ships of the United States Navy all start with USS, for **United States Ship.** Example: *USS Philadelphia.*

(British ships start with HMS for His/her Majesty's Ship. Example: *HMS Victory*)

6) Landlubber vs. Seadog

Lubber" is an old term for a clumsy person, and beginning in the 18th century sailors used it to describe a person who was not a good seaman. So the pirate expression of scorn for those who don't go to sea is not "land lover" but "landlubber." The opposite of a landlubber might be called a **sea dog**, defined as "a sailor, especially an old or experienced one." The term can also refer to a pirate, a harbor seal, or a luminous appearance near the horizon, such as a meteor, regarded by mariners as an omen of bad weather.

7) Commonplace or Plantation books

Plantation owners and mistresses of the manor kept these historic, handwritten journals which are essentially scrapbooks filled with items of every kind: recipes, remedies, how to make dyes, household hints, weights and measures, financial and household accounts, agricultural notes, livestock and gardening notes, travel diaries, letters, poetry and even beloved sermons. They were passed down in families. The dozen or so existing copies of pre-1820 commonplace plantation books offers a composite picture of domestic and medical practice and life. Half appear to have been penned by women. Cookery and medical recipes were intermingled with other household concerns in the domestic notes of people like Eliza Lucas Pinckney and Harriet Pinckney Horry. This mother and daughter, at the death of Harriet's husband, assumed the full responsibility for managing the family plantation and servants. The anonymous author of the commonplace book from the Waring Historical Library covers a broad range of notes related to household and plantation management. Many plantation books included remedies for dropsy, colic, fever, ague, poisoning, stomachache, and women's disorders in this era of "every man his own doctor." Two of the most popular domestic medical guides were William Buchan's *Domestic Medicine* and the Rev. John Wesley's *Primitive Physick*. (See *Southern Folk Medicine* in Sources for more on this subject of commonplace books and early medical remedies).

VOCABULARY APPENDIX

Given the start of these type journals during the Renaissance, it should come as no surprise that the practice of keeping a commonplace book is still carried on today by some modern colleges as a teaching tool for students to learn how to capture and build upon knowledge gained from books.

Sources studied for this novel:

Brian Kilmeade & Don Yaeger. *Thomas Jefferson and the Tripoli Pirates,* New York: Sentinel, an imprint of Penguin Random House, 2015.

Hopkins, Dr. Mark. *Pirates, Privateers and the U.S. Navy.* Indianapolis: Dog Ear Publishing, 2018.

Toll, Ian W. *Six Frigates, the Epic History of Founding of the U. S. Navy.* New York, London: W.W. Norton & Co. 2006.

Zacks, Richard. *The Pirate Coast, Thomas Jefferson, the First Marines, and the Secret Mission of 1805.* New York:

Moss, Kay K. *Southern Folk Medicine 1750-1820.* Columbia, South Carolina: University of South Carolina Press, 1999.

Don't miss *The Gamekeeper's Reluctant Bride*, book 6 in the Charleston Brides series!

Chapter 1

CHARLESTON, SOUTH CAROLINA - 1805

Pulling aside the heavy damask drapes from her upstairs window, Helen Allston stiffened. The lovely white stallion and the rider she hated pranced up the front drive as if the man owned it. She stamped her foot, then flipped around in her luxurious boudoir and snagged her lower lip between her teeth. How dare George Beauregard arrive this early? Today, right now, she would enact her escape plan. She would have the time she needed while he met with her father to draw up the marriage contract.

How could her father do this to her? She'd never marry George Beauregard.

Drawing on a common green cloak over her riding frock, not her maroon velvet wrap she loved, she pulled the hood over her pinned-up hair and glanced in the mirror. A simple servant girl with large green eyes looked back at her with determination—or was it fear? One auburn curl escaped the hood and danced at her pale cheek. She pushed it behind her ear and grabbed up her riding crop. With one last glance at her lavender silk and satin décor room and her curtained bed with pineapples carved atop its tall posts, she strode from the room. The jewels and small pouch of gold coins sewn into the lining of her riding skirt bumped against her boots as she hurried down the servants' entrance at the back of the house.

Nothing could go wrong. She'd put everything in place days ago—the rowboat she would catch two miles down the Ashley River from their own dock to take her to the English ship waiting in the Charleston Harbor. The young man who would ride Stormy home would be with the small boat. She'd met the friendly, older British captain, a relative of her dearest friend, when he took her trunk under his care three days earlier. Everything fell into place so well. Someone in heaven must be looking out for her. Her sweet mother's face came into her mind as clear as the day she'd left them, victim to the fever.

Crossing the backyard toward the stable, she avoided the path taken by the servants, most of whom would already be at their various morning posts at the plantation house and fields. Her personal maid and dear friend Belle crossed her mind. For her servant's own protection, she'd not told the girl her plan. Who knew what her father would do to her to get information when they discovered she'd fled? But Belle would be telling the truth. Everyone in the house respected her truthfulness. Helen had told her she would sleep late today and not to come to her until much later in the morning. Maybe she would write to Belle after she arrived in England. Perhaps she could even send for her. Dear Aunt Aggie would never mind another maid added to her large household in Yorkshire.

The smell of hay and feed teased Helen's nose as she entered the stable. She took a deep breath and inhaled the pleasant scents. Several horses nickered and pushed their curious faces over their stall doors as she approached. She patted a few soft noses but kept walking to the end of the corridor to Stormy's stall. The dapple-gray Arabian mare lifted her head and gave a happy whinny at her approach. Helen patted the satiny muzzle and slipped the mare a piece of sugar.

"Okay girl, we've a very important ride this morning, and I'm happy you're glad to see me, but please be quiet." She slid the bit into Stormy's mouth and buckled the English saddle on the shining silver back. Drawing the horse into the corridor, she mounted and rode out the back entrance toward the river on a little-used path. With luck, no one from the house would see her leave. Her father, probably still at the breakfast table, would be busy reading the *Charleston Times*. Servants would be busy with their many morning duties.

She followed the riverbank at a slow pace until she came to the river road. Pulling Stormy up the small incline, she started down the passage and urged her into a canter.

Around the next bend, pounding hooves behind her shot a tremor up her spine. Glancing back, Helen stiffened in the saddle and tightened her knees. George Beauregard and his thoroughbred, reportedly the fastest horse in Charleston, pursued her. How had he seen her leave the house?

Well, she'd show him. She knew these woods along the Ashley River a lot better than he did. She reined Stormy into the trees and raced through them, dodging limbs and jumping small gulleys, like she'd done since she was twelve. The tip of a limb snagged Helen's hood. Her hair sprang free from its pins, but she didn't slacken Stormy's pace. Behind, she saw the white stallion also turn off the road in pursuit. Drat George Beauregard. She'd give him the ride of his life.

At one point she galloped back to the road and crossed to the other side, into a forest less familiar, but with the river always to her left, she'd be fine. Finally, realizing she no longer heard hoof beats or saw flashes of white behind her, she crossed the road again and sailed back down near the river. She looked around. Where was the boat? Had she passed the rallying point? Maybe she'd overshot it, or had she not reached it yet? She guided Stormy farther down the riverbank, thinking the meeting place was more distant. She passed through thick scrub trees, then galloped into an open area where the river turned away from her and flowed by rice trunks she didn't recognize. Stormy's sides heaved after the hard gallop, and Helen slowed her, then stopped to give the mare a chance to catch her breath. Had they entered the next parish during the wild run?

A sound behind her made her stiffen. She reined her mount around. Smiling, George Beauregard broke through the scrub trees. His mount scarcely breathed hard. "What a lovely sight you are, Helen, astride that gray streak with your gorgeous hair flying about your shoulders." He dismounted and started toward her. "I love an adventure like this, my girl. Why don't we just seal it with a kiss—or maybe more? Then you'd be ready to marry me, no doubt." He tied the stallion's reins on a tree limb and turned toward her, a tall figure in his blue satin morning suit now with snags on the shoulders and arms undoubtedly from passing through the trees and bushes in the chase. Confidence lined his tanned, handsome countenance, and his black eyes shone like two pieces of coal in his bearded face.

Without hurrying, George walked toward her. A seductive smile crossed his lips. "Come now, Helen, you've nowhere to go with the river at your back and me blocking your escape." He extended his jeweled hands and strolled toward her.

Panic welled in Helen's throat, and her heart pounded against her ribs. But she threw her head back and gave him her most disdainful challenge. "How dare you accost me like this, George Beauregard? My father will hear of this, and that will be the end of your suit. You're proving yourself no gentleman."

He paused and folded his thick arms. His smile widened across his smirking face. "Your father signed all the marriage papers with me last week, my little dear. And when I saw you out the back window riding away, I guessed your intention. Where can you go? Believe me, lovely Helen, you cannot escape me." He drew closer.

A whiff of his stale tobacco, rum, and heavy cologne sent shivers of revulsion through her. The isolation of the place pressed upon her. What could prevent him from having his way with her in this deserted place? Who would hear her loudest scream?

Stormy pawed the ground and tossed her head at the man's approach.

Helen tried to swallow, but her mouth dried up like a potsherd. Taking a deep breath that ended with a sob, she gathered the reins tight and leaned down to whisper to the mare. "Forgive me, dear friend. Jump high and wide. If we die, we die together. *Please God, help us get over the rice trunks and into the deep river.*

Stormy blew through her nose, arched her back, and sidestepped from the approaching figure blocking the way back to the road.

"That's a good girl, Stormy." George stepped forward and extended his hand to reach for the mare's bridle.

With a gut-wrenching cry, Helen wheeled Stormy around and swung her riding crop down on the powerful rump. The mare reared with a high-pitched squeal and shot forward toward the river, flinging mud up on the surprised man from her back hooves digging into the damp riverside.

Curses exploded behind them as horse and rider leaped high over the rice trunks. Helen's forehead banged against the hard, arched neck, and a scream exploded from her lips. The cold Ashley River closed over the two of them and shut out sound, sight, and breath.

***

Gideon Falconer, carrying a hunting gun across his cloaked shoulder, emerged among the trees and scrub bushes farther down the same side of the river. He heard the scream and saw the flying horse with a female aboard soar into the rushing river. He stiffened and dropped the gun. The large brown hound with him whimpered, but Gideon quieted him. "Sit, Samson," he whispered.

He marked a richly dressed man stomp up to the river's edge and blackened the morning with curses when only the horse surfaced and swam to the far bank. The person hit his high boot with his riding crop and kicked at a rice trunk. Then, after glancing up and down the river a few seconds, he returned, ripped his horse's reins from a limb, mounted, and galloped off.

Tearing off his cloak and boots, Gideon ran to the river's edge and dove in. He searched underwater until he found the rider, her skirt caught on a rock. Jerking the fabric free, he rose to the surface with her in his arms. He strode from the river, laid her across his shoulder, and thumped her back like he'd once seen his father do in England when a child fell into the lake on their estate. She spat water from her nose and mouth, then gasped. He rejoiced. She would live. But then she fainted in his arms.

With gentle care, he laid her on a mossy bank. The hound came to sniff around her, and Gideon patted the large, soft head. "We've caught a very special fish today, Samson." He brushed long, dark, auburn strands of hair from the girl's face, beautiful even in deathly white and with a darkening bruise across her forehead. He tapped her thin shoulder. "Miss? Can you hear me?" She didn't respond, but regular breaths continued to fan her soft lips.

Quickly, he pulled on his boots and shouldered the gun. Then he wrapped the cold, wet form in his cloak and picked her up in his brawny arms. "Come, boy, we've got to see what we can do for this lassie."

Miles away, he kicked open the door of his gamekeeper's cottage at Brighton Plantation and laid her on the bed near the fireplace. He stoked up the fire he kept going in the chilly spring mornings. Still, she didn't awaken. Concerned, he touched her icy hands, then her cold cheek. He stood and paced across the floor, then ran his hand through his thick, dark hair. Right or not, he must get her out of her wet clothing. For a fleeting moment, he thought of his dear mother in England. How he wished she were here to help with this. But she wasn't. And there were no servants up at the main house, which was now closed up while awaiting its new owner.

Closing the curtains to make the cottage dim for the young woman's modesty, Gideon removed her clothing. He tried to shut his eyes away from her beauty. As he removed her skirt, he felt the heavy weight in the hem and a secret pocket sewed inside the garment, but he laid it aside. He dressed the girl in a set of his own clothes, which swallowed her from head to toe, then wrapped her in a warm blanket. He threw another log on the fire in the hearth and placed her clothing on chairs to dry. As he lifted the heavy riding skirt, a red ruby necklace slid out onto his wooden floor.

Samson came to sniff the shining object, then padded to his bed near the hearth and plopped down. He dropped his thick head onto his paws and rolled large, soulful eyes from his master to the still form on the bed.

Gideon retrieved the necklace and held it up to a ray of sunlight entering through a slit in his window curtains. "Well, my boy, what have we here?"

A movement on the bed drew his attention. He placed the necklace back in the secret pocket of the girl's clothing and strode to her. "Hello, there. Are you awake?" He sat near her in a chair.

The girl opened her eyes and stared up at him with lovely tawny

SNEAK PEEK: THE GAMEKEEPER'S RELUCTANT BRIDE

eyes that widened with confusion. But she didn't speak. The next moment, her eyelids closed again.

He leaned down and touched her shoulder. "I'm Gideon Falconer. I fished you out of the Ashley River. What's your name?"

The exquisite face creased into a frown, and a tear slipped from under the long lashes. Finally, a weak voice muttered three words. "I don't know." Then her chin dropped, and she fell back to sleep. Or had she lost consciousness again?

WATCH FOR *THE GAMEKEEPER'S RELUCTANT BRIDE* **RELEASING IN 2024!**

GET ALL THE BOOKS IN THE CHARLESTON BRIDES SERIES

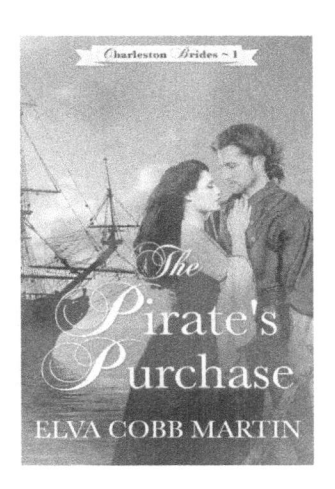

Book 1: The Pirate's Purchase

GET ALL THE BOOKS IN THE CHARLESTON BRIDES SERIES

Book 2: The Sultan's Captive

Book 3: The Petticoat Spy

GET ALL THE BOOKS IN THE CHARLESTON BRIDES SERIES

Book 4: The Sugar Baron's Governess

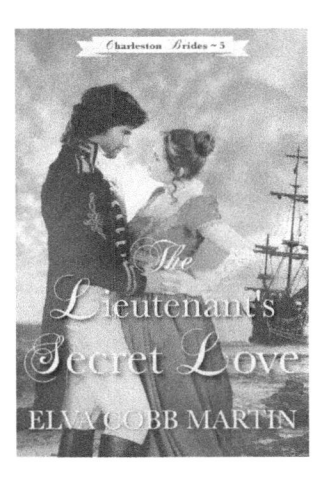

Book 5: The Lieutenant's Secret Love

ABOUT THE AUTHOR

Elva Cobb Martin is a retired school teacher, a mother, and grandmother who lives in South Carolina with her husband and high school sweetheart, Dwayne. She grew up on a farm in South Carolina and spends many vacations on the Carolina Coast. Her southern roots run deep.

A life-long student of history, her favorite city, Charleston, inspires her stories of romance and adventure. Her love of writing grew out of a desire to share exciting love stories of courageous characters and communicate truths of the Christian faith to bring hope and encouragement. She always pauses for historic houses, gardens, chocolate, and babies of any kind.

If you'd like to keep up with Elva's escapades, find her and a newsletter sign up at http://www.elvamartin.com or stalk her on

Facebook, Twitter, and Pinterest. She'll be glad to alert you when future books are available.

And guess what? She loves to hear from readers! Feel free to drop her a note at elvacmartin@gmail.com

In addition to the Charleston Brides Series, Elva Cobb Martin is author of:

The Barretts of Charleston Series
Book 1: In a Pirate's Debt
Book 2: Summer of Deception

Non-fiction
Power Over Satan: A Bible study on the believer's authority

Want more?

If you love historical romance, check out our other Wild Heart books!

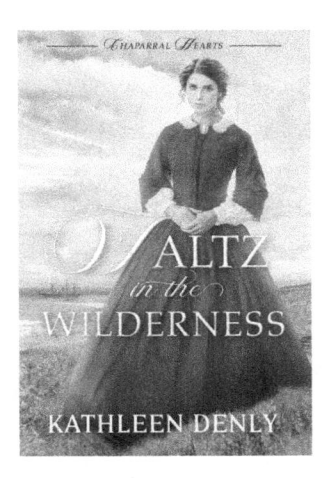

Waltz in the Wilderness by Kathleen Denly

She's desperate to find her missing father. His conscience demands he risk all to help.

Eliza Brooks is haunted by her role in her mother's death, so she'll do anything to find her missing pa—even if it means sneaking aboard a southbound ship. When those meant to protect her abandon and betray her instead, a family friend's unexpected assistance is a blessing she can't refuse.

Daniel Clarke came to California to make his fortune, and a stable job as a San Francisco carpenter has earned him more than most have scraped from the local goldfields. But it's been four years since he left Massachusetts and his fiancé is impatient for his return. Bound for home at last, Daniel Clarke finds his heart and plans challenged by a tenacious young woman with haunted eyes. Though every word he utters seems to offend her, he is determined to see her safely returned to her father. Even if that means risking his fragile engagement.

When disaster befalls them in the remote wilderness of the Southern California mountains, true feelings are revealed, and both must face heart-rending decisions. But how to decide when every choice before them leads to someone getting hurt?

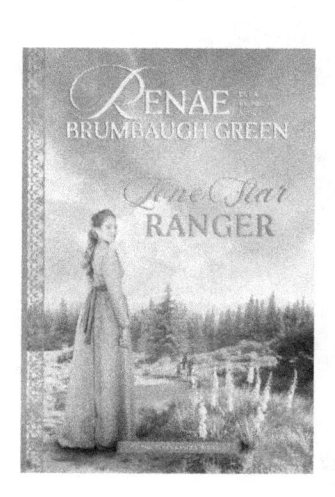

∼

Lone Star Ranger by Renae Brumbaugh Green

Elizabeth Covington will get her man.

And she has just a week to prove her brother isn't the murderer Texas Ranger Rett Smith accuses him of being. She'll show the good-looking lawman he's wrong, even if it means setting out on a risky race across Texas to catch the real killer.

Rett doesn't want to convict an innocent man. But he can't let the Boston beauty sway his senses to set a guilty man free. When Elizabeth follows him on a dangerous trek, the Ranger vows to keep her safe. But who will protect him from the woman whose conviction and courage leave him doubting everything—even his heart?

∼

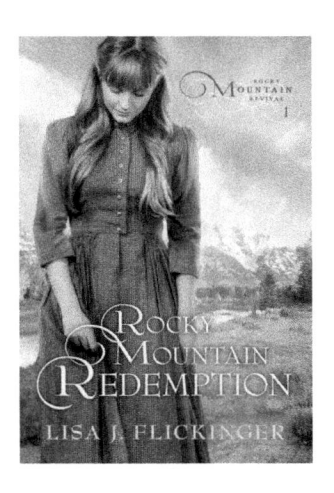

Rocky Mountain Redemption by Lisa J. Flickinger

A Rocky Mountain logging camp may be just the place to find herself.

To escape the devastation caused by the breaking of her wedding engagement, Isabelle Franklin joins her aunt in the Rocky Mountains to feed a camp of lumberjacks cutting on the slopes of Cougar Ridge. If only she could out run the lingering nightmares.

Charles Bailey, camp foreman and Stony Creek's itinerant pastor, develops a reputation to match his new nickname — Preach. However, an inner battle ensues when the details of his rough history threaten to overcome the beliefs of his young faith.

Amid the hazards of camp life, the unlikely friendship growing between the two surprises Isabelle. She's drawn to Preach's brute strength and gentle nature as he leads the ragtag crew toiling for Pollitt's Lumber. But when the ghosts from her past return to haunt her, the choices she will make change the course of her life forever—and that of the man she's come to love.

CPSIA information can be obtained
at www.ICGtesting.com
Printed in the USA
JSHW020801170323
39056JS00010B/293

9 781942 265696

BUILDING
LOUISIANA

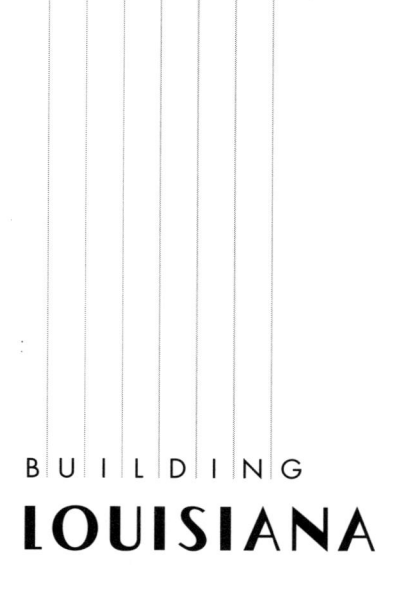

BUILDING
LOUISIANA

THE LEGACY OF THE
PUBLIC WORKS ADMINISTRATION

Robert D. Leighninger Jr.

UNIVERSITY PRESS OF MISSISSIPPI
Jackson

www.upress.state.ms.us

The University Press of Mississippi is a member of the Association of American University Presses.

Photo Credits
Greg Gilman, Geeman Photo, geemanphoto@cox-internet.com: pages 78, 83, 119, 120, 135, 136, 146, 149, 150, 152, 153; Archives and Special Collection, Noel Memorial Library, Louisiana State University, Shreveport: 154; Microfilm Copies of Records of the Public Works Administration, 1933–1947, Docket #La.5914, Record Group 135, National Archives II, College Park, MD: 158; R. D. Leighninger: all others.

Copyright © 2007 by University Press of Mississippi
All rights reserved
Manufactured in the United States of America

First edition 2007
∞

Library of Congress Cataloging-in-Publication Data

Leighninger, Robert D., 1941–
    Building Louisiana : the legacy of the Public Works Administration / Robert D. Leighninger, Jr.—1st ed.
        p. cm.
    Includes bibliographical references and index.
    ISBN-13: 978-1-57806-945-3 (cloth : alk. paper)
    ISBN-10: 1-57806-945-9 (cloth : alk. paper) 1. Public works—Louisiana—History. 2. United States. Public Works Administration. I. Title.
    HD3890.L8L45 2007
    363.0976309′043—dc22

2006027646

British Library Cataloging-in-Publication Data available

The duty of public works was to build permanent and socially desirable projects that would be assets of the communities which they would serve for many years to come.

—HAROLD ICKES

CONTENTS

List of Tables ix
Acknowledgments xi
Introduction xvii

PART I. A BRIEF HISTORY OF THE PWA IN LOUISIANA
1. How to Respond to a Great Depression 3
2. Harold Ickes Goes to Work 12
3. Huey Long Versus the PWA 28
4. The Second Louisiana Purchase 45
5. Scandal 56

PART II. CULTURAL INFRASTRUCTURE: REDEVELOPING COMMUNITY
6. Schools 71
7. Universities 92
8. Courthouses 108

PART III. PHYSICAL INFRASTRUCTURE: BUILDING A MODERN ECONOMY
9. The U.S. Marine Hospital at Carville and Other Federal Projects 129
10. The New Orleans Charity Hospital 138
11. The French Market 149
12. The Shreveport Incinerator 157
13. Sugar 162
14. The New Orleans Sewer and Water Project 166
15. Beyond the Bayous 180

APPENDIX. THE LEGACY: AN INVENTORY OF NONFEDERAL PWA PROJECTS IN LOUISIANA 187

Notes 269
Index 291

TABLES

TABLE 1. PWA Nonfederal Projects Approved in Louisiana Prior to the Freeze   43–44

TABLE 2. Total Allotments for Nonfederal Programs in Selected Southern States   55

TABLE 3. School Projects by Parish   90–91

TABLE 4. University Projects   107

TABLE 5. Courthouse Projects   124

TABLE 6. Era of Construction of Current Twentieth-Century Parish Courthouses in Louisiana   125

TABLE 7. Sewer and Water Projects   177–78

TABLE 8. Components of Docket #4284, New Orleans Sewerage and Water Board   179

ACKNOWLEDGMENTS

One of the most pleasurable parts of this project was the fieldwork. After identifying all of the Louisiana Public Works Administration (PWA) projects, I set out to discover how many were still around and what shape they were in. At first I could do this only on weekends. Later I was able to visit buildings during business hours and got to meet people who used them. Invariably, they were eager to tell me about their buildings and find out what I knew about them. They enjoyed pointing out the architectural features that they liked. They corrected my misimpressions and filled in the background. Most of all, they made it clear that these buildings had indeed made a mark on their communities. In my haste to see as much as I could and my enthusiasm to hear all they had to say, I sometimes forgot to write down their names. Here are some of them. I apologize for not being able to acknowledge everyone who helped me find my way around Louisiana and understand its history.

Paul Abram, Grandison Hall, Southern University; Gerald A. Bantaa, principal, Maurepas High School; Vic Bender, principal, Ponchatoula High School; Gary Black, Jackson Parish Middle School superintendent; Roosevelt Black, custodian, Ogden Primary Center, Liddieville; Pauline Blakley, director of admissions, Grambling State University; Yvonne Blunt, receptionist, Franklin Parish School Board; Ann Brown, Jefferson Davis Parish School Board; Emily Bruno, owner, Emily House Cafe, St. Joseph; Renard Cage, custodian, Ferriday Educational Center; Jo Caldwell, principal, Baskin High School; Lynda Cantu, secretary to the superintendent, Concordia Parish; Domenica Carriere, Noel Memorial Library, University of Louisiana–Shreveport; Rebecca Z. Carter, principal, L. S. Rugg Elementary School, Alexandria; Lieutenant Cooper, Avoyelles Correctional Center; Rishea Corvin, Caddo Parish School Board; June Cottle, coordinator, Pine Belt Community Action Agency; Sharon Cowser, receptionist, Jackson Parish School Board; Connie Credeur, receptionist, Mire Elementary School; R. E. Crowe, Jonesboro; Ruby Daigle, Iberville Parish School Board; Anita Daily, home economics teacher, Bell City

High School; Lilly Davis, principal, Marion High School; T-Joe DiStefano, retired maintenance director, Iberville Parish School Board; Pat Donovan and staff, Lake Charles City Waste Water Division; Juliette Dumond, secretary to the supervisor, Vermillion Parish School Board; Kay Easley, superintendent, Red River Parish Schools; John E. Ellis, principal, Linville High School; Archie Evans, Stirlington Senior High School; Mr. Facen, East Carroll Parish superintendent of schools; Mamcy Fox, Lacassine High School; Homer Free, principal, Marthaville Elementary and Junior High School; Margie Gaspard, custodian, Bell City High School; Eddie Gibson, Newellton High School; Larry Gilbert, principal, Brusly Middle School; Terry Hayden, principal, Chatham High School; Carolyn Hayes, Welsh High School; Iantha Hayes, retired English teacher, Ferriday High School; Joey Hebert, superintendent, Vermillion Parish School Board; Joyce Durr Hendricks, Marthaville Elementary and Junior High School; Frank Horrell, Kaleidoscope Panels, Inc., Eros; Terry Jackson, custodian, Bienville Parish Head Start Center; Raymond Jeffrees, Jonesboro; David Jones, business manager, Red River Parish School Board; Betsy Jordan, Robeline Town Hall; Odell Key, mayor of Gibsland; Shelton Kavalir, principal, Crowville High School; Wayne King, assistant superintendent, Webster Parish School Board; Carl J. Kowitz, office manager, Madison Parish School Board; Carl Langley, principal, Hathaway High School; Vic Labarbara, principal, and staff of Amite High School; Officer Lee, Avoyelles Correctional Center; Linda LeBlanc, Welsh town clerk; Ken Lejeune, principal, Richard Elementary School; Harry Lopez, director of facilities and maintenance, Iberia Parish School Board; Tommy Massy, Heritage Manor Nursing Home; Judy Matte, Acadia Parish School Board; Linda Matthews, receptionist, Jackson Parish Middle School; Carolyn McDonald, principal, Kelly Elementary School; Merella Melancon McFalls, principal, Rayne High School; Linda Melton, transportation secretary, Union Parish School Board; Taffy Morrison, Chatham High School; Robert Naquin, maintenance head, Avoyelles Manor Nursing Home; Charles Nevels, principal, Kinder High School; Keith Norwood, director of planning and purchasing, Bossier Parish Schools; Jesse Oubre, maintenance supervisor, St. John the Baptist Parish Schools; Darlene Pace, Bossier Parish School Board; Richard Partain, First Baptist Church of Greenwood; Marie Potts, assistant principal, Ferriday High School; Connie Richardson, custodian, Ponchatoula High School; Jeanette Rushing, Pine Belt Multi-Purpose Agency, Gibsland; Aubrey Sayes, principal, Plain Dealing Junior High School; Charles Scriber, principal, Ruston High School; Dusty Shenofsky, public relations officer, Louisiana National Guard; Angela Sims, Red River Family Center, Coushatta; Wavylon Smith, principal, Coushatta Elementary School; Ginger Stuckey, principal, Simpson High School; Jean Taylor, teacher, Linville High School; Larry Towner, Charlotte Mitchell Educational Center; Melanie Venable, principal, Mire Elementary School; Lori Wallace, principal, Eastside Elementary School, Bastrop; Gail Weems, receptionist, Crowville High School; Mary Wells, Facilities Planning, Southern University; Roger Whatley, principal, Hornbeck High School; Les Whitt, director, and Stephanie Smith, Alexandria Zoo; Doris Wilson, Bienville Parish Head Start Center; Gail Young, receptionist, Iberia Parish School Board.

I am also grateful to Officers Colas and Webre, St. John the Baptist Sheriff's Office, who rescued me when I locked my keys in my car; to Mike Boyd and Butch Jones, who gave me a pickup truck escort to Fort Necessity from Liddieville; and to Darnell Marie Brunner Beck, for post-Katrina reconnaissance in New Orleans.

Jerry Wise, editor of the *Dequincy News* and the *Cameron Pilot*, provided historical background, reconnaissance, and contacts for the southwestern part of the state. The contacts included John Blanchard and Pauline Norwood, who helped me in trying to trace the elusive Hunter High School.

Much of the primary research for this project was done with Record Group (RG) 135, the microfilm records of the PWA in the National Archives. When the films were stored in the Pennsylvania Avenue building, archivist Bill Creech was my guide. I spent almost a year staring into the one microfilm reader in the main reading room. On Saturdays and other days when staff shortages made that machine inaccessible, I had to compete with hundreds of amateur genealogists in the Microfilm Room. I overhead many interesting conversations about the ancestors of the eager researchers. My favorite was a father-daughter team following a relative in the Confederate army. Periodically, one of them would say: "Oh, he deserted again."

When RG 135 moved to College Park, Maryland, I was in the care of archivist Gene Morris. Then the collection went into storage, first in Pennsylvania and then Kansas, so that film had to be ordered days in advance. Gene kept me apprised of the whereabouts of the material, provided me with the finding aids to request the reels I wanted, and had them ready for me on arrival. His knowledge, service, and good humor were invaluable.

On many of my shorter trips to the archives, I was sheltered and fed by William Barnes and Eva Dömoter. Bill is senior policy analyst at the National League of Cities and was a sounding board and steadfast supporter throughout the project's ups and downs.

I'm grateful to the Louisiana Endowment for the Humanities (LEH) and its director, Michael Sartisky, for the award of a Book Completion Grant. This provided, in part, for the photographic services of Greg Gilman, who entered into the project enthusiastically and donated much more time and creativity than I could pay him for. Karen Kingsley, emerita professor of architecture, Tulane University, was the evaluator for the LEH grant and became an invaluable source of information and encouragement as my work continued. Celeste Uzee, LEH's assistant director, also became a stalwart adviser, informant, and supporter. A fringe benefit to this relationship is her wealth of information on Louisiana food, which has provided another way to maintain contact with these places that I love. Thus I have become a part of what she calls the Louisiana diaspora.

Charles Grenier encouraged me from the beginning, made connections for me, and read an earlier version of the manuscript. He is a fellow sociologist and has recently retired from a long teaching career at the Louisiana State University (LSU) School of Social Work to a second as apprentice restorer of New Deal murals at the State Exposition Building in Shreveport. J. Michael Desmond, professor of architecture at LSU, was one of the first people Charlie introduced me to. He was enthusiastic about the idea and has continued to be a most valuable adviser and supporter. Another of Charlie's contacts was Rick Speciale, of the Baton Rouge United Way, which is housed in a PWA building. Rick is a superlative advocate of anything related to art deco, and I was fortunate to receive his enthusiastic support.

Barry Blose, recently retired as acquisitions editor, University of South Carolina Press, gave me crucial advice on restructuring this book in its early stages and, while I was waiting for the publisher to which I had originally submitted it to decide its fate, suggested I write another book on the entire New Deal public building program. I did, and he saw me through the process while at the same time encouraging me not to give up on the Louisiana book.

Craig Gill, University Press of Mississippi, rescued me from despair, recognized the importance of illustrations for this work, recruited an outside reader who provided many useful suggestions for expanding my focus, and kept things moving along.

Donna Fricker, of the Louisiana Historic Preservation Office, helped me unravel the several phases of the Winnsboro High School project with fieldwork, photographs, and maps. Mary Fitzpatrick, editor of *Preservation in Print*, was immediately and consistently appreciative of my work and gave me a chance to make it accessible to readers during the years when I was not able to get it out in book form. She helped me keep up my faith.

My wife, Leslie, and daughter, Maggie Hopkins, both edited earlier versions of the manuscript and parts of the revision. My son, Matt, and daughter-in-law, Pamela Swett, each read a chapter of the revision, despite commitments to books of their own. Hal Swan helped me select the illustrations. He also read the entire manuscript and offered helpful suggestions. His photographer's eye was useful in framing the contours of an argument as well as a landscape.

Returning to fieldwork, I should report that while it is enjoyable as a solitary activity, it is much more fun with a companion. I made one trip with Greg Gilman and was very sorry I couldn't have had more. But I was fortunate that my wife shared this passion, and we made many expeditions together, despite her administrative and scholarly obligations. I particularly prize the title she gave me as she watched me broadcast information across the state on the accomplishments of the PWA: "Johnny Appleseed."

This image carries a corrective. Johnny Appleseed wore a tin pot for a hat. It is sometimes difficult to contain this enthusiasm within the necessary constraints of scholarly objectivity. This is a celebratory book because there is not only much to celebrate objectively but also because such celebration is long overdue. However, the New Deal had many failings. It was confused and erratic at its best. Its agricultural policies were devastating to tenant farmers and sharecroppers. Its work relief programs reached only a fraction of the unemployed. African Americans and Native Americans were included in federal aid policies to an unprecedented degree, but the efforts came nowhere near to meeting actual need. Its corporatist industrial policy was a clear failure. Its housing initiative, innovative and universal at the beginning, devolved into a two-tiered establishment that aided those better-off while stigmatizing the poor. Even its prime achievement, Social Security, left out domestic and agricultural workers. Economists continue to debate whether its polices helped end the Great Depression or simply marked time until World War II could do it. But amid this confusion and dubious battle, the backbone of our physical and cultural infrastructure was built. That has to be taken into account, and has yet to be, in any final assessment of the New Deal. That must be celebrated even as it is subjected to critical scrutiny.

INTRODUCTION

We are surrounded by facilities constructed for us over half a century ago at public expense. We use them or drive by them every day, yet most of us are totally unaware of how they got there. We would be surprised to learn that they were built within a brief period of six or seven years, not accumulated gradually over a century. They are the legacy of the public works programs of the Franklin Roosevelt administration's New Deal. Rarely has so much been built for so many in so little time and been so thoroughly forgotten.

This frenzy of construction happened as a response to the Great Depression. In the years of deflation following the stock market crash of 1929, industrial production declined to half its former level and construction to one-fifth. Workers were laid off or suffered drastically reduced wages and salaries. Businesses closed. Banks went under. Mortgages on homes and farms went unpaid, and foreclosures left many families homeless. Farmers in the Midwest were blown out of their homes and harried along the roads by ferocious, drought-induced dust storms. By 1933, a quarter of the workforce, as many as 15 million people, were unemployed. Many others were working only part-time. Skilled and unskilled workers alike were affected. Even men with college educations stood in soup lines. In a desperate search for work, men rode freight trains from city to city. Kansas City estimated 1,500 homeless men passed through each day. Shantytowns called Hoovervilles mushroomed beside the tracks. It was a time of fear and despair. Some politicians foresaw a revolution.[1]

When Franklin Roosevelt was elected president in 1932, he did not have any kind of comprehensive program for combating the Depression. His campaign promises were vague and grounded in the prevailing economic orthodoxy of limited government and balanced budgets. But he also realized that new departures were necessary. He assembled a wide variety of advisers, known to reporters as the brain trust, and entertained an even wider variety of ideas. He was willing to experiment.[2] This book will concentrate on only one of the manifold New Deal experiments, the use of public works to relieve unemployment and revive the economy; on only one of the many public building agencies: the Public Works Administration (PWA); and on only one state: Louisiana.

The PWA is often confused with another New Deal public works program, the Works Progress Administration (WPA). Harold Ickes, the administrator of the PWA, thought the confusion was deliberate. While the PWA was created in 1933, the WPA did not arrive until two years later. Ickes thought the head of the new agency, Harry Hopkins, wanted to borrow his favorable public image. There was a logic to the WPA's title, however. One of the functions of the new agency was to monitor the progress of all public works programs. It was, incidentally, to sponsor its own projects, which were to be more labor intensive and involve less skilled labor than the PWA's. This second function ballooned into a major public works effort of its own, hence Ickes's jealousy.[3] The two programs continued to exist side by side until the end of the New Deal, sometimes cooperating, often competing, but both contributing to the investment in infrastructure, as the products of these programs are now known.[4]

Infrastructure can be roughly divided into "physical" and "cultural" components. Physical infrastructure constitutes the basic underpinnings of modern, industrial society: the roads, bridges, canals, airports, sewer systems, waterworks, dams, and electrical power plants that we use to produce goods and services, to move them and ourselves across the landscape, and to keep us safe and healthy at work and at home. Cultural infrastructure consists of the facilities that allow us to educate our children and ourselves, conduct government, administer justice, and otherwise transmit our culture through museums and other venues for art performances and displays.

Though public works programs were first and foremost conceived as instruments to employ millions of people idled by the Great Depression, to feed families, and to revive the economy, there were also larger hopes behind them. They were investments in the future that would operate on two levels: they would build or rebuild communities, and they would build a modern economy. One can attempt to understand this investment through statistics or institutional histories, but let me introduce it in a more personal way, the way most citizens have experienced it.

On a typical day I used to drive to work at Louisiana State University (LSU) past a lake reclaimed from swampland by WPA workers. Retirees fish from its banks while students jog, cycle, or rollerblade around it and families with small children play in the adjacent park. The traffic was

INTRODUCTION XIX

Lafayette City Hall, now the French Cultural Center. An example of cultural infrastructure, then and now. It was designed by Favrot and Reed.

Baton Rouge Public Library by L. A. Groz, now the offices of the Capitol Area United Way. Another example of cultural infrastructure, then and now.

St. Joseph Community Center by J. W. Smith and Associates. Proceeds from a slot machine helped pay the city's portion of the project. More cultural infrastructure.

sometimes slow on the causeway because cars, trucks, and trailers were getting off the interstate highway and heading for a livestock show or rodeo at Parker Coliseum (also a WPA project) at the southeastern edge of campus.

As I entered the campus, I passed the Student Health Center (WPA) and Himes Hall (a PWA classroom building). Turning into my parking lot, I passed the northern enclosure of the football stadium (WPA). If I walked to lunch at the Faculty Club (PWA), I might pass Atkinson Hall (PWA), a math and physics building complete with observatory. If I walked a slightly wider loop, I'd pass the Geology Building (PWA) and three women's dormitories (PWA). A walk after lunch toward the Mississippi River levee would take me past Alex Box Stadium (WPA), home to LSU's three-time Division I championship baseball team. If I had to go to the credit union, I'd walk past the School of Agriculture's Sugar Factory, a major research facility that was given modern equipment by the PWA, installed by the WPA.

Demonstrations and rallies on the steps of the state capitol are not uncommon. Those attending see the Capitol Annex, an imposing office

Himes Hall, Louisiana State University. Weiss, Dreyfous, and Seiferth designed it.

building in the PWA moderne style, to the west of the capitol. The state troopers guarding the capitol have their headquarters, built by the WPA, a few miles to the east. From the observation deck at the top of the capitol, one can see the gleaming tower of the Port Allen Middle School, an art deco gem across the river built by the PWA.

When I visit my brother in St. Paul, Minnesota, in the summer, we can walk to the Como Park Zoo. Its administration building came from the WPA. A walk in the other direction takes us to the Minnesota State Fairgrounds, where the WPA contributed a livestock building, the 4-H headquarters, a concession building, and the promenade up to the stadium. On

Faculty Club, Louisiana State University, also by Weiss, Dreyfous, and Seiferth.

the nearby University of Minnesota campus are a student union, a natural history museum, an adult education center, a women's gym, and several dormitories constructed by the PWA.

On a recent vacation to Skyline Drive in Shenandoah National Park, I enjoyed the work of the Civilian Conservation Corps (CCC), yet another New Deal public works program. Its young men prepared the roadbeds, built the retaining walls, and erected a number of park shelters and service buildings. Skyline Drive itself and the park headquarters were done by the PWA. Skyline Drive continues south as the Smoky Mountain Parkway, also courtesy of the PWA.

Even my in-laws in rural northern Vermont are not far from New Deal public works. A simple white clapboard school in Cabot was constructed by the PWA. A large civic auditorium in Barre was a PWA project. In nearby Stowe, a major tourist attraction and revenue source, the original ski trails on Mt. Mansfield were cut by CCC "boys." They also built the Base Lodge, where you buy your lift tickets and have lunch. The bathhouse at Crystal Lake State Park in Barton was a CCC project. Four dams were constructed by the CCC to stop floods that had ravaged the Lamoille River watershed, costing many lives and millions of dollars.

There is scarcely a community of any size in the 1930s that did not

Capitol Annex, Baton Rouge, by Neild, Somdal, and Neild.

benefit in some way by this brief but prodigious period of public investment.[5] An assessment of this impact is long overdue.

I have chosen to begin such an assessment with one state and one agency. While it would be easy to skim the surface and point out the more spectacular projects, I think it better to begin with a more solid, if less flashy, base. We ought to know about the elementary schools in small towns, the unglamorous but necessary sewage treatment plants, and the modest but dignified courthouses, as well as the towering hospital and the world-famous market. We need to see everything by one agency in at least one state before we can begin to reckon the importance of all New Deal public works programs to America.

Port Allen Middle School, originally the high school. An art deco gem by Bodman and Murrell.

Most people are surprisingly ignorant of the scope of New Deal public works. Even historians can be wonderfully myopic. The authors of a highly respected history of the development of the city of Chicago assert that, except for housing and land-use planning, "most of the new federal programs for municipalities involved relief and jobs for the distressed and left no physical mark on the city."[6] In fact, the authors probably drive daily past major "physical marks" made by the New Deal. The Lake Michigan shoreline was stabilized by the WPA, which also built the ocean-liner-shaped bathhouse on the North Shore. The Outer Drive Bridge, a PWA project, connected the northern and southern stretches of the Outer Drive, ending the congestion that their diversion to Michigan Avenue had caused. Farther west, the PWA provided a new bridge over the Chicago River at Ashland Avenue. Five large high schools, including DuSable, visible from the Dan Ryan Expressway, were PWA projects. Cook County Hospital gained a seventeen-story nurses' home, an orthopedic hospital, and a laundry building. Nearby, the University of Illinois erected a nine-story dental school. A $56 million sewage project, one of the biggest in the country, cleaned up most of south Chicago. All were PWA projects. If the historians could not see these imposing structures, it is understandable that they should overlook the thirteen new elementary schools and the post offices, libraries, and municipal buildings the PWA distributed across the city.

Louisiana historians can be equally unobservant. After a lecture on New Deal murals recently rediscovered and installed at the University of Louisiana at Hammond, one said he was unaware of any New Deal architecture on his campus. In fact, the stadium was erected by the WPA. The music and drama building, the art museum (formerly the library), the president's house, a gym, and three other classroom buildings were built by the PWA.

Ignorance among the lay population is more understandable. For one thing, there was no official style by which to recognize New Deal buildings. They were designed by local architects at the request of local city councils or school boards, who chose whatever style suited them. For the majority, this was some variation of colonial revival. A building in that style could have been constructed anytime between the 1890s and yesterday, so there is no reason to connect it to the late 1930s. Many projects reflect local vernacular styles: clapboard in New England, adobe in the Southwest. The only stylistic clue that a building might come from this period is if it happened to be in a style briefly popular in the 1930s. This style, which was a blend of commercial art deco and beaux arts classicism, went under many names: "stripped classicism, "starved classicism," and "Greco-deco" among them. Since public buildings dominated construction during this period, one of those names was "PWA moderne." (Art deco will be discussed in chapter 6 and PWA moderne in chapter 8.) Otherwise, since most people don't make a habit of inspecting cornerstones or plaques, there is no other way to know when and by whom something was built. And plaques have a way of disappearing in maintenance or remodeling.

The PWA received 537 project proposals from Louisiana. Of these, 228 were approved and built. When the PWA was being closed down, 17 others were transferred to the WPA. Many of these proposals involved more than one building. One from the University of Louisiana at Lafayette involved twelve structures. Proposals from school boards frequently requested several new buildings or additions to old ones. The total contribution of these 228 projects approaches 400 structures distributed across fifty-five of Louisiana's sixty-four parishes. The excluded parishes are those with very low populations. Even today St. Helena has fewer than 10,000 people, and yet it was not really excluded; two applications for school projects originally sent to the PWA were transferred to the WPA when the PWA was closing shop. The WPA also built its courthouse. Other parishes have few population centers, being largely pine forest or swamp. Thus, with few exceptions, the PWA reached every corner of the state.

These buildings are now in their seventh decade of use. They were well built. Even with, in some cases, shamefully minimal maintenance, they continue to serve their original purposes or new ones. They maintain our health, provide for the transmission of our culture, and support our economy. Some of these services can be calculated in dollars; some are beyond such calculation. But the legacy is there, before our eyes. It's time we looked at it and appraised it. This book will show you where to look.

There is no institutional history of the PWA. Harold Ickes, who headed it, offered his own midway account, *Back to Work*, in 1935. Ickes's biographers and his diaries discuss the program. There is one very useful analysis of its operation that was undertaken shortly after its dissolution, and a doctoral dissertation that stops earlier, but there has been no detailed assessment of its successes and failures since that time. This book will not fill that gap, but I hope it will provide a useful case study that may inspire someone who can.

This book is divided into three parts. The first provides an overview of the PWA in Louisiana. The second deals with cultural infrastructure and community development, while the third focuses on physical infrastructure and the development of the broader economy. An appendix offers an annotated inventory of what the PWA built in Louisiana.

The first chapter provides a very brief introduction to the challenges of the Great Depression and the New Deal response. Chapter 2 gives an account of how Harold Ickes, Roosevelt's secretary of the interior and a Chicago lawyer who liked to refer to himself as a "curmudgeon," built the PWA and defended it against detractors and rivals inside and outside the administration. Chapter 3 describes some of the battles that developed between Louisiana senator Huey P. Long and his enemies when PWA money became available to the state. Long did not want his rivals bolstered by the popular support they would receive in securing PWA projects, so he used his control of the governor and the legislature to make it difficult for communities to initiate proposals without his approval. He was also beginning his own presidential campaign, which gave Ickes little desire to play this game. Therefore, in the early years of the PWA program, Louisiana had few projects under way.

In October 1935, Long's career was stopped by an assassin's bullet (or perhaps a stray from one of his bodyguards). A new governor, Richard Leche, took office in 1936 and decided that New Deal public works were a good thing. He went to Washington. His courtship unblocked the funding streams, and what became known as the "Second Louisiana Purchase" began. This will be recounted in chapter 4.

Ickes was known even to his enemies as "Honest Harold." He was determined to be an exemplary steward of federal money, even if it meant slowing down the PWA's impact on Depression unemployment. His Investigations Division pursued any allegation of wrongdoing in the letting of contracts, the hiring and paying of laborers, the purchase of materials, and the methods of construction. His special agents exposed and, where necessary, prosecuted fraud, collusion, kickbacks, cheap substitutions, and any kind of corner cutting. Louisiana kept them busy interviewing, taking depositions, and recommending settlements. This kept the PWA free of scandal, despite a major investigation of activities of the WPA swirling around it. This inquiry soon led to grand jury proceedings that ultimately sent the governor, LSU's president, and other prominent figures to jail. This story will be told in chapter 5.

The basic structure of the PWA funding process began at the bottom and worked up. Local communities decided what they needed and applied for support. Thus a great deal of the PWA legacy is seen at the community level and is largely what I am calling cultural infrastructure. The review of cultural infrastructure will begin with school buildings, which left a particularly important mark on Louisiana (chapter 6). They were the most numerous projects in the state. Before the PWA, students and teachers did their work in environments that were not only crowded and uncomfortable but also life threatening. Winds and rain blew through crumbling walls and roofs. Old and faulty heating and wiring started fires. Open latrines polluted drinking water. In addition to making schools safe for Louisiana's children, the PWA offered innovations in curriculum that educators had only dreamed about. Science and agriculture laboratories, machine shops and home economics rooms and cottages, music and art rooms, gymnasiums, auditoriums, and libraries became standard parts of new, consolidated elementary and high schools.

In the early 1930s, Louisiana's universities were mostly new and struggling institutions operating in old and borrowed buildings. The PWA provided them with major jolts of adrenalin (chapter 7). Laboratories, music and drama complexes, libraries, classroom buildings, dormitories, stadiums, and health centers popped up on campuses across the state. In several cases, the PWA produced what amounted to an "instant campus" kit. This accommodated the growing number of students with a new breadth and depth to the curricula that would have been impossible earlier in the decade. The state's two African American universities, Grambling and Southern, were included in the construction of the backbone of the state's higher education system.

Parish courthouses constructed through the PWA gave strong support to the administration of justice in Louisiana (chapter 8). In just four years, eleven were erected and others overhauled or added to. This is more courthouse construction than in any other period in the state's history, before or after the New Deal. Here we see some outstanding examples of PWA moderne architecture.

In moving to physical infrastructure, we are looking at facilities that figuratively, and sometimes literally, undergird society. These facilities, while serving a local population, also improved life well beyond it. New Orleans's Charity Hospital drew patients from the entire state. The LSU Sugar Institute supported a national industry. The French Market in New Orleans was not only an outlet for regional farmers but also an international tourist destination.

The Roosevelt administration knew that this piecemeal economic development should be part of a larger plan, and it began to see the economic development of the South as a critical part of reviving the nation's economy. In 1938 it issued a sixty-four-page "Report on Economic Conditions of the South," which the president declared in his introduction demonstrated that "the South represents right now the Nation's No. 1 economic problem."[7] This was a political document as much as it was an economic plan. It was intended to influence the elections of 1938; the administration hoped to bolster its southern supporters in Congress, who had been key actors in passing the legislation of the first "Hundred Days," and to purge some of its chief obstructionists. Yet a lot of serious economic analysis went into the report, and it stimulated a lively debate on the place of the southern economy in national operations. This accomplishment somewhat offset its utter failure as a political instrument.

The physical infrastructure section of the book begins with an overview of "federal" projects and an examination of one of them, the hospital for people with leprosy at Carville (chapter 9). Federal projects were those conducted through government agencies like the Treasury Department, which built post offices, and the Bureau of Public Roads, which constructed major highways and bridges. They were handled differently from the "nonfederal" projects that make up the bulk of this book, and they are much more difficult to document because their records are spread among, and in most cases have been lost by, these federal agencies. There are, however, enough scraps of information to convey some of the extent of these projects.

Chapter 10 tells the story of "Big Charity," the twenty-story hospital improbably erected on the peat and mud of New Orleans's former back swamp. It was a political and engineering achievement whose survival after Hurricane Katrina is now in doubt. Its construction incited an intense battle within the medical community and featured Huey Long in the unlikely role of peacemaker. Not far away is another landmark that came through the hurricane and flood in good condition: the French Market in the city's historic French Quarter, reviewed in chapter 11. A market had existed there for over a century, but the one we experience now was assembled by the PWA.

One of the most unusual PWA facilities in the state was the Shreveport incinerator (chapter 12). Its function was not out of the ordinary, but its design was. Sam Wiener, the incinerator's architect, had gone to Europe to see the works of the European modernists: Le Corbusier in France, Walter Gropius and the Bauhaus in Germany, and the De Stijl group in the Netherlands. Upon his return, he had several opportunities to put what he had learned into practice. He designed the Bossier City High School complex in the clean, modernist style. If you ask locals how old the building is, they usually say the 1960s or later. The Shreveport incinerator, a project he became involved in late in its development, drew international attention as an example of the aesthetic purity that functional design could achieve. It was written up in the architectural press, and photographs of it were included in an exhibit at the Museum of Modern Art in New York.

Another unique project, the LSU Sugar Factory, discussed in chapter 13, was a contribution both to education and to the national economy. A grant from the PWA helped the university acquire modern equipment that would allow it to conduct research on new types and methods of sugar production.

Finally, we will go underground in chapter 14 to explore the multimillion dollar improvement and extension of the New Orleans sewer, water, and storm drainage system. Like Big Charity, the system was a political battlefield. Huey Long and the Old Regulars fought to control it, and it took Long's assassination to clear the way for its completion.

In the last chapter I raise questions about the relevance of this history to contemporary debates about infrastructure, long-range public investment, and "big government." I also note a few examples of PWA work across the nation.

With this background, we can then proceed to the book's appendix and confront the legacy of the PWA in Louisiana, community by community, project by project, building by building. It will be an eye-opening tour even to those, perhaps particularly to those, who are familiar with the state. It documents what was accomplished by one federal agency in one southern state during a period of less than seven years. Indeed, much of the work was accomplished in three, 1936–1939, since most projects got under way only after Long's assassination and were completed before 1940.

People from outside the state, while they may have no prior acquaintance with these structures, with the possible exception of fond memories of café au lait and beignets in the French Market in New Orleans, will have a new awareness of the impact of one New Deal program on the face of the country. They will, I hope, begin to look around with sharper eyes and rediscover the familiar landmarks in their own communities that came to them through New Deal programs. These buildings, and the activities they made possible, are an investment our ancestors made in us. We have been enjoying the dividends for over six decades now. It is time to give the legacy a closer examination.

PART I

A BRIEF HISTORY OF THE PWA IN LOUISIANA

CHAPTER 1

HOW TO RESPOND TO A GREAT DEPRESSION

The Franklin Roosevelt administration's response to the greatest depression in American history was one of massive and inspired improvisation. The new president took office with a lot of valuable experience—work relief and conservation being just two problems he had dealt with as governor of New York—but without a clear philosophy or even an integrated set of theories about what to do. In fact, he didn't like theories and tended to be suspicious of those who offered them. He turned away the advice of John Maynard Keynes, the British economist who would later become famous for a theory of deficit spending that explained much about why some New Deal policies worked and some didn't. "He hated abstractions," said James MacGregor Burns, "his mind yearned for the detail, the particular, the specific."[1]

As one adviser, Raymond Moley, later put it: "to look at [New Deal] policies as the result of a unified plan was to believe that the accumulation of stuffed snakes, baseball pictures, school flags, old tennis shoes, carpenter's tools, geometry books, and chemistry sets in a boy's bedroom could have been put there by an interior decorator."[2] The important thing was that while Roosevelt never entirely shook free of economic orthodoxy, he was able to see its limitations and experiment with new ideas.

In fact, he saw experiments as imperative. In an address to the graduating class of Oglethorpe University, he stated: "This country needs and, unless I mistake its temper, this country demands bold, persistent experimentation. It is common sense to take a method and try it. If it fails, admit it frankly and try another. But above all, try something." Their challenge, he told the graduates, was not to make their way in the world before them, but to remake it.[3]

Roosevelt was ready to embrace new ideas, but New Deal programs did not spring full-blown from the mind of Roosevelt or his advisers. Most had antecedents in earlier times, particularly the Progressive Era at the beginning of the century, and even in the conservatism of Herbert Hoover. There is a long history of federal involvement in the development of cultural and physical infrastructure. Federal lands were granted to the states for schools in the nineteenth century. In 1887 the Hatch Act provided annual cash grants for agricultural experiment stations, and in 1890 the second Morrill Act did the same for land-grant colleges. The Smith-Lever Act of 1914 created the Cooperative Extension Service, which not only provided research and consultation to farmers but also offered "home economics" advice to their spouses and families. The Country Life movement preceded the New Deal's efforts to promote a sense of community among the isolated and individualistic farmers and reorganize agriculture along cooperative lines. President Theodore Roosevelt established a U.S. Country Life Commission in 1909 to support farming cooperatives. Marketing cooperatives flourished in the 1920s but soon became centrally controlled, big business enterprises beyond the reach of individual farmers.[4]

Rural poverty, in the South and elsewhere, was a concern of Progressives, and they looked to schools as the key to modernizing rural life. New, clean, and attractive school buildings would be built and students taught to transform their homes into similarly clean, efficient, and comfortable environments where education would be nurtured. The Progressives originally hoped that the farmers' wives and daughters would lead the farmers to more modern attitudes and practices, which would pull them out of poverty. However, by the end of the 1920s the reform movement had given up on motivating women to change men and hoping the home would change the rural economy. It withdrew to an entirely domestic and gender-specific agenda.[5] The home economic cottages with model kitchens, living rooms, laundries, and bedrooms that were added to many Louisiana high schools were the result of this movement.

Concern for the education of African Americans was also visible in the Progressive Era. One of its most important manifestations was a private initiative sponsored by the Julius Rosenwald Fund. Rosenwald was the president of Sears, Roebuck, and Company, the famous mail-order catalog corporation, and his organization helped black communities build their own schools throughout the South.[6] Attention to African Americans came gradually in Louisiana but nonetheless had important results.

One of the most significant initiatives of the New Deal, and the one central to this book, also had earlier origins. The idea of using public works as counterforces against a downturn in the business cycle had emerged in the 1920s and was championed by, among others, Herbert Hoover. He was, however, far too hesitant to act on this. In the last year of his administration he created the Reconstruction Finance Corporation (RFC) to offer emergency loans to banks, corporations, and railroads. A few months later he added the Emergency Relief and Construction Act (ERCA), which provided loans to states and communities for public works. But it had so many restrictions that it proved of little use. By the time Roosevelt was elected, ERCA had spent only $20 million of the $1.6 billion appropriated.[7]

One genuine New Deal innovation was the introduction of "cooperative federalism," whereby the federal government took direct responsibility for solving problems in the states and cities. Prior to the New Deal, local, state, and federal governments had essentially gone their own way, in what was called "dual federalism." Between 1931 and 1938, the number of federal grant programs doubled. Many of these grants went directly to local governments. Some have called this a "defining moment" in American history, and though it brought a significant expansion of the federal government, it was also a de-centralizing effort because local governments played major roles in these programs and had considerable authority within them.[8]

Another reason why there was never a monolithic New Deal was Roosevelt's administrative style. The president liked not only to delegate considerable authority to those running his programs but also to encourage some competition and overlap in organization. He tried "to create a planetary system wherein many would have a place in the sun."[9] Roosevelt learned from watching the clashes in his cabinet. He also believed that "too much emphasis on rigid organization and channels of responsibility might have suffocated the freshness and vitality he loved."[10] The structure of major New Deal programs differed greatly, as did the personalities and philosophies of their administrators.

The Civilian Conservation Corps (CCC), the first of the New Deal public building agencies, was a marvel of synergy and organizational improvisation. It addressed two huge problems simultaneously: the cumulative destruction of farmland and forest and the likely destruction of jobless young men with minimal education, few skills, starving families, and plenty of time on their hands for criminal pursuits. Roosevelt patched together four cabinet departments—Labor, Interior, Agriculture, and War—and created the most popular program in the entire New Deal. Held together by a modest and diplomatic labor negotiator, Robert Fechner, the CCC fought forest fires and soil erosion and built a vast array of state and national parks, while transforming the lives of the "boys" who labored under its banner.[11]

Harry Hopkins, the spark plug behind first the Federal Emergency Relief Administration, next the Civil Works Administration, and later the Works Progress Administration (WPA), was concerned first and foremost with getting people fed and clothed. He spent appropriations as fast as he could, did business by telephone and telegraph because printing policies took too long, kept tabs on his far-flung operations by personal reports from roving emissaries, and made compromises with politicians he disapproved of as long as the job got done. The WPA concentrated on smaller, more labor-intensive projects in order to employ more people (and more unskilled people) than the Public Works Administration (PWA) was able to do. It did, however, execute some large and impressive projects, like Parker Coliseum at Louisiana State University (LSU). Hopkins's attitude toward planning might be summed up in his famous reply to someone who proposed a complicated project that would work out "in the long run": "People don't eat in the long run," he said, "they eat every day."[12]

Rex Tugwell, on the other hand, believed that human and natural resources could be far better used if some rational planning could be brought to bear. He cherished the idea of cooperation but thought that people had to be taught how to do it. He had the participants in his Resettlement Administration farm communities and suburban "new towns" carefully screened, and assigned managers to help them plan their budgets and work their land. This desire for control was intrusive enough to inspire a comparison between his efforts and Mussolini's. When problems arose, particularly in the farm communities, that might be ascribed to bad planning, his successors in the Farm Security Administration (FSA) were inclined to place blame on the stubborn, ornery farmers. Despite this, both the farms and the new towns were much more successful than the FSA or its critics realized.[13]

The Tennessee Valley Authority (TVA) was, like the CCC, another organizational anomaly, led by not one but three dynamic personalities. A. E. Morgan, the first of the triumvirate, was a civil engineer full of visionary ideas for planned communities and the preservation of mountain

Parker Coliseum, Louisiana State University. An unusually large project for the WPA.

crafts, as well as for the construction of massive hydroelectric and flood control projects. David Lilienthal was a public utilities lawyer, master publicist, and field general of the administration's campaign for public power. Harcourt Morgan, an agricultural school dean, was also well connected in local politics. Lilienthal and Harcourt Morgan regarded A. E. Morgan as a crackpot. He, in turn, tried to get Congress to charge them with corruption. Ultimately, Roosevelt had to fire him. Yet the three men managed, together and separately, to revolutionize an entire watershed, bringing electricity to farms and cities, eliminating disastrous floods, greatly extending river navigation, conserving farm and forest land, developing recreation, conducting research, nurturing new industries, inspiring modern architects, and providing an unimagined market for electric appliances. Of the New Deal agencies discussed here, the TVA is the only one still in existence.[14]

As all of these programs were doing very concrete things with dirt, stone, steel, and cement, another thrust of the New Deal was in the abstract world of finance. "State capitalism" was the belief that markets could be built and the economy rescued by the strategic investment of public funds. With banks stabilized and protected by the Federal Deposit Insurance Corporation, they could be encouraged to pump new capital into the economy. This hope of reviving private investment was only minimally successful, but state capitalism succeeded hugely in replacing it. Leading the way was Jesse Jones, head of the revived RFC. State capitalists saw a key part of the economic crisis in the confinement of capital to the Northeast, and wanted to put it to work in the West and South. Jones, a Texan, planted thirteen of the thirty-one RFC field offices in the South.[15]

These New Dealers, among other things, "sought to make Americans and capitalists everywhere more creative by using public capital to capture and tame the power of rivers and thereby create a demand for refrigerators, milking machines, aluminum, aircraft and atomic energy for even more power and more growth."[16] Thus the abstract reached the concrete with the TVA and the gigantic power projects developed by the PWA in the West, most dramatically Boulder (later Hoover) Dam. Though Jones is not as well known as Hopkins, Fechner, Tugwell, or Harold Ickes, his behind-the-scenes influence as head of the RFC, as well as the Federal National Mortgage Association (Fanny Mae), the Electrical Home and Farm Authority, the Commodity Credit Corporation, the Import-Export Bank, the Federal Housing Administration, and the Home Owners Loan Corporation, may have equaled theirs in redirecting the economy toward growth and prosperity.

Harold Ickes, the PWA's administrator, shared with Tugwell a belief in careful planning and a desire for central control, but his planning was more circumspect, rarely going beyond particular projects, and his control was focused on ensuring that projects were soundly, honestly, and efficiently executed. He did not tell local communities what they should build or how it should look. He did not intrude into the lives of those using the projects. Although three of the proposed six criteria for project approval were "social desirability," "economic desirability," and "relationship to coordinated planning," they were never used. Legal, financial, and engineering soundness, the other three, were the important measures. In practice, the PWA was inclined to "assume that every *bona fide* proposal was for a project that would supply a useful piece of equipment to the community, relieve unemployment, and constitute a desirable local improvement."[17] Of all the New Deal agencies, the PWA embodied arguably the best integration of local initiative and federal oversight. It erected thousands of structures nationwide, including 1,085 in communities that had never had a federal building of any kind. The Treasury Department, which in normal times had primary responsibility for public buildings, found itself in control of twice as many buildings as it had prior to the activities of the PWA.[18]

The New Deal assault on the Depression was thus made up of many arms and legs punching and kicking, with many heads shouting or whispering but rarely talking with one another. And the assault was supported or obstructed by an equal variety of local organizations and individuals. As we will see, New Deal activities in Louisiana became enmeshed in Senator Huey Long's struggles with his opponents and, increasingly, with the Roosevelt administration. Georgia's governor Eugene Talmadge was a similar impediment, while Alabama's Lister Hill, Florida's Claude Pepper, and a young Lyndon Johnson in Texas were stalwart supporters. Thus "there was no generic New Deal affecting all communities, states, and regions equally, rather the collision between national laws and local conditions determined the degree of change."[19]

There are, however, certain things peculiar to the South as a region that influenced the New Deal's impact on it; chief among these was the legacy of its pre–Civil War plantation-based economy and its dependence on slavery. This caused particular problems for the New Deal's various attempts to stimulate economic development in the South. Both production and consumption were weaker than in other regions.

Southerners did appreciate that economic development required infrastructure, and since local entrepreneurs were providing it only sporadically in the 1920s, they turned to government. States began major highway and electrical power projects. They were slower to appreciate that health and education were important infrastructural components of economic development as well. However, because states were increasingly receptive to federal government aid, they could recognize the opportunities that the New Deal programs provided to improve both their physical and cultural infrastructure.[20]

The closest the New Deal came to a comprehensive plan for the economic development of the southern states came in its 1938 "Report on Economic Conditions of the South." Created to help understand and deal with the fact that the conditions of poverty afflicting the nation were even worse in the South, the report was also an attempt to mobilize southern voters in support of the New Deal in the upcoming election and to manifest this support by voting out of office some of the major opponents of New Deal legislation.

The South's plantation economy had inherent structural deficits that obstructed economic development. These deficits were still salient in the 1930s. Plantations had depended on outsiders for nonagricultural needs, used cities mainly as connections to their distant markets, and generally stunted the growth of trade within the region. The fact that most of the workforce was enslaved deprived the South of another economic engine: consumption. When industrialization did begin, it was in areas like cotton textiles, which were already well established elsewhere. This not only meant that southerners faced stiff competition but also that, once again, the South was dependent on outsiders for basic needs: machinery, design, marketing, and finance. The last factor was particularly important to further development. Plantation economics did not have much of a place for venture capitalists. What capital there was came from family and friends, who were likely to want a safe return on investment, not a high-risk adventure. Southern industrialism also tried to compete with the North by offering cheaper labor. Though its workforce was no longer enslaved, it was still largely impoverished. Deliberately keeping industrial wages down perpetuated the problem of underconsumption.[21]

Another blow to consumption was the plight of farm workers. Roosevelt had campaigned on the issue of chronic rural poverty, and his effort at agricultural reform was the Agricultural Adjustment Act, which aimed to stabilize farm prices by controlling supply.[22] It was a mixed blessing for the South. Landowners were paid to curtail production and were compensated for lost income. This money was also intended to help the sharecroppers and tenant farmers who worked the land. The landowners' response, however, was to send the sharecroppers and tenants packing and buy tractors, thus exacerbating the already crushing problems of resettlement and poverty.[23]

Because of the southern economy's grounding in the extraction of natural resources and its reliance on outside sources for most of the infrastructure of capitalism, some analysts saw it as caught in a kind of colonialism. This explanation had a certain amount of truth to it, but it also served to channel southern resentment of the North and obscure the contributions southerners themselves might have made to the situation.[24]

Even though the various programs that would help the South develop infrastructure were already well at work by 1938, the "Report on Economic Conditions of the South" made no attempt to weave them into its analysis or recommendations but did touch on a variety of problems that these agencies were addressing. It noted that water pollution was not only a public health threat but also a deterrent to the development of recreation and industry. It promised great commercial benefits from the hydroelectric potential in the region's rivers. It pointed out that many areas lacked the most basic school facilities. But the possibility of solving the problems of poverty and underconsumption through massive injections of human capital investment is never explicitly mentioned in the report.[25]

The president's introduction to the report declared that the South's economic plight was a problem not just for the region but for the entire nation as well. An economic imbalance existed between the North and South that must be set right in order for the nation to prosper. The report adopted to some extent the colonial analogy, which might have appealed to southerners and allowed the president to make common cause with them against their traditional enemies, the northern bankers and railroads. Instead, however, the report stirred up southerners' resentment at being made a public spectacle by outsiders. The attempt to purge the anti–New Deal congressmen in the 1938 election failed completely, and the report was pushed aside.[26]

The lack of a comprehensive New Deal plan to rebuild southern communities or provide the infrastructure to bring the South into the national economy nonetheless did not prevent the New Deal from doing just that. The CCC helped restore the timber industry to its status as the region's number one cash crop by planting millions of trees and encouraging private and public conservation efforts and federal protection of forests.[27] The WPA went on building schools and sidewalks. The Resettlement Administration created new communities and enabled farmers to own their own land. The RFC continued pushing state capital investment.

Moreover, the PWA went on transforming Louisiana and the rest of the nation with enduring community assets. Harold Ickes knew that his first job was to revive the economy and relieve unemployment, but he also appreciated the value of these projects as long-range public investment. For example, his own account of the PWA shows the connections between simple components of physical infrastructure like roads and larger economic and social development issues. Roads allow school consolidation, bring in tourists, get people to libraries and hospitals. He observed in 1935, when the PWA was only two years old and had seven more to run: "Each dollar spent will not only return many times its value in immediate benefits through the lessening of unemployment and the supply of some community need; it will continue to pay incalculable social dividends to generations of Americans still unborn."[28]

CHAPTER 2

HAROLD ICKES GOES TO WORK

The personality of Harold Leclair Ickes dominated the Public Works Administration (PWA). A good clue to that personality is the fact that he titled his published memoirs *The Autobiography of a Curmudgeon*.[1] He prized his independence, guarded his integrity, and loved a good fight. He grew up a Republican in Altoona, Pennsylvania, and moved as a young man to the bare-knuckle, largely Democratic city of Chicago. Young Harold was a reformer and a believer in honest government. He could not approve of the graft and corruption that were a central part of the urban political machine. But the Chicago Republican Party was rarely the party of reform. Many of its members had their own stake in the status quo. The reformers in its midst were frequently defeated or double-crossed in primaries.[2]

The principal Republican reformer was Charles Merriam, a young University of Chicago political science professor. Ickes had organized Merriam's successful campaign for city council in 1909 and tried unsuccessfully for a position himself the following year. In 1911 he headed Merriam's bid for mayor. Merriam won the Republican nomination but lost to the Democrat because of weak support from his own party.[3]

Ickes's law career also allowed him the chance to crusade for reform and champion underdogs. Early one morning in 1908, an eighteen-year-old Russian Jew was shot by the Chicago chief of police. The chief claimed it was in response to an assassination attempt. The newspapers called for the banishment of anarchists, most of whom were assumed to be Jewish, and the police began raiding suspected Jewish anarchists' hangouts. Jane Addams, head of the Hull House settlement, called a meeting to find ways to quell the panic. She wanted a lawyer to represent the dead boy's sister at the inquest. All those at the meeting refused; Ickes accepted. He had the body exhumed and a second autopsy performed. He discovered that the coroner had not only mishandled evidence, failing to notice, for example, that the alleged assailant had a bullet hole in his back, but also that the boy's brain had been removed and taken away for study. Ickes threatened to make this public if the authorities did not call off the anarchist hunt. His actions, his biographer T. H. Watkins believes, prevented a dangerous anti-Semitic hysteria from dividing the city. Ickes's own conclusion about the cause of the incident was that the chief had been drunk and fired without provocation.[4]

In 1911 Ickes once again came to the aid of Hull House, which had joined with the Women's Trade Union League in defense of seamstresses on strike against sweatshop conditions at the factory of the famous clothier Hart, Shafner, and Marks. Ickes's wife, Anna, joined the picket line. The police were rough in arresting immigrant women pickets but avoided the upper-class supporters until one day when they picked up Addams's friend Ellen Gates Starr. Addams asked Ickes to defend Starr, who was charged with assaulting a police officer. Ickes had the alleged victim, a "hulking clod of a policemen," stand beside the diminutive Starr. The courtroom burst out laughing, and the case was over.[5]

Other minority groups received Ickes's support. He was briefly (1922–1924) president of the Chicago branch of the National Association for the Advancement of Colored People (NAACP) and worked for antilynching legislation, but found both black and white members of the NAACP discouragingly passive. He also developed a strong interest in the rights of Native peoples. Because of his wife's asthma, they had built a small adobe house in New Mexico near the Navajo Reservation in 1916. This led to meeting John Collier, an advocate for the Pueblo Indians who was to become commissioner of Indian affairs during the New Deal. Ickes became involved with Collier in a fight with white ranchers over Native water rights and was a board member of the American Indian Defense Association. Though Ickes's politics remained focused on Chicago during the 1920s, he and his wife continued their involvement in American Indian rights.[6]

Thus, as Ickes gained experience campaigning for and managing Republican reform candidates in the first decades of the century, he was also establishing connections with a growing number of people, known as Progressives, who stood outside both parties. The Progressives were predominately middle-class citizens who were increasingly disturbed by the excesses of the "robber barons" of American industrialism. They saw this new wealth corrupting the political system as much or more than the machines of the big-city bosses. Many Progressives were from the West, where they could easily see the exploitation and ruin of the nation's natural resources by large corporations. They also responded sympathetically to the miserable living conditions of the urban poor. To get control of these growing problems, they looked for strong leaders and a stronger central government.

Theodore Roosevelt was a vigorous leader who shared many of the Progressives' concerns. He championed conservation, opposed business monopolies, and espoused a strong central government. Elected vice president in 1900, he assumed the presidency the following year when William McKinley was assassinated. He was elected president in 1904 and worked to get William Howard Taft the Republican nomination in 1908. Roosevelt expected Taft to continue his policies, but Taft instead became allied with the conservatives in the party. Roosevelt challenged him at the Republican Convention in 1912 and lost. He walked out of the convention to make an independent race for the presidency. The Progressives became his base and Harold Ickes his enthusiastic supporter.[7]

When Roosevelt arrived at the hastily convened Progressive Convention, he proclaimed himself as strong as a bull moose, so the Progressive Party quickly became known as the Bull Moose Party. The name, as well as the principles the party espoused, fit Ickes. Though short, Ickes was sturdily built and had a bellow that could shake the trees of any bureaucracy.

Teddy Roosevelt defeated Taft, his Republican opponent, but both were swamped by Democrat Woodrow Wilson. The Progressives nominated Roosevelt again in 1916, but he refused to run. Ickes returned to the Republican fold after the Progressives dissolved as a third party. During the First World War, Ickes, an ardent patriot but unacceptable for military service because of a damaged inner ear, managed to get to France as a YMCA administrator. He enjoyed the fevered activity and sense of purpose, and was most reluctant to return home when the fighting was over. The political landscape in America after the war was increasingly distasteful. Teddy Roosevelt was dead, the Progressives were scattered, and Ickes could find no worthy leaders in either major party. He supported Republican Charles Evans Hughes in 1920 but could not stomach Warren G.

Harding. Robert La Follette tried to reignite the Progressive Party, but Ickes thought he had moved too far from Roosevelt. In 1924 Ickes reluctantly supported the Democrat John W. Davis for president.[8]

During the war, a friend had invited Ickes to lunch with Herbert Hoover. Hoover ignored him, a snub Ickes never forgot. He voted for Hoover's opponent, Al Smith, in the presidential election of 1928. By now, being on the losing side was almost a habit. When the Depression hit, Ickes saw Hoover's response as largely rhetorical and "particularly wanting in qualities of leadership." He tried earnestly to get one of the old Progressives like Hiram Johnson to run against Hoover in 1932; he supported Gifford Pinchot, who soon dropped out. So Ickes was once again ready to vote for a Democrat. But this time it was not in the spirit of the lesser of two (or three) evils. He was "head over heals for the nomination of Franklin D. Roosevelt."[9] He had found a man with the strength and vision to battle the Great Depression.

Ickes was asked to organize a Western Independent Republican Committee for Roosevelt. He accepted, even though his wife was now seeking reelection to the Illinois legislature as a regular Republican. He told her that no one would be surprised; he had always been a "wobbly Republican."[10]

Ickes's campaign efforts on Roosevelt's behalf, his credentials as a leader of a revitalized constituency in American politics, and his experience as an organizer qualified him for a role of some kind in the new administration. His first thought was to seek to become the commissioner of Indian affairs; he still had a home in New Mexico and had fought for Native American rights for many years. But he decided to set his sights higher: secretary of the interior. A cabinet post was a long shot, but FDR was looking for a western Progressive to fill the post. When Senators Hiram Johnson and Bronson Cutting declined, Ickes became a reasonable choice. Ickes had established interests in conservation and hydroelectric power as well as Indian affairs. He was a good organizer and administrator, and he was a certifiable workaholic before the term had been invented. His loyalties, as amply demonstrated by his political career, were to people and principles, not party. Roosevelt had never met Ickes, but he sized him up quickly and gave him the job. An avid sailor, Roosevelt explained to adviser Raymond Moley: "I liked the cut of his jib."[11]

As secretary of the interior, Ickes wasted no time in putting his principles into practice. He was the first cabinet officer to de-segregate the public facilities of his department, he appointed African American advisers, and he tried hard to establish and enforce nondiscrimination in employment. This does not mean that Interior or the PWA was free of racism, but it does set him apart from most public officials of his day. In fact, in the eyes of one biographer, Ickes "did more to further the rights of minorities than any other official in the administration." Historian Harvard Sitkoff agrees, noting that "the totality of money spent on blacks by PWA was a quantum leap in . . . comparison to anything previously appropriated by public or private agencies."[12]

Interior was a large department with a wide variety of responsibilities. Its secretary did not need another job, particularly something as complicated and risky as the PWA. But Ickes soon proved himself one of the ablest of New Deal administrators. He earned Roosevelt's confidence and was entrusted with such a variety of responsibilities that he became known as "Secretary of Things in General."[13] Probably the most important of these extra assignments was to be named administrator of the PWA.

The PWA was not the first New Deal agency created to combat the Depression using public works. The Civilian Conservation Corps (CCC) has that distinction. Created March 31, 1933, the CCC was designed to provide useful employment for young men aged seventeen to twenty-five. The CCC workers sent most of their wages home to their struggling families. The "boys," as they were commonly referred to and as they still call themselves,[14] were organized in companies of 200 and put to work planting trees, stopping soil erosion, fighting forest fires, and building rural roads and bridges. Thus their accomplishments were usually not visible to the average citizen, but their record of public building, particularly in state and national parks, is as impressive and enduring as any New Deal agency.

The PWA followed the CCC a few months later. It was created by Title II of the National Industrial Recovery Act (NIRA).[15] Title I created the National Recovery Administration (NRA), which was to organize the heads of American industry and labor to adopt and enforce codes of uniform wage and price standards that would ensure the cooperation of producers, workers, and consumers in the effort to revive the stalled economy. Title II would give the economy something to do immediately: public works. Roosevelt was convinced that the two components were inseparable.[16] This may have been so in the beginning, but it did not prove so for long.

Inspired by the experience of the War Production Board during World

War I, which had successfully brought government coordination to the stimulation of defense industries, the NRA received the support of many industrialists, such as Gerald Swope of General Electric. The wage and price codes were devised in the major sectors of the economy, and a popular campaign to enforce them was adopted. The NRA's symbol was a blue eagle, and its motto was "We do our part." The logo was displayed prominently on products and in stores and factories. But widespread support did not materialize, and noncompliance was common. "Free traders fought with protectionists, big firms battled smaller competitors; buyers collided with suppliers. The result was chaos."[17] Apart from a wartime emergency situation, America had no experience with this kind of corporatist cooperation and no state capacity to carry it off.[18] When the Supreme Court declared the NRA unconstitutional on January 1, 1936, on the grounds that the agency had no authority to regulate interstate commerce, there was no attempt to revive it.

Title II of the NIRA, the PWA had the opposite experience. Though it, too, was an enterprise with no precedent, it moved resolutely through the decade to accomplish its purpose. The agency it created was called the Federal Emergency Administration for Public Works, and the plaques on the structures it built usually bear this name; but in popular discourse and even in its own paperwork it was always known as the PWA.

The PWA was a public jobs program. People who were out of work might have been saved from starvation through direct relief payments, which was known as "the dole" at that time and more recently as "welfare." This would have been cheaper in the short run. But New Deal strategists preferred publicly created jobs to keep workers going until the private job market recovered. There were several reasons for this. One was that direct relief would only stimulate consumption. Families would buy food, clothing, and other essentials. But early New Deal thinking placed more emphasis on the stimulation of production. The production of building materials was a good beginning. Another reason for preferring work to relief was the belief that it was better for national morale. Being out of work was humiliating. Honest work would restore a person's self-confidence as well as help the individual maintain and develop skills.[19]

The PWA was not a "work relief" program like the later WPA. Such programs required that participants be unemployed and qualified for direct relief. Applicants were also subjected to home visits by social workers to determine what they needed to survive. In contrast, you didn't have to be unemployed to work for the PWA. You were not subjected to a means test, and you were paid a regular wage, not one pegged to subsistence. Work relief programs were often stigmatized as "make work" efforts. This implied that their projects were not have ordinarily been undertaken. The distinction, however, was more ideological than practical. Both the PWA and the WPA did things of enduring benefit to the nation.

The PWA was guided through its infancy by a Special Board for Public Works consisting of the secretaries of war, agriculture, treasury, commerce, labor, and interior; the director of the Bureau of the Budget; and the attorney general. Ickes chaired the board, which met once a week. Congress had given it $3.3 billion to work with, a staggering amount of money, understandable only in the context of the desperation of the times. Ickes was duly impressed by the enormity of the responsibility entrusted to the board. To help him grasp the reality of the numbers, he came up with this image: he could drive a fleet of trucks across the country, shovel out a million dollars at each milepost, and still have enough money to build a fleet of battleships when he reached the coast.[20]

First call on the money was naturally given to federal agencies that already had machinery in place for building public works. Treasury's Public Buildings Administration was used to erect post offices and other structures. The Bureau of Public Roads could put people to work immediately on labor-intensive projects. The army and navy, with the prospect of war just over both east and west horizons, badly needed ships and planes and better support facilities.

But there were other, "nonfederal" projects that could be also started immediately. The federal/nonfederal categorization came from PWA temporary administrator Colonel Donald Sawyer's early filing system. Everything that didn't apply to the federal agencies got labeled "nonfederal." But the omnibus notation stayed in use even after the nonfederal side of the PWA ballooned.

The first nonfederal proposals were water and sewerage projects that had been submitted to the Reconstruction Finance Corporation during the last days of the Hoover administration. As the Depression deepened, Hoover had realized that public works might be a useful antidote. But he had insisted that to be worthy of federal loans, projects had to be "self-liquidating." That meant that they had to pay for themselves. Since you could bill consumers for water and sewer services, such facilities could qualify. Schools couldn't.[21]

Water projects therefore didn't have to be solicited; they were already in the pipeline for pipelines, and the hastily organized staff of the PWA got busy reviewing them. But within the Special Board, there was a debate under way about how much of the appropriation, if any, should be spent on nonfederal projects. Rex Tugwell, representing the Department of Agriculture, was content to concentrate on federal projects, believing that work was work and it didn't matter where it was done. Secretary of Labor Frances Perkins argued that it was better to employ workers on projects that would have a direct effect on the quality of life in their own communities than on, say, army bases they would never inhabit. Why not improve the quality of health or education in the process of keeping workers from starvation? Perkins won the argument, probably not realizing she was transforming the face of America.[22]

States, municipalities, and other political subdivisions such as school boards were invited to submit proposals. In order to prevent a deluge of proposals from raining on Washington, a state and regional structure was needed. A state engineer and a three-person advisory board were appointed in each state. They reviewed the applications and passed them on to Washington with a thumbs up or down recommendation. A grant of 30 percent of labor and costs would be made available to states, municipalities, or other community bodies like school boards. If the makers of the proposals, called "owners" in PWA contracts, could not come up with the remaining 70 percent, the PWA would loan it to them. This was adjusted in 1935 to a 45/55 split of total costs, though by that time most contracts were for grants only. By then, communities had reestablished their credit by paying off earlier PWA loans and were now attractive to local private lenders.[23]

After much debate on the criteria to be used in approving nonfederal projects, the board settled on a bottom line of three essentials: the project had to be legally, financially, and structurally sound. Matters of social desirability or appropriateness to local or regional planning would be left to the community. This tripartite standard dictated the creation of the Legal, Finance, and Engineering divisions within the PWA.[24]

There was also a concern for connecting projects as much as possible with areas with the highest concentrations of unemployment and with having an even geographic distribution of projects. No formulae were ever worked out for this. There was generally enough unemployment to go around, so any project was probably needed for relief. Since the PWA was under constant pressure to get to work as quickly as possible, it was difficult to justify slowing down states and communities that were organized well enough just for the sake of getting projects into less well organized communities with higher unemployment rates.

The Special Board members had a number of important policy issues to confront. How would they recruit workers? They decided to give union locals first crack but created a United States Employment Service to provide workers if unions couldn't staff approved projects within twenty-four hours. The board had to decide what standards there would be, if any, for the wages to be paid. It set minimums for skilled and unskilled work broken down by three geographic regions and created the Board of Labor Review to arbitrate disputes. It wanted to give preference to unemployed workers, so that it wouldn't just be shifting people from one job to another, but it also had to decide whether to give preference to local workers, union workers, and veterans. It agreed on such preferences in roughly that order. Racial discrimination was forbidden but hard to enforce.[25]

The Special Board also had to decide how stringent to be in its demands for local participation in the financing of the nonfederal projects, since the NIRA gave the president considerable leeway on this. Assistant Secretary of the Treasury Lawrence Robert reminded the board that banking theory and practice sometimes diverged, and bankers commonly gave loans to businesses without adequate security simply because the bank was already in too deeply to cut loose. This, he said, was not unlike the position of the president, whose first concern was the survival of communities, not just ensuring a return on investment. Moreover, like the bank, he got no return if the enterprise went under. Nonetheless, the board decided that it would insist on obligating communities to secure their loans. This might require a special bond election but, if so, would probably not slow down the projects much.[26]

The board had to set the interest rate on the loans. The compromise arrived at was 4 percent. This was thought high enough that communities that were doing well financially would continue to seek normal bank financing, but not so high as to discourage struggling communities from making a proposal.

Most important to Ickes, and probably to the political and historical fate of the program, was the issue of how careful to be in the disbursement of funds. The board was in a hurry. Board members knew mistakes would be made. But they also knew that the faster they moved, the easier it would be for local officials, contractors, labor leaders, and businessmen to get an illegal cut of the action. Municipal graft was a familiar component in American politics. Bribes, kickbacks, collusion by contractors in bidding, invoice padding, theft of materials, substitution of cheaper components for those specified, lax bookkeeping, sloppy construction, and other kinds of manipulations from simple corner cutting to bold-faced fraud were all associated with public works to different extents in most communities. Would the PWA be faulted for ignoring these threats and going swiftly forward with no more protection than crossed fingers?

Raymond Moley, who was fairly conservative when it came to fiscal matters, took the view that "public works, if they were going to do any good, should be got under way with incredible speed—even at the risk of inefficiency and perhaps occasional dishonesty." Ickes and the board, however, were not inclined to compromise on honesty in the interests of speed. Assistant Secretary Robert pointed out that citizens would be far less likely to vote for bond issues if they thought a portion of their taxes would be raked off in graft. But such tactical considerations were secondary influences on Ickes. His entire political career had been a crusade for honest government. This was reinforced, if any reinforcement were necessary, by his awareness that the Interior Department had been under a cloud since its secretary, Albert Fall, had in 1922 accepted $400,000 from two of his friends, heads of major oil companies, for allowing them to drill on public land. One of the sites, Teapot Dome, gave its name to the scandal. Ickes was determined to restore the department's reputation and maintain his own as "Honest Harold." Though he claimed to despise the nickname, it was politically useful, and he was too canny not to appreciate this.[27]

To help avoid any potential problems, Ickes created two more divisions of the PWA: Inspection and Investigations. Inspection would involve not only PWA oversight from Washington but also a resident engineer-inspector (REI) on each job site. The position of the REI was not an easy one. His salary came out of the project's budget, but he was responsible to the PWA, not the owner.[28] He was on the site almost every day, interacting with the contractor and the project's laborers. It might be easy to sympathize with their pressures working against deadlines and bad weather. It might be easy to accept favors from the contractor or the owner in order to look the other way when some corner was being cut.

When the Cameron Parish courthouse was being built, REI P. M.

Davis reported that contractor A. Farnell Blair asked what it would take for Davis to "go fishing every day and spend more time on the river and less inspecting his work." Would he like a new $600 boat to put his outboard motor on? Davis declined and reported the bribery attempt.[29] This, of course, made his task of supervision all the more difficult. Miles Hutson, the REI on the Shreveport fire alarm project, may have been less stalwart in resisting temptation. He was suspected of having "improper social relations" with the engineer Edward Brass and contractor John Maple, which resulted in his failure to report false invoices Maple submitted with Brass's knowledge. He was charged with "obvious laxness and inefficiency," but not with a criminal offense. He resigned.[30]

The REIs were men with experience as engineers, contractors, or even architects. This in itself might lead to friction with the contractors. The REIs had their own ways of doing things and sometimes found it hard to restrain themselves from taking over the job. One was described charitably as "almost too helpful."[31]

The Investigations Division was headed by Louis Glavis, who had been fired when he exposed an attempt by Taft's secretary of the interior, Richard Ballinger, to sell land in national forests to a private coal-mining syndicate. This made Glavis Ickes's kind of man.[32] The division employed engineers, accountants, and private investigators as special agents to probe any accusation of misconduct or malfeasance on a PWA project. Many project files have a Confidential Investigation section, which includes the charges and all depositions and exhibits produced by the special agents. Sometimes the allegations were groundless, made by unsuccessful bidders, disgruntled employees, scam artists, or political opponents. Sometimes they arose from simple misunderstanding of PWA regulations or careless bookkeeping. Sometimes there was evidence of intent to defraud. Depending on the seriousness of the infraction, the PWA could decide to withhold payment until the discrepancies were cleared up. It could also initiate court proceedings, though it usually managed to resolve problems before this was necessary.

After project proposals were sent by state engineers to Washington, they were logged in by the Projects Division, and copies were sent to the Engineering, Finance, and Legal divisions. Those surviving this triple gauntlet were forwarded by the Projects Division to Ickes, who took them to the Special Board and then on to the president. When nonfederal projects were first logged in, they were numbered sequentially and given a two-letter prefix to designate the state of origin. By April 1935, the end of four digits was approaching, so the PWA decided to start over. From that point, numbering was sequential within each state, starting with 1000. The highest completed docket in Louisiana was #1317, a school in Jennings. Most states did not get far into the 1300s. Trusting Ickes's thoroughness, the Special Board routinely approved the projects that reached it. But the president was no rubber stamp. He would disapprove or hold up a project and sometimes green-light projects that had not been approved by the PWA divisions.[33]

Once it became known that new projects might be proposed, there was no lack of new ideas for spending. "A mayor in the Middle West wanted to redecorate his office; a telegram from a promoter urged construction, at the cost of twenty billion dollars, of a moving road, something like an escalator, from New York to San Francisco, along which were to be built drug stores, theaters, churches, etc; a preacher in Kansas wanted money to buy Bibles for his congregation." A passenger rocket to the moon was proposed.[34]

The first wave of proposals included the practical as well as the visionary. But they were not always well thought out. A maternity hospital, alleged to be self-liquidating, could have paid for itself only if every woman in town would have a baby every year for the next twenty years. A graveyard could have been liquidated only if the town proposing it was also: all of the town's residents would have to die within seventeen years.[35]

On July 8, 1933, Roosevelt appointed Ickes administrator of the PWA. As chair of the Special Board, Ickes had exerted considerable influence on the policies of the new agency, but he didn't believe it could move forward confidently with a temporary head. He expressed surprise at the choice, but no reluctance to get going. He appointed Colonel Henry Waite, an engineer who had been city manager of Dayton, Ohio, and supervisor of construction for the new Union railroad terminal in Cincinnati, as his deputy and began moving personnel into the Interior Department.[36]

Organizing and staffing the new agency were the first challenges. As was typical under Roosevelt, several groups had begun drafting plans for the new agency. Several embryo staff rosters and no less than four tables of organization had been prepared. Other people had been expecting to be appointed administrator, including General Hugh Johnson, head of the NRA. Johnson had gone so far as to have drafted telegrams to people he wanted to appoint. According to Secretary of Labor Frances Perkins, when

Roosevelt told Johnson that he was giving the position to Ickes, Johnson turned "red, then dark red, then purplish." Roosevelt told Perkins to stick with Johnson after the meeting broke up. She drove him around Washington for an hour while he calmed down.[37] Ickes put together a structure to his liking and put the PWA in high gear.

Ickes's definition of "high gear," however, was not fast enough for some people. Large public works projects require planning, the assembly of heavy equipment, and the procurement of materials like stone and steel that can't be picked up at the corner store. Indeed, the need for such materials was one of the economic arguments for the PWA's existence. It was not just going to put people to work at a job site, but it would also enable suppliers of raw materials, manufacturers, and distributors to recall laid-off workers and get cracking to supply the contractors. This ripple or multiplier would "prime the pump" enough, the New Dealers hoped, to revive the economy. No immediate payoff could be expected. Of course, this didn't stop observers inside and outside the administration from wanting one. The PWA was under pressure from the beginning.

Another reason why the PWA could not start immediately with nonfederal projects was the decision of the Special Board members to look carefully at the legal and financial ability of localities to accept and repay loans. Some thought they looked too carefully. Said one critic, "They're trying to run a fire department [like] a conservative bond house."[38]

Ickes contributed to the deliberate pace of approval by insisting that he had to sign off on every project before it went to the president. He expected the Legal, Finance, and Engineering divisions to be very thorough in their review of proposals. To find out how thorough they were, he prepared a fake proposal into which he inserted a large section of text from *Alice in Wonderland*. When all three divisions approved the proposal without noticing the participation of characters like the Mad Hatter, Ickes raised the roof. He was determined that no one could accuse the PWA of misusing the taxpayers' money.[39]

This fierce guarding of the PWA's reputation, with its corps of REIs, its vigilant Investigations Division, and its careful review of proposals, would pay off by the end of the decade; when other agencies like the WPA were tainted with scandal, the PWA emerged unscathed.[40] But in the short term, the carefulness of the PWA and the delayed impact on the economy that resulted cost the agency some of its appropriations.

When it became clear that the combined efforts of the PWA and the

CCC could not pull enough people, particularly unskilled ones, out of unemployment fast enough to relieve the misery of the Depression, Roosevelt had to add other measures of relief. As the winter of 1933 approached, he created the Civil Works Administration (CWA), a federal employment program to provide work for men and women at all skill levels. It looked particularly for projects like road building that were labor intensive and required minimal skills and equipment. With Ickes's blessing, Roosevelt diverted money from the PWA to fund the CWA. For four and a half months the CWA put four million people to work. The program was ended in the spring of 1934, but served as a dress rehearsal for the WPA, created in May 1935.[41]

Roosevelt pulled the plug on the CWA because of its great expense and because he thought the recovery had begun. By early 1935, it was clear that it hadn't and that another large works program was needed. The Emergency Relief Appropriations Act of 1935, which created the WPA, also gave the PWA a new appropriation of $900 million for nonfederal projects.[42] While the PWA and the WPA ran on parallel tracks, the main difference between them remained one of labor intensity and skill level. But the boundary was frequently blurred. Initially, there was an attempt to set a dividing line in dollars: the WPA would take on projects under $25,000, and the PWA would take on anything larger. This didn't work. Large projects could be subdivided into $25,000 units to get around the limit, so there was no further attempt to separate the agencies by cost of project. Many of the PWA's school projects were small. The home economics building at Kinder High School in Allen Parish, #1155, cost less than $10,000. On the other hand, some WPA buildings were quite ambitious from an engineering standpoint, requiring every bit as much planning, materials, heavy equipment, and skilled labor as a PWA project. Parker Coliseum on the Louisiana State University (LSU) campus, the largest domed structure in the South at the time, was built by the WPA.

Harry Hopkins, the head of the Federal Emergency Relief Administration, took charge of the WPA. He saw his responsibility as getting as many people employed as fast as possible, and he worried far less than Ickes about procedure and protection. The amount of local participation in WPA projects was flexible. It was usually under 20 percent and could be in-kind contributions of materials or labor.[43] Communities might have to put up far less than the 55 percent required by the PWA. To prevent "shopping around," Ickes made it clear that projects submitted to the PWA could not be withdrawn in hopes of a better deal from the WPA.

In 1939, when the PWA was winding down and had stopped taking on new projects, the PWA and the WPA were consolidated into the Federal Works Agency (FWA). Though the PWA continued to exist until 1942, its activities past 1939 consisted primarily of closing out the completed projects, settling disputes, and pursuing those who had tried to defraud the agency. At this point, some projects that had been approved were transferred to the WPA for construction. In Louisiana, there were at least fifteen such projects.[44]

The PWA had two other divisions that were important nationally but did not operate in Louisiana. One was a program for slum clearance and low-income housing construction. This was the first federal construction of public housing in peacetime. The Housing Division created fifty-five housing estates in thirty-nine cities across the country and funded eight more through a program inherited from the Hoover administration. Apartments had amenities like stoves and refrigerators that even middle-income housing often lacked. They were so well built that most of them, despite indifferent maintenance, are still in use. Almost half of them were built for African Americans. New Orleans submitted a proposal to the PWA's Housing Division, but it was not approved.[45]

A second branch of the PWA that did not operate in Louisiana was the Subsistence Homesteads Division. This was one of several efforts to resettle families forced off their farms by soil depletion and dust storms, "stranded workers" like miners whose employers had shut down and who had no other places to find work, and farmers who had come to cities and failed to find work there. The idea was that colonies of families located on the fringes of cities could be able to survive by a combination of growing some of their own food and having part-time work elsewhere. There were no subsistence homesteads in Louisiana, though there were farm communities founded by the Resettlement Administration in Terrebonne and East Carroll parishes.[46]

Debate continues on the contribution public works programs made to ending the Depression. Assessment is complicated by the overshadowing impact of the Second World War. Preparation for the war was increasing as the New Deal programs were closing down. However, there was considerable overlap as both the PWA and the WPA increased construction on military bases, warships, and airplanes. The CCC also worked on military bases toward the end of its life and, more important, trained and toughened thousands of young men to work with cooperation and discipline, an experience that made them invaluable as recruits in the armed services.

On the production side, stimulus to the economy was slow. On the consumption side, however, the stimulus was clearly significant. Although the combined efforts of all the public jobs programs did not come close to eliminating unemployment, these programs still provided incomes for millions of families who would otherwise have had none. The brief retail spurt after the creation of the CWA late in 1933, the depression of 1937 that hit after Roosevelt cut back the public works programs, and the recovery once they were restored show the importance of consumption to economic stimulus.[47] But whether or not these programs did anything to mitigate the effects of the Great Depression is less important than the fact that they made an enormous public investment in physical and cultural infrastructure and left behind community assets that have been paying dividends ever since.

CHAPTER 3

HUEY LONG VERSUS THE PWA

Huey Long was a figure without parallel in American political history. Between his election as governor of Louisiana in 1928 and his death in 1935, he amassed so much power in the state that it scared even him. He told associates that if he died suddenly, they should not attempt to use the power he had created. For two years he simultaneously held the offices of governor and U.S. senator. He was on the cover of *Time* twice in one year. As a candidate for president in 1936 he was taken quite seriously by Democratic strategists. James Farley, Franklin Roosevelt's campaign manager, estimated that Long might take three million votes away from the president and tip the balance of power. Raymond Moley, another of the president's advisers, said of Long, "I have never known a mind that moved with more clarity, decisiveness, and force."[1] If Long could pull enough votes away from Roosevelt, a Republican could win. The reaction to this might, in turn, create enough turmoil to sweep Long into office in 1940. It didn't happen. But what did happen was amazing enough.

Huey Pierce Long was remembered as a boy for his energy, curiosity, remarkable memory, and ability to sell anything to anybody. As a young man he once got a job as a stenographer despite the fact that he knew no shorthand. He simply remembered the letters dictated to him. He showed great promise selling Cottoleen, a cotton-seed cooking oil, door to door. He would quote the Bible in support of his product and, if necessary, march into the kitchen and bake a cake to demonstrate it. But the company was in trouble. Long survived one mass layoff, but was cut down by the next. He studied part-time at the Tulane University Law School, and in less than a year passed the bar examination.[2]

Like Harold Ickes's, Huey Long's early law practice was notable for his defense of underdogs. He took on what seemed to be the hopeless case of a widow making an insurance claim against a local bank. He dressed his client's children in rags and sat them in front of the jury. The bank settled. Long pioneered in gaining compensation for workers who were injured on the job. His underlying passion was not sales or law, however, it was politics. Before he was twenty, he told his bride-to-be that he would be governor, senator, and president. She said it gave her "cold chills." She was not the only one. In the words of his Pulitzer Prize–winning biographer, T. Harry Williams, Long aroused every emotion in the political spectrum, "amazement and admiration, disbelief and disgust, love and hatred, and, with many individuals, cold apprehension."[3]

Legally underage at twenty-three for most state offices, Long discovered that the Railroad Commission had no minimum age. The commission regulated other public utilities as well as railroads. He ran for commissioner, won, and spent the next six years limiting the power of utilities and improving services. He attracted enough attention thereby to mount a campaign for governor in 1923. He lost, but did surprisingly well for a thirty-year-old, particularly in the poorer parishes. He won in 1928 with the slogan "Every Man a King, But No One Wears a Crown." Instead of king, Long crowned himself "Kingfish of the Lodge" after a character in the popular radio program *Amos and Andy*.[4]

Huey Long's campaign promises included improved roads and bridges and free school textbooks. Unlike previous Louisiana politicians, he actually made good on his promises. He financed the roads with a bond issue backed by an increase in the gasoline tax. It was the biggest public works project in state history. He added almost 3,500 miles of paved highways, another 4,000 miles of gravel roads, and thirty-seven new bridges. The construction was of poor quality, however. Contractors paid bribes for the jobs and overcharged the state for materials. Long put Oscar K. "O.K." Allen, who would later become his puppet governor, in charge of seeing that friends were rewarded with contracts and enemies punished.[5]

As impressive as this public works effort was at the time, it was small compared with the New Deal programs that were to come later. Long's program at its height employed 22,000 workers. The Civil Works Administration put 80,372 people to work in its short life. The Works Progress Administration (WPA) had 40,143 workers per month on its payroll in 1936 and kept similar numbers employed through 1940.[6]

After only two years in the governor's office, Long was elected to the

U.S. Senate. He waited until 1932 to take office because he no longer trusted his lieutenant governor, Paul Cyr, to take over. He waited until he could engineer the election of someone he could control. O.K. Allen was the man. According to a popular joke, Allen would sign a leaf if it blew onto his desk. Long also appointed his twenty-four-year-old mistress, Alice Lee Grosjean, as secretary of state. Long could now continue to control Louisiana while exploring new horizons in Washington.[7]

Long campaigned vigorously for FDR in 1932 and helped him gain support in other southern states. He supported early New Deal legislation, but soon concluded that it did not go far enough and that his own campaign for president should begin with a bolder policy. He had been thinking about income redistribution since 1916. He called his program "Share the Wealth." It promised an annual income of $2,500 to every citizen and a one-time payment of $5,000 to establish a homestead. It included old age pensions, veterans' bonuses, free college education, and a guaranteed job for everyone. By 1934, he was organizing clubs nationwide to support the plan.[8]

Huey Long did not intend to go to war with Harold Ickes and the Public Works Administration (PWA) when it first entered his state, but given the battles he was fighting at the time and the dreams of national conquest he was nurturing, the war was unavoidable. Because of his early support of Roosevelt, Long initially hoped for some patronage through the New Deal programs. Failing that, he seemed content to keep them neutral. He could not, however, let them be controlled by his enemies. Even as late as 1935, he told Robert W. "Pete" Hudgens, the regional director of the Resettlement Administration (RA), a program to aid displaced farmers and workers: "All I'm concerned about is that you help those poor people. . . . As long as you stick to that job, I'll never bother you. . . . The first time I catch you appointing somebody because one of those sons of bitches told you to I'll run you out of Louisiana."[9]

The threats to RA neutrality were entirely from the anti-Long forces. As an aide described it, the new RA director "had hardly got to town before they moved in on him and proposed to take him over, and the proposals that they began to make to him were as bad or worse than Huey could have thought of. . . . He was sent down to keep Huey from wrecking it, and found that what he had to do was to keep Huey's political *opponents* from wrecking it too."[10]

Long had numerous enemies across the state. He was a definite threat to the status quo—the planter aristocracy and the New Orleans business elite—because he was mobilizing poor people. He had made an enemy of the state's major corporate power, Standard Oil, by trying to impose a manufacturing tax as well as a severance tax on it. He had crossed or double-crossed every living former governor in the state. Some who were not bothered by his ideology just didn't like his style, his flamboyance and vulgarity. But his chief enemies were the Old Regulars of New Orleans, the "only substantial concentration of wealth in the state and the only effective political machine in the South." The Old Regulars were also "one of the most business-oriented machines in the country." They were conservative and protected corporate interests, particularly oil and gas. They were thus the natural enemy of a populist like Huey Long. But more important, they could deliver a large bloc of votes.[11]

The leader of the Old Regulars was Mayor T. Semmes Walmsley of New Orleans. He was not notably brilliant or politically shrewd, but had been a five-letter athlete at Tulane University and came from an old New Orleans family. For an aristocrat, he had a wider-than-usual streak of noblesse oblige and the ability to express it in popular gestures. He recruited a fifteen-year-old orphan to sit with him on the Mardi Gras grandstand and present the key to the city to King Rex. When the parade was rained out, he promised to have her back the next year. And he did. When the city's solvency was questioned in June 1930, he had city employees paid in cash to protect them from bounced checks. He bore the names of a former state attorney general and a Confederate admiral. Tall, thin, and balding, he also had a beaky nose. Long called him "Turkey Head."[12]

Patronage is the currency of the urban political machine. It was also a tool that Huey Long had learned to use effectively.[13] People you owed your job and livelihood to, it was assumed, were people you voted for, or with. In a depression that had put a quarter of the workforce on the streets, jobs were more precious than ever. New Deal work relief programs offered jobs, some paying decent wages. If the wages weren't decent, they were at least better than nothing. Therefore the ability to control these programs was a very important political asset.

The Old Regulars had surrendered to Long after his election to the Senate in 1930. Their best efforts had failed to deprive him of substantial support in New Orleans. He accepted the capitulation with unusual magnanimity, and they worked together for the next three years. But the prospect of federal work programs offered the Old Regulars an opportunity for rebellion. Indeed, it might be their last chance to be "rescued from political oblivion."[14]

The degree to which New Deal programs remained neutral in local patronage struggles differed from place to place and agency to agency. In many cities run by political machines there was no contest for patronage, and the Roosevelt administration was happy to let the local bosses get credit for the new jobs because the gratitude was usually repaid in Democratic votes at election time. If federal programs kept corrupt regimes in office, federal administrators could tolerate this as long as federal dollars were spent for their intended purposes. In Kansas City and Memphis, for example, the relationship between the Roosevelt administration and notorious bosses survived alleged improprieties.[15]

In cases of contested patronage, neutrality was sometimes possible. The RA was able to maintain it in Louisiana. Harry Hopkins, head of the WPA, attempted it for a while by bringing in Harry J. Early from out of state to direct the Louisiana WPA. In some cases, neutrality was maintained by Long-appointed officials. Rufus Foster, the state director of the National Reemployment Service, which provided the workforce for the PWA, was a friend of Long's, yet he played no politics with work assignments.[16]

But staying neutral in Louisiana was a problem for Roosevelt. First, Long's critics were often people well connected and even well regarded by members of the administration. Former governor John Parker had worked with Harold Ickes in the Progressive Party. The New Deal's five strongest Louisiana supporters in Congress, including John Sandlin and Cleveland Dear, were anti-Longites. Another former governor, J. Y. Sanders Sr., was a personal friend of the secretary of state and the secretary of commerce. Former senator Edmund Broussard, who had been defeated by Long ally John Overton, retained many friends in the Senate. It was hard to ignore such influential people.[17]

A second, and perhaps stronger, reason was that by 1934, Long was not only withdrawing his support for the New Deal and becoming one of its loudest critics, but he was also beginning to organize a challenge to Roosevelt for the presidency. Thus Roosevelt had little incentive to allow Long control of any patronage jobs and increasing interest in giving them to Long's enemies.

Roosevelt called Long to the White House in June 1933 to explain his position. According to Postmaster General James Farley, who was present,

Long tried to assume a commanding position by keeping his hat on except when using it to poke Roosevelt's knee to make a point. Roosevelt, however, refused to be offended and even seemed to be enjoying the test of wills. Long finally took his hat off. He made his case for patronage consideration, saying he had supported New Deal legislation better than many other senators. This had some truth to it; he spoke against many of the New Deal bills, even made fun of some of them, but usually backed them when the vote was called. Roosevelt replied that his only interest was appointing worthy people. Long told Farley after the meeting: "What the hell is the use of coming down to see this fellow? I can't win any decision over him."[18]

Long was right. To Roosevelt, "worthy people" were Long opponents. Hodding Carter noted in January 1934: "Without exception, every federal job in Louisiana has gone to an out-and-out anti-Long Democrat."[19] The PWA received a number of such appointments. Its advisory board was packed with Long's enemies and chaired by Edward Rightor, an old courtroom adversary. The PWA state attorney, Roland B. Howell, had spoken against Long in the Senate race. Orloff Henry, the PWA state engineer, was not a member of any anti-Long group, but was known to be friendly with some of them.[20]

But these appointments did not cause problems for Long immediately. Hiring for PWA jobs was nonpolitical. More important, the PWA projects that had been approved were moving slowly. There was little political capital to be made for the moment. On Ickes's part, there seems to be a similar unconcern. Long does not appear in his *Secret Diary* until January 1935.[21] Several New Orleans projects, including proposals for a dock, a dam, and a new city hall, were stalled because the city could not supply its share of financing for the projects. A $10 million bond issue had failed in a special election.

The New Orleans Sewerage and Water Board was able to pass a $1.8 million bond issue, however, thus qualifying for a $700,000 PWA grant. A housing proposal was under way; financing this was possible because future rents could secure the PWA loan. A proposed renovation of the French Market made it through because commercial revenues could be expected. A new Charity Hospital was also proposed, to be financed in part by adding some paying beds to the plan. But this had been met by stiff opposition from the medical community, which wanted no competition for paying customers.

It is hard to find evidence for federal political involvement in the progress, or lack thereof, in the PWA projects of this period. The city of Shreveport, a conservative and generally anti-Long stronghold, did fairly well in getting approval for its proposals in the first year of operation. Of the thirty-three Louisiana projects approved by the end of 1934, twelve were in Shreveport.[22] But it is entirely possible that this was less a matter of political favoritism than of careful preparation. These proposals appear to have been both thorough in content and slickly presented.[23]

Baton Rouge, in the shadow of Long's skyscraper capitol building, was also known for anti-Long sentiments. Its $50,000 city hall project, actually a renovation of the old post office to convert it to a city hall, was approved in mid-1934.

However, other anti-Long strongholds did not fare so well. Several places became known for gestures of hostility during a Long speaking tour in late 1933. In Minden, one victim of Long's verbal attacks was prepared to answer with bullets. Harmon Drew and a group of armed men, each assigned to shoot one of Long's bodyguards, came to the November 10

Municipal Auditorium, Shreveport, completed by the PWA. Home of the popular radio program *Louisiana Hayride* and venue for a young Elvis Presley. One of twelve early Shreveport projects. Samuel Wiener did the original design; Seymour Van Os finished it.

speech. The plan leaked to the Louisiana State Police, so they and the bodyguards were ready for a confrontation. Long made a short speech without mention of Drew and got out of town. Long was not known for his physical courage, so the appearance was noteworthy for both what did and didn't happen. He actually showed up, but carefully avoided provoking violence.[24] Minden thus became associated with the opposition. Its courthouse repair proposal to the PWA was approved, but its sewer project was not. One explanation for the success of the courthouse project was that it was small ($18,536) and was for a grant only ($5,246); the PWA did not have to put up the remaining $13,290 as a loan.[25]

Alexandria was another prominent rallying point of opposition to Long. Shortly after the Minden incident, Long found himself the target of rotten eggs. The chief of police, Clint O'Malley, would not let Long's bodyguards into the bank building that housed the egg hurlers. After Minden's threat of a pistol fusillade, eggs probably seemed less intimidating, so Long finished a two-hour speech.[26] He got his revenge a year later by creating a state civil service commission that allowed him to fire O'Malley. But there was no PWA reward for the city's anti-Long stance. Its forest development, clinic building, and water and gas proposals, along with a sewer project from neighboring Pineville, were all rejected.[27]

On the same tour Long decided not to enter Hammond at all. It was the home of former governor J. Y. Sanders, who had gotten into a well-publicized fistfight with Long in 1927. Its newspaper, the *Daily Courier*, edited by respected journalist Hodding Carter, was consistently critical of Long. But its school and waterworks proposals were both disapproved.[28]

One of the first PWA projects to be approved in Louisiana, a bridge upriver from New Orleans, could have helped either side. Begun in 1931 with the help of Hoover's Reconstruction Finance Corporation, it was originally to be called the Public Belt Railroad Bridge because part of it was to be used by that enterprise, whose chairman was none other than T. Semmes Walmsley. However, Long's intervention was necessary to continue the project, and because of that Long believed he could have it named in his honor. But there was still not enough money available to finish the project. By the time the PWA was asked to finance the completion of the bridge, Walmsley had broken with Long, and the original name reappeared in the proposal. Nonetheless, observers at the construction site noticed large cloth banners on the approach towers near Jefferson Highway proclaiming it the "Huey P. Long Bridge." When word of this reached Philip Fleming, PWA executive officer, he dispatched State Engineer Orloff Henry to investigate. By the time Henry arrived on the scene, the banners were gone. He inquired about the name with the Public Belt Railway and was assured that Long's name would not be on the completed bridge. Given the public perception that this was Long's bridge, however, it is not clear that Walmsley would have received credit for the project.[29]

The one project that was most directly under Long's control, a bridge across the Mississippi at Baton Rouge, was stalled. Initially, this was a matter of noncooperation from the railroads that were to share it.[30] But eventually the project became another venue for charges and countercharges. When Ickes threatened to investigate its finances, state highway commissioner A. P. Tugwell reminded him that the PWA had yet to spend any of its money on the project. "The records of your department will disclose the fact that your total contribution to the undertaking has up to date been nothing more than a voluminous file of correspondence." He further accused PWA Advisory Board chair Edward Rightor of demanding that a crony be hired as a consulting engineer. He claimed "no further interest" in the project. Ickes rescinded it.[31]

Given Long's interest in Louisiana State University (LSU), the difficulty encountered by LSU's proposal for several buildings might be seen as political. However, the complex and frequently changing financing of the university's share was probably more than enough to cause it to be given special scrutiny by PWA's careful Finance Division.[32]

Long worked hard to get the "Big Charity" hospital project approved even though it was in the heart of Old Regular territory. In June he "invaded" a state Judiciary Committee meeting, took over the microphone, and announced his solution to the financing problem. He replaced the contentious pay-bed scheme with an increase of the corporate franchise tax. In August he wrote Ickes to assure him that the loan would be repaid.[33] In this case, completion of the project could have benefited either side. However, it was not approved until after Long's death.

Even had federal programs continued to operate without showing political favoritism, they were becoming a problem for Long because of his increasing attacks on Roosevelt. Whether anyone called their attention to it or not, it would have been obvious to most relief workers that they were employed in Roosevelt's programs. And there was no lack of voices to call it to their attention. Said Hodding Carter: "Though there is an honest effort to keep these organizations nonpolitical, it isn't dishonest to tell the workers that the man Huey is fighting is the man who made their jobs possible."[34]

In September 1934 Ickes announced that Louisiana had exhausted its share of PWA funds, which he stated was $14 million. The amount surprised Louisiana politicians, who had been promised $28–30 million by Rightor a year earlier. Half of the $14 million was allocated to the Baton Rouge bridge. Because of the difficulties with the railroads, state officials thought they might cancel it in order to have money for other projects. Ickes, however, said the money would return to the general PWA fund and could not be set aside for Louisiana. The other $7 million was divided among forty smaller projects.[35] However, only thirty-one had actually been approved at the time of the announcement, and only two more small projects were approved in November. They would be the last until July 1936.

While making no direct moves against the PWA, Long had begun passing state legislation that caused federal officials, and particularly Harold Ickes, concern. Long's main aim was to consolidate power in Louisiana and bring the Old Regulars back to their knees. As U.S. senator, he should have been otherwise occupied. But his successor in the governor's office, O.K. Allen, although completely obedient to Long, was ineffective in moving Long's legislation. Long could only get what he wanted when he was present in person to intimidate the legislators.[36] In three special legislative sessions in 1934, he fired barrage after barrage of bills aimed at giving him complete control of the state, including, most particularly, New Orleans. Some of these looked to Ickes like threats to his program.

One bill reorganized the New Orleans Sewerage and Water Board, removing most of the city-appointed board members and adding appointees from state-controlled bodies. If carried through, this would give Long control of one of the state's biggest PWA projects. Another bill provided for a moratorium on private debts. It was aimed at giving debt-strapped individuals time to recover. But Ickes saw it as a prelude to a moratorium on federal government debts. Ickes suspended all PWA projects not already under construction. This gave Long a chance to cry "politics." If the New Orleans sewer project was worthy while it was controlled by his enemies, why wasn't it still worthy if controlled by his friends? Ickes backed off, ostensibly having been reassured that the private debt bill was no threat. He lifted the suspension on all of the PWA's projects but the sewer extension, which was enmeshed in court challenges to the board reorganization.[37]

Huey P. Long Bridge, New Orleans. Initiated by the RFC and completed by the PWA, but Long got the credit.

The war with the feds was now really heating up. In February 1935 Roosevelt put the word out that any non–civil service Long supporter should be fired. In April 1935 Hopkins decided that the Louisiana WPA director Harry Early was too pro-Long and replaced him with Frank H. Peterman, an administrator who had an established record for inefficiency but was decidedly anti-Long. This threatened to give a large patronage gift to Long's opponents. The response was obvious. If Long couldn't control patronage jobs and couldn't prevent his enemies from controlling them, then he best keep them out of the state all together. Thus Long put a bill through the legislature creating a state Bond and Tax Board with the power to approve any locality's move to borrow money.[38]

In a WPA project, local financial participation was negotiable. Some projects were completed without any local money involved, but there was a strong desire for some degree of local involvement. With PWA projects, local participation of at least 70, and later 55, percent was absolutely required. Since bond issues were the principal means by which communities could come up with their share of federal projects, Long's Bond and Tax

Board could stop the PWA in its tracks. Ickes didn't wait. He froze all PWA projects already in the pipeline.[39]

This was followed by a colorful exchange between the two. Long told Ickes to go "slap-damn to hell." Several days later, he appeared on the Senate floor, "a sartorial aurora borealis" dressed in tan suit, checked lavender shirt, mottled red and green tie, and white and tan shoes, to denounce Ickes as the "cinch bug of Chicago." Ickes called a press conference and told the reporters that Long had "halitosis of the intellect."[40] Ickes thought this was a real zinger. He remarked in his diary that it had "made a great hit with the correspondents. I have never seen them so interested and amused."[41] But given the malignancy that Ickes believed characterized Long's quest for power, it is hard to see that a comparison with bad breath was exactly on target.

Anti-Long forces pressured the PWA to get the sewer and hospital projects moving again despite Ickes's conflict with Long. The latter project had finally found support by all sides, thanks in part to Long's new financing method. Since Long wanted the project, no problem was expected from the Tax and Bond Board. A delegation including LSU president

Maurepas High School, designed by William R. Burk, allotted before the 1935 freeze.

James Monroe Smith was sent to make the case. Ickes noted in his diary for July 16, 1935: "I explained we would not allow ourselves to be put in the position of being permitted to go ahead with a project in Louisiana merely by grace of one of Huey Long's boards." He pointed out that he'd imposed a similar freeze in Massachusetts in 1933. When Smith asked about the LSU proposal, Ickes told him many people thought LSU "wasn't so much a educational institution as a political institution." Smith took "great exception" to this, but Ickes refused to mollify him.[42]

In the third special session of the Louisiana legislature in July 1935, Long's steamroller was moving at top speed. Twenty-five bills were passed by both houses with no explanation and no debate in a total of seventy minutes. The anti-Long representatives didn't bother to vote. Included in this blitz were bills making it impossible for New Orleans to collect any standard revenues or taxes or to appoint any officials. Even the district attorney could not select his own staff. The Old Regulars were helpless, and most deserted to the Long camp. The mayor was left with "nothing but his title and office furniture."[43]

One might think this would have been enough to ensure that federal patronage held no further threat. It wasn't. Another special session was called in September. Among the forty-two bills introduced was one that Long portrayed as protecting the public against the political use of government money. In effect, it meant that any federal official could be accused of "political purposes" and hauled into jail for disbursing money through any relief program. In reply, Ickes announced that no new Louisiana projects would be accepted and that work would stop on any of those less than 95 percent complete. Such was the state of paralysis already existing in Louisiana PWA operations that this affected only two projects.[44]

The political-use-of-federal-money law was most likely aimed at the WPA rather than the PWA. It was probably just further insurance that federal patronage could not be used against Long in the next election.[45] Perhaps it was also a bargaining chip to throw into future negotiations with Ickes to get some of the projects that Long wanted, and knew his state needed, started again. We'll never know. The day after the bill was introduced, Huey Long was shot to death.

It seems clear overall that the PWA took some part in the war between Long and his enemies. Ickes followed Roosevelt's wishes and gave patronage positions to prominent anti-Longites. He also allowed himself to be drawn into rhetorical combat. That, of course, wasn't hard; Ickes loved a fight. In addition to trading barbs with Long, he also stopped or threatened to stop Louisiana projects several times. These threats were usually responses to Long legislation that Ickes thought would threaten the operation of his agency. The announcement on September 29, 1934, that Louisiana had exceeded its "quota" came after a Long initiative of another kind, however.

From the end of July until after the congressional election on September 11, Long had New Orleans under "partial martial law," occupying the building containing the Registrar of Voters' office, next door to city hall, with National Guard troops. Three thousands troops were encamped in the city. The mayor mobilized 400 policemen and quickly bought new arms and equipment for them. Before civil war erupted, however, both sides agreed to stay away from the polls, and the election went through without incident. The Long candidates won handily, and the Guard went home. Ickes's announcement of the quota two weeks later may have been unrelated, or it may have been the first sign of an intended withdrawal from Louisiana.

The reason to be suspicious of a connection is that the PWA had no policy of establishing quotas. They were talked about. A year earlier, there was a subcommittee report to the Special Board that used the term in reviewing allotments to thirty-four states.[46] The quotas were based on population and percentage of unemployment in each state. But no quota system was pursued after that. There was general concern to balance aid as fairly as possible across the states. There was also general concern to get projects under way as quickly as possible. It was therefore hard to deny states that were organized enough to complete well-drawn proposals for worthy projects in order to spread money over the less-organized states. Therefore the closest the PWA came to invoking quotas was to find ways to get projects going in states that were lagging, not states that were high performers.[47] The New Orleans sewer project, a multimillion dollar endeavor, had been approved in June, and the Baton Rouge bridge had not yet been rescinded, so there were sizable amounts of money committed to Louisiana at this point. But other states had drawn similar amounts of PWA money.[48] Had the political situation been different, it seems unlikely that a "quota" would have been invoked.

Instead, judging from the rate and dates of project approval, the PWA had decided to drastically slow further involvement in Louisiana almost a year before the actual freeze came. Of the 534 PWA projects proposed in

Louisiana during the life of the program, over 100 were initiated before the end of 1934. But after June 1934, when 11 projects were approved, only 1 in July, 2 in September, and 2 in November got through (see table 1). From November 11, 1934, until Long's assassination, no projects were approved. Thus, during the year of threatened or actual stoppages or withdrawals, things were already on hold.

The pattern of early project approvals shows no clear indication of partisanship. Projects seem to have been approved on their merits rather than who could take credit for them. As Ickes became drawn into the war with Huey Long, his service seems to have been mostly rhetorical. The agency itself responded by slowing and then stopping approval of Louisiana projects rather than trying to reward anti-Long forces. This could have come from a desire on Ickes's part, despite his personal partisanship, to defend the agency entrusted to him from political debasement. It could also have been simple prudence, for which he was famous. The web of restrictive legislation that Long spun was probably reason enough in itself for the PWA to pull back. A conscientious administrator without a political bone in his or her body might have done likewise.

For whatever reason, the impact of the PWA on the Louisiana landscape was modest in the agency's first years of its operation. Only thirty-three projects had been approved. Of these, twenty-one had reached completion before Long's death. And his shadow remained after he was gone. No new PWA project could break ground in Louisiana until July 21, 1936.

TABLE 1.
PWA Nonfederal Projects Approved in Louisiana Prior to the Freeze (in order of approval)

Date	Docket	Location	Type	Loan	Grant	Total Cost	Completed
\multicolumn{8}{c}{1933}							
12/26	2020	Gretna	waterworks improvements	$207,000	$78,839	$235,839	2/22/35
12/26	3908	New Orleans	toll bridge	369,856	0	369,856	12/31/35
12/28	1794	Houma	incinerator	12,000	4,463	16,463	5/16/35
\multicolumn{8}{c}{1934}							
1/9	3069	Zachery	gas distributor	12,500	4,551	17,051	12/18/36
1/11	4635	DeSoto Parish	school	0	3,894	3,894	6/2/34
2/1	3068	Shreveport	incinerator	129,030	51,128	180,158	7/31/35
2/1	3068.2	"	police radio	3,560	1,225	5,005	6/17/35
2/1	3068.3	"	auditorium	26,800	10,232	37,032	10/31/34
2/1	3068.4	"	streets	104,980	43,153	148,133	2/6/35
2/1	3068.5	"	courthouse	12,260	4,755	17,015	12/21/34
2/1	3068.6	"	fire department	7,690	2,317	10,007	10/4/34
2/1	3068.8	"	fire alarm	40,600	17,454	58,054	12/5/35
2/1	3068.9	"	city hall	30,970	9,058	40,028	1/12/35
2/1	3058.10	"	fire department	15,200	4,815	20,015	12/21/34
2/7	3068.1	"	park improvements	60,700	24,375	85,075	2/19/35
2/21	4391	St. Joseph	courthouse	10,000	4,032	14,032	10/31/34
2/28	3068.7	Shreveport	market	38,300	11,736	50,03 6	12/20/34
6/20	4522	E. Jefferson	waterworks improvements	226,326	86,674	313,000	12/31/38
6/20	4531	Baton Rouge	city hall	36,400	13,600	50,000	8/7/35
6/20	5062	Shreveport	school	0	25,000	25,000	5/8/35
6/20	5123	Greenwood	school	0	6,400	6,400	11/26/34
6/20	5638	Caddo Parish	highway improvements	181,000	88,258	269,258	2/6/35
6/20	6235	Bastrop	courthouse addition	0	10,500	10,500	12/31/35
6/20	6373	Logansport	waterworks	30,700	12,300	43,000	3/23/38

TABLE 1. (Continued)

PWA Nonfederal Projects Approved in Louisiana Prior to the Freeze (in order of approval)

Date	Docket	Location	Type	Loan	Grant	Total Cost	Completed
6/20	6422	Minden	courthouse repairs	0	5,246	5,246	10/11/35
6/20	7675	LaFourch	school	52,700	20,300	73,000	9/17/35
6/27	3840	Maurepas	school	24,300	9,590	33,890	8/27/35
6/27	4284	New Orleans	water/sewer	1,800,800	769,200	2,570,000	6/30/38
7/18	5914	New Orleans	market	300,000	0	300,000	1/24/38
9/5	6702	Sunset	waterworks	20,900	8,100	29,100	7/12/37
9/5	8801	Ringgold	waterworks	28,800	10,368	39,168	7/31/37
11/7	9203	Jackson	waterworks	30,300	9,643	39,643	11/16/37
11/7	4887	St. Joseph	filter plant	4,800	2,098	6,898	3/19/37

Source: List of All Allotted Non-Federal Projects, All Programs, by State and Docket, as of May 30, 1942, 65–66, Federal Works Agency, Public Works Administration, Record Group 135, National Archives II, College Park, Md.

CHAPTER 4

THE SECOND LOUISIANA PURCHASE

Relations between Louisiana and the Roosevelt administration were not patched up immediately after Huey Long's assassination. The Long organization saw its future in keeping Long's name alive, and that meant maintaining most of his attitudes and policies. This included skepticism, if not outright hostility, toward the New Deal. And Washington saw no need to woo Long's successors as long as there were genuine New Deal candidates to promote in the election of 1936.

Cleveland Dear, a New Dealer in good standing, opposed Richard Leche, Long's chosen candidate for governor. Part of Dear's platform was to bring the Public Works Administration (PWA) back to Louisiana. He claimed that the state had lost $60 million and 60,000 jobs because of Long's war with Ickes. Dear seems to have gotten substantial support from the New Deal agencies still operating in the state. Ickes kept PWA projects frozen, but new Civilian Conservation Corps (CCC) camps were opened, and 7,600 Works Progress Administration (WPA) projects were approved. Anti-Long congressmen announced WPA projects even when they weren't in their districts. John Sandlin from Shreveport told the state about new projects in New Orleans and Lake Providence.[1]

But this federal largesse did not influence many voters. They had no problem accepting the New Deal's jobs and voting for its presumed opponents.[2] In the January 1936 election, the Long candidates won easily. Both Louisiana and Washington had to reassess their positions.

Some observers concluded that the new governor was putting out peace feelers. When one prominent Long lieutenant, Gerald L. K. Smith, went to Georgia to discuss with Governor Eugene Talmadge the possibility of an anti-Roosevelt coalition, Leche said Smith was not speaking for him.

From Washington came the news that the tax fraud cases that were being built against Long supporters were being dropped because the government thought that convictions were unlikely in the "changed environment since the death of Long."[3]

Other developments occurred in the "changed environment." The state WPA was overhauled, probably less to make peace with the victors than because Harry Hopkins thought that local WPA administrators had overstepped their roles. He had dismissed several before the election because they were running for office. He accepted the resignation of the inefficient but anti-Long Frank Peterman and appointed Joseph H. Crutcher, an out-of-stater and a professional social worker who had worked under both the anti-Long Peterman and the pro-Long Harry Early. Crutcher replaced eight district administrators—Peterman appointees—with social workers and made the WPA an efficient, nonpolitical relief organization again.[4]

Governor Leche had no trouble adapting to a "changed environment." He had campaigned against "federal intervention" but not against New Deal programs themselves and had endorsed Social Security just before the election. So he did not have to dissemble too much when he decided to go hat-in-hand to Washington. He called on Hopkins, Ickes, Jim Farley, Frances Perkins, Rex Tugwell, and other New Deal notables. He visited the White House. He even opened an "embassy" in Washington to expedite applications for federal assistance. At home, Leche changed the policies of the state Bond and Tax Board to suit the PWA. He worked toward the repeal of other Long antifederal laws.[5]

Leche also seems to have inherited some of Long's operatic flair. When Roosevelt visited Dallas to attend the Texas Centennial Exposition, Leche packed up both houses of the Louisiana legislature, along with the Louisiana State University (LSU) band, and took them to the exposition to help welcome the president.[6]

With the repeal of the obstructing legislation, Ickes was ready to resume business in Louisiana. The floodgates opened, and the backlog of proposals surged toward approval and groundbreaking. Congressman Usher Burdick of North Dakota, referring both to the tax fraud cases and to "certain patronage heretofore withheld from the Long machine," called it "the second Louisiana Purchase." New Orleans journalist Harnett Kane explicitly included public works as one of the "results of the Second Purchase" in his exposé of Long and Leche, *Louisiana Hayride*.[7]

James Farley argued that there was no need to purchase Louisiana; it was safely in the Democratic camp by 1936. Kane countered that there was no assurance at this time that Louisiana votes could be relied on to support critical New Deal programs. It is indeed true that southern support was increasingly hard to hold on to in Roosevelt's second term, but how much was this problem apparent in early 1936? The presidential election produced a Roosevelt landslide.[8] Was the campaign tight enough to warrant a purchase of Louisiana votes, or was Roosevelt simply tired of fighting Louisiana politicians? The anti-Long forces with whom Roosevelt had allied were mostly conservatives of the old planter aristocracy and not natural New Deal supporters. Doing them favors by continuing to prosecute their enemies was in all likelihood a thankless task.

What part had the PWA played in this? Was the approval of PWA projects a payoff for Louisiana's support in the election and in Congress, or was it simply an artifact of the backlog of frozen projects? It is important as far as possible to separate patronage and political appointments from the awarding of contracts. Giving politicians jobs and allowing them to take credit for providing jobs for others are on a different level from depriving communities of essential facilities or granting them things they don't really need on political grounds.

There is no evidence, however, that the PWA's customary thoroughness was being relaxed. Louisiana projects were engineered, constructed, and inspected with the same care as buildings in other states. Their current survival rate testifies to that, if the evidence in the files is not itself enough. There are no frivolous projects to be found. A high percentage of these dockets were education related, and Louisiana needed them badly. Louisiana was simply given its due, not purchased. Or, rather, if there was a purchase, the PWA was not part of the deal.

In addition to the proposals submitted or being prepared at the time of the freeze, there were probably also ideas for proposals accumulating but not put on paper because of the freeze. There was bound to be a disproportionate number of proposals to deal with in the 1936–1938 period. As noted earlier, Louisiana's overall share of PWA funds was not disproportionate to that of other southern states (table 2).[9] But seeing so many projects sprout in a short period rather than being spread over three years as in other states must have heightened the perception of outside observers that a great deal of favoritism was being shown.

While relationships between Louisiana and the PWA were suspended, the federal agency had been given more money to spend and new directives on how to spend it. The Emergency Relief Appropriations Act of 1935 had created the WPA because the PWA, with its emphasis on careful planning and skilled labor, was not getting to enough unskilled workers fast enough to relieve their destitution. Accordingly, the WPA got most of the money from this legislation, $1.4 billion. But the PWA was not left out. It received $313 million plus another $395 million from the revolving fund to spend on loans.[10]

A revolving fund had been created in 1934 from proceeds from the sale of securities held as collateral for loans to the nonfederal projects or from repayments of those loans. At first, such money was returned to the treasury, but Public Resolution 412 made it available for further PWA loans. This would prove to be an important supplement to the PWA's later efforts. And because it was a "revolving" fund—loans brought repayments and interest, which made it possible to make more loans—the PWA could maintain a certain level of operation without going back to Congress for new appropriations.[11]

The very existence of the money in the revolving fund is a tribute to all the cities and towns that undertook these projects and taxed themselves to pay for them. It also is a resounding answer to the skeptics, including Huey Long, who predicted widespread default on government loans. Actual defaults were few and profits considerable. The profits on loans made in 1934 alone ($674,532) exceeded all defaults in four and a half years of program operation ($599,879).[12]

The first projects to emerge from the reopened pipeline in Louisiana were a waterworks for Independence and new sidewalks for Cottonport, allotted on July 21, 1936. In August two more water projects were approved, one in Bernice and one in Franklinton. From September to November, five school projects—three in Shreveport and one each in Kelly and Crowley—and a courthouse/jail in Covington were approved. Most important of the eleven projects to get started in 1936 was the New Orleans Charity Hospital.[13]

These grants and loans were supported by the First Deficiency Appropriation Act passed on June 21, 1936, which allowed the PWA to spend $300 million from the revolving fund for grants (money from the fund had previously been available only for loans). The act also specified that projects had to be completed by the beginning of July 1937, which was the expected termination of the PWA. This deadline put particular pressure on LSU's proposal to modernize its Sugar Factory, which was pending at the end of 1936. LSU officials assured the PWA that the project could be completed in three to four months after funds were received.[14]

Another fourteen projects received allotments on February 12, 1937. This group included a number of important civic buildings. Four parish courthouse/jails were supported (Cameron, Caldwell, East Carroll, and Terrebonne). The Capitol Annex in Baton Rouge and the State Exposition Building in Shreveport were approved. The women's dormitories for LSU finally got off the drawing board, and the Sugar Factory proposal was allotted. A pipeline to bring fresh drinking water to Berwick was authorized. The rest were school projects, including the wonderful art deco high school in Port Allen.[15]

The landslide election of 1936 seemed a broad national endorsement of the president and his policies; but the mandate, while broad, was thinner than it originally seemed. Confident that he now had the support to confront one of the major impediments to New Deal legislation, the Supreme Court, Roosevelt had conceived a radical plan to obviate further Court challenges to his proposals, such as the striking down of the National Industrial Recovery Act and the Agricultural Adjustment Act. He would add new members for every justice who did not retire at age seventy. Along

Louisiana State Exposition Building, Shreveport, designed by Neild, Somdal, and Neild.

Louisiana State Exposition Building, Shreveport. The murals were restored recently.

with conservatives, many middle-of-the-road citizens found this a bit scary. The proposal may have succeeded in encouraging moderation in the Court, but it seriously weakened Roosevelt's political support across the country.[16]

A second blow to administration confidence was the recession that appeared in the summer and grew in the fall of 1937. This wound may have been self-inflicted. Roosevelt had campaigned on a balanced budget in 1932 and again in 1936, and despite the huge amounts of money he had spent to revitalize the economy, he still maintained the hope that when the emergency was over, he could return to economic orthodoxy. Whatever his opponents might think, Roosevelt was not a radical and had no sense that there might be basic structural problems with the economy. Even as late as 1929, he had shared Hoover's belief that business and government should be separate.[17]

Of his advisers, Treasury Secretary Henry Morgenthau, was particularly passionate about balancing the budget. By April 1937, he had convinced the president that the economy was far enough along to afford cutting back on emergency programs like the PWA, the WPA, and others. But instead of furthering the recovery, this brought the recession.[18]

On June 29, 1937, during this new move to budget balancing, the life of the PWA had been extended another two years, until June 30, 1939. It was allowed to increase its use of money from the revolving fund from $300 to $359 million. But no new applications could be accepted, and allotments could be made only to projects that had already passed the examining divisions. The extension seemed designed to serve only to close out the program.

By October, the recession had reached frightening proportions. Production, employment, and the stock market were in sharp decline. Comparisons were being made to the crash of 1929. The administration seemed paralyzed. Morgenthau blamed it on a lack of "business confidence" rather than his own recommendations for cutbacks in work programs. He and others within the administration pushed Roosevelt to seek accommodation with business leaders outside of the New Deal orbit. This meant still greater efforts to balance the budget. Others, including Adolph Berle and Rex Tugwell, members of the Roosevelt brain trust, had a vision of cooperation between corporations, labor unions, and government planners to achieve an orderly economy without cutthroat competition. Still others, Harold Ickes prominent among them, saw the recession as a "capital strike," a refusal of corporations to invest and to hire. Rather than placating business, they wanted a public investigation of monopolies. Positive public response to Ickes's speeches may have inclined the president toward this view, but he spent a long time making up his mind.[19]

Though he had accomplished much in his initial assault on the Depression, Roosevelt was improvising and was not sure how far he could stray from conventional wisdom. He was distrustful of abstract schemes and had none of his own. He was more comfortable with pragmatic accommodation and political compromise. Having a new idea did not require throwing out all the old ones.[20]

The role of public works in economic recovery was still seen by many backers of the New Deal as central to social stability and economic recovery. But their economic arguments explaining why this was so were changing. In the beginning, they argued that government spending, particularly on public works, would stimulate production. Building required building materials and construction machinery. Lumber, steel, cement, gas, and oil were major industries that must be fired up. The construction workers at the jobs sites, and the many other workers involved in primary production, would all go back to work. This would give people money to spend, which would in turn increase demand for other goods and stimulate further production. But as economists observed the process, some came to the conclusion that consumption drove the recovery more than production. Thus work relief programs could not be cut back. The more consumers who could be brought back into the economy, the healthier the economy would become.

These ideas are usually associated with the English economist John Maynard Keynes, but in fact their influence in the United States predates Keynes's major publications on the subject. It came from domestic sources. A 1928 book—*Road to Plenty* by William Foster, a college president, and Waddill Catchings, an industrialist—made the argument for public spending, particularly on public works, as an antidote to underconsumption. These ideas gradually infiltrated the Roosevelt administration, articulated especially by Utah banker Marriner Eccles, chairman of the Federal Reserve Board. Eccles was particularly supportive of the PWA. Instead of cajoling businessmen to invest, he argued, making it possible for consumers to buy would pull the economy out of recession, bringing the businessmen along.[21]

By 1936, Keynes's ideas about government spending as an anti-Depression strategy were well known and were being absorbed and propagated in the United States by Harvard economist Alvin Hansen. They focused on the relationship between private and public investment throughout history, arguing that private investment had been stimulated in the past by geographic expansion, population growth, and technological change. The first two had now slowed to a halt, and the third was insufficient to stimulate enough investment to keep an economy healthy. A "fourth pillar" was necessary: public investment. This would provide the necessary stability to encourage private investment again. Private consumption was not enough; community consumption—investment in education, health, housing, recreation, social services—was required as well.[22]

As Roosevelt watched the debate within his administration over the relative importance of production versus consumption, of public versus private investment, he might have recalled that the policies advocated by his now-dead rival Huey Long were grounded in a theory of underconsumption. Long's Share the Wealth plan is easily dismissed as a crackpot scheme designed to win votes but lacking in substance. But its basic theme, "the insufficient distribution of purchasing power among the populace [and] the inability of the economy to provide markets for the tremendous productivity of American industry and agriculture," says historian Alan Brinkley, "was not without elements of economic truth." As this economic truth was being reinforced by his advisers in 1938, Roosevelt might have thought about its appeal to voters in 1935 when Long was mounting his challenge to the New Deal.[23]

In any case, the argument for consumption finally won out. On April 14, 1938, Roosevelt asked Congress to reauthorize the PWA and the WPA. On June 21, Congress passed the PWA Reappropriation Act of 1938, authorizing the expenditure of $965 million, of which $200 million could go to federal projects. The new deadline for receipt of proposals was September 30, 1938.[24]

The response was immediate. The last projects were whisked from drawing boards, and the last frenzy of construction began. Included in this wave were eight more Louisiana parish courthouses, almost all of the higher education projects, and many more schools. The Avoca ferry, the Adeline drawbridge, and the Alexandria swimming pool were also among the 1938 efforts. Communities rushed to meet the deadline. Three Lake Providence officials chartered an airplane to deliver their proposal for a $170,000 power and water project. They made it on time; however, the project was later transferred to the WPA. The last proposal the PWA accepted came from a small town in Texas, delivered just five minutes before the deadline by two men on a motorcycle.[25]

There would be no further extensions for the PWA. Some in Congress made an effort to set up a permanent public works program to guarantee employment in future recessions and to ensure that public projects could be realized when they were needed and not deferred. But the votes in Congress to support New Deal legislation were no longer sufficient. Southern Democrats who had been core supporters of the first wave of New Deal legislation were now fearful of the support these programs were giving to people they saw as adversaries: urban northerners, particularly immigrants, and African Americans.[26]

Roosevelt's Reorganization Act of 1939 amalgamated the PWA and the WPA, now called the Work Projects Administration, into a single agency

Avoca Ferry, Morgan City. Still in operation but with a newer ferry boat.

titled the Federal Works Agency under the direction of John Carmody, an engineer and former trouble-shooter for the CWA. Carmody was succeeded in 1941 by Major General Philip B. Fleming, who had worked as Ickes's deputy from 1933 to 1935. Fleming made an energetic and eloquent defense of the need for a permanent federal public works agency but ran into opposition from the Army Corps of Engineers. There was little public support. Americans in general were relieved to see the end of the Depression in sight and disinclined to further experimentation. The new schools, courthouses, university campuses, and other community facilities they had helped build probably seemed enough of an accomplishment for one generation. Besides, there was a war to think about. Their energies would be required elsewhere.[27]

TABLE 2.

Total Allotments for Nonfederal Programs in Selected Southern States

State	Number of Projects	Loans	PWA Funds Grants	Total	Estimated Cost
Alabama	330	$13,907,400	$17,735,934	$31,643,334	$46,936,821
Arkansas	235	11,761,271	10,810,708	22,472,979	29,699,049
Georgia	516	3,034,600	16,486,635	19,521,235	39,329,151
Louisiana	228	4,170,972	19,607,376	23,778,348	52,292,697
Mississippi	231	4,274,953	29,469,178	33,745,131	68,311,347
South Carolina	243	37,636,257	36,057,727	73,693,884	86,473,382

Source: List of All Allotted Non-Federal Projects, Projects by State and Docket, as of May 30, 1942, Table Number SP 1865, Federal Works Agency, Public Works Administration, Record Group 135, National Archives II, College Park, Md.

CHAPTER 5

SCANDAL

In June 1939, as most of the last round of Public Works Administration (PWA) projects were nearing completion, a reporter and a photographer from the *New Orleans States* observed workmen in Metarie unloading window frames from a Louisiana State University (LSU) truck. They were at the site of a house being built by Mrs. James McLachlan, the wife of one of Governor Richard Leche's staff members. The men and materials were believed to be part of a Works Progress Administration (WPA) project. Soon the entire nation was informed of the delivery by Drew Pearson and Robert Allen in their syndicated column "Washington Merry-Go-Round." The *Shreveport Journal* printed it as a front-page story.[1] This flare splashed phosphorescent light on a range of activities and relationships that would come to be known as the "Louisiana Scandals."

After uncounted grand jury sessions, reports, charges, denials, counter-charges, investigations, indictments, and verdicts, some of the state's most illustrious citizens were in jail. Governor Leche, LSU president James Monroe Smith, prominent architect Leon Weiss, megacontractor George Caldwell, and LSU business manager E. N. Jackson had to move from their mansions to more modest quarters in the federal penitentiary in Atlanta. Contractor Monte Hart died before he could serve his sentence. Dr. Clarence Lorio, president of the Louisiana State Medical Society, had his two-year sentence suspended.

It was the climax of the pageant of malfeasance that Huey Long had both organized and warned against. "If I don't live long enough to undo the centralization of government I've built up in this state," he said, "all these men around me are going to end up in the penitentiary."[2] The prophecy was fulfilled in less than five years.

The pageant was undeniably colorful while it lasted. A sportsman and gentleman horse breeder, Governor Leche built a stud farm on the north shore of Lake Pontchartrain that was reportedly embellished by outbuildings prefabricated in Parker Coliseum by WPA labor and trucked to the site in the same manner as Mrs. McLaughlin's window frames. This was petty crime, however, compared to his illegal oil leasing deals, which finally put him in jail.

Perhaps even more colorful, literally and figuratively, was the general contracting firm of Caldwell Brothers and Hart, which played a major part in building public facilities in Louisiana during the 1930s and for two decades thereafter. It was founded in the little town of Abbeville by Summerfield Caldwell, known as "Summa," with his brothers, Vernon and Tom. Summa was the center of the firm, the one with a keen sense of business. Vern was more interested in agriculture and took little part in building. Tom was a master bricklayer and content to work under Summa's, and later his nephew's, direction.

Summa Caldwell was gregarious and liked a good story. He made modest investments in a wide range of stock schemes, not because he believed he'd get a good return but because he admired the pitchman's tale. He also enjoyed a little personal drama. He wore the same outfit to every bid opening: a tailcoat, blue pin-striped pants, a red shirt, a red vest with green buttons, and red socks. (He wore red socks even when there wasn't a bid opening.) A bowler hat, cane, and spats completed the ensemble. The uniform must have brought him luck, because the firm prospered. Probably the brain under the bowler had something to do with it, too.[3]

Of the next generation of Caldwells, only Summa's nephew George took an active role in the firm. George's parents died while he was a boy, and he lived with his uncle Summa during his youth. Summa's own son, Jimmy, was nominally part of the firm but preferred the life of a playboy in New Orleans. George had a talent for organization. He was able to mobilize people and materials and get the job done swiftly. The Panhellenion, a WPA project on the LSU campus, was completed in thirty days. Building "G" went up in ten. However, neither is still standing, so perhaps some compromises were made in the interests of speed.

George also had a talent for living extravagantly. By the mid-1930s, he had a mansion on Baton Rouge's Highland Road with gold-plated bathroom fixtures, a clothes closet bigger than most bedrooms, and a mirror over the bed. He liked to entertain, and set such an example in the consumption of food and drink that he attained a body mass of over 300 pounds. He more than earned his nickname, "Big George." In order to help introduce his girth behind the wheel of his car, he had half the steering wheel cut off. This worked well until he had to make a turn, at which point the cutoff ends of the steering wheel were rather painful intrusions. So he engaged a chauffeur.

At some point, the electrical contractor Monte Hart entered the partnership, and the firm became Caldwell Brothers and Hart. Caldwell family members blame Hart for the firm's involvement in the scandals. Indeed, the indictments in the PWA files bear his name more often then either Summa's or George's. The center of the scandal in the LSU dormitory project was a piece of electrical equipment, Hart's province. But family members also do not deny that Big George was a wheeler-dealer and lax bookkeeper. His great wealth most likely had illegal augmentation. At the time the scandal broke, Big George was serving as LSU's superintendent of construction, a position that he used to rake off 2 percent of the cost of all building projects.

Leon Weiss, architect of the Louisiana state capitol, collaborated with Caldwell and Hart to pad the costs of state buildings. The administration building at Louisiana Polytechnic Institute, named, appropriately, after Governor Leche, proved to be their undoing. They were charged with defrauding the university of $56,914. They were also indicted for $62,486 worth of fraudulent repairs to an LSU Medical Center building, for a $37,232 overcharge in moving a Charity Hospital building to make way for a proposed dental building, and for $23,696 in fraudulent foundation work for the dental building. Though no charges were pressed, the cost of the law school at LSU, also temporarily named after the governor, ballooned from $675,000 to $905,000.[4]

President James Monroe Smith's sins were in even larger figures. He played the commodities market with LSU bonds, some of which he printed himself. He was also in the habit of amending the minutes of the meetings of the LSU Board of Supervisors to reflect approval of actions the supervisors hadn't discussed and salary increases for himself and his friends they hadn't approved. Huey Long had appointed Smith in 1930. Long confided: "There ain't a straight bone in Jim's body. But he does what I want him to." Long kept careful watch on Smith's administration of LSU, but after Long's death Smith had a free hand. One of his nicknames on campus was "Jingle Money." When word got out of his commodities trading, he and his wife fled the country. He was found in Canada "on vacation," and the Royal Canadian Mounted Police shipped him home.[5]

The role of the PWA in these Louisiana luminaries' downfall was peripheral, despite the fact that all of these individuals had some involvement in PWA projects. The reason is probably that the PWA's Inspection and Investigations divisions allowed little room for shady dealing. They did not wait for newspaper columnists to point out some infraction. As mentioned, each project had a resident engineer-inspector (REI) assigned to it. He saw to it that proper construction techniques were employed; that the materials specified in the contract, and not cheaper substitutes, were the ones used; and that the contractor adhered to the PWA's labor policies. Often, the REI had more than one project to oversee, so there were opportunities to sneak something past him. And sometimes the opportunities were taken, as in the case of the LSU Geology Building. But for the most part, the PWA's system of scandal detection was highly efficient.

The second line of defense in maintaining project integrity was the Investigations Division. In response to any complaint, a special agent was dispatched from Washington. These men had varied backgrounds—law, engineering, private investigation, accounting—and could be selected according to the needs of the case. Since contractors were dealing with the individual project sponsors and not the PWA, the agency itself could not take them to court. It could, however, withhold grant payments. This was usually enough to ensure compliance.[6]

Looking at the kinds of things the PWA investigated provides some idea of its thoroughness. Some of the matters were quite small, some petty. Some involved individual con artists blaming a contractor for a small, perhaps feigned, injury. Some involved contractors trying to take advantage of desperate workers. Personal jealousies and small town politics sometimes produced accusations of fraud or bribery. The PWA investigated them all and usually reached a settlement.

The labor policies the PWA developed were designed to spread work around as widely as possible. Accordingly, there were limits to how many hours an individual could work each week. At the Gillis Intermediary School, a construction superintendent allowed three workers to put in two extra hours each one week because weather had prevented them from working part of the previous week. It made sense to the superintendent, who was new to the PWA and did not know how straight-laced an organization it was. The investigation involved interviewing nineteen witnesses and producing eleven exhibits. The amount in dispute was $3.30.[7] The PWA made them give it back. But the PWA went to equal lengths to protect workers. At the Hathaway High School, after talking with twelve witnesses and reviewing eighteen exhibits, a contractor was required to restore a grand total of $24.00 to underpaid workers.[8]

Misclassification of workers was a frequent bone of contention. Pay levels were set by the PWA according to skill. If workers hired at one level performed work at a higher level, they were entitled to higher pay. This could be a few cents an hour, but could mount up in the course of a long job. A common laborer who worked as a plumber's helper at the Natchitoches courthouse gained $455.80 through a PWA investigation.[9]

Having a government agency stand up for them against contractors must have been a new experience for workers. The Natchitoches case may have emboldened laborers at Marthaville to report that they were doing structural steel work on the new gymnasium there. This was considered skilled work. The construction supervisor denied their claim. Two REIs vouched for the integrity of the contractor and said that with three certified structural steel men on the job, there should have been no need for others. But contrary evidence came in from school bus drivers who lingered near the building site after dropping off their students. An important part of the classification of a structural steel worker is that he climbs on the girders and uses tools. The drivers testified that they saw the workers in question on the structure and using tools. The contractor settled with the plaintiffs in order to get on with the job. He even paid higher wages to one worker who had done (or not done) the same things as the plaintiffs but who had not joined the complaint. But he clearly felt wronged.[10]

Such cases didn't always go against the contractor. At the Alexandria pool, the PWA investigation found that a business agent of the Common Laborers' Union persuaded six workers to accuse the contractor of having them do skilled work and paying them common labor wages. Special Agent Doyle H. Willis found other workers who had been asked to join the plot but had refused. Part of the charge was that the contractor had folded the pay sheets so that workers could not see the wage rates when they signed the sheets. Willis found the pay sheets: no folds.[11]

Discrimination against various classes of workers was investigated. Usually this was more rumor than substance, fueled by the hunger for jobs and the fear of there not being enough to go around. In Red River Parish, discrimination against veterans was alleged by officials of the local American Legion. At the outset of the investigation, it was discovered that one of the projects where the discrimination was supposed to be taking place was actually a WPA project. On the PWA project, the special agent found veterans to be working. All workers had been referred by the Louisiana State Employment Service and were hired according to the skills needed. The agent also interviewed a veteran who had not been hired. This individual said it was not discrimination, he just didn't have the qualifications for the available jobs.[12]

When the Caldwell Parish courthouse was begun, the rumor spread that the contractor, who was from Tennessee, was bringing in "foreign" labor. The foreigners, of course, were Tennesseans. The investigation found that, apart from certain supervisory and specially skilled technicians—categories exempted from PWA policies on the use of local labor—the contractor was using local men.[13]

Racial discrimination was a constant possibility. The labor policies of the PWA were unusual in requiring equal pay for black and white workers, but even more unusual because the PWA attempted to enforce them. The WPA had similar policies but rarely tried to apply them in the South.[14] Ickes was sometimes forced to compromise, but at least he made the effort. The Investigations files of the Louisiana projects contain several examples of efforts to enforce nondiscrimination. In the conversion of the old Baton Rouge post office to a city hall, contractors were accused of paying white plasterers $1.00 per hour but black plasterers only $.75. REI Edmund B. Mason was able to correct this.[15]

Proving discrimination is difficult if the presumed victims won't testify. A contractor building the school at Maurice insisted on employing people he had worked with before, including several African American painters. It was alleged that he was paying them $4.00 a day rather than the PWA rate of $1.00 per hour. When asked, the painters insisted that they were paid at the PWA rate. It is possible that the allegation was made by people who wanted to make trouble for the contractor because he had not employed enough local people. It is possible that the contractor was in fact underpaying the painters and knew they would not testify against him out of loyalty for past employment. The matter could be taken no further.[16]

Community politics sometimes entered into the execution of PWA projects. The Jeanerette sewer project involved street and sidewalk improvements. When it became apparent that the budget would not allow for the paving of all proposed streets if concrete was used, some city council members suggested other materials. The mayor refused to consider it. It turned out that his street was one of the few that would be paved. Rather than accept a pavement of lesser quality for his street, he was willing to leave other streets unpaved. When the special agent came to town, the mayor told him not to bother talking with council members. It would just stir up trouble, he said, and they didn't know anything about construction anyway. The agent did talk with them, but the mayor must have prevailed. The contract specified concrete.[17]

A more convoluted tale of conspiracy was spun around Hanna Junior High School in Red River Parish. The principal noticed an employee of one of the school board members hauling lumber from the building site. He also noticed a truckload of bricks being delivered to the board member's farm. Furthermore, he noticed cracks in the walls and discoloration in the stone surrounding the front door of his school. The grounds of the school contained unsightly holes and trenches. He assumed the board member must be taking bribes to ignore construction defects in his building.

After thirty-five interviews and thirty-seven exhibits were assembled, the investigator discovered other explanations for all of these mysterious occurrences. The lumber was scrap. It was splintered and full of nails, useful only for firewood. The contractor was happy to have someone haul it away; otherwise he would have to do it. Several people other than the school board member had obliged him. The load of bricks, declared at first to be 4,000 by the principal and then reduced to a much smaller number, was not part of the project. It had been bought by the board member from the supplier in a separate transaction. The cracks in the plaster were the result of the location of the school next to a rail line. They were being repaired. The discoloration of the stone, said the architect, was normal for this kind of stone. It would even out over time. Best of all, the scars in the landscape, so testified the school janitor, were in preparation for the planting of shrubs ordered by the principal himself.[18]

Collusion among bidders and kickbacks by successful bidders to persons who might have influenced their selection were common complaints, and the PWA investigated a number of them. The Monroe High School gymnasium involved both. Two special agents were unable to prove either charge in an investigation that involved sixty-three witnesses and ninety-

Hanna Junior High School. Imaginative brickwork enlivens a simple design by William T. Nolan. The school is now abandoned.

one exhibits, including the bank accounts of the accused. There was a possibility that one firm had prepared two bids, their own and one slightly higher that they got another contractor to sign. But there was no conclusive evidence.[19] In the case of "Big Charity" hospital, collusion was in fact uncovered and the contractors prosecuted. In most cases, however, the PWA did not find evidence of collusion. In some, disgruntled high bidders seemed to be at the heart of the charges.

In several cases, contractors were caught in other kinds of frauds. In Mooringsport, contractors concealed subcontracts and submitted false invoices. They also tried to bribe the mayor. In New Orleans, payrolls were falsified. The contractor had workers putting in excess hours both daily and weekly. He had a second payroll for the excess hours, which was not shown to the PWA. When investigators arrived, some payrolls were altered and others destroyed.[20]

Contractors had more opportunities to make big money in shady dealing and may have been better at covering up, but workers sometimes tried to use the PWA to make a quick buck. On the site of the Shreveport Exhibition Building, W. R. Myers claimed serious injury from falling off

Ouachita Parish School Board offices in the former Monroe High School gymnasium, by H. H. Land.

some low, wooden steps. He also claimed that the construction supervisor took kickbacks from workers and loaned money to black workers (he called them by another name) at 25 percent interest.

The REI, Marcus D. Weeks, inspected the stairs and found only part of one tread missing (one exhibit is a diagram of the steps). Myers had not claimed any injury until considerably after the fact. None of his coworkers noticed any impairment on the job. No employee, white or black, could be found who had delivered a kickback or accepted a high-interest loan. Thirty-two people were interviewed, and forty-six exhibits were examined. Further checking on Myers disclosed that ten years earlier he had won a settlement of $10,000 from the Missouri Pacific Railroad for a "permanent disability." He also had an earlier career as a police officer in Muskogee, Oklahoma, where he had taken protection money from brothels and bootleggers. So he was apparently not an inexperienced shakedown operator. But the PWA prevented him from collecting from the contractor in this case.[21]

Sometimes it was hard to tell who was conning whom. A night watchman at the Amite High School addition site claimed he was on the job fourteen and a half hours each day but was paid for only ten. The foreman agreed the watchman was there but said he was not asked to be. He assumed that the early arrival and late departure were due to the fact that the watchman lived some distance from Amite and was at the mercy of infrequent bus schedules. The watchman asserted that he was ordered to be at work at 4:30 P.M., not 7:00. He said he could have taken a later bus and still arrived on time. The construction superintendent was evasive when interviewed, and the company president confirmed, after initially denying it, that the watchman had been fired for complaining. This may have been enough to persuade the PWA investigator to side with the watchman.

However, the company refused to pay, and the watchman took them to court. He lost. It turned out that during the first six months he was on the job, there was indeed no bus that could have gotten him to the job later than 4:30. But then a later bus was added. It appeared that he kept taking the earlier bus and used the existence of the new schedule to support his claim.[22]

In these examples, we can see the kind and level of scrutiny that the PWA gave its projects. Occasional malefactors may have gotten away with something, but the list of those who did not is impressive. Perhaps as important, rumors of malfeasance or corruption that might have damaged the PWA's ability to operate, however misinformed, were put to rest by thorough investigation. But in Louisiana, the PWA had its hands full, and it could not avoid some role in the Louisiana scandals.

One early test came in LSU's first PWA project, the three women's dormitories. Electrical equipment supposed to be installed in Louis Garig Hall was instead placed in Annie Boyd Hall, a pre-PWA building. The equipment from Annie Boyd went to Strawberry Stadium in Hammond, a WPA project. The contractor on all these projects was Caldwell Brothers and Hart. Why this switch was made is unclear. Probably the used equipment was sold as new to the WPA, but how did Caldwell and Hart think that no one would notice the absence of equipment in Louis Garig? We don't know because Caldwell quickly refunded the cost of the equipment to LSU, and no further questions were asked.[23]

An even more interesting mystery was uncovered midway through the construction of the Geology Building. REI Horace R. Brown realized that the building going up was not the building whose plans had been approved by the PWA. He found there were two sets of plans. Harnett Kane tells this story but makes it sound like a simple scheme to pad expenses.[24] The

Women's dormitories, Louisiana State University. The contractors attempted a mysterious equipment swap with Strawberry Stadium in Hammond. All three dormitories were designed by Weiss, Dreyfous, and Seiferth.

architect and contractors had managed that on other buildings without going to the trouble of creating two sets of plans. The truth was more complicated.

The situation arose because the building was to be occupied jointly by the LSU Geology Department and the State Conservation Department, but the initial plans were drawn up with the consultation of only one party. When Conservation officials saw what the Geology Department had provided for them, they were not pleased. Since they were putting up a goodly share of the local financing of the project, their wishes were accommodated in a revision of the plans. But since the original plan had already received PWA approval, and because Leon Weiss feared that processing a change order at that point would delay the project beyond the point tolerable to the PWA, it was agreed to proceed on the first set of plans. By the time the PWA realized what was going on, its money would have been spent.[25]

Because the revision required only internal adjustments and no changes in the outer shell of the building, it took Brown two months to notice what was happening. He later offered the defense that he was inspecting twenty other projects at the time and was spread too thin. The whistle was actually blown after Traveling Engineer-Inspector Barnet Brezner came to town. Traveling engineer-inspectors were regional monitors and troubleshooters. It seems that Brown had some trouble making up his mind what to do. Brezner must have convinced him that investigators had to be called in.[26] In any case, the system worked. The PWA investigation was initiated in February, long before the Pearson and Allen column on the WPA appeared in June.

The investigation concluded that the difference in cost between the building as approved and the building as completed was $85,988. Had the changes been officially requested and reviewed according to standard procedure, it is possible that the PWA would have approved them. But it did not, so the PWA's first grievance was blatant violation of the contract. And in the course of developing a second set of plans and expense records, some additional offenses were committed. This may have been encouraged by the atmosphere of duplicity already established. It is also possible that once the deceit came to light, the books were inspected with extra care. In any case, the special agents discovered that in the $86,000 change order, $11,568 was padding.[27]

Summa Caldwell and Monte Hart had on several occasions requested two sets of invoices from subcontractors, explaining that this would simply "offset their loss" for other work on this project, expenses they were not getting paid for. But one item they snuck in was millwork that went to the residence they were building for LSU business manager E. N. Jackson. As their bookkeeping was being deconstructed, Caldwell and Hart voluntarily reduced their claims by over $10,000. This did not prevent a federal grand jury from indicting them in September 1939 on conspiracy to defraud the U.S. government and on five counts of "making false and fraudulent representations to the PWA."[28]

After James Monroe Smith's arrest, Law School dean Paul Hebert was named acting president of LSU. Not long after he took the helm of the storm-tossed institution, he fired the firm of Weiss, Dreyfous, and Seiferth because they had

> *failed to protect the interests of the university properly insofar as change orders and extras for [three LSU projects] . . . and failed to give necessary cooperation to the Public Works Administration in these matters. Addi-*

tionally, the university's unfortunate experience in the past, when it accepted buildings upon your recommendation and certificate that all work had been performed satisfactorily and has been discovered subsequently that these buildings never should have been accepted in their then state, leads the Executive Committee to a very serious doubt as to whether it can rely upon your recommendations in the future.[29]

The reference to the acceptance of buildings refers to the standard practice of an inspection by the architect of the completed building to ensure that all work had been properly done. On PWA projects, the REI was part of this inspection. Obviously, Hebert had concluded that Weiss's firm had not done proper inspections when left on its own. Frederick Von Osthoff, the architect LSU brought in to inspect the Geology Building after the scandals broke, seems to have relied on an inspection done by PWA special agent Willis when referring to four pages of problems as minute as frayed sash cords that were "called to my attention."[30]

In addition to being aided by the example of careful PWA inspection of its projects, LSU also benefited from the agency's practice of withholding the last grant payment until all parties had inspected the building. In his attempt to recover what he believed the architects and contractors owed LSU on the non-PWA buildings, Hebert used the PWA's last payment to them as leverage.[31] Thus not only were the PWA's buildings victimized much less than non-PWA projects, its procedures were also an important instrument for redress on these other projects.

Public concern about the potential for fraud and profiteering on public works projects was one of the factors that motivated Harold Ickes to move carefully and prudently in spending the public's money through the PWA. In Louisiana, this public concern was well founded, and Ickes's stewardship of public money prevented or minimized abuses and ensured that abusers would be exposed and prosecuted. Ickes maintained his reputation as "Honest Harold," and the PWA earned its reputation for diligent management. By inspecting projects as they went along and withholding funds rather than using threats of legal action, PWA staff were usually able to see a problematic situation as it developed and correct it before it became a criminal case. They provided the ounce of prevention that saved the owner from wearisome litigation after violations had been committed.

PART II

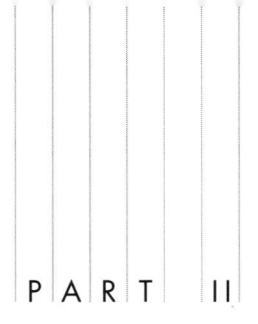

CULTURAL INFRASTRUCTURE

REDEVELOPING COMMUNITY

CHAPTER 6

SCHOOLS

School projects were by far the most numerous of the Public Works Administration (PWA) contributions to Louisiana. These efforts added 175 new buildings to parish school systems, built additions to twenty-eight existing buildings, and repaired twelve others. The new structures ranged from one-room, wood-frame schools with outhouses to a million dollar vocational school like Francis T. Nichols (now Frederick Douglass) in New Orleans or high schools in Houma, Natchitoches, Bossier City, and Ruston, each costing over half a million dollars.

The impact of these new buildings was multifaceted. First, they improved the health and safety of thousands of children and their teachers who had been working in genuinely life-threatening situations. Second, they greatly accelerated a trend in consolidation of schools. The one- and two-room buildings built through the PWA that simply maintained the status quo were few compared with the substantial elementary and secondary buildings that brought in pupils from scattered sites across the state. This, in turn, made possible the third and most important impact: expansion and enrichment of the curriculum.

Even the most talented and resourceful of teachers could not be expected to be equally adept at teaching English, history, geography, mathematics, science, and the arts. No two-room building could possibly offer a chemistry laboratory, a football team, or an orchestra to its students. In a consolidated school, teachers could specialize, and large numbers of students could make expanded facilities more economical. Better facilities, the chance to develop intellectually in one's specialty, and a larger community of educators made it easier for small towns and rural areas to attract and keep qualified teachers who might otherwise go to the cities. The opportunities for both teaching and learning were expanded exponentially in consolidated schools.[1]

In the period after the end of the First World War, the need for better education systems was recognized. Furthermore, greater resources were required to support a growing population even without improving the system. The prosperity of the 1920s helped efforts to meet these challenges. In Shreveport, a building plan supported by a $6 million bond issue was begun in the late 1920s. In other places, the need was apparent, but remedies were not yet under way. The Depression brought everything to a stop.

Most of the thirty-three proposals approved by the PWA during the Huey Long era were for physical infrastructure projects, particularly public utilities like gas, water, and sewerage. Only five of this first batch were for schools. DeSoto Parish led the way, followed by Shreveport, Greenwood, Lafourche, and Maurepas. Shreveport, using the remainder of its $6 million bond issue to put up its 70 percent contribution, had six other proposals ready, but they did not make it under the wire when Ickes froze PWA activities in Louisiana.

The Shreveport proposals were for combination gymnasium/auditorium buildings to add to the elementary schools the city had just built. Such facilities provided educational opportunities otherwise unavailable in the ordinary classroom buildings. It meant that physical education and recess play could take place even on rainy days. Plays could be performed and musical groups heard in concert. Students and teachers could be brought together for convocations and assemblies of all kinds. The space could also be used for community meetings.

Thus the gym/auditorium was a big step up from the minimal physical plant that could provide a basic education. Following the example of Shreveport, many schools made this addition to their programs when the PWA reopened for business in the summer of 1936. The reduction of the required local financial contribution for PWA projects from 70 to 55 percent made it easier for poorer communities to participate.

Though some facilities like those at the Franklinton High School gave separate spaces to the gymnasium and the auditorium, allowing permanent seating and perhaps dressing rooms and locker rooms, the combined version was more economical and more common. The basic model was a wooden basketball floor with a stage at one end. Folding chairs filled the floor for assemblies, plays, and concerts, and were stacked or moved to the

SCHOOLS 73

White Castle High School gym/auditorium, now used for city recreation programs. The architects were William T. Nolan and Ulisse Nolan.

Fort Necessity High School gym/auditorium by John A. Baker.

sidelines for games. The basketball hoops were on movable poles or swung down from the ceiling.

Seventeen new gymnasiums, seven auditoriums, and thirty-two combination gyms/auditoriums were added to Louisiana school grounds. Another six were built as additions to existing buildings. Most are still serving their original purposes. Others have new lives. The Ouachita Parish School Board offices are in a converted PWA gym. The First Baptist Church of Monroe uses the old Okaloosa High School gym as the focus of its Seeker Springs Ministry Retreat Center. In addition to its function as a regional retreat center, other services like the church's latchkey program are available to the local community. The director told me of a third-grade girl who used to go home alone and now comes to Seeker Springs to play kickball and draw pictures under adult supervision. "We are blessed to have this building," he said.

Another popular addition, particularly in high schools that already had a gym/auditorium, was the home economics cottage. This was a kind of laboratory for teaching the "domestic sciences" of nutrition, cooking, sewing, child care, and home maintenance. It always featured a large kitchen and frequently a sewing room. Some versions were organized to resemble an ordinary middle-class house with a dining room and bedroom. Six freestanding home economics buildings were constructed, and a number of home economics rooms were included in the new high schools.

The rise of home economics parallels to some extent the growth of the women's movement of the late nineteenth century. The increased emphasis on home economics was spurred by two rather contradictory impulses. On the one hand, some thought that the status of women might be improved by stressing the complexity of homemaking and child rearing. Terms like "home economics" and "domestic science" called attention to the extent to which these taken-for-granted activities drew from more exalted fields of knowledge like biology, psychology, and economics. One the other hand, antifeminists could also endorse this route to higher status for women because it kept women in their "proper" domestic sphere—in other words, at home.[2]

As discussed in chapter 1, the Country Life movement that developed during the Progressive Era promoted home economics as a means of reducing poverty and modernizing life in rural areas. The initial hope was that a focus on a better planned and more efficient domestic sphere brought about by girls and women would broaden to encompass men and

Ward Elementary School cafeteria, originally the Jennings High School home economics cottage. William R. Burk was the architect.

communities. By the end of the 1920s, the broader goal had been abandoned, and the focus narrowed to concentrate on girls.[3]

Demographic changes during the 1920s and 1930s saw many families leaving farms for cities, thus separating the generations and generally dispersing the extended family. Also, while it was still unusual for women with children to be in the labor force, it was not unknown. The lack of jobs for men sometimes made it essential for women to take work outside the home. In such an atmosphere, it was understandable that communities might be beginning to worry about their girls losing the opportunity of learning traditional home-making skills from their mothers, grandmothers, and aunts.

The Depression gave a new edge to one of these domestic skills: canning. Canning was a traditional way of making fruits and vegetables grown in the summer and fall last through the winter and spring. With so many families losing the income to buy food, it became essential to see that nothing that was harvested was wasted. To put food preservation skills taught in the DeSoto Parish home economics cottage to work immediately, school officials planned for the cottage to be large enough to support a community-wide canning effort.[4]

Ruston High School Special Education Building. It was originally a home economics cottage. Home economics mansion might have been more accurate.

The gyms/auditoriums and home economics cottages were important enrichments to education for the more fortunate communities, but in many places basic classroom buildings were a pressing need. One indication of how great that need was can be found in a report made by the PWA's traveling engineer-inspector Fred L. Hargett on July 27, 1937. He was sent around the state to verify the claims of local school officials that existing buildings posed substantial health and safety risks to students and teachers. He covered eleven communities in that report and substantiated health or fire hazards in all but one. He also noted severe overcrowding in some places.

In Shreveport, Liddieville, Winnsboro, and Natchitoches, Hargett confirmed that the schools there were fire hazards. The school at Winnsboro had already caught fire twice. Its open-flame heater was unshielded from the dry pine lumber around it. There were no fire escapes. The building at Liddeville also had no fire escape and had also suffered fires.[5] High schools in Franklinton and Lake Providence and a school at Hunter in DeSoto Parish had already burned to the ground. Some of the walls of the Franklinton school were salvaged.

The other schools posed health risks because of deteriorating building structure, poor ventilation, or contaminated water. At Monticello and Liddieville, open-pit toilets were located perilously near the well where students drank. In a separate report on Liddieville, PWA director of engineering Arthur J. Bulger described the toilets as "filthy" and measured the distance to the well as only 100 feet. He also noted that students who could not fit into the existing four-room building had to hold class in a nearby church, which was impossible to heat in winter.[6]

Schools for African Americans were even worse. Another of Hargett's reports described a fifty-five-year-old "Negro School" in Lake Providence as "leaning" and "about rotted down." It "would take very little wind to blow it over," he added. It had "very unsanitary toilets" and only one light. It was "dangerous," he concluded, "and should not be used as a school."[7] The situation in Jennings was among the worst, if only because of the incredible overcrowding. John M. Whitney, M.D., the director of the Parish Health Unit, reported to the school superintendent on the "Training School," which served as both the elementary and high school for African Americans:

> [Its] siding is either rotted or warped beyond repair, several pieces are hanging loose or tied together with bailing wire. A number of window lights are missing. . . . The window shades are ragged and torn and afford no protection against the sun's rays, the doors are warped, the hinges rusty, and the locks in poor condition. Several steps are rotted away.
>
> The water supply consists of a drilled well and hand pump which accommodates approximately 600 children, whereas the source of city water supply is but two blocks away. The toilet facilities . . . consist of two sanitary pit privies which are practically full to overflow.
>
> . . . During a rain the roof leaks and if the wind blows at all the building rocks to and fro. Termites are noted in both buildings as well as bats and lice in the attic from which a very strong odor emits.[8]

In replacing schools like this, the PWA was a true lifesaver for many communities. In addition to the gyms/auditoriums and home economics cottages discussed above, a total of ninety-one new elementary schools were built. Another nine were repaired, and eighteen got new additions.

High schools were also needed. Seventeen new ones were built. They

CULTURAL INFRASTRUCTURE

Mermantau Elementary School, an unusual design by Baron and Roberts that anticipates postmodernism by fifty years.

included Francis T. Nicholls Vocational School (now Frederick Douglass High School) in New Orleans; Bossier High School, a sleek modernist composition; Ruston High School and Port Allen High School (now Middle School), both art deco gems; Franklinton High School (now junior high); Natchitoches High School (now the Louisiana School for Math, Science, and the Arts); and high schools in Bell City, Bonita, Clayton, Hathaway, Kelly, Martin, Monticello, Rayne, Simpson, Thibodaux, and Winnsboro. Another four schools received additions, and three more were repaired.

The art deco style, which gets its name from the 1925 Exposition Internationale des Arts Decoratifs et Industriels in Paris, was very popular in the 1930s. It was felt in the design of furniture, jewelry, ceramics, wallpa-

L. S. Rugg Elementary School, Alexandria, with streamline deco touches by Baron and Roberts.

Terrebonne High School, Houma, at $750,000, the most expensive of the Louisiana PWA high schools. The architects were Wogan and Bernard.

Franklinton Middle School, originally the high school. The Tudor entrance and castellated cornice by John A. Baker are unusual for the time and place.

per, and women's clothing. Hollywood movies placed their stylish stars in deco interiors. In architecture, commercial buildings and hotels that were intended to catch the eye of potential customers used deco motifs to say to the world: we are hip, we are sophisticated, we are where the action is, where the fashionable people congregate.

There were several branches of art deco design. The one most often seen in PWA buildings is known as "streamline deco." Simple geometric forms predominated. Mechanical elements, borrowed particularly from airplanes and ocean liners, gave the buildings a feel of motion. Strong horizontal moldings added to this effect; indeed, they were sometimes called "speed lines." Rounded corners made the buildings more aerodynamic. Pointed towers shaped like rockets and vertical fins punctuating the facade and rising above the roofline also conveyed motion. A world of the future, like that seen in the Buck Rogers and Flash Gordon comic strips and movies, was being created.

This commercial flamboyance is toned down considerably in the Louisiana schools, but the rounded corners, the aerodynamic surfaces, and the proud verticality can be seen in the Port Allen and Ruston high schools and in many of the gyms/auditoriums around the state. In the latter, the

Frederick Douglass High School, originally Francis T. Nicholls Vocational School. Damage by Hurricane Katrina leaves its fate in doubt. Its architect was Edgar A. Christy.

barrel or elliptical arch of the roof is preferred to a flat or pitched roof. This orientation toward the future, along with a sense of adventure and fun, seems entirely appropriate to a school building. We can look at them and feel the hope for a better tomorrow that Depression-era parents felt for their children.

Central to this future were the dramatically new educational opportunities that these buildings made possible. Libraries, science and agricultural laboratories, art and music rooms, industrial arts shops, home economics rooms, and other special facilities that existed only in the dreams of educators before the Depression now became realities even in small communities.

Along with the elementary and high schools were a new junior high

82 CULTURAL INFRASTRUCTURE

The Louisiana School for Math, Science, and the Arts; originally Natchitoches High School. Designed by Weiss, Dreyfous, and Seiferth.

North Iberville Elementary-High School, originally Shady Grove High School. Another creative use of brick by William T. Nolan.

SCHOOLS 83

Labadieville Middle School, originally an elementary school, with a nice art deco entrance by Bodman and Murrell.

Ruston High School, an impressive art-deco composition by J. W. Smith and Associates.

Baton Rouge Police Department administration building, originally the Louisiana State School for the Deaf, a neoclassical design by Favrot and Reed.

school and six vocational schools. The Louisiana State School for the Deaf got a large new classroom building, now used by the Baton Rouge Police Department. It also received a swimming pool addition to its gym/auditorium. An amazing total of 182 school buildings were added to the Louisiana educational system. Another forty buildings were expanded or repaired.

It seems odd that with schools blooming across the state, there should be so little activity in its largest population center. New Orleans had only one school project, which contributed just three buildings. True, it was an effort of over $1.2 million. But one would expect a city that had so recently fought Huey Long so hard for patronage would have jumped to take advantage of the PWA's assistance in school construction. Perhaps the other large projects—the bridge, the hospital, the market—were enough to fill the need for jobs. But perhaps the real answer lies in the attitude of the city to public education. There was little support for it. There was not much interest in it before the Civil War and even less after. Whites went to private, usually religious, schools. Blacks were not educated above the fifth grade. What schools the city had were largely the product of one benefactor. John C. McDonough served in Beale's Rifles at the Battle of New Orleans and became a wealthy landowner. He was a penny-pincher, rowing to his home on the West Bank to save the cost of a ferry ticket. However, he was very generous to good causes. In 1850 he willed over $1 million in property to the city for the purpose of financing public schools. This produced forty schools between 1861 and 1951.[9] So, while the rest of the state was feverishly building PWA schools, large and small, New Orleans was satisfied with one PWA project.

There was, as might be expected, a certain racial bias in these educational efforts. Schools for African Americans were included in many parish proposals, but they were usually smaller, less expensive, and proposed later. Caddo Parish superintendent of schools E. W. Jones, in a letter to PWA assistant administrator Horatio Hackett about eight Shreveport school proposals, complained that "the eighth one is in the hands of the New Orleans office and, like all building programs in the south, being one for Negroes it was left to the last." The Training School in Jennings is an example of this. Jennings had already put through three school projects for a total of $101,124 worth of construction. The Training School barely made the final application deadline. The Hathaway High School is another example. The school board had a two-phase plan. The new $115,000 high school was phase one; schools for black students were phase two. After phase one was completed, however, the money had run out.[10]

Schools for white students were usually solid brick buildings; ones for black students were often frame, without plumbing or electricity. The one- and two-room schools that were being happily abandoned by white students were being reproduced in some parishes for black students. The lack of plumbing in these buildings is made brutally clear in the PWA microfilm records of the Bossier Parish schools: there are drawings of architect-designed outdoor privies.[11]

One example of the unequal distribution of resources is in Docket #1077, a Lake Providence proposal for two schools, one for blacks, one for whites. They seem intended for roughly the same number of students: the school for whites was to have eighteen classrooms, the school for blacks fourteen. Both included gyms/auditoriums. The school for whites had two music rooms, a nurse's room, and steam heat. The school for blacks had a library, a book storage room, a separate shop building, and gas heat. While the buildings might at first seem roughly comparable, they are not. The school for whites was made of brick and stone and cost $146,375; the school for blacks was made of weatherboard and cost $29,567.¹²

Red River Parish constructed a new high school at Martin, a new junior high at Hanna, new gymnasiums at East Point and Grand Bayou, combination gym and shop buildings at Hall Summit and Coushatta, and an administration building in Coushatta. They were all brick and stone. The Negro Training School at Coushatta was wood frame, as were four small school and shop buildings for blacks placed around the parish. When rising costs required cutbacks, the board eliminated proposed equipment from the seven buildings for whites and cut down the size of those for blacks.¹³

Bossier High School is one of the most impressive of the PWA high schools with its clean, modernist design by Sam Wiener for Jones, Roessle, Olschner, and Wiener. It has eighteen classrooms; an auditorium seating 1,000; a cafeteria; biology, chemistry, and general science laboratories; a study hall; a combination conference room and library; a manual training room; bookkeeping, typing, and business practice rooms; sewing, fitting, and cooking rooms; a home economics apartment; and a book storage room. It is made of brick and limestone and has gleaming hallways of

Springville Education Center, Coushatta; originally the Negro Training School. Designed by William T. Nolan.

vitrified tile and marble toilets. A new "colored high school" was built at the same time. Its size and amenities are not specified, but its excavation requirements were 230 cubic yards versus 4,750 for the school for whites. It was built of brick, not weatherboard, and had heat and electricity. But instead of marble toilets, it featured "out of doors sanitation."[14]

It was not unusual for projects to face cutbacks once they had been approved and bids had been solicited from contractors. Poor planning or higher than expected bids would require reassessment. Sometimes communities would seek extra money from the PWA. If that didn't work, something would have to be cut out. The likely candidates were facilities for blacks. A minor example of that occurred in Red River Parish. Crowley is another. It wanted six school projects; one was to be a four-room, brick addition to a school for blacks. When forced to scale back to four projects, this school was one of those abandoned.[15] Parks picked for improvements in Shreveport included Lincoln, used by blacks. When the budget had to be adjusted, Lincoln took the biggest hit.[16] Its appropriation was cut from $2,421 to $921. The funds for Thomas Park, a park for whites slated for similar improvements, were reduced from $2,127 to $1,627.

The picture that emerges from the examination of the PWA elementary and secondary school projects in Louisiana is not one of equal treatment for African American students. The best that can be said is that they were not entirely excluded. Some of these buildings were built to last, and some of them were quite attractive. The Training School at Jennings, though last in line and built of wood rather than brick, is a handsome building with classical pilasters flanking the entrance. And it cost $31,644, which is a respectable investment when compared with the total cost of the other three projects at $101,000.

Nor were all such projects tacked on to proposals that featured schools for white students. The Industrial Training High School for Negroes in Clinton was a project all to itself. It produced an eight-room frame building with an auditorium accented with a columned portico and other classical details. Unfortunately, it has fallen victim to fire. A similar separate project was the Napoleonville Colored School. It is a frame structure given elegance by its V-shaped plan and tall central chimney. It had steam heat and indoor plumbing and contained five classrooms, a manual training room, a science and agriculture laboratory, a cooking room, and a sewing room. It was proposed at the same time as the Napoleonville gymnasium and cost $54,000 compared to $88,000 for the gym. Both are still in use.

One of the two elementary schools in the New Orleans project, Marie C. Courvent (now Alfred P. Tureaud), was for African Americans. It has graceful art deco detailing and is of the same size and cost as the school for whites.[17]

Some PWA schools were replacements for older structures, but others were new buildings, erected where none had existed. Even modest buildings could represent an improvement of considerable magnitude. They created educational opportunities for African Americans that simply did not exist before the PWA came to Louisiana. The net result, then, is that education for both blacks and whites took a giant step forward during the New Deal.

Alfred P. Tureaud Elementary School, New Orleans, originally Marie C. Courvent Elementary School, built for African Americans, beset by Formosan termites, and recently flooded by Hurricane Katrina.

The impact of these facilities on education in Louisiana is impossible to measure, but we can make a start. Begin with the lives saved from potentially disastrous school fires or outbreaks of disease. Then consider the hundreds of thousands of students who passed through these doors in the last seven decades, better able to lead productive lives after graduation. Think of the increased breadth and depth of learning they were exposed to in the laboratories, shops, and music rooms offered by the new, consolidated buildings. The opportunities for young bodies to develop physically and for individuals to learn to cooperate in team sports offered by the gymnasiums should not be overlooked. What contributions to the state and nation did these young people make that might have gone unrecognized and undeveloped in one-room schoolhouses? These things cannot be given dollar values, but they have undeniably improved our lives. And they continue to do so.

TABLE 3.
School Projects by Parish

Parish	New Buildings	Additions	Repairs
Acadia	10	1	
Allen	2		
Assumption	5		
Avoyelles	3		
Bienville	1		
Bossier	26 incl. 18 one- and two-room schools		1
Caddo	12	2	
Calcasieu	3	1	
Caldwell	1		
Concordia	2		
DeSoto	1		
E. Baton Rouge	3		
E. Carroll	3		
Franklin	8	3	1
Iberia	9	1	
Iberville	3		
Jackson	6	1	
Jefferson Davis	9		
LaFourche	1		
Lincoln	2		
Livingston		1	
Madison	1		1
Morehouse	2	2	
Natchatoches	7		3
Orleans	3		
Ouchita	4		
Point Coupee	1		
Rapides	1		
Red River	12		

TABLE 3. (Continued)
School Projects by Parish

Parish	New Buildings	Additions	Repairs
St. John the Baptist	1		
St. Tamany		1	
Tanigpahoa	3	3	
Tensas	1		
Terrebonne	1		
Union	9	2	1
Vermillion	6		1
Vernon	2		
Webster	4		
Washington	7		
W. Baton Rouge	2		
W. Carroll	3		
Winn	1		

CHAPTER 7

UNIVERSITIES

In the early 1930s Louisianans' interest in higher education was growing rapidly. The state's colleges and universities, most less than a decade old, were housed in makeshift quarters. Few had permanent buildings. Louisiana State University (LSU), the flagship in Baton Rouge of this newly carpentered fleet, was making progress toward adequate facilities on its new suburban campus when the Depression began. The institution had moved from its original downtown site and was settling into new Italian Renaissance–style buildings and grounds designed by Theodore C. Link, the architect of St. Louis's grand Romanesque revival Union Station.[1]

But momentum was not lost during the national economic crisis, because in 1930 Governor Huey Long took an interest in LSU. Only two years into his term, Long saw the university as a venue for political theatrics that might propel him to higher office. He tripled the size of the marching band and marched at its head in parades. He cheered for the football team and, to the growing irritation of its coach, tried to design new plays for it to run. Most important, he engineered a scheme for new construction.[2]

Long wanted to build a new capitol on land recently vacated by the university, so he had the university sell it to the state for a handsome, some said inflated, price. The questionable legality of one branch of the government selling land to another was brushed aside, and LSU was able to continue building. One of the products of this windfall was a field house named after Long and sporting a swimming pool that he made certain was the longest in the country. Another was a music and drama building, designed, like the field house, by the state's premier architects: Weiss,

Dreyfous, and Seiferth. This facility would provide an inspiration to the regional colleges that, with the help of the Public Works Administration (PWA), would soon be able to construct their own performing arts centers.

The other institutions of higher education in the state, not enjoying Long's personal attention, were in much poorer shape. The science building at Hammond Junior College (later Southeastern Louisiana University)[3] was a former barn with a leaking roof, termites, and a rotting foundation.[4] When asked whether he had inspected the engineering building at the Louisiana Polytechnic Institute in Ruston, State Superintendent of Education T. H. Harris replied: "I went in that building once before and I was lucky to get out alive."[5]

Despite the obvious need for new facilities, the regional institutions were slow to take advantage of the opportunity posed by the PWA. But LSU was not reticent. It launched a proposal in 1934 for four women's dormitories, a classroom building, and an addition to the student store in the field house. The total cost of the project was over $1 million.

Approval, however, was not soon in coming. The PWA's Finance Division had doubts about the university's ability to cover the loan it was seeking. The initial concern was the university's authority to issue bonds. That question was rendered moot by Long's state legislation requiring the state's approval for any borrowing or any spending of federal money and by the PWA's responding freeze of all Louisiana projects.

While LSU's proposal was in limbo, the university took advantage of the Civil Works Administration (CWA), which, with its emphasis on labor-intensive activities, was a natural for a project that involved taking a building apart, moving it, and reassembling it in another location. LSU was moving to its new campus. Most of the downtown buildings were left behind, but there was one, Alumni Hall, that university officials wanted to take with them. Workers hired by the CWA moved it, bit by bit, to the bluff west of the quad and next to the gym/armory. It is now home to the School of Journalism.

The reason the state's institutions of higher education moved slowly to use the PWA to expand their facilities might be found in popular opinion that elementary and secondary education had more pressing needs. An August 23, 1934, editorial in the *New Orleans States* denounced LSU's collaboration in Long's financial extravagances and his "exploitation of higher education at the expense of community institutions, the kindergarten, primary, grammar and high schools which have been so sorely neglected by the administration that pretends to be a friend of the masses."[6]

When the state reestablished relations with the PWA in 1936, the LSU women's dormitory proposal was put forth again. In fact, it went through several more iterations with different buildings and financial arrangements. Final approval came in February 1937 for three women's dorms: Evangeline, Grace King, and Louis Garig. The classroom building and bookstore extension were taken over by the WPA. The path to approval was smoothed by removing the loan request and asking only for a grant. The local portion was funded by loans from City National Bank.

The state's second higher education proposal to the PWA was also from LSU. It involved new equipment for the Sugar Factory. This was a particularly interesting combination of contributions to education and to the regional economy.

Southern University was next to ask the PWA for assistance. In August 1937 it received approval from the PWA to construct a gym/auditorium. In the building it replaced, ceiling plaster was falling, and several students had been injured. A week after the gym project was approved, the State School for Deaf and Blind Negro Children received support to build a brick school and dormitory building on the Southern University campus. It had tiled bathrooms and a slate roof. Prior to this time there had been no facilities for African American children with hearing or visual impairments.[7]

In 1938 LSU opened a junior college in Lake Charles. It became McNeese Junior College and later McNeese State University. A proposal jointly funded through a Calcasieu Parish bond issue and an appropriation by the state legislature brought two large buildings to the junior college and a stock exhibit pavilion to the community. One college building was a combination administration and classroom structure. The other was an auditorium with a seating capacity of 2,500. Both feature smooth surfaces with simplified classical details and were designed by Weiss, Dreyfous, and Seiferth.[8]

In the summer of 1938 the real building boom for higher education began. Northwestern State Normal School in Natchitoches led the construction march with two proposals, the first for a stadium and the second for a men's dormitory.[9] At the same time as the second Natchitoches project was approved, LSU's junior college in Monroe was given the go-ahead for two buildings of its own. One was a library, the other a music building.

F. G. Bulber Auditorium, McNeese State University, Lake Charles, one of three buildings at what was McNeese Junior College.

Both are dignified art deco buildings vertically designed in gray brick with limestone trim by architect J. W. Smith. Smith made one important error in drafting the music building, however. His stairways were not designed with the transport of pianos in mind. Only with great difficulty could workmen get them up to the practice rooms.[10]

Three new projects from LSU were forwarded next: a faculty club, a commerce classroom building, and a geology building. The first was described in the application as a "dormitory" because it was "designed to house unmarried members of the faculty." The "dormitory" project was also to provide facilities for a faculty club. Perhaps the label was purposeful. LSU might not have wanted to call it a "faculty club" because of possible connotations of self-indulgence on the part of the university's administration. The commerce building was to become Himes Hall. The local contributions for both were obtained through state appropriations raised through the corporate franchise tax. The tax provided debt service to the Board of Education's $6 million bond issue, which had already made possible the application to the PWA for so many elementary and secondary schools. Any tax revenue left over after servicing the debt could be used for further construction. State highway commissioner A. P. Tug-

Kaufmann Hall, McNeese State University, Lake Charles. Architects of all three McNeese buildings were Weiss, Dreyfous, and Seiferth.

well told George Bull, PWA regional director, that this would amount to $325,000 per year between 1938 and 1940.[11]

The Geology Building was financed in a more complex, and ultimately problematic, manner. The building was to be shared with the Louisiana Department of Conservation, which therefore would put up part of the money. Unfortunately, the department wasn't consulted in the design of the building and discovered only after the PWA had approved the project that the space allotted to it was inadequate. The architects redrew the plans but didn't tell the PWA.[12] But, as mentioned in chapter 5, this was only one of the famous firm's indiscretions.

Grambling University began as the Lincoln Parish Training School and

Biedenharn Hall, University of Louisiana–Monroe. Although J. W. Smith knew he was designing a music building, he neglected to make the stairwells large enough to bring in the pianos.

became, with the backing of Huey Long, the Negro Normal and Industrial School in 1928. It consisted of five wooden buildings: an eight-room classroom building, a dining hall, an elementary school building, and two dormitories. They were served by well water, oil lamps, and wood heat. The PWA brought Grambling its "first permanent buildings" in 1939: a classroom building, women's dormitory, library, gym/auditorium, dining hall, and president's house. They were brick, colonial revival structures with cypress sash and tile and marble bathrooms.[13]

The financing for the Gambling project came from the same Board of Education bond issue that supported the other school and university projects, despite the fact State Superintendent of Education T. H. Harris was not a Grambling fan. He had opposed the upgrading of the training school to a normal school by Long and had made Lincoln Parish continue paying for it until 1930, when a state appropriation of $9,000 was made. According to one observer, Harris harassed the school until his retirement.[14] This attitude notwithstanding, Grambling got a construction project of over $420,000, almost twice the cost of Monroe's.

By far the largest project in the northern part of the state was undertaken by the Louisiana Polytechnic Institute at Ruston (Tech). Subjected

Long-Jones Hall, Grambling University, administrative offices, once a classroom building.

to enrollment increases of almost 60 percent in the five years prior to the application and over 18 percent in the previous year alone, it was bursting at the seams. Buildings designed for 500–600 students were now used by 1,625. Senator John Overton informed the PWA by telegram that "the young people are temporality housed in barns." Tech lobbied hard for its proposal. The crowded and crumbling conditions of its buildings were documented by photographs in a pamphlet archly titled "*Picturing Woeful Affairs*." The state's efforts paid off in the PWA's approval of a project of over $2 million.[15]

The centerpiece of the Tech project was an auditorium and fine arts building that rivaled LSU's. Tech also built a new engineering building,

Bogard Hall, to replace the one Superintendent Harris was afraid to inspect. In addition, an agricultural building, two dormitories, a dining hall, and a power plant were added to the campus.

Campuses in the southern part of the state were also blooming. Hammond Junior College, established in 1925 and made a four-year program in 1937, had only two "permanent or worthwhile structures" on its grounds when the PWA arrived. It had one "well designed and economically constructed" building that was "taxed far beyond its proper capacity." The library was in one room of this building.[16] The other "worthwhile structure" was Strawberry Stadium, a recently completed WPA project. It contained thirty-six dorm rooms, but a quarter of them were being used for classrooms. So the core of what became Southeastern Louisiana University was established by New Deal programs. The PWA's contribution was Clark Library, which now houses the university museum and the Visual Arts Department; Mead Hall, a laboratory school building; McClimans Hall, now home to math and computers; a gym; a women's dormitory; a music and drama building; and the president's home.

The architects—Weiss, Dreyfous, and Seiferth—showed their modest

McClimans Hall, Southeast Louisiana University. All PWA Hammond buildings were the work of Weiss, Dreyfous, and Seiferth.

modernism again in some of these buildings. The president's house is a simple composition of geometric volumes. The Ralph A. Pottle Music Building has more complex geometry, with some art deco trim. Campbell Hall is notable for its corner windows, which wrap around the corners without any muntins (glazing bars) where the glass panes meet. Instead, the glass has mitered edges, leaving a clear, unbroken surface suggesting space cut out of the mass of the building. Frank Lloyd Wright used this unusual window treatment in his Los Angeles houses built in the 1920s.

In addition to the buildings, the Hammond project provided for service tunnels, walks and roads, lighting, and landscaping. The PWA's efforts would form the university's basic identity for many years to come.

As dramatic as was this blossoming of infant universities on the other regional campuses, the record for the most PWA buildings on a single campus goes to Southwestern Institute, the future University of Louisiana at Lafayette. Like Hammond and Tech, the most expensive structure on the Lafayette site was the Fine Arts Building. But there were also substantial academic, sciences, and elementary/junior high buildings. A library, now the home of the Computer Center, was built. An infirmary, women's dormitory, women's gym, and industrial arts building were solid structures

Ralph A. Pottle Music Building, Southeast Louisiana University.

Campbell Hall, Southeast Louisiana University, with Frank Lloyd Wright–inspired corner windows.

as well. A house for the president, a dining hall addition, and a stadium incorporating men's dormitory rooms brought the total to twelve major construction efforts. In addition, there were tennis courts, a track and football field, covered walkways between buildings to protect students from the heavy rains, and general landscaping. It was a true "instant campus" kit.[17] Once again, the architects of the Lafayette buildings were Weiss, Dreyfous, and Seiferth. But they display here none of their art deco or modernist leanings. The buildings are all in traditional, colonial revival style.

Completing the 1938 Louisiana investment in higher education was an addition and renovations to the LSU Medical Center building in New

Broussard Hall, University of Louisiana–Lafayette. More work by Weiss, Dreyfous, and Seiferth.

Orleans. Two wings were added to the eighth floor, and renovations were made to the main building in order to make proper use of the new spaces.[18]

But the PWA's involvement in Louisiana higher learning was not over yet. The summer of 1939 saw a final round of proposals. Natchitoches, which had planned only two buildings and a utilities extension in the first round, came back with a larger package this time. It consisted of five new buildings and additions to two others. Following the leads of Hammond, Tech, and Lafayette, Natchitoches, too, built a fine arts building, now named after Albert Fredericks, the president who oversaw the project. A geometric brick design by Edward F. Neild Jr., it compromised its modernism with classical sculptures over the three main portals. It contains two theaters, one seating 750 people and the other, 300. A men's dorm (Varnado Hall), a men's gym, a student center, and a swimming pool, not called a pool but a natatorium, were also added. Additions to the infirmary and power plant completed the PWA package.[19]

Southern University also found support for more construction in 1939. It built a stadium and three more dormitories with PWA help. One dormitory was a modest, one-story brick home for freshmen. The other two were more impressive compositions. A long, two-story women's dorm and

Fredericks Auditorium, Northwestern State University, Natchitoches, an interesting juxtaposition of classical sculpture with modernist massing, by Edward F. Neild Jr.

a more compact, three-story men's dorm were designed by William T. Nolan and his son, Ulisse, in light brick and green limestone. They have a restrained but definite streamline deco character, with terrazzo floors and marble bathrooms. Each dormitory cost about $200,000.[20]

While there were racial imbalances in the elementary and secondary school projects, African Americans got a better deal in higher education. At both Southern and Grambling, handsome and lasting structures were erected. In the number of buildings constructed and dollars spent, Grambling and Southern were both more favored than Monroe, and at $702,000, Southern was not too far behind Lake Charles at $904,000 and Hammond at $1 million. It was not equal treatment, but conferred some measure of respect while providing valuable support.

The PWA was not the only New Deal agency to work on Louisiana campuses. At Natchitoches, the WPA did renovations, the National Youth Administration built five wood dormitories, and the Federal Emergency Reconstruction Agency did landscaping and installed sewers.[21] At Hammond, as noted, the WPA built Strawberry Stadium. At LSU, the WPA was even more active. It built Alex Box Stadium, the northern enclosure of the football stadium, the student health center, the physics building

104 CULTURAL INFRASTRUCTURE

Natatorium, Northwestern State University, Natchitoches, not just an ordinary swimming pool.

(Nicholson Hall) complete with observatory, and the Agricultural Administration building. The Panhellenion, an office building for sororities, since torn down, was a WPA effort. WPA workers dug the lakes below City Park that border the campus on the east, paved roads and sidewalks, installed sewers and drainage canals, and built tennis courts and a running track. Their most impressive structure, rivaling many PWA projects in scale, is Parker Agricultural Center, once the largest copper-domed coliseum in the country.[22]

The biggest beneficiaries of the PWA's investment were Louisiana Tech, Lafayette, and Natchitoches, each gaining $2 million in new facilities. But from one corner of the state to the other, higher education was,

Bradford Hall, Southern University, Scotlandville, a women's dormitory. Streamline deco features with the characteristic brickwork by William T. Nolan and Ulisse Nolan.

in a few short years, given a foundation that would serve it for the rest of the century. And most of these buildings are serving the next millennium. The school for students who were deaf or blind at Southern has burned down, the student union at Natchitoches was razed to make room for new construction, and McNaspy Stadium at Lafayette is also gone. But with these three exceptions, every building that the PWA helped construct on Louisiana's college campuses is still standing and in use. What would higher education in Louisiana be today without them?

Grandison Hall, Southern University, Scotlandville, also by William T. Nolan and Ulisse M. Nolan.

TABLE 4.
University Projects

University	Classroom Buildings	Dorms	Arts/Music	Libraries	Gyms	Stadiums	Clinics	Heat/Util.	Pres. House	Other
Baton Rouge, Louisiana State Univ.	2	3								Faculty Club, Sugar Factory
Grambling, Grambling Univ.	1	1		1	1			1	1*	
Hammond Southeastern Louisiana State	2	1	1	1	1				1	
Lafayette, Univ. of Louisiana	4	1	1	1	1	1		1	1	pool, dining hall addition
Lake Charles, McNeese State	1**		1							stock arena
Monroe, Univ. of Louisiana, Monroe			1	1						
Natchitoches, Northwest Louisiana State		2	1	1	1	1	addition	improvements (2)		Student Center.
Ruston, Louisiana Technical Univ.	2	2	1					1		dining hall
Scotlandville, Southern Univ.		3			1	1				

* combined with dining hall
** combined with administrative offices

CHAPTER 8

COURTHOUSES

Next to education, the Public Works Administration (PWA) probably made its greatest impact in Louisiana on the administration of justice. New courthouse and jail buildings were constructed in eleven parishes, new jails were constructed in four others, and additions to existing courthouses were built in another two parishes. This represents major construction in over 25 percent of Louisiana's sixty-four parishes. On top of that, the PWA supported repairs to courthouses in three more parishes (table 5). This effort represents not only a revival of civic building in a time when it had come to a halt, but it also was a return to an earlier tradition of sound construction and planning with an eye to the future. At the same time, the style in which most were built brought a modest breath of modernity to communities accustomed to looking backward for cultural references.

The antebellum courthouses, of which four survive, display a sense of style and solidity indicating that they were true centers of government and were intended to be around for a while. But parish boundaries often shifted in the nineteenth century, and new parishes were created, leading to a short lifespan for many courthouses of the period. Fire, sometimes set intentionally by parties who wanted to move the parish seat, and poor construction hurried this process along. The 1899 Vernon Parish courthouse was so poorly built that it required shoring up within three years of its dedication. Six years later, despite several attempts at repairs, it was declared unsafe for occupation.[1] Only two of the courthouses from the second half of the century survive.

In the period after the First World War, courthouses tended to be short-lived for a different reason. Taxpayers were inclined to support meeting only the most immediate needs. At the same time, parish officials often took the position that new construction was more practical than renovation. "The combination of these two approaches resulted in the appearance of several parish courthouses with a life expectancy of one generation."[2] Better times in the 1920s produced a few more substantial buildings, but many more parishes met their problems of overcrowded offices by putting up temporary annexes and outbuildings.

In contrast, all the PWA courthouses, following established PWA policies, were built to last. All are still standing, and all are still the focus of parish judicial life. Two other courthouses were build by the WPA, in Concordia and St. Helena parishes. Both are still in use, though the Concordia building is no longer the main courthouse. Further testimony to the structures' solidity can be found in Cameron Parish, where its courthouse was one of the few buildings in town to weather Hurricane Audrey in 1957 without serious damage. In 2005 Hurricane Rita leveled almost the entire town, but the courthouse is still standing.

Incredibly, these structures were all put up in a period of three years. This effort is unmatched in the history of the state. Even the later periods

Cameron Parish courthouse has survived two hurricanes while the buildings around it were flattened. The battered corners in Herman J. Duncan's design hint at Mayan architecture, popular in the 1920s and 1930s.

of prosperity did not produce as many lasting buildings in the average decade (see table 6 for a historical comparison).

This frenzy of construction was caused in part by the fact that projects proposed earlier in the decade were delayed by the conflict between Huey Long and President Roosevelt. East Carroll made its original courthouse proposal in 1935, and Tangipahoa had asked for its jail addition in 1934.[3] Two of the repair projects and one of the additions were actually carried out in 1934 and 1935. But proposals for larger projects were piling up. Once the logjam was broken, they leaped off the drawing board. But even if more projects had been approved earlier and construction spread more evenly over the lifespan of the PWA, this work would still represent a larger contribution to Louisiana civic infrastructure than that undertaken in any comparable period in state history.

Beyond their function in the administration of justice and the support of government and commerce, the PWA courthouses made aesthetic contributions. All but one of the eleven PWA courthouses broke with the tradition of using past historical styles. The Greek revival style, much admired by plantation owners and Garden District merchants, was a common antebellum courthouse form. In the later part of the century, Romanesque and more ornate versions of neoclassicism popularized by Paris's Ecole des Beaux Arts, the model for many American schools of architecture, were popular. But by the 1930s, a revolt was brewing.

New materials were becoming available to supplement or compete with traditional wood, brick, and stone. Steel, aluminum, concrete, and glass offered the possibility of taller, stronger, lighter, and less expensive construction. And to display the new materials, new forms were appearing. Some architects were declaring that simple, geometric shapes without ornamentation were the only proper expression of the modern world. A radical split from the past was necessary, they argued. These new ideas were developing in Germany, France, and the Netherlands and became known collectively as modernism.

A less radical development, though also "modern" in spirit and encompassing all the arts, was the art deco style (described in chapter 6). It featured the new materials and favored simplified shapes, though often artificially streamlined. Suburban villas that looked like ocean liners and urban buildings that seemed to be moving down the street at high speed or about to launch into space grabbed attention. But giving up ornament was not part of the art deco program. Flat surfaces could be decorated with zigzags or geometric designs, sometimes also simplified floral patterns that were an outgrowth of the French art nouveau. Decorative terra cotta panels and even bas-relief sculpture were allowed.

While many American architects embraced art deco, particularly in their commercial work, they could not make the leap into European modernism. The manifestos of De Stijl, the Bauhaus, the constructivists, and Le Corbusier were too bold and disruptive on this side of the Atlantic. The severe geometry of the modernist housing developments in Rotterdam, Berlin, Vienna, and Stuttgart was too sharp and abrading for American architects. They found no comfort in Corbusier's villas, described by their creator as "house machines" or "machines for living." Those doing residential construction were also constrained by the conservative tastes of mortgage bankers, echoed by the newly created Federal Housing Administration.[4]

The application of modernist ideas to public buildings was particularly problematic for American architects. Industrial materials and machine imagery hardly seemed appropriate settings for conducting government or administrating justice. Some sense of continuity with the past was felt desirable in all these institutions. Even industrial buildings bore classical ornament. But Americans had always had faith in "progress." And the new materials were useful, interesting, and sometimes attractive. Moreover, in the 1930s budgets were tight, and carved stone was expensive. As a result, many American architects were drawn to a compromise.

The compromise went by various names: stripped-down classicism, starved classicism, American moderne, and Greco-deco. Because this style came into popularity at the time when most construction projects were government-supported public buildings, is also known by some architectural historians as PWA moderne. It allowed a retention, though simplified, of the basic elements of the classical facade: base, column, and entablature. It permitted some ornament: simple bas-relief sculpture panels and similar low carving of capitals and cornices. It also embraced a limited display of new materials, particularly glass and aluminum in windows and light fixtures. The design of these latter features followed the energetic style of commercial art deco, which was definitely "modern" but more playful than the stark European modernism. Ten of the eleven PWA courthouses in Louisiana feature this style.

It was not a style imposed from Washington. There was no attempt by the PWA to tell communities how their buildings should look. They were locally initiated and locally designed. Thus a great many public buildings across the country were done in the ever-popular colonial revival style. Some followed vernacular styles characteristic of their region: clapboard in Vermont, adobe in New Mexico, Spanish colonial revival in southern California. But the debate in the architectural magazines about the proper style for a public building favored the PWA moderne compromise.[5]

The Louisiana PWA moderne courthouses offer an interesting, if subtle, range in their mixture of classical and deco or modernist components. One of the standard features of Greco-deco buildings is in the treatment of columns. In a classical building, these would be freestanding and decorated at the top, or "capital," with carving following standard Greek or Roman patterns, or "orders." The Doric order is the simplest, with a capital consisting of one curved and one square, flattened cap. The Ionic order involves scroll shapes that look a little like horns or ears. The Corinthian features an elaborate mass of leaves and flowers. The shafts of the columns are often grooved, or "fluted."

In a PWA moderne building, the columns are sucked back into the surface of the building, no longer free of the wall. They are squared off into a shape called a pilaster. The pilaster may be left flat or fluted, in stone or concrete. If brick, the fluting may be suggested by patterns in the brick. The capital is usually decorated with a simple, geometric pattern. Sometimes there is no capital at all. The more complex the surface detail is, the more "classical" it is. The smoother and simpler it is, the more "modern."

The Terrebonne Parish courthouse is the most classical of the Louisiana buildings. It has six freestanding Doric columns decorating the second and third floors of the main facade. The surface is mostly unornamented, which is a modernist touch, and there is a band of zigzag deco ornament above the columns and windows, but the columns grab your attention. The principal deco features are the lampposts in front, which look like party-going ice cream cones.

The most modernist courthouse is A. Hays Town's Iberia Parish building. The walls are white stucco, a treatment Le Corbusier would have approved of, and the window openings just cut into the wall surface without accented sills or moldings. The building has a symmetrical mass, which is classical, and there are pilasters at the entrance. However, these are smooth, triangular projections, as if a square pier (half inside the building) had been pivoted ninety degrees. Thus the classical supporting func-

COURTHOUSES 113

Terrebonne Parish courthouse, Houma. Wogan and Bernard's aesthetic is more classic than modern, however.

tion of the column is retained symbolically, but is abstracted much more than the usual PWA moderne pilaster, a very modern statement.

Another feature of PWA moderne design is its vertical window strips. The space in between the pilasters is usually all window, with opaque panels, called spandrels, found only between floors. The spandrels are sometimes ornamented with bas-relief sculpture. The windows themselves are often composed of deco-patterned pane arrangements. The panes are usually framed in aluminum. Doors are also often aluminum and frequently ornamented with deco bas-relief. The Iberia courthouse makes dramatic use of this window, door, and spandrel combination. The Terrebonne courthouse features windows of standard size with plain rectangular panes, as might be found in a factory or office building.

The other Louisiana PWA moderne courthouses are somewhere between these two examples. With its smooth, light plaster walls and relatively undecorated surfaces, the Cameron courthouse is more similar to Iberia's. The Caldwell courthouse cleverly expresses the classical fluting of columns in its brick pilasters. St. Bernard is at the center, with a nice balance of classical pilasters and deco scrollwork in the windows.

The Jackson courthouse is a relatively simple and sedate composition,

These light fixtures in front of the Terrebonne Parish courthouse are emphatically art deco.

with deco bands above the first and third floors and window strips confined to the second and third. The first floor is stone, and the upper two are brick. This, plus the window strips, suggests that the architect, D. Curtis Smith, wants us to read the ground floor as the classical temple base and the upper two stories as the peristyle or temple colonnade. If so, the windows and door in the ground floor undermine its symbolic supportiveness. The top part of the building seems to be pressing down on its base.

The St. Landry Parish courthouse is more deco than Greco. First, there are the lipstick-case lamps in front. But the building itself continues this deco theme. Instead of the pilasters and window strips hinting at a classical

COURTHOUSES 115

Iberia Parish courthouse, New Iberia, an early work by celebrated residential architect A. Hays Town. It is the most modernist of the Louisiana PWA courthouses.

Caldwell Parish courthouse, Columbia, by J. W. Smith and Associates, has classic fluted pilasters with deco molding.

St. Bernard Parish courthouse, Chalmette, also has fluted pilasters with more assertive deco windows. This is Weiss, Dreyfous, and Seiferth's only PWA courthouse.

colonnade, there is a center mass with a stepped-back top. This suggests not Greek architecture but Mayan. Mayan pyramids were a popular feature in art deco design, noticeable in jewelry, ceramics, and graphic arts as well as architecture. There were full-blown Mayan-style movie theaters in Los Angeles, Detroit, and Denver, and Mayan ornament in other kinds of buildings, but stepped-back towers of this kind, sometimes tapering slightly from base to top, were the most common architectural expression of the Mayan theme. This can also be seen in the pylons flanking the entrance to the Cameron courthouse. The Mayan influence was felt not only in art deco but also in the 1920s southern California work of Frank Lloyd Wright.[6]

Though bas-relief sculpture is a standard PWA moderne feature, it is used sparingly or not at all in most Louisiana courthouses. Two wonderful exceptions are found in Natchitoches and Rapides parishes. The entrance to the Natchitoches building is flanked with two huge American Indian chiefs. At Rapides, two bas-relief panels bracket the front doors. One features a superbly streamlined Justice, her hair and robe streaming behind her and her out-thrust scales. She also wears the traditional blindfold,

St. Bernard Parish courthouse, interior.

which, given the speed she is traveling, should cause malefactors to get well out of the way. The other panel features a more stationary Moses, staring sternly forward, law books in his lap, and the bundled fasces, a Roman symbol of community power, in his hand.

Moses and Justice inform us that serious business goes on inside. If you think the aerodynamic form of Justice detracts from her seriousness, don't forget the maxim: "Justice delayed is justice denied." Like these traditional figures, the classical proportions of PWA moderne courthouses connect us with the past. This continuity with the past reassures us that the world is orderly and stable. Precedence, a form of continuity and stability, is an important underpinning of our judicial system. Law and architecture con-

118   CULTURAL INFRASTRUCTURE

Jackson Parish courthouse, Jonesboro, by D. Curtis Smith.

St. Landry Parish courthouse, Opelousas, with deco light fixtures and Mayan setbacks at the top. The architect was Theodore L. Perrier.

Natchitoches Parish courthouse, Natchitoches. J. W. Smith posted both American Indian chiefs and deco lighting to guard the doorway

nect us with our ancestors. "Chronological connectivity," says one recent analyst of community design, "lends meaning and dignity to our little lives."[7]

But the past can also be oppressive, and elaborate classical architecture can be intimidating. It can remind us of past excesses and failures, like the collapse of the stock market. Talbot Hamlin, a noted scholar of the Greek revival, concluded in 1938 that "archeological architecture is dead."[8] It is no accident that the World's Columbian Exposition of 1893 featured beaux arts classicism, but all the world's fairs of the 1930s tried to bring optimism to the Depression with "worlds of tomorrow" created in bold deco and modernist forms.

CULTURAL INFRASTRUCTURE

Rapides Parish courthouse, Alexandria. A stern Moses demonstrates that the law binds the community.

PWA moderne courthouses don't encourage us to dance and sing like the world's fairs or the Miami Beach hotels do, but neither do they try to intimidate us with the heavy hand of the past. They present a dignified front, remind us of our connection with our forebears, but also give us hope for a better future. The glow of the tile is friendly; the matte aluminum invites your hand on the railing and supports you as you enter; the zigzags convey vibrancy. It is a delicate but important balance. The best PWA moderne buildings achieve it nicely.

It is useful to remember that the size of these projects required a considerable local contribution. The parishes were putting up 55 percent of the funding for the project, which they had to do by issuing bonds. And bond issues required elections. Parish citizens had to be willing to commit themselves to service these bonds out of their future taxes. In almost all cases

Rapides Parish courthouse, Alexandria. On the other side of the door, a streamlined Justice promises speedy action. Edward F. Neild designed this high-rise building.

they were. St. John the Baptist was an exception. The parish administrators wanted a new courthouse, but the bond issue was defeated.[9] They had to settle for a new jail.

Eleven other parishes approved bond issues for courthouse construction. It could be argued that this was a matter of anxiety about the present rather than investment in the future. You have to have an income before you can worry about paying taxes. But judging from newspaper ads supporting the Rapides Parish courthouse bond issue, there were also practical concerns for parish needs and a sense of community progress.

There is a full-page ad in the *Alexandria Town Talk* on September 11, 1937, that features testimonials and endorsements by organizations like the Italian Union of Rapides Parish; politicians like "Mr. Bob," commissioner of streets and parks; and individuals like "a taxpayer," who says "unless we vote a bond issue for a new courthouse and jail we shall wake up some morning and find most of our parish records in Red River." Another cries: "Refuse to place yourself in the stick-in-the-mud class." M. Neustadt says: "Let's go forward with the trend of the times and be progressive."[10] The reference to Red River was not a casual jest. The old courthouse stood right on the river; in fact, the levee curved out around it. High water placed it at considerable risk.

The campaign was successful. The headline of the September 15, 1937, *Alexandria Town Talk* reads "RAPIDES VOTES NEW COURTHOUSE-JAIL." The paper goes on to report a "sweeping victory" of 735 to 499. Three years later the parish had a seven-story courthouse/jail of reinforced concrete sheathed in Indiana limestone with sculptures of Moses and Justice greeting all who come through its front doors. Seventy years later they are still continuing to offer testimony that their community is both stable and progressive.

However, the courthouses had a retrogressive side as well. They were an embodiment of the Jim Crow laws. Racial segregation by law did not derive from slavery or from Reconstruction. Under slavery, slave owners controlled where slaves could be and needed no legal reinforcement. In fact, segregation would have been inconvenient because the presence of slaves was required in all sorts of places. After the Civil War, public space was open to all, and freed slaves made use of it. African Americans rode trains and steamboats and dined in restaurants. At the International exposition in New Orleans in 1885, one observer reported that "white and colored people mingled freely, talking and looking at what was of common interest . . . and the races mingled in the grounds in unconscious equality of privileges."[11]

African Americans voted and held office. Louisiana governor Francis T. Nicholls made a point of including them on boards and commissions. The conservative whites who brought Reconstruction to an end in 1877, and thus became known as Redeemers, generally maintained a conciliatory and paternalistic attitude toward the freed slaves. All of this changed when these whites were challenged from below by poor farmers rebelling against the banks and railroads that oppressed them. This Populist revolt was biracial. To maintain power, the conservatives turned the poor whites against blacks, letting loose the more virulent expressions of racism that they had heretofore kept in check.[12]

This led to an institutionalization of white supremacy, beginning with political disenfranchisement and ending in total segregation of public life. Poll taxes, property requirements, and other restrictions on voting brought African American participation in politics to a halt. In 1894 there were 130,334 registered African American voters in Louisiana; by 1904 there were only 1,342. Laws were passed restricting seating on trains, streetcars, and steamboats. Waiting rooms, restrooms, parks, sports venues, even drinking fountains were segregated. What was not spelled out in law was enforced through unofficial terrorism. The Ku Klux Klan was turned loose to burn and lynch. At one point mobs took over New Orleans for three days, attacking and robbing black residents. The system became known as Jim Crow after a character in a popular song and dance. By the 1920s, it had become a way of life regarded as eternal despite its recent origins.[13]

The period of the New Deal, according to historian C. Vann Woodward, brought a diminution of racial tension. It also brought African Americans into the Democratic Party. The Southern Conference on Human Welfare, established in 1938 in the wake of Roosevelt's "Report on Economic Conditions of the South," advocated on behalf of the poor of all races. A full-scale attack on Jim Crow did not get under way for another twenty years, but when it finally came, a good part of its success, said Woodward, was due to the influence of the federal government. So, in an important way the courthouses not only embodied Jim Crow laws, they also embodied the new relationship between federal and local government, the system of "cooperative federalism" that got them built and which eventually restored all Louisiana's citizens to equality before the law.[14]

TABLE 5.
Courthouse Projects

Parish	Project	Completed	Cost
Caddo	jail addition	12/21/34	$19,549
Caldwell	new courthouse/jail	12/14/37	129,984
Cameron	new courthouse/jail	2/23/38	134,522
East Carroll	new courthouse/jail	9/17/38	100,589
Iberia	new courthouse/jail	5/6/40	410,863
Jackson	new courthouse/jail	1/31/39	248,529
Madison	new courthouse/jail	9/14/39	134,790
Morehouse	addition	12/31/35	37,289
Natchitoches	new courthouse/jail	3/29/40	261,110
Point Coupee	new annex w/jail	3/9/40	185,971
Rapides	new courthouse/jail	7/27/40	588,528
St. Bernard	new courthouse/jail	2/24/40	433,495
St. James	additions/alterations	11/28/39	67,570
St. John the Baptist	new jail	4/29/39	47,523
St. Landry	new courthouse/jail	3/1/40	481,794
St. Tamany	repairs	7/10/37	36,528
Tangipahoa	new annex w/jail	7/26/38	84,502
Tensas	repairs	10/31/34	15,262
Terrebonne	new courthouse/jail	8/28/38	369,961
Webster	repairs	10/11/35	18,536

Source: List of All Allotted Non-Federal Projects, Projects by State and Docket, as of May 30, 1942, 65–66, Federal Works Agency, Public Works Administration, Record Group 135, National Archives II, College Park, Md.

TABLE 6.

Era of Construction of Current Twentieth-Century Parish Courthouses in Louisiana

1901–1905	2
1906–1910	2
1911–1915	5
1916–1920	1
1921–1925	2
1926–1930	6
1931–1935	0
1936–1940	12
1941–1945	0
1946–1950	2
1951–1955	5
1956–1960	5
1961–1965	3
1966–1970	6
1971–1975	3
1976–1980	3
1981–1985	2

This does not include buildings like the Concordia courthouse that survive but are no longer the primary parish courthouse. It does not include buildings erected and torn down during this period or annexes or additions to existing courthouses.

Source: Carl A. Brasseaux, Glenn R. Conrad, and R. Warren Robinson, *The Courthouses of Louisiana*, 2nd ed. (Lafayette: Center for Louisiana Studies, 1997).

PART III

PHYSICAL INFRASTRUCTURE
BUILDING A MODERN ECONOMY

CHAPTER 9

THE U.S. MARINE HOSPITAL AT CARVILLE AND OTHER FEDERAL PROJECTS

The projects reviewed thus far have all been what the Public Works Administration (PWA) called "nonfederal" projects. They were initiated at the state and local levels. Communities decided what facilities they needed, hired their own architects and engineers to design them, and, if the proposals were approved by the PWA, employed local contractors and laborers to build them. But nonfederal projects were only a part of the PWA's responsibility. It also had "federal" projects.

Federal projects were carried out by other agencies of the federal government that needed to construct and maintain facilities but couldn't finance them out of their current regular budgets. The Treasury Department needed new post offices. The Commerce Department needed beacons and radios to guide airplanes carrying people and freight across the country. The Agriculture Department had research facilities studying crop production, soil conservation, insect control, and drug safety that needed maintenance and improvement. The Interior Department had to maintain national parks, historic sites, and military cemeteries. The U.S. Coast Guard, a division of the Treasury Department, needed boats and airplanes to patrol coastal waters and rescue imperiled ships. The War Department was repairing and expanding bases and airfields as the prospect of war grew. The PWA aided all of them. It even built aircraft carriers, destroyers, and fighter planes for the navy.[1] One of the carriers, the USS *Yorktown*, was sunk at the battle of Midway after playing a key role in the sinking of four Japanese fleet carriers.

In deciding what federal projects to fund, the PWA had a running start. The Employment Stabilization Act of 1931, at the end of the Hoover administration, created a Stabilization Board, which in June 1932 asked government agencies to prepare plans for construction and repair projects for the next six years. Seventy agencies replied.[2] What a second Hoover administration might have done with this list will never be known. The Roosevelt administration gave it to the PWA, which proceeded to build.

The short-lived Civil Works Administration also contributed to the PWA's federal agenda. When this wide-ranging work relief program was terminated in the spring of 1934, many projects were left uncompleted. Among them were many airport projects. These included 537 airfields begun but still needing work, 404 sites where land had been purchased for fields but work had not begun on them, and 488 existing fields that remained torn up when the money ran out before repairs could be completed. Apparently, the PWA supplied materials to complete them, and the Federal Emergency Relief Administration supplied the labor.[3]

We may never know the full extent of the PWA federal projects because the files have been mostly lost.[4] It might be possible to trace them on an agency-by-agency basis, but that would be a daunting task. The best picture we have of them is a series of weekly reports issued by the PWA in 1933 when the agency was just getting started and the federal programs were the center of attention.[5]

One of the biggest of Louisiana's federal projects was at Shreveport's Barksdale Field. Land suitable for an airport was acquired by the city in 1929 through a 1.65 mil bond issue for the purpose of hosting an Air National Guard unit. As the threat of war increased, it was turned over to the developing U.S. Army Air Corps. It became the headquarters of the Third Wing in 1935. One of only three divisions of the air corps, this unit was assigned to protect the entire Southeast and Gulf Coast. Basic facilities were constructed from 1931 to 1933.[6]

The PWA financed a sizable expansion of Barksdale; more than $2 million went into housing alone. The Signal Corps installed $4,800 worth of underground cable. A hospital, a headquarters and wing operations building, a garage, a warehouse, and night lighting were added. A barracks building and noncommissioned officers' and officers' quarters were begun.[7]

Barksdale Field continues to play a major role in U.S. Air Force operations. Units based there were an important part of the North Atlantic Treaty Organization (NATO) attack in the 1999 Kosovo conflict. It sheltered President George W. Bush, who spent the night here on his way back to Washington, D.C., after the attack on September 11, 2001. In 1992 Barksdale Field was placed on the National Register of Historic Places.[8]

Another War Department project that was to have long-range impact—peaceful economic benefits in this case—was the Army Corps of Engineers' work on the Intracoastal Waterway from New Orleans to Galveston, Texas. In Louisiana, Petite Anse, Carlin, and Tigre Bayous were dredged for the project. The PWA spent $807,704 on it. By 1934, this section was finally complete and open. The corps also put $1.25 million of PWA money into flood control projects in Louisiana.[9]

The Interior Department sponsored several topographic survey projects in Louisiana. One in Kisatchie National Forest cost $12,000. The department also prepared tactical maps for the War Department of Johnson's Bayou, Hackberry Bayou, Bayou Bois Courier, and Lake Miserie that cost $57,000. The Coast and Geodetic Survey worked in forty-six different parishes and spent over $137,000.[10]

Airmail service, and later all manner of airborne commerce, was aided by the installation of beacon lights from New Orleans to St. Louis. This "lighted highway," built by the Aeronautics Council of the Commerce Department, cost $161,169. Commerce Department fish hatcheries in Natchitoches received $5,000 worth of repairs. The Commerce Department was also active in New Orleans' waterways. It built a new lighthouse depot at New Orleans costing $117,250 and a new $150,000 lighthouse tender, and it replaced engines on the lighthouse tenders in Magnolia and Camellia. Another $23,000 was spent on stone protection and lighting for the depot. After the Bureau of Lighthouses was transferred to the Treasury Department in 1939, the Eighth Lighthouse District in Louisiana got almost $37,000 worth of new radio equipment, buoys, beacons, and improved sanitation.[11]

The Agriculture Department's Bureau of Animal Industries added laboratories and a slaughter, cutting, and curing building to its facility at Jeanerette, along with road, fence, drainage, and shed repairs. The total package was $65,000. Another $700 was spent on painting the Soil Fertility Laboratory in Houma and building a new hard-surfaced road to the main highway. To enforce migratory bird legislation, the department spent $4,000 on new boats.

Houma, Bastrop, and Plaquemine got new post offices through the Treasury Department. The Plaquemine building is now enjoying a second career as a cabinet and gift shop. Although plaques crediting the PWA under its official name, the Federal Emergency Administration of Public Works, appear on most of the structures it erected, this is not the case with post offices. Treasury Secretary Henry Morgenthau and Harold Ickes were not on the best of terms, and apparently Morgenthau disliked giving any credit to Ickes for "his" buildings. Post office plaques credit only Morgenthau and Treasury's supervising architect, Louis Simon. Rarely is a local architect listed, and, unlike PWA plaques, a contractor's name never appears.

More than $300,000 of the money the PWA sent to the Bureau of Public Roads was spent in Louisiana for highways and bridges.[12] Most of this work cannot be recognized by those who benefit from it. However, one very important bridge for which the PWA was responsible is identifiable: the northern span across the Mississippi River that connects Vidalia with Natchez.

A project that probably seemed like it was created just for the purpose of employing people involved spending $35,000 to improve roads and grounds at the Chalmette battlefield outside New Orleans, where Andrew Jackson, Jean Laffite, and a ragtag army of pirates, New Orleans business-

Plaquemine post office, now a gift shop. The Treasury Department gave no credit to the PWA on its cornerstones or plaques.

Vidalia-Natchez Bridge crossing the Mississippi. The PWA built the north span.

men, Tennessee squirrel hunters, Cherokee Indians, and free men of color defeated the British in the last battle of the War of 1812. The site's enduring contribution to tourism, however, has long since paid off this small investment in the future New Orleans economy.

One of Louisiana's more interesting federal projects was the Gillis Long Hansen's Disease Center, then known as the National Leprosarium. In Louisiana, it is known simply as "Carville." In 1934 the PWA completed Federal Project #50: a new hospital for the treatment of and research on the crippling disease then called leprosy. The "leper colony" had been established at Carville in 1894 when five men and two women disembarked on the grounds of the old Indian Camp Plantation. They had come up from New Orleans on a barge during the night to maintain secrecy. The state had evicted them from the "Pest House" there and transferred them to this new "hospital," which consisted of a rotting plantation house and slave cabins. The slave cabins were in better shape, so the patients settled in there. Local residents were told that the state had leased the plantation for an ostrich farm.[13]

This out-of-the-way location was thought appropriate for people with leprosy for two reasons. First, the disease was believed to be highly contagious. This mythology has biblical roots and was so powerful that few bothered to notice that the nuns and doctors who treated patients with leprosy never contracted the disease themselves. The misunderstanding was the result of a series of translation errors from Hebrew to Greek to Latin to English. The Bible refers to a number of repellant diseases, none of them, judging by the symptoms described, modern leprosy. Unfortunately, a translator chose to use the Greek word "*lepra*" for the Hebrew catchall disease term. "*Lepra*" also does not mean "leprosy" in Greek, but was considered equivalent to "stricken" by a translator who rendered it "Leprosarium" in Latin. It finally became attached to a specific set of symptoms we now know as leprosy. The Old Testament horrors of contagion and disfigurement, and the persecution and banishment of the "unclean" that followed from this, were thus accidentally funneled into leprosy.[14]

The second appeal of this obscure location grew out of the first. Because of this fear of contagion, and the stigma attached to anyone who aroused it, people with leprosy were encouraged to cut themselves off from their families. Relatives of those with leprosy risked ostracism, economic boycott, even arson. To protect their families, Carville inmates took new names. Sidney Maurice Levyson became Stanley Stein when he was diagnosed and moved to Carville. He spent the rest of his life disseminating accurate medical information about the disease and crusading against the stigma attached to it, but he never gave up his pseudonym entirely.[15] A Carville resident who won international attention with her autobiography wrote a sequel, largely to explain why she could not use her real name. "We belong with a secret people," she concluded. "There are thousands like us, who for one reason or another must walk carefully, that no one may know we walk in a secret world."[16]

In 1896 four members of the Daughters of Charity of St. Vincent de Paul, more commonly known as the Daughters of Charity, moved into two rooms of the crumbling Indian Camp Plantation house and took up the care of the banished. The state of Louisiana bought the plantation in 1905 and replaced the slave cabins with twelve cottages and a dining hall. In 1921, when the site had ninety patients, the U.S. Public Health Service took over. In 1938, with the help of the PWA, it built a new hospital.

The new hospital was designed by the Public Buildings Branch of the Treasury Department and was one of a chain of U.S. marine hospitals. Despite the name, they had no connection with the U.S. Marine Corps.

CARVILLE AND OTHER FEDERAL PROJECTS 135

Gillis Long Hansen's Disease Center, Carville, North America's only hospital for those with "leprosy."

Marine hospitals were built in port cities beginning in the nineteenth century to deal with the health problems of merchant seamen and immigrants. The chief problem such a clientele posed was exotic diseases. Therefore it was reasonable that the marine hospital system take over the National Leprosarium. The marine hospitals were the core of the Public Health Service.

The Carville facility became "the best equipped leper colony in the world."[17] It had sixty-five bedrooms, staff quarters, research laboratories, an operating room, a pharmacy, and treatment rooms offering hydrotherapy and electrotherapy. Across the front is a two-story, screened porch to protect patients from the sun, which was believed to complicate the disease. The facility's international status can be quickly confirmed by a walk through its cemetery, where the headstones show birthplaces throughout the hemisphere.

The PWA was not the only New Deal agency to contribute to the National Leprosarium. In 1940 the Works Progress Administration completely rebuilt the center's dormitories, dining facilities, and the two-story, screened and covered walkways that connected all the buildings. The walkways are broad enough that residents could use them to bicycle around the

Gillis Long Hansen's Disease Center, Carville, interior courtyard.

complex. They also sometimes served as dining annexes. During a period when hospital administrators became strict about gender segregation, men and women were not allowed in each other's rooms. They could share a semiprivate meal, however, by putting a table in the doorway and having the men sit in the corridor.[18]

In 1873 the bacillus causing leprosy was discovered by a Norwegian physician, Dr. Gerhard Henrik Armauer Hansen, but the discovery of an agent to control it awaited another seventy years. This happened at Carville when Dr. Guy H. Faget began experimenting with sulfa-based drugs. They did not cure leprosy, but arrested or reversed the symptoms in 80 percent of those who took them.[19] Ulcers and skin lesions and inflammation of the eyes and throat disappeared. It was, to those who had studied Hansen's bacillus or suffered from its effects, a miracle.

Naming the disease for Hansen was partly recognition for his accomplishment and partly to eradicate the stigma associated with the old name. Symptoms can now be controlled and disability prevented. Contagion was never a great problem. Even close family members are unlikely to contract the disease. Tuberculosis is far more contagious.[20] Treatment can be given on an out-patient basis, so there is no compulsion for patients to continue to reside at Carville. However, some residents choose to stay on. They learned to live with their imposed isolation and now find no desire to leave this separate world. Some who left for a while have returned. They are working toward establishing a museum on the grounds. The Hansen's Disease Center at Carville is officially closed, and its research facilities are now housed in the Louisiana State University School for Veterinary Medicine. The Carville facility is undergoing a transformation. But for the present, at least, this is going on around the elderly residents.

The center is now home to 168 cadets in the Louisiana National Guard's Youth ChalleNGe Program for teenagers. A Job Corps program provides skills to go along with their boot-camp conditioning. Thus the facility provides an opportunity to build new lives as it did for the original Carville inhabitants.

Though we do not, and probably never will, have a complete list of federal projects, these fragments of information provide some idea of what was accomplished. One thing that is obvious is that the federal projects considerably broadened the PWA's impact on both the physical and cultural infrastructure in Louisiana.

CHAPTER 10

THE NEW ORLEANS CHARITY HOSPITAL

Louisiana is the only state in the Union with hospitals providing medical care to those who cannot pay for it. The original New Orleans Charity Hospital was built in 1736 with an endowment from a French shipbuilder. The institution wore out or lost to fire four buildings. The fifth, built in 1832, was falling apart in 1933 when its board of administrators asked that the Public Works Administration (PWA) fund a replacement. In order to cover its 70 percent of the project, the board proposed adding paying beds.

Paying beds in a charity hospital? Betrayal of a tradition almost 200 years old? The idea provoked a howl of protest from members of the Orleans Parish Medical Society. They could not deny that many of the buildings being used by Charity Hospital were in bad shape. The leaking roofs, termite-eaten walls, and caving floors were obvious to casual inspection. Nor could they ignore the overcrowded wards where patients slept two to a bed, in chairs, and on floors.[1] They could, however, argue that the overcrowding was unnecessary.

One problem was that patients came to Charity from all parts of the state. They often, argued the Medical Society, stayed after treatment was completed, while transportation was being arranged. If the patient was a child or an elder, a family member might be staying with him or her in the hospital. This could be dealt with, the Medical Society suggested, by adding charity wards to other hospitals throughout the state. Another cause of crowding, alleged the society, was widespread abuse of Charity facilities by people who could afford to go elsewhere. These were people with political connections, particularly friends of Huey Long's.[2]

An underlying reason for the Medical Society's rush to find explanations for overcrowding other than genuine need was probably fear of competition for paying customers. Hospital historian John Salvaggio reports that "Southern Baptist Hospital and Touro Infirmary claimed that paying wards would put them out of business."[3]

Alfred Danziger, head of the board of administrators, replied that patients at Charity stayed on average 16.6 days, no longer than those at other city hospitals. He agreed that some prominent people and their relatives had been treated at Charity, but said they were emergency cases. He denied widespread abuse. He noted that the hospital had an average daily occupancy of 2,185 patients in 1932 and had beds for only 1,756. At the time of writing, November 1933, the hospital housed 2,400 patients. In the preceding five years, he said, the number of people served had increased 70 percent.[4]

The proposal was disapproved by the PWA in December 1933. The financial arrangements were judged inadequate even with the paying beds. The PWA was not sure Charity had the authority to issue revenue bonds. Nor was it sure the state would back the bonds if the revenue did not meet expectations.[5]

The board then made a second attempt. It tried to mollify the opposition by scaling down the size of the proposal, cutting back from $9.85 million to $8 million. The board had originally asked for 2,930 beds; this was reduced to 2,370. The Orleans Parish Medical Society replied with a list of forty-eight abuses involving treatment of those unqualified for charity. It included Huey Long's niece, Governor O.K. Long and his nephew, the son of House Speaker Allen Ellender, a police captain, and a variety of state and Louisiana State University employees. A new charge was added: hospital use figures had been inflated by mass tonsillectomies given to schoolchildren.[6]

In June Huey Long entered the dispute. He marched into a state Judiciary Committee hearing and took over the microphone. He announced that he had a new plan to finance the hospital. The pay beds would be withdrawn, and in their place the state's corporation tax would be raised from $1.00 to $1.50 per thousand dollars of income. He drafted a committee of doctors, lawyers, and labor union officials and told them to get busy on a new proposal.[7] Long then prodded Ickes, assuring him that the loan to the hospital was now "gilt-edged and so secure that there should be no difficulty." He claimed that the opposing physicians were now converted because he had withdrawn the plan for paying beds.[8]

But the Medical Society had not withdrawn from the field. It saw in the situation an opportunity to gain some control over Charity Hospital. The society announced that it would be willing to accept a total of 2,300 beds, including 360 in the units that would not be replaced. However, there were conditions. The society wanted two members of the hospital board of supervisors appointed from a list approved by the state medical society and two appointed from the Orleans Parish Medical Society. It also wanted to deny the hospital the right to enter into any contracts for medical services.[9]

Ickes's own staff was inclined to favor the project and found little substance in the medical establishment's opposition. State Engineer Orloff Henry met with the Orleans Parish Medical Society in August 1934. He found "few, in any, of its members have given serious study to the proposed plan." He confirmed Danziger's claim that the prominent physicians opposing him had no recent experience with the hospital.[10] Henry also noted that although the argument for decentralizing Charity and dispersing beds throughout the state had merit, the Medical Society had done nothing to realize this proposal. He could find no evidence to support the charge of mass tonsillectomies and other abuses. The forty-eight alleged political favors covered six years.[11]

Engineer-examiner Lester Marx, visiting the city the same month, came to the same conclusions as Henry had. The opponents, he thought, "displayed a surprising lack of knowledge regarding the details of the proposed project. None of those who object to any phase of the project appear to have studied it sufficiently to offer any constructive suggestions." He also noted that forty-eight abuses out of 50,000 admissions wasn't all that damaging a charge.[12]

Henry concluded that the Medical Society membership was "entirely incompetent to express an opinion." He said their opposition was motivated by fear of "state medicine" and a threat to their financial interests. Their concern with the possible competition was clear enough. The threat of "state medicine" was less clear. Unlike other states, Louisiana had a tradition of charity hospitals extending back to 1793. Its physicians had lived comfortably with this. Perhaps the expanding of federal and state government during the early New Deal raised the prospect of greater socialization of health care.

However, the arguments between the hospital and the Medical Society were no longer the main issue. The political situation in the state was near the boiling point. Long had ordered the National Guard to occupy the voter registration headquarters in New Orleans, and its machine guns now faced 400 city policemen across the street in city hall. Long's battle with the Old Regulars had reached the point of possible armed conflict. This was not a situation into which the PWA wanted to pump millions of dollars.

The election of September 1934 was held without violence, however. The factions negotiated a truce and presided over a relatively fair election.[13] Long's forces overwhelmed the Old Regulars. The troops went home.

Some hope remained for approval of the hospital proposal into 1935. The legislature had authorized Charity to issue bonds. This authority, said the PWA, had to be tested by the state supreme court. The court test was arranged, and the hospital's authority was upheld on March 22, 1935. But in the following month Long created the state Bond and Tax Board, and Ickes embargoed new Louisiana projects. Even though Long wanted the hospital, he wanted even more to be able to keep federal projects out of the hands of his enemies.

Delos Smith, an attorney for the hospital, paid a visit to Colonel Horatio Hackett, PWA assistant administrator, to promote the project. During their conference, Hackett told Smith not to expect PWA money as long as Huey Long controlled the state. Smith tried to get Hackett to confirm this in writing, but Hackett replied that "the political activities of any one man have nothing to do with PWA actions." He did, however, say that he couldn't approve projects where "a situation of legal uncertainty exists such as has been created in Louisiana."[14]

After the assassination of Huey Long and the reestablishment of the state's relationship with Roosevelt in 1936, the laws Long had passed to keep federal agencies at bay were repealed. The way was cleared for a third Charity Hospital proposal. This time only a grant was requested, which freed the PWA from concerns about hospital bond issues. Matters were further helped by the new regulations increasing the size of the grant from 30 to 45 percent. For the state's share of the project, the Charity administrators could rely on funds from the corporation franchise tax that had been dedicated to it and which, a newspaper noted as early as March 1935, had been "piling up in the banks and . . . not doing anybody any good."[15] The project was approved on September 14. The contract went to the state's favorite firm: Weiss, Dreyfous, and Seiferth.

The new hospital was to be the second largest in the country. It would

Charity Hospital, New Orleans. At twenty stories, it was the tallest building in the city at the time it was built and the second tallest hospital in the country. Weiss, Dreyfous, and Seiferth designed it. Because of mold germinated by Hurricane Katrina, hospital administrators want to tear it down.

rise twenty stories, the tallest building in the city. With it came a fifteen-story nurses' building, ambulance house, laundry, incinerator, repair shop, and power house addition. The approved cost of the project was $8 million. It soon appeared that it would actually cost $12.5 million. Governor Leche got the legislature to come up with the additional $4.5 million. Weiss, Dreyfous, and Seiferth wanted their fees increased accordingly. After some consultation with well-known architects around the country, the PWA decided to stick to the original contract allowing 6 percent on the $8 million. It argued that all the work was done before construction costs went up. However, it had no objection if the state wished to pay the architects more out of its own funds. The state did.[16]

The growing cost of the project emerged gradually. The ambulance house and laundry were built first with some cost overruns. It got worse when bids were let for the main building. Orloff Henry decided it was time for a "showdown." He stopped the bidding until the state assured him that additional money would be available.[17]

Henry suspected that the building was designed at $12 million but budgeted at $8 million because that was the PWA's limit. Members of the

The Nurses' Building was recently rehabilitated. After Hurricane Katrina, its fate is uncertain.

board of administrators maintained, however, that the architects had assured them that an $8 million building could be built. Lester Marx thought the original specifications were "bare essentials." The $12 million version was more in line with other modern hospitals. He found no wasted space.[18]

The finished building was a grand monument to public health, but it had feet of clay, or, more accurately, sand. No one had attempted to erect such a huge building on New Orleans's spongy soil. So it was not altogether a surprise when Big Charity began to sink. By January 1939 it was nine inches below its starting point, more than two and a half times the average settlement in the city. Cracks, separations, and distortions prolif-

Ambulance house, laundry, and shops behind the hospital.

erated, and the PWA regional engineer Alexander Allaire became concerned that the building's structural steel frame might be damaged. Allaire, PWA chief engineer Harry M. Brown, and Resident Engineer-Inspector (REI) Edmund B. Mason met with architects Weiss and Seiferth. Brown found them "quite complacent."[19]

Consultants were sought. Karl Terzaghi of Harvard University was retained at $75 an hour. Weiss agreed to pay the fee, probably gnashing his teeth. Allaire wanted a "structural man," so Hardy Cross of Yale was hired. His services were secured for a lump sum of $6,000. Test borings cost another $4,651.50.

Terzaghi concluded that the architects were not at fault. Longer pilings, which some critics said should have been used, wouldn't have helped. The gradual consolidation of material under them would have happened in any case. Cross affirmed that the structural steel was undamaged. It would, however, require another $70,000 to repair the building. By the end of 1939, the building had sunk 12 3/4 inches and was still going. Terzaghi had originally thought that 80 percent of settlement had occurred. In his final report, he revised it to 70 percent and predicted it might continue until 1950. He was right about the percentage but overly conservative about the time. The building would continue to sink for another three and a half years, coming to rest almost eighteen inches down. Rumors that the second story had now become the entry level were a slight exaggeration.[20]

The Ivy League experts did not impress everyone. Charles Fowler, an engineer who had been among those originally recommended for the inspection, called their reports a whitewash and proclaimed himself willing to straighten things out (for only $2,500). He claimed experience on over 4,000 projects from 1886 to 1939 and to have authored thirty books. Had he known what he was doing, it would have been a bargain. We'll never know; despite his impressive credentials, the PWA declined the offer. Another volunteer fixer was a young Tulane graduate named Claiborne Perrilliat. He was no more successful than the veteran Fowler.[21] The crisis passed, the experts were paid and went home to New England, and the hospital opened for business.

Though Huey Long was not able to get Big Charity built before he died, the structure contains a tribute to him and his system of government. Sculptor Enrique Alferez designed an aluminum grill over the main entrance to the hospital. In the center is a flying duck. It is a reference to the deduction, or "dee duct," box into which state employees put cash "contributions" to Long's campaigns. They were required to remit a percentage of their salary on designated paydays. When this was called for, the word was passed that "de ducks were flying." Richard Leche continued the practice and was not amused at Alferez's reference. According to Alferez, a man with a hacksaw was sent to excise the offending bird. He was intercepted by *Times-Picayune* reporters who told him that since the PWA had helped pay for the building, his duck hunting would be a federal offense. The duck remains.[22]

Alferez had another interesting story about the building of Big Charity. He claims that Leon Weiss was asked "almost every day" to take money in amounts of $2,000 to $10,000 out of hospital funds to pay off people who were owed money by Governor Leche. He alleges that fire escapes were omitted to save money. In one case, Weiss is said to have approved the omission of one of the six screws in each door hinge at a savings of $5,000. It's a good story, and it might well have happened on one of Weiss's other buildings. But it probably didn't on this one. Even though there is some suggestion that REI Mason was sometimes willing to turn his back on corner cutting, this project was inspected and audited in excruciating detail.[23] Anything that might have escaped notice or been willfully

Sculptor Enrique Alferez placed a reminder of the kickbacks government employees were required to "contribute" during the Long and Leche eras in this screen over the front door. Leche was not amused.

overlooked during construction would have been caught in the postconstruction investigations.

There were at least four investigations of the bidding process, most having to do with equipment. When the PWA decided that the bidding for the contract to provide sterilizing equipment was improper, its cost ($101,800) was eliminated from the grant. The most serious bidding irregularity involved the contract for the pilings undergirding the main building. It was discovered that the competitors for this contract had all included an "estimating fee" in their bids. This was paid by the winning contractor, Farnsworth and Company, to the New Orleans chapter of the

Associated General Contractors of America, which divided it among the losing contractors. This led to prosecution and conviction of Farnsworth and the association.[24]

As of the end of 1939, 357 change orders had been submitted for approval. The PWA analyzed 339 of them. Their total cost would have been over $850,000. Almost $150,000 of this was disapproved by the PWA; the rest were withdrawn. In the final reckoning, all these change orders had added only $17,732.50 to the total cost of the $12 million project. The investigation noted that Weiss authorized numerous changes himself without the knowledge of the PWA or the hospital. Many of these were due to the architects' "inadequate research or investigation of conditions to be encountered, lack of coordination of the respective technical staffs of the offices of the consulting engineers and the office of the architects, . . . and a situation approaching incompetence with respect to the mechanical layouts and analysis of substitute costs involved in the reissue of pile layouts." Investigators found various corners cut by contractors, for which the contractors had to reimburse the hospital. However, they found no "evidence of graft in connection with the actions of the Owner, its architects or other officials relating to the subject matter of this investigation."[25] Alferez's picture of daily hemorrhaging of thousands of dollars from the budget would not have escaped notice.

Not only were the architects and contractors scrutinized, subcontractors were audited as well. Even those who had been eliminated from the project or paid directly by the hospital rather than through the PWA were audited by the PWA. They included some projects as low as $1,400 as well as those of several hundred thousand dollars.

The building itself was gone over thoroughly by PWA special agent Gilbert B. Carter. His twelve-page report goes into great detail, listing things like aluminum trim omitted in phone booths.[26] Consistent omission of hinge screws would most likely have been noticed in an inspection at this level.

In another study of the hospital's finances covering this period, Stella O'Conner concluded that "despite wholesale scandals which later resulted in prison sentences for high state officials as well as contractors and architects associated with the project, comparatively little fraud was connected with the hospital construction." She notes further: "A force of thirty Federal Investigators was unable to find factual evidence of graft."[27]

Though it took years of struggle within the state and between the state and the federal government, Big Charity was built. It became "one of the world's great hospitals" and continues to stand (though a bit lower than intended) as "a model of health care for indigents years before modern federal health-care programs were put into effect."[28] It was open to all, providing "separate but roughly equal wards for blacks and whites."[29]

How long it will continue to stand, however, is an open question. Because of damage from flooding and subsequent infestation of mold, officials of the Louisiana State University Hospitals, which now runs Charity, want to replace it. After Hurricane Katrina, doctors, nurses, military personnel, and civil engineers from Germany worked with hydraulic pumps to clean up the building. But once the first three floors were scrubbed and the doctors pronounced them ready for use, the medical personnel were ordered out of the building. Dr. Juliette Saussy, director of emergency medical services for New Orleans, believes the building is usable. Hospital officials have declared it unsafe.[30]

New construction is always appealing, but its apparent financial advantages over renovation may be deceptive. Bringing down such a solid building may be more difficult and costly than it first appears. Whether Big Charity comes down or survives to continue its service to the city, its three-quarters-of-a-century contribution should not be forgotten.

CHAPTER 11

THE FRENCH MARKET

There was a market in New Orleans's Vieux Carre long before the Public Works Administration (PWA) arrived, but the form it now presents to us was the product of PWA project #La.5914. Old buildings were remodeled or reconstructed, new buildings were added, and the whole complex was united by columned arcades, lantern towers, and a common stucco finish.

The project is unusual because, unlike schools or courthouses, it serves private, commercial interests. The market was run by a private corpora-

French Market, New Orleans. There was a market here since 1784, but the way it ooks today was put together by Sam Stone Jr. for the PWA.

PHYSICAL INFRASTRUCTURE

A characteristic lantern feature on all the buildings of the French Market, New Orleans.

tion, and the PWA was hesitant to become involved in it for this reason. Opponents of New Deal public works programs were greatly concerned that the government not compete with or take over activities that could be undertaken by private enterprise. In fact, however, there has always been a great deal of overlap between the public and private sectors. Traditional public projects like roads, bridges, airports, and tunnels are as much an aid to commerce as they are to civic welfare. Real estate developers rely on public bodies to provide their gas, water, electrical, and sewerage facilities. The support for commerce provided by such facilities as the Triborough Bridge, Hoover Dam, LaGuardia Airport, and San Antonio's River Walk since they were built over seven decades ago by the PWA and the Works Progress Administration (WPA) is incalculable.

In the case of farmers' markets, the provision of market halls by a city government is a tradition that goes back at least to sixteenth-century England.[1] Since the PWA was willing to support "any projects of the character heretofore constructed or carried on either directly by public authority or with public aid to serve the interests of the general public," there was no reason not to fund a farmers' market.[2] It is one of two built by the PWA in Louisiana. The other is in Shreveport but no longer functions as a market. But it is still useful; the stalls are enclosed and now house shops for the Department of Water and Sewerage.

The decision to support the French Market was made easier in this case because the members of the French Market Corporation were appointed by the city council, and the property was owned by the city and leased to the corporation. Any profits went to the city. Therefore the PWA could consider the French Market Corporation a public body.[3]

When the original market was built in 1784, it sprung from city officials' desire to monitor the quality and price of farm produce. The corporation's concern in 1933 was rehabilitating or replacing the deteriorating market buildings and improving access for farmers and wholesale and retail buyers. The corporation also aspired to new standards of health and cleanliness. It envisioned, and obtained, refrigerated glass and steel counters to keep meat fresh at the point of sale, and water heaters able to deliver fifty gallons per minute to sluice the terrazzo floors. The new facilities centralized operations then conducted in Westwego, Harvey, and other outlying areas.

As one approaches the French Market from Jackson Square, the first building encountered is the Meat Market, or Old Butchers' Building. Built in 1813 to replace a meat market built by the Spanish and destroyed in a hurricane in 1812, it is the oldest surviving structure in the Market.[4] It required the least restoration work by the PWA.

The next building, known as the Bazaar because it displayed a wide variety of imported clothing and dry goods, was a reconstruction by the PWA of a building destroyed in a 1917 hurricane. The Old Vegetable Market at the confluence of Decatur and N. Peters streets dates from 1823 and required extensive remodeling by the PWA. It housed Morning Call, one of two coffee shops then in the Market. Nearby is a flagpole with the PWA plaque at its base.

Farther east are two traditional Market buildings, roofed but open along the sides. Built by the PWA, they were intended to allow regional farmers to display and sell their produce. The first building is still devoted to foods,

Old Butchers' Building, French Market, New Orleans, dating from 1813, is the oldest surviving structure in the market. It required minimal restoration by the PWA.

though the fresh produce is now mixed with tourist-oriented convenience foods like jambalaya mixes and unique fast foods like alligator-on-a-stick. The second building shelters a flea market displaying a wide variety of goods: T-shirts, sunglasses, leather bags, jewelry, crafts, and souvenirs.

The PWA also built a new Wholesale Seafood Shed on the river side of the Vegetable Market on the site now occupied by the Red Stores, a three-story building that houses offices, including those of the French Market Corporation. It is a 1976 reconstruction of an 1833 building that was razed by the PWA. The Riverside Market is another 1976 addition on the side of a PWA market shed. It includes an office of the National Park Service, which offers guided tours in the French Quarter. Further

FRENCH MARKET 153

The Farmers' Market and Flea Market sheds were new construction by the PWA.

remodeling was done in 1991, and a new facelift was scheduled in 2005, just prior to Hurricane Katrina.

The overhaul of the French Market was not universally welcomed. Some farmers complained that they were being squeezed by the wholesalers. When the project was first being considered, Mrs. A. V. Smith of Paradis wrote a letter to Mayor T. Semmes Walmsley complaining that farmers were forced by wholesalers to sell low because otherwise produce would spoil. She also noted that while police kept order for the tourists during the day, the Market was a "tough spot" at night when the farmers customarily made their deliveries. "No man of any decency would think of taking his family on an outing to the market." She next took her grievance to the *Times-Picayune*, where she is pictured with a handful of vegetables over the caption: "Cowpeas Shrink Between Producer and Consumer." When the project got under way again, she resumed her crusade, sending a telegram to the PWA denouncing the corporation as "a bunch of speculating wholesale merchants and shippers . . . [who] pauperize farmers and fisherman by manipulating retail prices."[5]

We don't know what Smith thought of the finished product. She may never have received what she considered a fair deal from the wholesalers, but at least one of her complaints was addressed. The Market became a place for a decent man to take his family for an outing.

The corporation was already aware that it had a potential tourist attraction, not just a city produce market. This awareness is reflected in the decision of the architects, brothers Sam Stone Jr. and Frank Stone, to unify the complex with a common style reflecting the old buildings of the Vieux Carre rather than erecting a group of purely functional sheds. It is very clear from their drawings in 1934 of the buildings and their patrons. One drawing, depicting the corner of St. Philip and Decatur, shows a woman in a fur-collared coat on the sidewalk in front of Morning Call followed by her chauffeur, identifiable by his cap and jodhpurs, carrying her packages. A couple, arm in arm, prepare to cross St. Philip. One truck proceeds down Decatur, but all the other vehicles on the street are touring cars or sedans, plus a coupe with a rumble seat. Another drawing looks down (then) Gallitin Street past the market shed. There are plenty of trucks here, but there are also women in stylish hats. A man crosses the street wearing a fedora and carrying a briefcase.[6]

This drawing of the French Market by Stone's firm demonstrates that he conceived it as a tourist destination even then and not just a place to sell vegetables. His vision has been amply fulfilled.

To spread the word about the new wonders of the French Market, the corporation produced a pamphlet in 1938. Farmers, butchers, and dockworkers needed no introduction to the Morning Call or Café du Monde. But the authors felt the need to wax eloquent in praise of Morning Call coffee. "And satisfying this particular demand of one's appetite [for a cup of coffee]," they said, "brings a surcease of nerve, of weariness, of boredom, and makes one at peace with the world." If one wanted more than peace with the world, one could go to Café du Monde, a "mecca of the elite in the social sphere and travelers from all states in the union and countless numbers from points across the two great oceans."[7]

The Morning Call has left the French Market and moved across Lake Pontchartrain, but Café du Monde remains at the upriver end of the Butcher's Market greeting tourists and locals twenty-four hours a day. The projected revenues for the Market when fully operational were then estimated to be $90,000 a year. The profit from café au lait and beignets since 1938 alone could probably repay the cost of PWA's French Market renovation many times over.

The new Market was dedicated on March 19, 1938, at 4:00 P.M. Roosevelt and Ickes were invited, but neither could attend. French Market Corporation president J. Richard Reuter oozed compliments for the PWA: "Throughout the period of rebuilding the ancient market place, the sponsors were given full and complete cooperation on the part of the Hon. Harold L. Ickes and the gentlemen in Washington and New Orleans and we cannot possibly be too high in our praise for their whole-hearted assistance."[8] He enclosed a copy of the pamphlet.

Ickes seemed pleased with the result as well. He wrote to Reuter: "I have long been aware of the position which good food and fine dining enjoys in New Orleans. It is particularly fitting therefore that PWA should have assisted in carrying through a project which will aid in perpetuating the epicurean traditions of your city. . . . I hope that the market will continue to offer its colorful services to the city for many more years."[9]

The French Market retains a token of its original function in the fruit and vegetable stalls in the Farmers' Market building, but it is now much more. It is a major tourist attraction within a major tourist attraction and was mercifully spared by Hurricane Katrina. Food, drink, and merchandise will again soon be dispensed nonstop. Entertainment, once almost as constant, ranging from clowns, mimes, puppeteers, and sidewalk saxophonists to café jazz combos, will also return. It will again be a venue for unlicensed entrepreneurs, the bottle-cap tap-dancers, guerrilla shoe-shiners, and joke hustlers hoping for a quick buck. The coffee may not produce peace with the world, but it does offer surcease from weariness and boredom. And you now can get it iced as well as hot.

CHAPTER 12

THE SHREVEPORT INCINERATOR

Designing an incinerator is not the sort of task that usually excites an architect. Nor are incinerators frequently written up in the architectural press. Nonetheless, the design by Jones, Roessle, Olschner, and Wiener for the Shreveport incinerator drew praise from architectural arbiter and *New Yorker* writer Lewis Mumford and was featured in major architectural and engineering journals in the United States, France, and the Netherlands. The New York Museum of Modern Art chose an image of it for a traveling photographic exhibition on modern architecture and displayed it in the U.S. Pavilion at the Paris International Exposition of 1937. At the San Francisco World's Fair a year later, it was named one of "the 25 best contemporary buildings east of the Rockies."[1]

The reason for all this attention was that the design was strikingly modernist, and there were few such buildings in this country at the time. Modernism was a European development about which most American architects were skeptical. The manifestos of De Stijl, the Bauhaus, the Constructivists, and Le Corbusier calling for a radical break with the classical past, a rejection of all its ornamentation, and not only the use but the prominent display of new construction materials like concrete, steel, and glass were too severe for this side of the Atlantic. And, as noted in chapter 8, they got no encouragement to experiment in residential buildings from mortgage bankers and the new Federal Housing Administration, even if they and their clients had wanted to try the new aesthetic.

One would think that when designing industrial buildings, American architects would have free rein to create a more modern aesthetic by openly celebrating the new materials of aluminum, steel, concrete, and glass. But even here they had trouble breaking with the past. It was not uncommon

Shreveport incinerator. It received international attention as a masterpiece of modern architecture, but that didn't save it from demolition in 1974.

to see factories with the same classical ornaments worn by banks or courthouses. Prior to the Tennessee Valley Authority, even such utilitarian structures as dams often had classical packaging.

The Shreveport incinerator began its life on the drawing board sporting classical detailing.[2] It is unlikely that this version would have attracted any notice from the architectural press. But somewhere along the line a transformation occurred. The partner who supervised construction was Clarence Olschner because, as he told the Public Works Administration (PWA) public relations officer Michael Straus after the building was selected for the Paris Exposition, his partnership "operated on the principle that the partner who was best acquainted with the client should give his personal attention to the work." In the same letter, he takes credit for making a "survey of all the modern incinerators in the United States and Canada and then personally drawing the plans." Indeed, Olschner billed the city $488.13 for the inspection tour.[3]

However, the recognized modernist in the firm was Samuel Wiener. Along with his wife, his brother William, and another Shreveport architect, Theodore Flaxman, he had made a pilgrimage to the Netherlands and Germany in 1931 to see the work of Walter Gropius, Ludwig Mies van der Rohe, J. J. P. Oud, Peter Behrens, Willem Dudok, and Eric Mendelsohn.[4] He is the likely creator of the look that brought international fame to the building. And there is a letter from Shreveport commissioner of accounts and finance John M. Ford to a PWA auditor pressing a claim on Sam Wiener's behalf for $185.81 for Wiener's plans and specifications, which Ford says saved the city $3,000. Still, it is Olschner who authored an article in *American City* describing the project. In it, no other architect is credited with the design.[5] The other features in architecture journals simply give credit to the firm. Wiener, however, has the last word chronologically. In responding to an inquiry from L. A. Hodges, chair of the PWA Committee on Architectural Surveys, in 1939, he presents a slightly longer list of citations in the international architectural press and offers to provide photographs and drawings. In the letter, Wiener neither takes nor assigns credit for the design. But it does maintain his association with the project and, given his established aesthetic preferences, makes it most likely that he is the author of the final exterior appearance.[6]

The incinerator incorporated engineering innovations as well as architectural ones. It featured two garbage-receiving bins, one on each side of the building, allowing one to be cleaned without having to shut down the furnace. Ash was deposited by gravity directly to trucks on the bottom floor. This floor was extended for use as a garage when the furnace was not operating. The stoking room had direct ventilation. Reinforced concrete rather than structural steel was used in construction.[7]

The designer of the furnace was H. E. Burns, a former vice president of the Superior Incinerator Company. He joined forces with the A. J. Rife Construction Company of Dallas to bid on the project. When their bid was accepted, other bidders did their best to smear him. The sales manager of the Pittsburgh–Des Moines Steel Company alleged that Burns's incinerator projects in Cincinnati and New York City had to be overhauled before they would work. A representative of the Nye Odorless Incinerator Company of Macon, Georgia, was even more agitated. In a letter addressed to the nonexistent PWA "Incinerator Division," he said his competitor knew nothing about advances in the field in the last twenty years. He stated flatly that the city had "thrown away $100,000 of the taxpayers' money" and prophesied that "when the plant is built it will be worthless as the City will not be able to operate it."[8] The projects in other cities were investigated, and the PWA could find no reason not to approve the Burns/Rife bid. The results, including acclamation of the finished project by engineering journals and the adoption of the plan by incinerator builders throughout the world, seem to answer the unsuccessful bidders.[9]

Thus the Shreveport incinerator shown forth to modernists as incontrovertible evidence that function was beauty. *Architectural Forum* praised it as a "strikingly clean piece of design." The window band, a modernist trademark, provided "an unusual amount of light and air." The "plan without precedent has quite logically resulted in a building as new as it is sound." The window also caught the eye of *New Yorker* architectural critic Lewis Mumford when he saw a photograph of the building at a New York Architectural League show. "This is one of the best examples of the rational use of the ribbon window . . . that I have come across—an excellent design, with no vulgar attempts at prettifying a form that needs no addition." He was, he said, ready to pin a medal on Jones, Roessle, Olschner, and Wiener.[10]

The mystery over who should get credit for the design of the building can be resolved if we conclude that Olschner drew the original plans and neoclassical elevations, and that Wiener later redesigned the shell of the building, giving it the modernist look that made it famous. Eliminating classical ornamentation was more economical, and cost savings were probably important as the project progressed. But this causes some problems for the modernist ideological conviction that the beauty of the building derives directly from the functions within. With the exception of the capacious windows on the third-floor stoking room, which provided welcome light and ventilation, there is not much articulation between plan and elevation. Marcus Weeks, who was the resident engineer-inspector on the project, gives some support to this conclusion when he notes that the architects designed the building so that it might accommodate any type of incinerator furnace.[11] On the other hand, this fits well with the kind of modernist design espoused by Mies van der Rohe, who built boxy buildings with a minimum of interior supports or services, so that clients could arrange the interior spaces any way they wanted and change them when the need arose.

We can leave this ideological argument to architectural historians. Perhaps it was a beautiful building because it worked well. Perhaps it was a beautiful building regardless of what went on inside. It is enough to say that it was a beautiful building and it worked well. Unfortunately, most citizens of Shreveport remained unaware that their garbage was being vaporized by a minor icon of modern architecture. They allowed it to be razed in 1974.

CHAPTER 13

SUGAR

The growing of sugarcane and the manufacture of sugar from it in south Louisiana goes back to at least 1795. Other cash crops were not suitable to the climate. After World War I, bitter competition forced most Louisiana refineries out of business. The surviving sugar plants concentrated on producing raw sugar for others to refine. However, the big refineries could import sugar from tropical countries where labor was cheaper, thus forcing down the price of raw sugar for domestic producers.

In the early 1930s a U.S. Department of Agriculture study suggested that there would be a regional market of "direct consumption sugar," a commodity cheaper than the granular sugar produced by the refineries but commanding a better price than raw sugar. Direct consumption sugar was used by canneries turning out sweetened food products and by makers of jellies and jams. The process of producing such sugar, however, was not well understood by Louisiana sugar plant operators.

The Audubon Sugar School was established by Louisiana State University (LSU) in 1891. It evolved from the Sugar Experiment Station, the first such research organization in the hemisphere, which began work in 1885. A four-year course of study became available in 1896 and was expanded to a five-year curriculum leading to a B.S. degree in 1899. The school was moved from Audubon Park in New Orleans to the Baton Rouge campus in 1925. The Department of Chemical Engineering assumed its direction five years later. It became known throughout the hemisphere as a center for research and education in growing sugarcane and producing sugar products. It also attracted students from sugar-growing countries in Asia.[1] It was therefore natural that area sugar producers, and indeed the entire sugar industry, would look to LSU for help as the Depression pushed them into further distress.

LSU responded in the form of a proposal to the Public Works Administration (PWA) for new milling and experimental equipment. At the center of the proposal was a report by Charles E. Coates, dean of the College of Pure and Applied Sciences, and Arthur G. Keller, dean of the College of Chemical Engineering.[2] This report put forth the case for direct consumption sugar. It enumerated the contributions that the new equipment could make in researching the techniques to efficiently manufacture and deliver such sugar to the packagers of sweetened food products. Finally, it outlined the impact that a revitalized sugar industry would have on the region.

A survey and census funded by the Works Progress Administration (WPA) had documented the amount of idle land in the sugar-producing area and found 70,000 people on relief in the twenty cane-producing parishes. It also found 5,000 idle farmers not on relief. Based on this information, Coates and Keller estimated that the 1934 sugar crop could be doubled. This would employ 30,000 extra regular workers along with 30,000 seasonal workers in the spring and 70,000 in the fall. It would not only absorb all the unemployed farm workers in the area but bring others in from outside the region.[3]

To make this project a success, sugar producers would have to learn how to control the manufacturing techniques and turn out a uniform product of higher quality than currently was reaching the market. They could also learn how to produce specialty sugars such as turbinado, used in making jams. This would free them from dependence on the large refineries.

Research tasks to be undertaken by LSU sugar scientists included determining the sucrose content of various varieties of cane and finding optimum conditions for milling the various canes. Researchers would also be documenting the power requirements for sugar plants; testing a new milling diffusion process used in other countries; finding new uses for begasse, a cellulose cane by-product; testing juice clarification processes; and finding ways to control boiling to get uniform sugar crystal size.[4]

Solid support for this proposal came from the sugar producers. The American Sugar Cane League testified to the current lack of scientific data on cane milling. When it was discovered during bidding that the needed equipment was going to be more expensive than estimated, the league came up with $14,000 to help cover the difference.[5]

The existing LSU milling equipment was forty years old. The replacement included revolving cane knives, a two-roller crusher, a shredder, and three three-roller mills with hydraulic pressure regulators driven by separate electric motors. It could grind 7.5 tons of cane an hour. The plant was built by George L. Squire of Buffalo, New York.

There was heavy lobbying for the project in the spring and summer of 1936. Some of it was a bit clumsy. Congressman W. G. Andrews wrote to Harry Hopkins, thinking it was a WPA project. Rose Long, who had replaced her dead husband as senator, made the same mistake. However, Senator John Overton and Congressman J. O. Fernandez were well acquainted with the PWA and made regular inquiries. Congressmen John Sandlin and J. Y. Sanders Jr. also weighed in. This was at the time when the Long legislation controlling bond issues and the use of federal money was being repealed. Fernandez assured Ickes that such laws had been retracted.[6]

One reason for the urgency was that the legislation authorizing the PWA was due to expire on July 1, 1937, and the PWA was being careful in making allotments to projects that might not be completed by that date. The LSU project was approved but, despite Coates's conviction that it could be completed in three to four months, encountered delays in getting the equipment. The recession of 1937, as we have seen, gave the PWA an extended life. So the project was able to continue to completion.[7] The equipment finally arrived in January 1938. It was installed with the help of workers hired under the WPA. Keller supervised the installation.

Paul Hebert, who was dean of the LSU law school and the university's representative for this project, was pleased with the results. "The project," he said, "has resulted in a great deal of good will throughout the state . . . by reason of the widespread interest of the people in the sugar industry and because the sugar industry itself has long felt the need for a model experimental cane sugar factory at the university." He concluded that LSU "would have obtained better buildings in other projects if they had been constructed under the PWA."[8]

The new equipment and the research program devised by Coates and Keller became an asset to education at LSU and the sugar industry in general for years afterward. But what saved the sugar industry during the Depression was another piece of New Deal legislation. The Sugar Act of 1934 established quotas based on supply and demand to keep prices stable. It paid benefits to growers from a tax on processors. In order to qualify for benefits, growers had to pay a minimum wage to field workers. They became the first farmers in the country to be covered by minimum wage

Sugar Factory, Louisiana State University. A center for research known throughout the hemisphere, it helped revitalized the local economy during the Depression.

legislation.[9] This is particularly significant in light of the neglect that tenant farmers and sharecroppers had experienced at the hands of the Agricultural Adjustment Administration.

Like the PWA's aid to the French Market project, the LSU Sugar Factory project was a contribution to the economy as well as to social and cultural infrastructure. Businessmen who might otherwise have denounced government intervention in any business-related activity were happy to have a partnership with the government and a state university to help them understand the cultivation, processing, and marketing of this very important regional crop.

CHAPTER 14

THE NEW ORLEANS SEWER AND WATER PROJECT

Up to this point, most of our attention has been directed above ground. The importance of the New Deal public works programs is most easily understood by looking at the structures that made possible the many improvements in education, health, recreation, the conduct of government, the administration of justice, and other aspects of civic life. But some of these improvements happened largely out of sight and often underground. Safe drinking water and the sanitary disposal of waste products are aspects of life we are inclined to take for granted. If they are not available, however, disease and death, sometimes on epidemic levels, are inevitable consequences. An underground water system is also an important contribution to fire protection. Finally, in some areas storm sewers and drainage canals are essential to prevent damaging floods. This chapter brings to light some of these hidden aspects of infrastructure.

The rapid growth of towns and cities in the early part of the nineteenth century created serious public health problems. Concentrations of people required more water and produced more waste. Wells were often inadequate to provide drinking water for the growing population and were subject to contamination if located near industrial sites. Rivers and streams faced similar pollution threats. Entire cities could be burned to the ground if a small fire got started amid the closely packed homes and businesses. Fire trucks bearing tanks of water were totally inadequate to such challenges. When fire insurance became available, it was much more costly in cities without water systems, a daily drain on the economy to go along with the potential for catastrophic loss.

In the early part of the century, cities often lacked the resources to meet the challenges thrown at them by a mushrooming population and explosive industrialization. Water and sewer needs were only part of the challenge. Children moving from rural areas were joined by others recently arrived in America, swelling schools to the bursting point. Population concentration and poverty also increased crime and required more police protection. City governments, however, could not easily provide the cultural and physical infrastructure to meet these needs. They were constrained by ideological and sometimes legal restrictions on borrowing or raising taxes to pay for services.[1]

Thanks to New Deal public building programs, and particularly the Public Works Administration (PWA), many cities made great progress in protecting their citizens from epidemics by introducing or expanding clean drinking water and sewage treatment facilities. For example, in 1930 a full third of the urban population was drinking untreated water; by 1940 it was down to 1 percent. In 1930 only 30 percent of the sewage in cities was being treated; by 1940 treatment had doubled.[2]

In Louisiana, the PWA supported thirty-five water and/or sewer projects in twenty-five parishes at a cost of over $6.3 million (see table 5).[3] This is a small amount of money relative to other PWA sewer projects. The sewage system for Chicago was one of the largest single projects the PWA attempted. It totaled over $56 million. The Ward's Island Treatment Plant was constructed to handle all the sewage on the east side of Manhattan from 72nd Street to 178th Street and cost $24.7 million. Cleveland, Buffalo, and Minneapolis/St. Paul all got new disposal plants costing approximately $15 million each.[4] Milwaukee received over $5 million and Cincinnati over $3 million for sewage treatment. The Potomac River was cleaned up with the help of a $4 million project in the District of Columbia. A $2.5 million plant at the end of Golden Gate Park ended the dumping of raw sewage into San Francisco Bay. But for a small state like Louisiana, $6.3 million was a huge amount of money and made major differences in the communities served.

In Lake Charles, for example, raw sewage was going directly into the lake and the Calcasieu River. Citizens swam and caught fish in both bodies of water. The State Board of Health had to condemn the lake. Worse, the city's water supply intake was only several hundred yards from the sewage outflow. A PWA project costing $257,612 replaced the original sewage system, which was twenty years old. Components are still in operation.[5]

Communities across Louisiana were reporting similar problems. In

Lake Charles Wastewater Treatment Plant. Raw sewage was going directly into the lake and the Calcasieu River, where people swam and fished.

Welsh, septic tanks regularly overflowed into ditches lining the city streets. The mayor of New Roads complained of "privies, cesspools and open drains" producing "foul stenches" and creating the "hazard of epidemic diseases." In Jackson, wells serving the large state hospital there were polluted, and an outbreak of typhoid fever was feared. The State Board of Health had declared the water quality of St. Joseph in need of "very urgent" attention. Citizens of Logansport feared malaria and typhoid fever because of their shallow wells. They had no sewer or water system and thus no fire protection. The failure of the artesian well in Independence left the town with no drinkable water. Townspeople there, too, had no sewer, water, or fire protection. Sunset and Ringold were in a similar situation.[6]

Some communities were not just looking at the immediate dangers they faced. They were looking beyond the current threats to their health and safety toward a more secure future. In Metarie, a rapidly growing suburb to the west of New Orleans, the sewer and water inadequacies had produced an ambiance that was "unhealthy and smelly." But, said Metarie's application to the PWA, the proposed million dollar sewerage disposal system "will no doubt aid materially in the development of this valuable area." Prophetic words.[7]

Safe drinking water, the sanitary treatment of sewage, and a more efficient system of fire protection meant for these communities not just improved health and safety for the current residents but also the possibility of economic growth. Clean lakes and rivers would welcome those seeking recreation as well as sport and commercial fishing. Safer cities would make possible the initiation and expansion of businesses. Sewer and water systems were an essential investment in the future.

New Orleans has been called "the impossible but inevitable city." The Mississippi River was the continent's central highway between the heart-

Mooringsport water supply and filtration system. None existed in the city prior to this.

land and the sea. The agricultural products of the interior headed for markets worldwide required a point of transfer somewhere near the mouth of the river. But unlike the mouths of other great rivers of the world, which ended in estuaries surrounded by solid land, the Mississippi ended in a vast delta of swamps and marshes. There was no reasonable place to put a city. So the city had to be built in an unreasonable place.[8]

For trade and exploration purposes, the site was reasonable enough. It was on the portage between the river and Lake Pontchartrain. The Choctaws showed it to the first French explorers, who appreciated the importance of this connection. But making it more than just a portage was a real challenge. Ridges, formed by eons of flooding over the banks of the Mississippi and its distributary bayous, constituted the only high ground remotely suitable for building. Back of that was swamp, and not just swamp, but swamp below sea level. The region's subtropical torrents of rain could fill the basin behind the ridges in a few hours. Expanding the settlement beyond the ridges was impossible without some means of initial drainage, and anything built there could not survive without ongoing drainage. So, for two centuries the city clung to the ridges and, because of its strategic location, prospered despite its precariousness. In 1810 it was the nation's fifth largest city and was close to being its second by 1850.[9]

The Carondelet Canal, dug in 1796 for commercial purposes to connect the French Quarter to Bayou St. John and thence to the lake, was also an effort toward basic drainage. But the gradient was small enough that any appreciable wind from the north could back up the flow of water (and sewage). Other canals were dug in the early 1800s, the largest being the "New Canal" in 1831, which went from Poydras Street to the lake; but stagnant water continued to pose a health threat to the city.[10]

The city leaders decided in 1893 to take a more systematic approach to drainage, covering not only the built-up areas but also places they thought would soon be built upon. The plan included several outlets to Lake Pontchartrain and one eastward to Lake Borgne, and added pumps to speed water over the shallow gradients. The plan was not immediately implemented, however.[11]

A yellow fever epidemic in 1895, not the first in the city's history, heightened awareness in New Orleans of the need for public sanitation. There were no sewers, and the only safe drinking water came from cisterns collecting rain water. The Sewerage and Water Board was created in 1899. Property owners agreed to tax themselves and back a $12 million bond issue in 1900, and by 1904 the first sewers were operating. The Sewerage and Water Board merged with the Drainage Commission in 1902. Another bond issue, this time for $8 million, was passed in 1906. Filtered water was available in 1909. The system of drains and sewers included the major drainage canals at Seventeenth Street and London Avenue, the ones that were to collapse during Hurricane Katrina. On April 17, 1911, fourteen inches of rain fell on the city in twenty-four hours. The flood prompted an $11 million improvement in the system that year.[12]

In 1917 A. Baldwin Wood, an engineer who would later become the director of the Sewerage and Water Board, invented a pump that "made it possible to raise huge volumes of debris-laden water a short vertical distance, and do it fast. It was one of those potent inventions that people in later years would take for granted, but just as high speed elevators changed the geography of New York City by making skyscrapers possible, the Wood pump revolutionized the urban geography of New Orleans by suddenly opening to settlement areas which were thought forever closed." The pumps could remove seven billion gallons of water a day, keeping these new neighborhoods from becoming periodic swimming pools. This also brought a dramatic drop in death from typhoid fever, from 38 people per 100,000 in 1910 to 7.5 in 1920.[13]

When the Dutch were first constructing their "polders," large areas of agricultural land reclaimed from the sea, they came to New Orleans to look at Wood's pumps. We might then have learned from them about keeping back the sea. After three drainage canals fell apart under the pressure of Hurricane Katrina, Louisiana governor Katherine Babineaux Blanco made a belated trip to the Netherlands to correct the oversight.[14]

Thus by the beginning of the Great Depression the city of New Orleans already had a well-developed sewer and water system. By 1920, 97 percent of the city's buildings had water connections, and by 1923, 93 percent of them were served by city sewers. The city was able to keep up with new construction during the early 1920s.[15]

On March 16, 1927, George G. Earl, the general supervisor of the Sewerage and Water Board, issued a report projecting a 100 percent expansion of the city in the next fifteen years, with a 40 percent increase in new buildings. More paving and roofing would mean more runoff of rain water and greater pressure on drains and storm sewers. Flooding above curb level was now frequent. He predicted that $65.5 million worth of improvements would be necessary to keep pace with this growth. He recommended $9.5 million be spent immediately.[16]

On April 17, 1928, voters approved a $9 million bond issue. By then the Depression was closing in, and chances for any further improvement dried up. The rain, of course, did not. So, when the PWA was created in 1933 and began to encourage physical infrastructure projects, the city saw new hope. President Herbert Hoover's last-minute public works program, the Emergency Relief and Construction Act run by the Reconstruction Finance Corporation (RFC), had briefly signaled similar hope, but it was short-lived. Hoover had insisted all projects be "self-liquidating," meaning that they had to be paid for out of fees charged for the services provided, not from general city funds.[17] Fees could be charged for water and sewer service and users made to pay fairly for the amount they used. But fire and drainage protection were services that had to be extended to the general public and paid for equally. So communities were ineligible for RFC loans for water, sewer, and drainage projects.[18]

The Sewerage and Water Board submitted a proposal to the PWA on October 13, 1933, for a combination of sewer, water, and drainage improvements across the city, including the West Bank. It asked for $7 million. The proposal ran into trouble with both the Finance and Legal divisions of the PWA. They doubted the board's authority to use its surplus from special taxes as security for the loan. The board responded with a revised and reduced application for $2.5 million, backed by a $1.8 million bond issue approved in an election on April 4, 1933.[19]

While negotiations with the PWA were proceeding, the Civil Works Administration (CWA) was created. Its emphasis on labor-intensive projects was perfectly suited to ditch-digging. New Orleans did not let this new opportunity pass. The CWA put in over 10,000 linear feet of sewer lines and 17,700 linear feet of water mains with an accompanying forty-six fire hydrants and twenty-six valves. It also cleared drainage canals and ditches.[20]

But just as the PWA project was finally getting under way, it sailed into a cross fire between Huey Long and the New Orleans Old Regulars. Long was trying to wrest control over city employees and the services they provided from Mayor T. Semmes Walmsley and his supporters. In November 1934 he secured passage of state legislation that not only created a state Civil Service Commission to oversee all police and fire chiefs but also reorganized the Sewerage and Water Board. This removed most of the city-appointed members, replacing them with state appointees he could control.[21]

Long also declared a moratorium on private debts for up to two years. Harold Ickes was immediately suspicious that this atmosphere of forgiveness might soon be extended to public debts as well and that he might be left holding a $2.5 million bag. He suspended all PWA projects in Louisiana not already under construction on November 16. The agreement for the sewer and water project was already in the mail, but neither the old board nor its replacement could put it to use.[22]

On January 4, 1935, Ickes concluded that the debt suspension law was no threat to the PWA and lifted the suspension of Louisiana projects. However, the sewer and water project remained frozen until it was clear with which board he should work. A flurry of court actions to test the legality of the reorganization legislation ensued that would last until August 1935, when all courts involved had rendered decisions and all injunctions were lifted.[23]

But the legality of the dueling water boards was only one problem for the Sewerage and Water project. In April 1935 Long had created a state Bond and Tax Board whose approval was required before any community could commit itself to financing a public works project. In September he put through a bill making it illegal for any federal official to spent pubic money for "political purposes." The legislation only furthered Ickes's fear that his project personnel would be subject to harassment and possible criminal charges. Even Long's assassination did not change his mind. Only in October 1935, when the Louisiana attorney general assured Ickes that the laws could not be applied because the allotment to the project had been made before the legislation was enacted, did Ickes release the funds to move the project forward.[24] Ickes, however, continued to suspend the other PWA projects until the laws were repealed and until after the elections of 1936, when the Long candidates defeated the New Deal loyalists.

Even as the shot and shell were exploding over the board, it managed in April 1935 to issue from its bunker a proposal for a change in the project's scope. The original proposal included provision for underground cable to transmit power to the pumping stations, thus protecting them from any interference from high winds. The cost of the cable proved too expensive. In its place, sewer extensions on Harrison Avenue, Lee Boulevard, Orleans Avenue, and the New Basin Canal were proposed. The amendment was approved on February 17, 1936.

When finally under way, the project spanned the city with sewer, water, and drain improvements. It involved the redredging, widening, and enlarging of outfall canals; the lining and covering of drainage ditches; and the laying of concrete pipe to extend the sewer and water system (see table 6). It was not the $7 million project originally hoped for, but it provided needed improvements that would not have been possible otherwise during the Depression. It brought water and sewer service to new neighborhoods, facilitating the growth of the city. It also gave protection to a "high value district," Canal Street. Even with new area to cover, the drainage improvements made it possible to handle three inches of rain or more.[25]

A second amendatory proposal for a change in scope was submitted to the PWA on September 5, 1936. It asked for an auxiliary waterworks pumping plant. Because of the low elevation of the city, water pressure was a problem. Demand was rising. In 1934, 81.5 million gallons a day were needed; by 1936 it was 102.5 million. Furthermore, the Board of Fire Underwriters required that the system be able to deliver 25 million gallons per day above peak demand with one pump out of service. Failing that test, insurance rates would be higher. With one pump out, the system could only guarantee 120 million gallons.[26]

The current plant had four pumps, one dating from 1907 and two others from 1917. They were also close together. On November 26, 1935, a steam explosion had shut down the entire plant for seventy-three minutes. A similar event, or a hurricane, could cut off the water supply for the entire city. Thus there was a need not only for an additional pump but also for one placed at some distance from the others.[27] The amendment was approved on December 9, 1936.

Even with the political warfare between Huey Long and the Old Regulars out of the way, the project was not without other kinds of strife. A labor union organized a strike against one of the contractors, and, perhaps coincidentally, one of the contractor's dredging boats was destroyed by fire, bringing work to a halt on the London Avenue Canal. A crane operator was beaten by workers who thought they should have gotten his job. A business agent for Local 406 of the International Union of Operating Engineers, H. D. Bannister, was accused of stealing documents from the office of Resident Engineer-Inspector C. L. Crowell. He was also arrested for the stabbing murder of one of the contractor's men during a card game.[28]

Discontent among property owners did not reach this level of mayhem,

Pumping Station #21, Filmore and Memphis streets, New Orleans.

but they were very angry with what one of the contractors, W. R. Aldrich and Company, did to their yards. Residents along General Taylor Street, Larmarque Street, Whitney Avenue, and Jefferson Avenue sued for over $9,000 in damages. Among the claimants was Bethany Evangelical Church, which wanted $1,355. The church, however, settled for $400.[29]

Finally, on June 30, 1938, after all claims were settled, all bills paid, and all investigations concluded, the PWA declared the project completed. It is difficult to estimate the value of the sewer, water, and storm drainage system to the people who live above it and, in general, take it for granted. It is essential to the economy because no business, industry, or private residence can exist comfortably and efficiently without it, and without businesses and a resident population there is no economy. It is vital to the health of the population because without it, diseases could reach epidemic proportions and ravage the city. It protects the city from fires that can easily get out of control in congested areas. And, in the case of a city that lies largely below sea level, comprehensive and immediate drainage is a matter of life and death. This unfolded before our eyes in the aftermath of Hurricane Katrina. The storm sewers, the drainage canals, and the Wood pumps were designed to combat extraordinary rainfall. They might even have coped with a moderate storm surge. They could not, however, drain the city if the levees failed. The results of that failure are still being reckoned. Loss of life in the hundreds at least, the destruction of whole neighborhoods, and the scattering of over half the population of the city are among the costs. It may also prove that among the casualties are some of the structures described in earlier chapters.

Physical and cultural infrastructure are interdependent. The buildings above ground are served and protected by the utilities below. The enormous amount of building that the New Deal accomplished in a few years across Louisiana has served for almost three quarters of a century. It formed the backbone of our public life in health, education, recreation, commerce, and the administration of government and justice. But a political and economic culture grew up that took these things for granted and turned its back on proper maintenance of them. In the words of one observer, "New Orleans was a beautiful machine that was left to rust." Now we know that this neglect can result in destruction that is equally enormous.[30]

TABLE 7.
Sewer and Water Projects

Community	Parish	Type of Project	Cost	Completed
Abbeville	Vermillion	sanitary sewer	$237,148	1939
Amite	Tangipahoa	waterworks improvements	44,009	1938
Bernice	Union	waterworks	50,880	1938
Berwick	Terrebonne	water pipeline	10,636	1937
Crowley	Acadia	sanitary sewer	333,282	1939
Delcambre	Vermillion	waterworks	29,140	1938
E. Jefferson Parish	Jefferson	waterworks	321,836	1938
Franklinton	Washington	waterworks	37,780	1937
Grambling	Lincoln	water tower	.	1939
Gretna	Jefferson	waterworks	285,839	1935
Gretna	Jefferson	waterworks improvements	43,270	1939
Homer	Claiborne	disposal plant	63,812	1939
Independence	Tangipahoa	waterworks	7,239	1937
Jackson	E. Feliciana	waterworks	37,579	1937
Jefferson Parish	Jefferson	waterworks improvements	34,000	
Jeanerette	Iberia	sanitary sewer	169,629"	1939
Lake Charles	Calcasieu	disposal plant	257,612	1938
Logansport	Desoto	waterworks	42,207	1937
Metarie	Jefferson	sewage disposal	1,022,667	1940
Mooringsport	Caddo	waterworks	38,031	1937
Natchidoches	Natchidoches	utilities improvements	23,921	1939
New Orleans	Orleans	water/sewer/drainage	2,285,312	1938
New Roads	Pointe Coupee	water/sewer	135,804	1939
Port Barre	St. Landry	waterworks	31,392	1938
Rayne	Acadia	water/light/power	86,169	1939
Rayville	Richland	water/sewer	26,921	1939
Ringold	Bienville	waterworks	39,417	1937
Ruston	Lincoln	waterworks	108,235	1939
St. Joseph	Tensas	filtration plant	36,098	1937
St. Martinville	St. Martin	sewage disposal	133,833	1939

TABLE 7. (Continued)

Sewer and Water Projects

Community	Parish	Type of Project	Cost	Completed
Sulpher	Calcasiue	sanitary sewer	134,997	1939
Sunset	St. Landry	waterworks	30,497	1937
Welsh	Jefferson Davis	waterworks	129,600	1939
Winsboro	Franklin	water/sewer addition	60,158	1938
Wisner	Franklin	waterworks	45,643	1938

* Part of the $421,260 Grambling University project
** Also includes streets and sidewalks

Source: List of All Allotted Non-Federal Projects, All Programs, by State and Docket, as of May 30, 1942, 6568, Federal Works Agency, Public Works Administration, Record Group 135, National Archives II, College Park, Md.

TABLE 8.

Components of Docket #4284, New Orleans Sewerage and Water Board

	Drainage Projects
London Ave. Outfall Canal	widened and deepened	Pumping Stn. #3 to Lake (12,400')
Orleans Outfall Canal	widened and deepened	Pumping Stn. #7 to Lake (12,000')
Main (Broad) St. Canal	widened and deepened	Bruxelles St. to Pumping Stn. #3
S. Claiborn Ave. Canal	lined and covered	Nashville St. to Monticello St.
S. Claiborn Ave. Canal	lined and covered	3rd St. to Napoleon St. (3,900')
Almonaster Canal	lined and covered	Roman St. to Florida Ave.
Lamarque St. Canal	lined and covered	Vallette St. to Whitney Ave. (3,600')
St. Charles Ave. storm sewer	concrete pipe laid	Lee Circle to Felicity St.
Olympia St. storm sewer	concrete pipe laid	Orleans St. to Baudin St.
Jefferson Ave. storm sewer	concrete pipe laid	S. Claiborn Ave. to McKenna St. (2,500')
St. Clause St. storm sewer	concrete pipe laid	Poland St. to Japonica St. (500')

Sanitary Sewer Projects	
sewage pumping station #21	Fillmore Ave. & Memphis St.
submain and smaller tributaries	Algiers below the Southern Pacific R.R. yards
submain and smaller tributaries	to Pumping Station B
submain and smaller tributaries	to Pumping Station D
submain and smaller tributaries	to Pumping Station 19
relief discharge main	6th St. to 15th St.
multiple small and scattered projects	
sewer extensions	Harrison Ave, Lee Blvd., Orleans Ave. and New Basin Canal*

Water Projects
East Bank, larger mains to improve service
West Bank, larger mains to improve service
extension beyond Industrial Canal along Gentilly Rd. and Lakefront
larger mains reinforcement
scattered services to unserved houses

* re: amendatory proposal of 4/11/35

Source: Reel 3528, Docket #4284, Box 295, Record Group 135, Microfilm Records of the Public Works Administration, National Archives II, College Park, Md.

CHAPTER 15

BEYOND THE BAYOUS

The Public Works Administration (PWA) was in existence for nine years, from June 16, 1933, to June 30, 1942. After 1939, however, most of the agency's time was devoted to closing out projects with legal or financial difficulties, so most of its building was done in seven years. In Louisiana, thanks to friction over patronage and the legal impediments Huey Long created to protect his power, the PWA's work was done mostly in three years.

In the introduction, I mentioned a few of the PWA works that I have encountered, sometimes by accident, in the course of my travels. In fact, it is hard to go anywhere and not come across a PWA project. Here are some of the more famous ones that you may have encountered. Getting in or out of New York City is usually a challenge, but imagine how much more challenging it would be without the Triborough Bridge, the Lincoln Tunnel, the Queens-Midtown Tunnel, the East Side Drive and Henry Hudson Parkway, and the Staten Island Ferry.[1] In New York City's Central Park, the zoo, conservatory gardens, and peripheral playgrounds were contributed by the PWA. The zoo has been recently remodeled, but you can still discern its PWA core.

If you're in Miami, Florida, you might attend a football game in the Orange Bowl and then drive to Key West over the Overseas Highway. Elsewhere in the South you might visit the Gold Depository in Fort Knox, Kentucky, where the nation's bullion is kept safe, or the chapel at the famous Citadel military school in Charleston, South Carolina. These experiences were made possible by the PWA. Historic Fort Pulaski in Georgia was restored by the PWA.

The PWA created animal habitats in many zoos throughout the country, including those in St. Louis, San Francisco, and Washington, D.C. While in St. Louis you might attend an opera in Kiel Auditorium, visit the War Memorial across the street, or see a floral exhibit in the Jewel Box in Forest Park, courtesy of the PWA. Kansas City's skyscraper city hall and municipal auditorium were PWA projects.

Houston's ten-story city hall has many fine art deco details. The Houston Federation of Garden Clubs has its own Garden Center in Hermann Park, thanks to the PWA. In commemoration of the state's birth, the PWA erected a tower crowned by a lone star at the site of the battle of San Jacinto. In Dallas, Fair Park, which was built for the Texas Centennial Exposition in 1936, retains most of its original New Deal buildings and hosts the state fair and year-round conventions and shows. Its Natural History Museum was built by the PWA. The Will Rogers Coliseum in Fort Worth is another venue for entertainment of all kinds. In Austin, the University of Texas's famous tower as well as a museum and several dormitories were made possible by the PWA.

Farther west in Arizona, visitors to the Petrified Forest and Painted Desert should stop at the Painted Desert Inn, a Civilian Conservation Corps (CCC)/PWA collaboration. Next to famous Window Rock is the Council Chamber of the Navajo Nation. In Phoenix, you might visit Encanto Park, graced with a clubhouse, boathouse, and golf club office. It now has a popular amusement park for children on the main island of its PWA-created lake. Then on to California, you cross the mighty Hoover Dam.

In San Francisco, you'll probably see the ocean-liner shaped Maritime Museum at the marina by Ghiradelli Square. You might attend a convention at the Cow Palace; both of the two national political parties have frequently convened there. If you're taking a cruise or just walking along the Embarcadero, you'll pass a PWA terminal building. You won't notice it, but a $2.6 million PWA sewage treatment plant constructed in Golden Gate Park ended the practice of dumping raw sewage into San Francisco Bay. To provide water to the city, the PWA doubled the size of Hetch-Hectchy Reservoir at a cost of $2.3 million. Crossing the Bay Bridge, a Reconstruction Finance Corporation project completed by the PWA, you'll see two massive hangers on Treasure Island that were to be part of a China Clipper airport and are now film studios. The tall Alameda County courthouse dominates Lake Merritt in Oakland. A little to the north is Berkeley High, the impressive art deco high school. But even more valuable to the continuing commercial life of the Bay Area is the Caldicott Tunnel, which daily conducts thousands of commuters to and from the suburbs beyond the coastal mountains.

A drive up the Oregon Coast is possible because of a series of PWA bridges over rivers that empty into the Pacific Ocean. The Oregon state capitol in Salem is worth a visit. In Seattle, at the foot of the iconic Space Needle, a PWA armory has been converted to a children's museum, food court, and offices for arts organizations.

For every spectacular monument, there are dozens of modest schools, hospitals, post offices, and other community buildings that will entirely escape your notice. Taken together, they are an unparalleled achievement in U.S. history. *Life* magazine concluded that

> *Franklin D. Roosevelt has made Cheops, Pericles, Augustus, Ch'in Shih Huang Ti, the Medicis and Peter the Great look like a club of birdhouse builders. For one Great Pyramid or Great Wall, PWA has raised up scores of tremendous dams. For one Parthenon, it has reared thousands of glistening city halls, courthouses, post offices, schoolhouses. For one 366-mile Appian Way, it has laid 50,000 miles of highways over the hills and valleys of America.*[2]

This achievement should inspire wonder, but it should also stimulate thought. It raises questions about the way we think about several important public policy issues.

The first question is: Is there really such a thing as long-range public investment? New Deal agencies like the PWA were first and foremost responses to the Great Depression. They were attempts to reemploy thousands of idle workers, provide their families with basic subsistence, and stimulate economic recovery. But they were also long-range investments. The notion of public investment has been subject to ridicule in recent years. Such proposals are usually labeled as "pork." Of course, this could be a matter of geopolitical perspective. The expenditure of public money in my district may be investment, but in your district it's pork. In general, public investment seems a dubious proposition these days. Yet we are surrounded by evidence, thanks to New Deal building programs, that public investment exists and works. The structures they built were contributions to a future where citizens are safer, healthier, better educated, and better administered. They are investments that have paid dividends for going on eight decades, and they continue to enrich the communities in which they were created because most are still in use.

The next question is: Can we afford long-range public investment? Looking at current income and immediate needs usually brings a negative answer. We tend not to ask about the consequences of not making the investment. A person with a mortgage to pay and small children to feed may decide he or she can't afford to go to the dentist. A decade or two later, that same person will pay thousands of dollars to salvage what's left of his or her teeth and will end up with eating equipment that is much less efficient and comfortable than the properly maintained original would have been. A generation of poorly educated children will guarantee billions of future costs in crime, economic inefficiency, scientific stagnation, and artistic sterility. Fortunately, the Depression generation decided they had to make this investment. Bond issues to finance the community share of a PWA project often passed with little opposition. In one place in Louisiana, Bunkie, there was none at all.[3]

We don't know how much people living during the Depression were thinking about the future and how much they were preoccupied with the temporary relief of unemployment. But we do know that they willingly undertook their share of the financing of these projects, which required the assumption of debt to be paid off later. This displayed both a faith in the future and a willingness to sacrifice for it.

Does this mean that all "pork" is really long-range public investment? Probably not. But currently, public spending projects are not debated publicly. Nor is there any individual or group, public or private, to oversee them. They are attached as riders or smuggled into pieces of legislation whose main purpose has nothing to do with them. Projects are "earmarked" for certain influential legislators and never seen by the public at large. PWA proposals were debated locally, usually when the vote had to be taken on the bond issue that would help finance them. And they were scrutinized by a national organization for financial and structural soundness. This decision-making process was much more open than the current one. It might not have been completely above pork barrel considerations, but we can judge by its results. The great majority of its products were undeniably useful to their communities. *Life* magazine, a Henry Luce publication, was no fan of the New Deal. It retained a conservative skepticism in its article on the PWA. "Time alone," it concluded, "can tell whether the nation could afford to spend four billion dollars for PWA's 34,000 projects. But nobody can look at a representative sample of those projects and deny that they are, in themselves, useful and good."[4] How can we bring public works back into the open so that we can again debate doing what is "useful and good" in public life?

Another question is: How should public building programs be administered? Our current political wisdom has declared that "big government" is bad. It is bloated, inefficient, and out of touch. The PWA was a "big government" program, one of the classic "big government" programs. It was centrally administered and was often slower to act than many wanted. But it was also based on local initiative. Communities decided what they wanted to build and hired local architects and engineers to do the designing. If the project was built, it was constructed by local contractors with local laborers. The federal government did not tell communities what buildings they needed or how they should look. As noted earlier, it did review all proposals for financial and structural integrity, and it also undertook oversight of their construction.

The question of accountability and oversight leads to a further question: Why not turn the whole process over to local decision making? As we have seen from the work of the resident engineer-inspectors and of the Investigations Division, there were enough attempts to compromise the projects that it was very useful to have some sort of outside watchdog. Sometimes the pressure for compliance was overzealous, and sometimes it was lax. But is seems clear that making accountability a strictly local matter would have resulted in more abuse than having it shared at the federal level.

Does this suggest that current impulses to dissolve federal responsibility and leave all implementation in local hands are simplistic and risky? As there are a variety of ways to structure partnerships between local and federal governments, there are also a variety of ways to invite cooperation between public and private bodies. Here, too, the New Deal offered experiments worth reexamining. Though most businessmen and women of the time preferred to keep government agencies out of the economy, there were many PWA projects that paid dividends not only in public life but also private wallets. The French Market and the Audubon Sugar School were key contributors to the state's long-range economic prosperity.

Perhaps the most important lesson worth remembering is that in a time of misery, fear, and despair, people worked together with great energy and creativity to assuage their difficulties and at the same time make their communities better places to live for years to come. We need to restore this legacy to public awareness. It will help us honor the courage of our ancestors and perhaps lend faith and courage to our own efforts to solve the large-scale problems that confront us today.

My admiration for the PWA is obvious. Perhaps historian T. H. Watkins's assessment is more balanced. "All these men and tools," he says, "were never quite enough, of course, to do everything that was expected of them, but for all its failings, it should be remembered that this kind of thinking got things done in a big way—never perfectly, sometimes badly, but almost always with a dimension of hope that is breathtaking to observe from the distance of more than fifty years."[5] If we cannot rediscover that hope for ourselves, let us at least honor our ancestors who had it.

APPENDIX

THE LEGACY: AN INVENTORY OF NONFEDERAL PWA PROJECTS IN LOUISIANA

ABBEVILLE

Williams Junior High School "old gym," 1105 Prairie Ave., originally an elementary school gym/auditorium
    architect: William R. Burke
    contractor: Caldwell Bros. and Hart
    REIs: J. J. Krebs, Emile Delaune
    cost: $73,376
    completed: 1939

streets and sewers
    engineer: J. B. McCrary
    contractor: T. L. James
    REI: J. J. Krebs
    cost: $281,064
    completed: 1939

elementary school, 1105 Prairie Ave., torn down to build Williams Junior High School
    architect: William R. Burk
    contractor: Caldwell Bros. and Hart
    REIs: J. J. Krebs, L. J. Higdon
    cost: $94,754
    completed: 1939

sanitary sewer system
   engineer: J. B. McCrary
   contractor: Drainage Const. Co.
   REI: J. H. Higdon
   cost: $237,148
   completed: 1938

special education building, S. Washington St., originally an elementary school and auditorium
   architect: William R. Burk
   contractor: T. Miller and Sons
   REIs: J. R. Krebs, John Kerper, Emile Delaune
   cost: $43,732
   completed: 1939

ADELINE

drawbridge, replaced 1989
   engineer: Kemper and Hanniford
   contractor: A. J. Hanson Co.
   REI: J. H. Higdon
   cost: $27,037
   completed: 1939

ALEXANDRIA

"Asian Temple ruins," part of tiger and leopard habitat, originally Alexandria Municipal Pool, Alexandria Zoo. Pump house is part of animal hospital.
   architect: Charles T. Roberts
   contractor: Gravier and Harper
   REI: William B. Robert
   cost: $98,151
   completed: 1939

L. S. Rugg Elementary School, 1319 Bush Ave.
   architect: Barron and Roberts
   contractor: Tudor and Ratcliff

REI: William B. Robert
cost: $199,798
completed: 1940

Rapides Parish courthouse/jail, 1701 Murray St.
   architects: Edward F. Neild, Barron and Roberts
   contractor: James T. Taylor
   REIs: Stephen P. Cooley, V. L. Logan
   cost: $588,528
   completed: 1940

AMITE

courthouse annex/jail, torn down 1969
   architect: Favrot and Reed
   contractor: J. Farnell Blair
   REI: Fred L. Hargett
   cost: $84,502
   completed: 1938

waterworks improvement
   engineer: Edward G. Freiler
   contractor: McEachin and McEachin
   REI: Fred L. Hargett
   cost: $44,009
   completed: 1938

Amite High School gymnasium, Laurel St.
   architect: Favrot and Reed
   contractor: Independence Lumber Co.
   REIs: Horace R. Brown, Fred L. Hargett
   cost: $155,000 including project below
   completed: 1938

Amite High School addition, two wings and rear extension, burned 1969, arson committed by a disgruntled student who had used up his athletic eligibility
   architect: Favrot and Reed
   contractor: Independence Lumber Co.

    REIs: Horace R. Brown, Fred L. Hargett
    cost: included in above project
    completed: 1938

ANGIE

Angie Junior High School gymnasium, 64433 Dixon St., originally Angie High School
    architect: Sam Stone Jr.
    contractor: Albert Seal
    REI: Jefferson L. Smith
    cost: $33,797 including project below
    completed: 1939

Angie Junior High School offices, 64433 Dixon St., originally agriculture and home economics building
    architect: Sam Stone Jr.
    contractor: Albert Seal
    REI: Jefferson L. Smith
    cost: included in above project
    completed: 1939

ANSLEY

Ansley school gymnasium, torn down in 1960s
    architect: D. Curtis Smith
    contractor: Meriweather and Adams
    REI: Solomon Finkelstein
    cost: part of Jackson Parish project totaling $277,999
    completed: 1939

ASHLAND

school addition
    architect: Neild, Somdal, and Neild
    contractor: Gravier and Harper

REIs: S. Logan McConnell, Charles D. Evans
cost: $17,688
completed: 1939

AVOCA

Avoca Ferry, Morgan City, still in operation, boat replaced
   engineer: P. C. Hannaford
   contractor: Intracoastal Shipyard
   REI: James C. Moore
   cost: $3,165
   completed: 1939

BASKIN

Baskin High School gymnasium, Hwy. 857 south of Hwy. 132, unused
   architect: John W. Baker
   contractor: Meriweather and Adams
   REI: Clyde V. Downing
   cost: $23,144 including project below
   completed: 1939

Baskin High School repairs
   architect: John W. Baker
   contractor: Meriweather and Adams
   REI: Clyde V. Downing
   cost: included in above project
   completed: 1939

BASTROP

Eastside Elementary School gym/auditorium and classroom addition, 102 McCreight St. The gym is now a cafeteria.
   architect: H. H. Land
   contractor: McBride and Son
   REIs: P. M. Davis, Charles D. Evans

cost: $82,291 including project below
completed: 1938

Morehouse Magnet School gym/auditorium addition, 909 Larch Lane, originally Westside Elementary School. The gym is now a cafeteria.
    architect: H. H. Land
    contractor: Delaney and Tatum
    REIs: P. M. Davis, Charles D. Evans
    cost: included in above project
    completed: 1938

courthouse addition
    architect: J. W. Smith and Assoc.
    contractor: Gravier and Harper
    REIs: P. R. Alford, Walter J. Ferguson
    cost: $37,289
    completed: 1935

BATON ROUGE

Capitol Annex
    architect: Neild, Somdal, and Neild
    contractor: Caldwell Bros. and Hart
    REIs: Neville Sattoon, William B. Robert, J. G. Wilburn, Horace R. Brown, Marcus D. Weeks
    cost: $1,190,521
    completed: 1938

Grace King Hall, Louisiana State University
    architects: Weiss, Dreyfous, and Seiferth; Edward F. Neild
    contractor: Caldwell Bros. and Hart
    REIs: Neville Sattoon, Walter J. Ferguson, Horace R. Brown
    cost: $667,520 including projects below
    completed: 1938

Louis Garig Hall, Louisiana State University
    architects: Weiss, Dreyfous, and Seiferth; Edward F. Neild
    contractor: Caldwell Bros. and Hart

REIs: Neville Sattoon, Walter J. Ferguson, Horace R. Brown
cost: included in above project
completed: 1938

Evangeline Hall, Louisiana State University
architects: Weiss, Dreyfous, and Seiferth; Edward F. Neild
contractor: Caldwell Bros. and Hart
REIs: Neville Sattoon, Walter J. Ferguson, Horace R. Brown
cost: included in above project
completed: 1938

Sugar Factory, Louisiana State University
engineer: Arthur J. Keller
contractor: LSU technical staff
REIs: Neville Sattoon, J. G. Wilburn
cost: $97,519
completed: 1938

Baton Rouge Police Department, administration building, 704 Mayflower St., originally the vocational building, Louisiana State School for the Deaf
architect: Favrot and Reed
contractor: Forcum and James
REI: Horace R. Brown
cost: $422,567 including project below
completed: 1940

Baton Rouge Police Department, Training Academy addition, west of administration building, originally the high school, Louisiana State School for the Deaf
architect: Favrot and Reed
contractor: Forcum and James
REI: Horace R. Brown
cost: included in above project
completed: 1940

Geology Building, Louisiana State University
architect: Weiss, Dreyfous, and Seiferth
contractor: Caldwell Bros. and Hart
REIs: Horace R. Brown, William B. Robert

cost: $424,721
completed: 1939

Himes Hall, Louisiana State University, originally called Commerce Building
   architect: Weiss, Dreyfous, and Seiferth
   contractor: R. P. Farnsworth
   REIs: Horace R. Brown, William B. Robert
   cost: $384,850
   completed: 1940

Faculty Club, Louisiana State University
   architect: Weiss, Dreyfous, and Seiferth
   contractor: Caldwell Bros. and Hart
   REIs: Horace R. Brown, William B. Robert
   cost: $168,214
   completed: 1939

Capitol Area United Way, 700 Laurel St., originally Baton Rouge Public Library
   architect: L. A. Grosz
   contractor: Pittman Bros.
   REIs: Horace R. Brown, Robert L. Gay
   cost: $101,570
   completed: 1939

City Club of Baton Rouge, 355 North Blvd., originally post office converted by the PWA to Baton Rouge city hall
   architect: L. A. Grosz
   contractor: L. W. Eaton
   REI: Edmund B. Mason
   cost: $56,242
   completed: 1935

BELL CITY

Bell City High School, torn down 1994
   architect: Herman J. Duncan

contractor: Herbert and Mutersbaug
REI: Charles D. Evans
cost: $91,550
completed: 1939

BELLE ROSE

Belle Rose Middle School, 7177 Hwy. 1, originally elementary and high school
   architect: Bodman and Murell
   contractor: Caldwell Bros. and Hart
   REI: John A. Brown
   cost: $204,949
   completed: 1939

BENTON

school gymnasium, now used for storage
   architect: J. Cheshire Payton
   contractor: McMichael Const. Co.
   REIs: W. C. Campbell, Fred L. Hargett, Marcus D. Weeks
   cost: $40,179
   completed: 1939

BERNICE

Bernice High School gymnasium, 119 Eighth St.
   architect: J. W. Smith and Assoc.
   contractor: Salley and Ellis
   REIs: P. M. Davis, Charles D. Evans
   cost: $48,650 including project below
   completed: 1938

Bernice High School addition, 119 Eighth St.
   architect: J. W. Smith and Co.
   contractor: Salley and Ellis

REIs: P. M. Davis, Charles D. Evans
cost: included in above project
completed: 1938

waterworks
engineer: S. E. Huey Monroe
contractor: B. and M. Const. Co.
REIs: Marcus D. Weeks, P. M. Davis, Walter J. Ferguson
cost: $50,880
completed: 1938

BERWICK

water pipeline
engineer: T. F. Kramer
contractor: Littrell Const. Co.
REI: William B. Robert
cost: $10,636
completed: 1937

BONITA

Bonita High School, Hwy. 165, boarded up because of concern about asbestos
architect: H. H. Land
contractor: Delaney and Tatum
REI: P. M. Davis
cost: $71,977 including project below
completed: 1938

Bonita High School gymnasium, Hwy. 165, burned
architect: H. H. Land
contractor: Delaney and Tatum
REI: P. M. Davis
cost: included in above project
completed: 1938

BOSSIER CITY

Bossier City High School, 777 Bearkat Dr.
    architect: Jones, Roessle, Olschner, and Wiener
    contractor: James T. Taylor
    REIs: W. C. Campbell, Fred L. Hargett
    cost: $571,741 including projects below
    completed: 1940

Bossier City High School ticket office
    architect: Jones, Roessle, Olschner, and Wiener
    contractor: McConnell and Whitaker
    REIs: W. C. Campbell, Fred L. Hargett
    cost: included in above project
    completed: 1940

colored high school
    architect: Jones, Roessle, Olschner, and Wiener
    contractor: McMichael Const. Co.
    REIs: W. C. Campbell, Fred L. Hargett
    cost: included in above project
    completed: 1940

elementary school remodeling
    architect: Jones, Roessle, Olschner, and Wiener
    contractor: Maple Const. Co.
    REIs: W. C. Campbell, Fred L. Hargett
    cost: included in above project
    completed: 1940

BOSSIER PARISH

Approximate addresses of these one- and two-room schools for blacks come from a report by Clifton D. Cardin, Bossier Parish historian, October 17, 2000, in the possession of Keith Norwood, director of planning and purchasing, Bossier Parish Schools.

Allentown School (1 room), near Haughton, below Clark's Shooting Range
   architect: J. Cheshire Peyton
   contractor: J. M. Brown
   REI: W. C. Campbell
   cost: included in above project
   completed: 1939

Atkins School (2 rooms), now Taylortown Masonic Temple
   architect: J. Cheshire Peyton
   contractor: J. M. Brown
   REI: W. C. Campbell
   cost: included in above project
   completed: 1939

Bear Point School (2 rooms), south of Ninock
   architect: J. Cheshire Peyton
   contractor: J. M. Brown
   REI: W. C. Campbell
   cost: included in above project
   completed: 1939

Belcher's Chapel School (1 room), Sylvan Lane and Benton–Bellevue Rd.
   architect: J. Cheshire Peyton
   contractor: J. M. Brown
   REI: W. C. Campbell
   cost: included in above project
   completed: 1939

Bodcau or Bodclaw School (1 room)
   architect: J. Cheshire Peyton
   contractor: J. M. Brown
   REI: W. C. Campbell
   cost: included in above project
   completed: 1939

Bright Star School (1 room), near Bright Star
   architect: J. Cheshire Peyton
   contractor: J. M. Brown

REI: W. C. Campbell
cost: included in above project
completed: 1939

Camp Zion School (1 room), Camp Zion Rd., northeast of Haughton
architect: J. Cheshire Peyton
contractor: J. M. Brown
REI: W. C. Campbell
cost: included in above project
completed: 1939

Elizabeth School (1 room)
architect: J. Cheshire Peyton
contractor: C. H. Treadwell
REI: W. C. Campbell
cost: included in above project
completed: 1939

Glover School (2 rooms), north of Plain Dealing
architect: J. Cheshire Peyton
contractor: J. M. Brown
REI: W. C. Campbell
cost: $43,381 including projects below
completed: 1939

High Island School (1 room), off Poole Rd., south parish
architect: J. Cheshire Peyton
contractor: C. H. Treadwell
REI: W. C. Campbell
cost: included in above project
completed: 1939

Indian Hill School (2 rooms)
architect: J. Cheshire Peyton
contractor: J. M. Brown
REI: W. C. Campbell
cost: included in above project
completed: 1939

Morning Star School (1 room), Hwy. 157, near Morning Star Cemetery, northeast parish
    architect: J. Cheshire Peyton
    contractor: J. M. Brown
    REI: W. C. Campbell
    cost: included in above project
    completed: 1939

Mount Zion School (2 rooms), Swan Lake Rd., east of Airline Drive
    architect: J. Cheshire Peyton
    contractor: J. M. Brown
    REI: W. C. Campbell
    cost: included in above project
    completed: 1939

New Zion School (2 rooms), east of Benton, near New Zion Church
    architect: J. Cheshire Peyton
    contractor: J. M. Brown
    REI: W. C. Campbell
    cost: included in above project
    completed: 1939

Providence School (1 room), Hwy. 3, south of Benton
    architect: J. Cheshire Peyton
    contractor: J. M. Brown
    REI: W. C. Campbell
    cost: included in above project
    completed: 1939

Simmon Grove School (2 rooms)
    architect: J. Cheshire Peyton
    contractor: J. M. Brown
    REI: W. C. Campbell
    cost: included in above project
    completed: 1939

St. Johns School (1 room), Bellevue–Red Chute Rd., near St. Johns Church
    architect: J. Cheshire Peyton
    contractor: J. M. Brown

REI: W. C. Campbell
cost: included in above project
completed: 1939

Stinson School (2 rooms)
   architect: J. Cheshire Peyton
   contractor: J. M. Brown
   REI: W. C. Campbell
   cost: included in above project
   completed: 1939

BRUSLY

Brusly Middle School classroom building, S. River Rd., next to a WPA gymnasium
   architect: Bodman and Murrell
   contractor: J. M. King
   REIs: Neville Sattoon, Horace R. Brown
   cost: $31,202
   completed: 1938

BUNKIE

Hass gym/auditorium, to be renovated as an alcohol and drug abuse center
   architect: J. W. Smith and Co.
   contractor: E. E. Rabalais
   REIs: J. H. Higdon, William R. Brown
   cost: $120,958
   completed: 1939

CADDO PARISH

highway improvements
   engineer: J. T. Bullen
   contractor: unknown
   REI: supervised by Bureau of Public Roads

cost: $301,144
completed: 1935

CAMERON

Cameron Parish courthouse/jail
    architect: Herman J. Duncan
    contractor: A. Farnel Blair
    REI: P. M. Davis
    cost: $134,522
    completed: 1938

CAMPTI

gym/auditorium, burned?
    architect: Neild, Somdal, and Neild
    contractor: McMichael Const. Co.
    REI: V. L. Ott
    cost: $45,971 including project below
    completed: 1938

Campti High School repairs, burned?
    architect: Neild, Somdal, and Neild
    contractor: McMichael Const. Co.
    REI: V. L. Ott
    cost: included in above project
    completed: 1938

CHALMETTE

St. Bernard Parish courthouse, west St. Bernard Hwy. between Parkenham Dr. and Fazzio Rd.
    architect: Weiss, Dreyfous, and Seiferth
    contractor: R. P. Farnsworth
    REIs: Clarence Olschner, Edmund B. Mason
    cost: $433,495
    completed: 1940

CHARLOTTE

school
    architects: Favrot and Reed, F. J. Nehrbrass
    contractor: Jay W. Taylor
    REIs: J. H. Higdon, J. J. Krebs
    cost: part of Iberia Parish project totaling $322,870
    completed: 1939

CHATHAM

gym/auditorium, burned 1975?
    architect: D. Curtis Smith
    contractor: Tudor and Ratcliff
    REI: Solomon Finkelstein
    cost: part of Jackson Parish project totaling $277,999
    completed: 1939

school addition
    architect: D. Curtis Smith
    contractor: Tudor and Ratcliff
    REI: Solomon Finkelstein
    cost: part of above project
    completed: 1939

CHURCH POINT

Church Point gymnasium, torn down 1995
    architect: Baron and Roberts
    contractor: E. E. Rabalais
    REI: Allen D. McCord
    cost: part of Acadia Parish project totaling $95,641
    completed: 1938

CLAYTON

Concordia Parish Head Start Center, 31539 Hwy. 15, originally Clayton High School

architect: J. W. Smith and Assoc.
contractor: Meriweather and Adams
REI: Irwin G. Morrow
cost: $45,285
completed: 1939

CLINTON

industrial training school, burned
   architect: Herman J. Duncan
   contractor: William M. Bozeman
   REIs: Allison Owen, Jefferson L. Smith
   cost: $16,012
   completed: 1939

COLUMBIA

Caldwell Parish courthouse/jail
   architect: J. W. Smith and Assoc.
   contractor: Nile Yearwood
   REIs: Fred L. Hargett, Charles D. Evans
   cost: $129,984
   completed: 1937

CONVENT

St. James Parish courthouse addition, torn down 1993
   architect: N. W. Overstreet and A. Hays Town
   contractor: J. C. Murphy
   REIs: John A. Brown, Robert M. Hunter
   cost: $67,570
   completed: 1939

COTEAU

3-room school
   architects: Favrot and Reed, F. J. Nehrbrass

contractor: W. J. Quick and Hudson East
REIs: J. H. Higdon, J. J. Krebs
cost: part of Iberia Parish project totaling $322,870
completed: 1939

COTTONPORT

sidewalks
   engineer: H. J. Daigre
   contractors: Gremillion Bros., C. R. Laborde
   REI: Clyde V. Downing
   cost: $35,267
   completed: 1937

COUSHATTA

Red River Parish School Board, administration building, 1922 Alonzo St.
   architect: William T. Nolan
   contractor: F. D. Welch
   REI: H. W. Hundley
   cost: part of Red River Parish project totaling $325,590
   completed: 1940

Springville Education Center, Springville Rd., originally a Negro Training School
   architect: William T. Nolan
   contractor: T. Miller and Sons
   REI: H. W. Hundley
   cost: part of above project
   completed: 1940

Coushatta High School gymnasium, 915 E. Carrol St.
   architect: William T. Nolan
   contractor: T. Miller and Sons
   REI: H. W. Hundley
   cost: part of above project
   completed: 1940

COVINGTON

St. Tamany Parish courthouse/jail repairs
   architect: Favrot and Reed
   contractor: Joe E. Anzalone
   REI: Frank C. Wilson
   cost: $36,528
   completed: 1937

CROWLEY

Crowley High School gymnasium, Hwy. 165
   architect: Baron and Roberts
   contractor: E. E. Rabalais and Sons
   REI: Allen D. McCord
   cost: part of school project totaling $218,717
   completed: 1938

Crowley High School athletic field and track
   architect: Baron and Roberts
   contractor: T. Miller and Sons
   REI: Allen D. McCord
   cost: included in above project
   completed: 1938

Crowley Kindergarten, N. Parkerson and 10th St., originally North Crowley Elementary School
   architect: Baron and Roberts
   contractor: E. E. Rabalais and Sons
   REI: Allen D. McCord
   cost: included in above project
   completed: 1938

South Crowley Elementary School, 1102 S. Parkerson
   architect: Baron and Roberts
   contractor: E. E. Rabalais and Sons
   REI: Allen D. McCord
   cost: included in above project
   completed: 1938

sanitary sewer
    engineer: Louis V. Voorhies
    contractors: Tellepson Const. Co., Drainage Const. Co.
    REI: Ralph C. Allor
    cost: $333,282
    completed: 1939

Acadia Parish Adult Education, 404 W. 12th St., originally Southwest Louisiana Trade School
    architect: Baron and Roberts
    contractor: E. E. Rabalais and Sons
    REI: Ralph C. Allor
    cost: $99,854
    completed: 1939

CROWVILLE

Crowville High School repairs, torn down
    architect: John W. Baker
    contractor: J. A. Harper
    REI: Clyde V. Downing
    cost: part of school project totaling $36,376
    completed: 1939

Crowville High School classroom building, burned 1960
    architect: John W. Baker
    contractor: J. A. Harper
    REI: Clyde V. Downing
    cost: part of above project
    completed: 1939

Crowville High School gymnasium
    architect: John W. Baker
    contractor: J. A. Harper
    REI: Clyde V. Downing
    cost: part of above project
    completed: 1939

DELCAMBRE

waterworks
   engineer: Randolph and Middleton
   contractor: McEachin and McEachin
   REI: J. H. Higdon
   cost: $29,140
   completed: 1938

DOWNSVILLE

Downsville High School, Domestic Science Building, 4787 Hwy. 151
   architect: J. W. Smith and Co.
   contractor: Cruise and McKeithen
   REI: P. M. Davis
   cost: $13,155 including projects below
   completed: 1939

Downsville High School, vocational/agricultural building, 4787 Hwy. 151
   architect: J. W. Smith and Co.
   contractor: Cruise and McKeithen
   REI: P. M. Davis
   cost: included in above project
   completed: 1939

Downsville High School repairs, 4787 Hwy. 151
   architect: J. W. Smith and Co.
   contractor: Taylor, Crawford, and Taylor
   REI: P. M. Davis
   cost: included in above project
   completed: 1939

DUBBERLY

domestic science cottage, torn down 2003
   architect: Edward F. Neild Jr.
   contractor: Mitchell and Eaves

REI: James A. Marmouget
cost: $14,542
completed: 1939

DUPONT

Avoyelles Manor Nursing Home, Hwy. 107, originally Dupont Junior High School
    architect: William T. Nolan
    contractor: E. E. Rabalais and Sons
    REI: William B. Robert
    cost: $30,104
    completed: 1938

EAST JEFFERSON PARISH

waterworks
    engineers: Scott and Bres, John H. Gregory
    contractors: John Reiss, Pittman Bros.
    REIs: Edmund B. Mason, C. L. Crowell
    cost: $321,836
    completed: 1938

EAST POINT

Riverdale Academy gymnasium, originally East Point High School gym
    architect: William T. Nolan
    contractor: R. J. Jones
    REI: H. W. Hundley
    cost: part of Red River Parish project totaling $325,590
    completed: 1940

EDGARD

St. John the Baptist Parish jail, torn down
    architect: Dieboll, Boettner, and Kessels

contractor: Jay M. Taylor
REI: Robert M. Hunter
cost: $47,523 including project below
completed: 1939

St. John the Baptist Parish courthouse addition, torn down
architect: Dieboll, Boettner, and Kessels
contractor: Jay M. Taylor
REI: Robert M. Hunter
cost: included in above project
completed: 1939

ENON

Enon Elementary School agricultural building, 14058 Hwy. 16, originally Enon High School
architect: C. Carter Brown
contractor: Green Bros.
REI: T. C. Larsen
cost: $13,223 including projects below
completed: 1939

Enon Elementary School home economics cottage, 14058 Hwy. 16, originally Enon High School
architect: C. Carter Brown
contractor: Green Bros.
REI: T. C. Larsen
cost: included in above project
completed: 1939

Enon High School repairs, 14058 Hwy. 16, originally Enon High School
architect: C. Carter Brown
contractor: Green Bros.
REI: T. C. Larsen
cost: included in above project
completed: 1939

EPPS

Epps High School gymnasium, 4044 Hwy. 134
   architect: J. W. Smith and Assoc
   contractor: J. A. Harper
   REI: Clyde V. Downing
   cost: $157,394
   completed: 1938

ERATH

Erath High School gymnasium, 800 S. Broadway
   architect: William R. Burk
   contractor: W. J. Quick and Hudson East
   REI: J. J. Krebs
   cost: $39,863 including projects below
   completed: 1939

Erath High School home economics cottage, torn down
   architect: William R. Burk
   contractor: W. J. Quick and Hudson East
   REI: J. J. Krebs
   cost: included in above project
   completed: 1939

Erath High School repairs, 800 S. Broadway
   architect: William R. Burk
   contractor: W. J. Quick and Hudson East
   REI: J. J. Krebs
   cost: included in above project
   completed: 1939

EROS

Kaleidoscope Panels, Inc. storage, Hwy. 34, originally Eros school gymnasium
   architect: D. Curtis Smith

contractor: Tudor and Ratcliff
REI: Solomon Finkelstein
cost: part of Jackson Parish project totaling $277,999
completed: 1939

ESTERWOOD

Esterwood gym/auditorium, 214 Jefferson Ave.
   architect: Baron and Roberts
   contractor: James McDaniel and Son
   REI: Allen D. McCord
   cost: part of Acadia Parish project totaling $95,641
   completed: 1938

FENTON

Fenton High School gymnasium, torn down
   architect: William R. Burk
   contractor: E. E. Rabalais and Sons
   REIs: Dick A. Hunt, Allen D. McCord
   cost: $33,427
   completed: 1939

Fenton Elementary and Junior High School, 1st St. and 3rd Ave., not in use
   architect: William R. Burk
   contractor: E. E. Rabalais and Sons
   REIs: Dick A. Hunt, Allen D. McCord
   cost: $12,367
   completed: 1939

FERRIDAY

Ferriday School gym/auditorium, Florida St., leased to city for recreational programs
   architect: C. Scott Yeager

contractor: Tudor and Ratcliff
REIs: Clyde V. Downing, Irwin G. Morrow
cost: $43,003
completed: 1939

FONDALE

Fondale School auditorium, burned
architect: J. W. Smith and Assoc.
contractor: Frank Masling, Inc.
REI: P. M. Davis
cost: $24,696
completed: 1939

FRANKLINTON

waterworks, gone
engineer: J. B. McCrary Co.
contractor: H. A. Forest
REI: Frank C. Wilson
cost: $37,780
completed: 1937

Franklinton Junior High School, 617 Main St., originally Franklinton High School
architect: Herman J. Duncan
contractor: Caldwell Bros. and Hart
REIs: Martin Shephard, Jefferson L. Smith
cost: $194,063 including project below
completed: 1939

Franklinton Junior High School gym/auditorium, 617 Main St., originally Franklinton High School
architect: Herman J. Duncan
contractor: Caldwell Bros. and Hart
REIs: Martin Shephard, Jefferson L. Smith
cost: included in above project
completed: 1939

FORT NECESSITY

Fort Necessity High School gymnasium, Hwy. 562 and Hwy. 871
    architect: John A. Baker
    contractor: Meriweather and Adams
    REI: Clyde V. Downing
    cost: $19,151 including project below
    completed: 1939

Fort Necessity High School alterations, Hwy. 562 and Hwy. 871
    architect: John A. Baker
    contractor: Meriweather and Adams
    REI: Clyde V. Downing
    cost: included in above project
    completed: 1939

GIBSLAND

gymnasium/home economics/agricultural building, S. Main St. and S. 11th St., not in use
    architect: Jones, Roessle, Olschner, and Wiener
    contractor: McMichael Const. Co.
    REI: James A. Marmouget
    cost: $55,786
    completed: 1939

GILLIS

Gillis Intermediate School auditorium, torn down
    architect: Herman J. Duncan
    contractor: T. Miller and Sons
    REI: Charles D. Evans
    cost: $29,260 including projects below
    completed: 1939

Gillis Intermediate School teachers' residence, sold, moved to Bundicks Lake
    architect: Herman J. Duncan
    contractor: T. Miller and Sons

REI: Charles D. Evans
cost: included in above project
completed: 1939

Gillis Intermediate School addition, torn down
architect: Herman J. Duncan
contractor: T. Miller and Sons
REI: Charles D. Evans
cost: included in above project
completed: 1939

GRAMBLING

water tower, Grambling University
architect: J. W. Smith and Assoc.
contractor: J. A. Harper
REI: P. M. Davis
cost: $421,547 including projects below
completed: 1939

dining hall and president's residence, Grambling University, burned
architect: J. W. Smith and Assoc.
contractor: C. E. Andrews
REI: P. M. Davis
cost: included in above project
completed: 1939

Lee Hall, Grambling University, originally the college library
architect: J. W. Smith and Assoc.
contractor: Tudor and Ratcliff
REI: P. M. Davis
cost: included in above project
completed: 1939

Womens' Memorial Gymnasium, Grambling University, originally the college gym/auditorium
architect: J. W. Smith and Assoc.
contractor: C. E. Andrews

REI: P. M. Davis
cost: included in above project
completed: 1939

Long-Jones Hall, Grambling University, originally a classroom building
architect: J. W. Smith and Assoc.
contractor: J. A. Harper
REI: P. M. Davis
cost: included in above project
completed: 1939

Jewett Hall, Grambling University
architect: J. W. Smith and Assoc.
contractor: C. E. Andrews
REI: P. M. Davis
cost: included in above project
completed: 1939

GRAND BAYOU

gymnasium, closed
architect: William T. Nolan
contractor: McMichael Const. Co.
REI: H. W. Hundley
cost: part of Red River Parish project totaling $325,590
completed: 1940

GREENWOOD

First Baptist Church of Greenwood auditorium, Howell St., originally Greenwood School gymnasium
architect: Edward F. Neild Jr.
contractor: G. H. Treadwell
REIs: John A. Brown, Marcus D. Weeks
cost: $38,265
completed: 1939

First Baptist Church of Greenwood Sunday school rooms, Nixon St., originally Greenwood School addition
    architect: Edward F. Neild Jr.
    contractor: Werner Co.
    REIs: Edmund B. Mason, Marcus D. Weeks
    cost: $22,848
    completed: 1934

GRETNA

waterworks
    engineer: Swanson-McGraw
    contractor: R. P. Farnsworth
    REIs: Walter J. Ferguson, Edward G. Freiler
    cost: $285,839
    completed: 1935

waterworks improvement
    engineer: George P. Rice
    contractor: A. N. Goldberg
    REI: Edmund B. Mason
    cost: $34,270
    completed: 1939

GUEYDON

elementary school, burned
    architect: William R. Burk
    contractor: Pittman Bros.
    REI: J. J. Krebs
    cost: $138,003
    completed: 1939

HALL SUMMIT

gym/auditorium, Duke Ave., closed
    architect: William T. Nolan

contractor: T. Miller and Sons
REI: H. W. Hundley
cost: part of Red River Parish project totaling $325,590
completed: 1940

HAMMOND

Intramural Recreation Center, Southeastern Louisiana University
  architect: Weiss, Dreyfous, and Seiferth
  contractor: Forcum and James
  REIs: R. S. Coupland, Jefferson L. Smith, Clyde V. Downing, William
    B. Gregory, Allison Owen
  cost: $1,004,363 including projects below
  completed: 1940

Ralph R. Pottle Music Building, Southeastern Louisiana University
  architect: Weiss, Dreyfous, and Seiferth
  contractor: Forcum and James
  REIs: R. S. Coupland, Jefferson L. Smith, Clyde V. Downing, William
    B. Gregory, Allison Owen
  cost: included in above project
  completed: 1940

president's house, Southeastern Louisiana University
  architect: Weiss, Dreyfous, and Seiferth
  contractor: Forcum and James
  REIs: R. S. Coupland, Jefferson L. Smith, Clyde V. Downing, William
    B. Gregory, Allison Owen
  cost: included in above project
  completed: 1940

Campbell Hall, Southeastern Louisiana University, originally a women's
dorm
  architect: Weiss, Dreyfous, and Seiferth
  contractor: Forcum and James
  REIs: R. S. Coupland, Jefferson L. Smith, Clyde V. Downing, William
    B. Gregory, Allison Owen

cost: included in above project
completed: 1940

McClimans Hall, Southeastern Louisiana University, originally the elementary training school
architect: Weiss, Dreyfous, and Seiferth
contractor: Forcum and James
REIs: R. S. Coupland, Jefferson L. Smith, Clyde V. Downing, William B. Gregory, Allison Owen
cost: included in above project
completed: 1940

Clarke Gallery, Southeastern Louisiana University, originally the university library
architect: Weiss, Dreyfous, and Seiferth
contractor: Forcum and James
REIs: R. S. Coupland, Jefferson L. Smith, Clyde V. Downing, William B. Gregory, Allison Owen
cost: included in above project
completed: 1940

Meade Hall, Southeastern Louisiana University
architect: Weiss, Dreyfous, and Seiferth
contractor: Forcum and James
REIs: R. S. Coupland, Jefferson L. Smith, Clyde V. Downing, William B. Gregory, Allison Owen
cost: included in above project
completed: 1940

HANNA

Hanna Junior High School, Hwy. 1, abandoned
architect: William T. Nolan
contractor: Hardy and Hardy
REI: H. W. Hundley
cost: part of Red River Parish project totaling $325,590
completed: 1940

HATHAWAY

Hathaway High School, struck by lightning and destroyed by fire 1989. Original entrance has been incorporated into the new building.
  architect: William R. Burk
  contractor: Pittman Bros.
  REIs: Dick A. Hunt, Allen D. McCord
  cost: $115,078
  completed: 1939

HODGE

Hodge Elementary School addition, closed
  architect: D. Curtis Smith
  contractor: Meriweather and Adams
  REI: Solomon Finkelstein
  cost: part of Jackson Parish project totaling $277,999
  completed: 1939

HOMER

disposal plant
  architect: Louis V. Voorhies
  contractor: B. and M. Const. Co.
  REIs: Erastus B. Welch, James A. Marmouget
  cost: $63,812
  completed: 1939

HORNBECK

Hornbeck High School gymnasium, 2362 Stillwell Ave., bears non-PWA plaque with later date, possibly a renovation
  architect: Herman J. Duncan
  contractor: A. Hoffpauir, Inc.
  REIs: L. P. McKnight, S. Logan McConnell
  cost: $18,376
  completed: 1939

HOUMA

incinerator, torn down
   engineer: John L. Porter
   contractor: Frederick Page Co.
   REI: Albert G. Garrett
   cost: $16,177
   completed: 1935

Terrebonne Parish courthouse/jail
   architect: Wogan and Bernard
   contractor: Caldwell Bros. and Hart
   REIs: C. L. Crowell, Clarence Olschner
   cost: $369,961
   completed: 1938

Terrebonne High School, N. Main St. and St. Charles St.
   architect: Wogan and Bernard
   contractor: Lionel Favrot
   REI: S. E. Calogne
   cost: $749,173
   completed: 1940

HUNTER

Hunter School, moved
   architect: J. E. Crain
   contractor: L. T. Lynn
   REIs: Walter J. Ferguson, S. R. Jones
   cost: $13,439
   completed: 1934

INDEPENDENCE

waterworks
   engineer: Edward G. Freiler
   contractor: Mercer-Runyon Drilling

REI: Frank C. Wilson
cost: $7,239
completed: 1937

IOTA

Iota School addition, torn down
   architect: Baron and Roberts
   contractor: E. E. Rabalais and Sons
   REI: Allen D. McCord
   cost: part of Acadia Parish project totaling $95,641
   completed: 1938

ISABEL

school, no sign of it
   architect: C. Carter Brown
   contractor: Green Bros.
   REI: T. C. Larsen
   cost: $9,653
   completed: 1939

JACKSON

waterworks
   engineer: P. F. Joseph
   contractor: Robert DeSelle
   REIs: Neville Sattoon, Frank C. Wilson
   cost: $37,579
   completed: 1937

JEANERETTE

sanitary sewer system
   engineer: J. B. McCrary Co.
   contractor: W. H. O'Toole

REIs: J. H. Higdon, J. J. Krebs
cost: $169,629 including project below
completed: 1939

streets and sidewalks
   engineer: J. B. McCrary Co.
   contractor: Flenniken Const. Co.
   REIs: J. H. Higdon, J. J. Krebs
   cost: included in above project
   completed: 1939

JENNINGS

Ward Elementary School gymnasium, originally Jennings High School, later Northside Junior High School
   architect: William R. Burk
   contractor: Pittman Bros
   REIs: Allen D. McCord, Dick A. Hunt
   cost: $65,541
   completed: 1939

Ward Elementary School stadium, originally Bulldog Stadium
   architect: William R. Burk
   contractor: Pittsburg–Des Moines Steel
   REI: Allen D. McCord
   cost: $18,152
   completed: 1938

Ward Elementary School cafeteria, originally Jennings High School home economics cottage
   architect: William R. Burk
   contractor: T. Miller and Sons
   REI: Dick A. Hunt
   cost: $17,425
   completed: 1939

Jennings Head Start Center, 1303 S. Cutting Ave., originally a Negro Training School, later Ward Elementary School
   architect: William R. Burk
   contractor: T. Miller and Sons

REI: Dick A. Hunt
cost: $31,644
completed: 1939

JONESBORO

Jonesboro High School gym/auditorium, 225 Pershing Hwy.
architect: D. Curtis Smith
contractor: Salley and Ellis
REI: Solomon Finkelstein
cost: part of Jackson Parish project totaling $277,999
completed: 1939

Jonesboro Elementary School addition, burned
architect: D. Curtis Smith
contractor: Salley and Ellis
REI: Solomon Finkelstein
cost: included in above project
completed: 1939

Jackson Parish courthouse, 301 Jimmy Davis Blvd.
architects: J. W. Smith and Assoc., H. H. Land
contractor: Tudor and Ratcliff
REIs: P. M. Davis, H. E. Bennett
cost: $248,529
completed: 1939

KELLY

Kelly High School, burned 1993, suspected lightning strike
architect: J. W. Smith and Assoc.
contractor: Salley and Ellis
REIs: Fred L. Hargett, Charles D. Evans
cost: $61,259
completed: 1937

KILBOURN

Kilbourn High School gymnasium, Hwy. 585
    architect: J. W. Smith and Assoc.
    contractor: J. A. Harper
    REI: Clyde V. Downing
    cost: part of West Carroll Parish project totaling $157,394
    completed: 1938

KINDER

home economics building, torn down 1972
    architect: Charles T. Roberts
    contractor: R. J. Jones
    REI: William B. Robert
    cost: $9,931
    completed: 1939

LABADIEVILLE

Labadieville Middle School, 2447 Hwy. 1, originally an elementary school
    architect: Bodman and Murrell
    contractor: Perrilliat-Rickey
    REI: John A. Brown
    cost: $139,071
    completed: 1939

LACASSINE

Lacassine High School gym/auditorium, Algonia Ave. and Dugas St.
    architect: William R. Burk
    contractor: Caldwell Bros. and Hart
    REI: Dick A. Hunt
    cost: $26,591
    completed: 1939

LAFAYETTE

Broussard Hall, University of Louisiana–Lafayette
    architects: Weiss, Dreyfous, and Seiferth; Favrot and Reed
    contractor: Caldwell Bros. and Hart
    REIs: Allen D. McCord, J. H. Higdon
    cost: $2,018,689 including projects below
    completed: 1940

Burke Fine Arts Building, University of Louisiana–Lafayette
    architects: Weiss, Dreyfous, and Seiferth; Favrot and Reed
    contractor: Caldwell Bros. and Hart
    REIs: Allen D. McCord, J. H. Higdon
    cost: included in above project
    completed: 1940

clinic, University of Louisiana–Lafayette
    architects: Weiss, Dreyfous, and Seiferth; Favrot and Reed
    contractor: Caldwell Bros. and Hart
    REIs: Allen D. McCord, J. H. Higdon
    cost: included in above project
    completed: 1940

Hamilton Hall, University of Louisiana–Lafayette
    architects: Weiss, Dreyfous, and Seiferth; Favrot and Reed
    contractor: Caldwell Bros. and Hart
    REIs: Allen D. McCord, J. H. Higdon
    cost: included in above project
    completed: 1940

Stephens Hall Computer Center, University of Louisiana–Lafayette, originally the university library
    architects: Weiss, Dreyfous, and Seiferth; Favrot and Reed
    contractor: Caldwell Bros. and Hart
    REIs: Allen D. McCord, J. H. Higdon
    cost: included in above project
    completed: 1940

INVENTORY OF NONFEDERAL PWA FROJECTS   227

O.K. Allen Dining Hall addition, University of Louisiana–Lafayette
    architects: Weiss, Dreyfous, and Seiferth; Favrot and Reed
    contractor: Robert Angelle
    REIs: Allen D. McCord, J. H. Higdon
    cost: included in above project
    completed: 1940

president's residence, University of Louisiana–Lafayette
    architects: Weiss, Dreyfous, and Seiferth; Favrot and Reed
    contractor: A. J. Rife
    REIs: Allen D. McCord, J. H. Higdon
    cost: included in above project
    completed: 1940

McLaren Gymnasium, University of Louisiana–Lafayette
    architects: Weiss, Dreyfous, and Seiferth; Favrot and Reed
    contractor: Caldwell Bros. and Hart
    REIs: Allen D. McCord, J. H. Higdon
    cost: included in above project
    completed: 1940

Parker Hall, University of Louisiana–Lafayette
    architects: Weiss, Dreyfous, and Seiferth; Favrot and Reed
    contractor: Norman Const. Co.
    REIs: Allen D. McCord, J. H. Higdon
    cost: included in above project
    completed: 1940

McNaspy Stadium, University of Louisiana–Lafayette, torn down
    architects: Weiss, Dreyfous, and Seiferth; Favrot and Reed
    contractor: Norman Const. Co.
    REIs: Allen D. McCord, J. H. Higdon
    cost: included in above project
    completed: 1940

Mouton Hall, University of Louisiana–Lafayette
    architects: Weiss, Dreyfous, and Seiferth; Favrot and Reed
    contractor: Caldwell Bros. and Hart
    REIs: Allen D. McCord, J. H. Higdon

cost: included in above project
completed: 1940

Evangeline Hall, University of Louisiana–Lafayette
architects: Weiss, Dreyfous, and Seiferth; Favrot and Reed
contractor: Robert Angelle
REIs: Allen D. McCord, J. H. Higdon
cost: included in above project
completed: 1940

power plant, University of Louisiana–Lafayette
engineer: Val E. Smith
contractors: Robert Angelle, J. W. Taylor, Archie Ducharme
REIs: J. H. Higdon, Allen D. McCord
cost: $163,294
completed: 1940

French Cultural Center, originally Lafayette city hall
architects: Favrot and Reed, F. J. Nehrbrass
contractor: W. J. Quick and Hudson East
REI: Allen D. McCord
cost: $138,222
completed: 1939

LAKE ARTHUR

home economics cottage, torn down in 1970s to build bank
architect: William R. Burk
contractor: Pittman Bros.
REIs: Dick A. Hunt, Allen D. McCord
cost: $15,462
completed: 1939

Lake Arthur High School gymnasium, torn down in the 1970s to build bank, contractor went bankrupt
architect: William R. Burk
contractor: E. E. Rabalais and Sons
REIs: Dick A. Hunt, Allen D. McCord, E. J. Corona

cost: $37,465
completed: 1939

LAKE CHARLES

paving
   engineer: James M. Fourmey
   contractor: Mills Engineering Co.
   REI: Charles D. Evans
   cost: $101,128
   completed: 1939

Ralph O. Ward Memorial Arena, McNeese State University, originally a stock pavilion
   architect: Weiss, Dreyfous, and Seiferth
   contractor: Caldwell Bros. and Hart
   REI: Charles D. Evans
   cost: $904,129 including projects below
   completed: 1940

Kaufman Hall, McNeese State University
   architect: Weiss, Dreyfous, and Seiferth
   contractor: Caldwell Bros. and Hart
   REI: Charles D. Evans
   cost: included in above project
   completed: 1940

F. G. Bulber Auditorium, McNeese State University
   architect: Weiss, Dreyfous, and Seiferth
   contractor: Caldwell Bros. and Hart
   REI: Charles D. Evans
   cost: included in above project
   completed: 1940

disposal plant, 128 W. Railroad St.
   engineer: James M. Fourmey
   contractors: Pittman Bros., Mike Mitchell and Sons
   REIs: Charles D. Evans, P. M. Davis

cost: $257,612
completed: 1938

LAKE PROVIDENCE

East Carroll Parish courthouse/jail
    architect: J. W. Smith and Assoc.
    contractor: M. T. Reed
    REIs: Fred L. Hargett, Clyde V. Downing
    cost: $100,589
    completed: 1938

Lake Providence Elementary and Secondary School, burned 1992
    architect: H. H. Land
    contractor: M. T. Reed
    REI: Clyde V. Downing
    cost: $210,260 including project below
    completed: 1938

E. Carroll Parish Training School, burned 1959, suspected arson
    architect: H. H. Land
    contractor: M. T. Reed
    REI: J. H. Higdon
    cost: included in above project
    completed: 1938

LANDRY

school
    architects: Favrot and Reed, F. J. Nehrbrass
    contractor: W. J. Quick and Hudson East
    REIs: J. H. Higdon, J. J. Krebs
    cost: part of Iberia Parish project totaling $322,870
    completed: 1939

LIDDIEVILLE

Ogden Primary Center, home economics building, Hwy. 135, closed, originally Ogden High School

architect: John W. Baker
contractor: Meriweather and Adams
REI: P. R. Alford
cost: $21,813 including projects below
completed: 1938

Ogden Primary Center gym/auditorium, Hwy. 135, closed, originally Ogden High School
architect: John W. Baker
contractor: Meriweather and Adams
REI: P. R. Alford
cost: included in above project
completed: 1938

Ogden Primary Center addition, Hwy. 135, closed, originally Ogden High School
architect: John W. Baker
contractor: Meriweather and Adams
REI: P. R. Alford
cost: included in above project
completed: 1938

LINVILLE

gym/auditorium, torn down in the 1980s
architect: J. W. Smith and Assoc.
contractor: A. G. McBride and Son
REI: P. M. Davis
cost: $26,218 including project below
completed: 1939

"Little Red School House," Linville High School, 2061 Hwy. 143, closed, originally a science building
architect: J. W. Smith and Assoc.
contractor: A. G. McBride and Son
REI: P. M. Davis
cost: included in above project
completed: 1939

LOGANSPORT

waterworks
    engineer: Joe A. Holland
    contractors: Layne-Louisiana Co., N. R. Forsong, J. B. McCrary
    REIs: Marcus D. Weeks, Clyde V. Downing
    cost: $42,207
    completed: 1937

LYDIA

school
    architects: Favrot and Reed, F. J. Nehrbrass
    contractor: W. J. Quick and Hudson East
    REIs: J. H. Higdon, J. J. Krebs
    cost: part of Iberia Parish project totaling $322,870
    completed: 1939

MARION

Marion High School addition, 3062 Taylor St.
    architect: D. Curtis Smith
    contractor: A. G. McBride and Son
    REI: George T. Littlefield
    cost: $56,043 including projects below
    completed: 1939

Marion High School vocational/agricultural building, 3062 Taylor St.
    architect: D. Curtis Smith
    contractor: A. G. McBride and Son
    REI: George T. Littlefield
    cost: included in above project
    completed: 1939

Marion High School principal's cottage, Taylor and Cox Sts., now a private residence
    architect: D. Curtis Smith
    contractor: A. G. McBride and Son

REI: George T. Littlefield
cost: included in above project
completed: 1939

Marion High School gym/auditorium, 3062 Taylor St., torn down 2000?
architect: D. Curtis Smith
contractor: A. G. McBride and Son
REI: George T. Littlefield
cost: included in above project
completed: 1939

MARTHAVILLE

Marthaville Elementary and Junior High School gymnasium, 10800 Hwy. 20, originally Marthaville High School
architect: Edward F. Neild Jr.
contractor: James McDaniel and Co.
REIs: Logan McConnell, Stephen P. Cooley, L. P. McKnight
cost: $54,167 including project below
completed: 1939

Marthaville Elementary and Junior High School classroom building, 10800 Hwy. 20, originally Marthaville High School
architect: Edward F. Neild Jr.
contractor: James McDaniel and Co.
REIs: Logan McConnell, Stephen P. Cooley, L. P. McKnight
cost: included in above project
completed: 1939

MARTIN

Martin High School, closed
architect: William T. Nolan
contractor: Humble and Humble
REI: H. W. Hundley
cost: part of Red River Parish project totaling $325,590
completed: 1940

MAUREPAS

Maurepas High School gym/auditorium and classroom addition, Hwy. 22
  architect: William R. Burk
  contractor: L. W. Eaton
  REIs: C. L. Crowell, Martin Shepard
  cost: $33,573
  completed: 1935

MAURICE

school, torn down to build new school
  architect: Favrot and Reed
  contractor: J. B. Mouton
  REI: J. J. Krebs
  cost: $38,792
  completed: 1939

MERMENTAU

Mermentau School, 405 Church St.
  architect: Baron and Roberts
  contractor: E. E. Rabalais and Sons
  REI: Allen D. McCord
  cost: part of Acadia Parish project totaling $324,301
  completed: 1938

METAIRIE

disposal plant
  engineer: George P. Rice
  contractors: John Reiss, Drainage Const. Co.
  REIs: Arthur M. Shaw, Ralph Earl
  cost: $1,022,667
  completed: 1940

MINDEN

Minden High School gymnasium, McIntire and Ash Sts., first gym in the state with an indoor pool
    architect: Edward F. Neild Jr.
    contractor: James T. Taylor
    REIs: James A. Marmouget, H. W. Hundley
    cost: $128,268
    completed: 1939

Webster Parish courthouse, repairs
    architect: Edward F. Neild Jr.
    contractor: McMichael Const. Co.
    REI: P. M. Davis
    cost: $18,536
    completed: 1935

MIRE (ORIGINALLY MIER)

Mire Elementary School, Hwy. 95
    architect: Baron and Roberts
    contractor: T. Miller and Sons
    REI: Allen D. McCord
    cost: part of Acadia Parish project totaling $324,301
    completed: 1938

MONROE

Bry Hall, University of Louisiana–Monroe, originally the university library
    architect: J. W. Smith and Assoc.
    contractor: M. T. Reed
    REI: P. M. Davis
    cost: $225,683 including project below
    completed: 1939

Biedenharn Hall, University of Louisiana–Monroe, the music building
    architect: J. W. Smith and Assoc.
    contractor: Salley and Ellis

REI: P. M. Davis
cost: included in above project
completed: 1939

Ouachita Parish School Board office, 100 Bry St., originally the Ouachita High School gym
    architect: H. H. Land
    contractor: Salley and Ellis
    REIs: Fred L. Hargett, Charles D. Evans
    cost: $108,979
    completed: 1938

MONTICELLO

Monticello High School, Hwy. 577
    architect: H. H. Land
    contractor: M. T. Reed
    REIs: Clyde V. Downing, S. Logan McConnell
    cost: $33,016
    completed: 1938

MOORINGSPORT

waterworks, Lake St.
    engineer: Huey and Gage
    contractor: H. A. Forest
    REI: Marcus D. Weeks
    cost: $38,031
    completed: 1937

NAPOLEONVILLE

Napoleonville Primary School, 1008 Hwy. 185, originally Napoleonville Colored School, later W. H. Reed High School
    architect: Bodman and Murrell
    contractor: E. E. Rabalais and Sons

REI: James C. Moore
cost: $53,878
completed: 1939

Napoleonville Middle School, 4847 Hwy. 1, originally Napoleonville High School gym
architect: Bodman and Murrell
contractor: Herman T. Makofsky
REI: John A. Brown
cost: $87,850
completed: 1939

NATCHITOCHES

Casperi Hall, Northwestern State University
architect: Edward F. Neild Jr.
contractor: Caldwell Bros. and Hart
REIs: Stephen P. Cooley, S. Logan McConnell
cost: $72,018
completed: 1939

university stadium, Northwestern State University
architect: Edward F. Neild Jr.
contractor: Caldwell Bros. and Hart
REIs: Stephen P. Cooley, S. Logan McConnell
cost: $95,860
completed: 1939

utilities improvement, Northwestern State University
architect: Edward F. Neild Jr.
contractor: Caldwell Bros. and Hart
REI: Stephen P. Cooley
cost: $23,921
completed: 1939

natatorium, Northwestern State University
architect: Edward F. Neild Jr.
contractor: R. P. Farnsworth

REI: Stephen P. Cooley
cost: part of project totaling $1,802,549
completed: 1940

men's gymnasium, Northwestern State University
architect: Edward F. Neild Jr.
contractor: Nathan Wolfeld
REI: Stephen P. Cooley
cost: included in above project
completed: 1940

Fredrichs Auditorium, Northwestern State University
architect: Edward F. Neild Jr.
contractor: Nathan Wolfeld
REI: Stephen P. Cooley
cost: included in above project
completed: 1940

student center, Northwestern State University, torn down to make room for new buildings
architect: Edward F. Neild Jr.
contractor: R. P. Farnsworth
REI: Stephen P. Cooley
cost: included in above project
completed: 1940

infirmary addition, Northwestern State University
architect: Edward F. Neild Jr.
contractor: R. P. Farnsworth
REI: Stephen P. Cooley
cost: included in above project
completed: 1940

Varnado Hall, Northwestern State University
architect: Edward F. Neild Jr.
contractor: R. P. Farnsworth
REI: Stephen P. Cooley

cost: included in above project
completed: 1940

power plant addition, Northwestern State University
   architect: Edward F. Neild Jr.
   contractor: Caldwell Bros. and Hart
   REI: Stephen P. Cooley
   cost: included in above project
   completed: 1940

art classrooms, Northwestern State University, originally Natchitoches Trade School
   architects: Weiss, Dreyfous, and Seiferth; Neild, Somdal, and Neild
   contractor: R. P. Farnsworth
   REIs: V. L. Ott, H. E. Bennett, S. Logan McConnell
   cost: part of a project totaling $563,498
   completed: 1939

Natchitoches Training School
   architects: Weiss, Dreyfous, and Seiferth; Neild, Somdal, and Neild
   contractor: C. H. Treadwell
   REIs: V. L. Ott, H. E. Bennett, S. Logan McConnell
   cost: included in above project
   completed: 1939

Louisiana School for Math, Science, and the Arts, originally Natchitoches High School
   architects: Weiss, Dreyfous, and Seiferth; Neild, Somdal, and Neild
   contractor: R. P. Farnsworth
   REIs: V. L. Ott, H. E. Bennett, S. Logan McConnell
   cost: included in above project
   completed: 1939

Natchitoches Parish courthouse/jail
   architect: J. W. Smith and Assoc.
   contractor: M. T. Reed
   REIs: Stephen P. Cooley, Marion J. G. Glodt, S. Logan McConnell

cost: $261,110
completed: 1940

NEWELLTON

Newellton High School, torn down, 1976
    architect: H. H. Land
    contractor: Humble and Humble
    REI: Clyde V. Downing
    cost: $98,369 including project below
    completed: 1939

Newellton High School, repair to existing building, torn down earlier
    architect: H. H. Land
    contractor: Humble and Humble
    REI: Clyde V. Downing
    cost: included in above project
    completed: 1939

NEW IBERIA

School Days Retirement Community, two two-story additions, 415 Center St., originally New Iberia High School
    architects: Favrot and Reed, F. J. Nehrbrass
    contractor: Clifford H. King
    REIs: J. H. Higdon, J. J. Krebs
    cost: part of Iberia Parish project totaling $322,870
    completed: 1939

Iberia Boys' and Girls' Club, 430 E. Pershing, originally Charles M. Bahon Gymnasium
    architects: Favrot and Reed, F. J. Nehrbrass
    contractor: Clifford H. King
    REIs: J. H. Higdon, J. J. Krebs
    cost: included in above project
    completed: 1939

New Iberia High School domestic science building, currently unused
   architects: Favrot and Reed, F. J. Nehrbrass
   contractor: Clifford H. King
   REIs: J. H. Higdon, J. J. Krebs
   cost: included in above project
   completed: 1939

Iberia Parish courthouse/jail
   architect: A. Hays Town
   contractors: Gravier and Harper, I. M. Goldberg
   REI: J. J. Krebs
   cost: $410,863
   completed: 1940

NEW ORLEANS

Charity Hospital, damaged by Hurricane Katrina
   architect: Weiss, Dreyfous, and Seiferth
   contractors: George A. Fuller, R. P. Farnsworth
   REIs: Edmund B. Mason, Clarence Olschner, Randolph Harrison, V. L. Ott
   cost: $12,866,376 including projects below
   completed: 1940

Nurses' Building, Charity Hospital, status uncertain
   architect: Weiss, Dreyfous, and Seiferth
   contractor: Burkes Bros.
   REI: Edmund B. Mason
   cost: included in above project
   completed: 1940

ambulance house, Charity Hospital
   architect: Weiss, Dreyfous, and Seiferth
   contractor: Caldwell Bros. and Hart
   REI: Edmund B. Mason
   cost: included in above project
   completed: 1940

laundry, Charity Hospital
    architect: Weiss, Dreyfous, and Seiferth
    contractor: Caldwell Bros. and Hart
    REI: Edmund B. Mason
    cost: included in above project
    completed: 1940

shop, Charity Hospital
    architect: Weiss, Dreyfous, and Seiferth
    contractor: R. P. Farnsworth
    REI: Edmund B. Mason
    cost: included in above project
    completed: 1940

power house, Charity Hospital
    architect: Weiss, Dreyfous, and Seiferth
    contractor: R. P. Farnsworth
    REI: Edmund B. Mason
    cost: included in above project
    completed: 1940

waterworks/sewer
    engineer: Bryson Villas
    contractors: John Riess, R. P. Farnsworth, Boh and Lagarde, W. R. Aldrich, R. J Reid
    REI: C. L. Crowell
    cost: $2,285,312
    completed: 1938

Huey P. Long Bridge, completed by the PWA, project initiated under the Reconstruction Finance Corp.
    engineer: unknown
    contractors: American Bridge Co., Siems-Helmers, McDonald Engineering Co., McClintock-Marshall Corp.
    REI: supervised by RFC
    cost: $470,000 (completion costs)
    completed: 1935

Old Butchers' Building restoration, French Market, now home of Café du Monde
    architects: Sam Stone Jr., Frank Stone
    contractor: John Reiss
    REIs: Clarence Olschner, C. L. Crowell
    cost: $323,750 including projects below
    completed: 1938

Bazaar Building reconstruction, French Market
    architects: Sam Stone Jr., Frank Stone
    contractor: John Reiss
    REIs: Clarence Olschner, C. L. Crowell
    cost: included in above project
    completed: 1938

Old Vegetable Market restoration, French Market, former home of Morning Call
    architects: Sam Stone Jr., Frank Stone
    contractor: John Reiss
    REIs: Clarence Olschner, C. L. Crowell
    cost: included in above project
    completed: 1938

Farmers' Market shed, French Market
    architects: Sam Stone Jr., Frank Stone
    contractor: John Reiss
    REIs: Clarence Olschner, C. L. Crowell
    cost: included in above project
    completed: 1938

Flea Market shed, French Market
    architects: Sam Stone Jr., Frank Stone
    contractor: John Reiss
    REIs: Clarence Olschner, C. L. Crowell
    cost: included in above project
    completed: 1938

wholesale seafood shed, French Market, demolished to build Red Stores building
    architects: Sam Stone Jr., Frank Stone
    contractor: John Reiss
    REIs: Clarence Olschner, C. L. Crowell
    cost: included in above project
    completed: 1938

Frederick Douglass High School, St. Claude, originally Francis T. Nichols Vocational School, flooded by Hurricane Katrina
    architect: Edgar A. Christy
    contractor: R. P. Farnsworth
    REIs: Alfred G. Garrett, Harry Sallinger
    cost: $1,230,467 including projects below
    completed: 1940

Alfred P. Tureaud Elementary School, 2021 Prauger St., originally Marie C. Courvent Elementary School
    architect: Edgar A. Christy
    contractor: Pittman Bros.
    REIs: Alfred G. Garrett, Harry Sallinger
    cost: included in above project
    completed: 1940

John A. Shaw Elementary School, 2518 Arts St.
    architect: Edgar A. Christy
    contractor: Gervais F. Favrot
    REI: Alfred G. Garrett
    cost: included in above project
    completed: 1940

LSU Medical Center addition
    architect: Weiss, Dreyfous, and Seiferth
    contractors: Gervais F. Favrot, Caldwell Bros. and Hart
    REI: Clarence Olschner
    cost: $141,392
    completed: 1939

NEW ROADS

waterworks/sewer
   engineer: Louis V. Voorhies
   contractor: J. B. McCrary Co.
   REIs: Arthur A. Defraites, William B. Robert
   cost: $135,804
   completed: 1939

Point Coupee Parish courthouse annex and jail
   architect: William T. Nolan
   contractor: E. E. Rabalais and Sons
   REIs: William B. Robert, Fred L. Hargett, Arthur A. Defraites
   cost: $185,971
   completed: 1940

OAK GROVE

Oak Grove High School gymnasium, 501 W. Main St.
   architect: J. W. Smith and Assoc.
   contractor: M. T. Reed Const. Co.
   REI: Clyde V. Downing
   cost: part of West Carroll Parish project totaling $157,394
   completed: 1938

OBERLIN

Oberlin High School gymnasium, torn down
   architect: Charles T. Roberts
   contractor: Gravier and Harper
   REI: William B. Robert
   cost: $21,490
   completed: 1939

OKALOOSA

Seeker Springs Ministry Retreat Center gym/auditorium, originally Okaloosa High School gym

architect: L. Milton King
contractor: Frank Masling, Inc.
REIs: V. H. Kyle, P. M. Davis
cost: $25,279
completed: 1939

OPELOUSAS

St. Landry Parish courthouse/jail
architect: Theodore L. Perrier
contractor: A. J. Rife
REIs: Irwin G. Morrow, Robert R. McBride
cost: $481,794
completed: 1940

PATOUT

Negro school (1 room)
architects: Favrot and Reed, F. J. Nehrbrass
contractor: J. W. Quick and Hudson East
REIs: H. V. Higdon, J. J. Krebs
cost: part of Iberia Parish project totaling $322,870
completed: 1939

PEEBLES

Peebles School heating plant
architects: Favrot and Reed, F. J. Nehrbrass
contractor: Jay W. Taylor
REIs: H. V. Higdon, J. J. Krebs
cost: included in above project
completed: 1939

PIERRE PART

Pierre Part Middle and Primary School, 3321 Hwy. 70 S.
architect: Bodman and Murrell

contractor: E. E. Rabalais and Sons
REIs: James C. Moore, John A. Brown
cost: $146,729
completed: 1939

PLAIN DEALING

Plain Dealing Junior and Senior High School activities building, E. Vance and N. Perrin Sts.
   architect: J. Cheshire Peyton
   contractor: C. H. Treadwell
   REIs: W. C. Campbell, Fred L. Hargett
   cost: $157,183 including projects below
   completed: 1939

stadium replaced
   architect: J. Cheshire Payton
   contractor: Maple Const. Co.
   REIs: W. C. Campbell, Fred L. Hargett
   cost: included in above project
   completed: 1939

school repair
   architect: J. Cheshire Payton
   contractor: Maple Const. Co.
   REIs: W. C. Campbell, Fred L. Hargett
   cost: included in above project
   completed: 1939

PONCHATOULA

elementary school, burned 1994, possibly because squirrels chewed electrical wiring
   architect: Favrot and Reed
   contractor: A. Farnell Blair
   REIs: Neville Sattoon, F. C. Wilson, Walter J. Ferguson
   cost: $110,027
   completed: 1937

Ponchatoula Junior High School gymnasium, 315 East Oak St., originally Ponchatoula High School
    architect: Favrot and Reed
    contractor: Dye and Mullins
    REIs: R. S. Coupland, Allison Owen
    cost: $56,792
    completed: 1939

PORT ALLEN

Port Allen Middle School, 610 Rosedale Rd., originally Port Allen High School
    architect: Bodman and Murrell
    contractor: Caldwell Bros. and Hart
    REIs: Neville Sattoon, Horace R. Brown
    cost: $169,694
    completed: 1938

PORT BARRE

waterworks
    engineer: Louis V. Voorhies
    contractor: J. B. McCrary
    REI: William B. Robert
    cost: $31,392
    completed: 1938

QUITMAN

Quitman High School gym/auditorium, Hwy. 167
    architect: D. Curtis Smith
    contractor: J. A. Harper
    REI: Solomon Finkelstein
    cost: part of Jackson Parish project totaling $277,999
    completed: 1939

RAYNE

water, light, and power project
   engineer: Louis V. Voorhies
   contractor: E. E. Rabalais and Sons
   REI: Allen D. McCord
   cost: $86,169
   completed: 1939

Rayne High School, 1016 N. Polk St.
   architect: Baron and Roberts
   contractor: A. Farnel Blair
   REI: Allen D. McCord
   cost: part of Acadia Parish project totaling $324,301
   completed: 1938

RAYVILLE

light plant
   engineer: C. A. Peerman
   contractor: Salley and Ellis
   REIs: Clyde V. Downing, George T. Littlefield
   cost: $77,464
   completed: 1940

waterworks/sewer
   engineer: C. A. Peerman
   contractor: Salley and Ellis
   REIs: Clyde V. Downing, George T. Littlefield
   cost: $26,921
   completed: 1939

RED RIVER PARISH

Negro school/shop
   architect: William T. Nolan
   contractor: Humble and Humble

REI: H. W. Hundley
cost: part of Red River Parish project totaling $325,590
completed: 1940

Negro school/shop
architect: William T. Nolan
contractor: Humble and Humble
REI: H. W. Hundley
cost: part of above project
completed: 1940

Negro school/shop
architect: William T. Nolan
contractor: Humble and Humble
REI: H. W. Hundley
cost: part of above project
completed: 1940

Negro school/shop
architect: William T. Nolan
contractor: Humble and Humble
REI: H. W. Hundley
cost: part of above project
completed: 1940

RESERVE

Leon Godschaux Accelerated Program gymnasium, Hwy. 44 and W. 10th St., originally Leon Godschaux High School
architect: Dieboll, Boettner, and Kessels
contractor: J. C. Murphy
REI: Robert M. Hunter
cost: $53,207
completed: 1939

REYNELLA

Negro school (1 room)
architect: Favrot and Reed

contractor: J. W. Quick and Hudson East
REIs: H. V. Higdon, J. J. Krebs
cost: part of Iberia Parish project totaling $322,870
completed: 1939

RICHARD

Richard Elementary School, Hwy. 1105
   architect: Baron and Roberts
   contractor: A. Farnel Blair
   REI: Allen D. McCord
   cost: part of Acadia Parish project totaling $324,301
   completed: 1938

RINGOLD

waterworks
   engineer: F. B. Joseph
   contractor: Robert DeSelle
   REIs: R. A. Boyce, Marcus D. Weeks, Clyde V. Downing
   cost: $39,417
   completed: 1937

ROANOKE

Welsh-Roanoak Middle School gymnasium, 2nd Ave. and Hwy. 395, originally Roanoke High School
   architect: William R. Burk
   contractor: Pittman Bros.
   REIs: Dick A. Hunt, Allen D. McCord
   cost: $31,598
   completed: 1939

ROBELINE

domestic science building, torn down, 1980s
   architect: Neild, Somdal, and Neild

contractor: Glassell General Const.
REI: S. Logan McConnell
cost: $47,891 including projects below
completed: 1939

classroom building, torn down, 1980s
architect: Neild, Somdal, and Neild
contractor: Glassell General Const.
REI: S. Logan McConnell
cost: included in above project
completed: 1939

school repairs
architect: Neild, Somdal, and Neild
contractor: Glassell General Const.
REI: S. Logan McConnell
cost: included in above project
completed: 1939

auditorium repairs
architect: Neild, Somdal, and Neild
contractor: Glassell General Const.
REI: S. Logan McConnell
cost: included in above project
completed: 1939

ROCKY MOUNT

gymnasium, privately owned
architect: J. Cheshire Peyton
contractor: C. H. Treadwell
REIs: W. C. Campbell, Fred L. Hargett
cost: $32,126
completed: 1939

RODESSA

Rodessa High School, Hwy. 168, abandoned
architect: Seymour Van Os

contractor: F. D. Welch
REI: W. C. Campbell
cost: $219,344
completed: 1939

ROSELAND

school addition, 12516 Time Ave.
   architect: Favrot and Reed
   contractor: Independence Lumber Co.
   REI: Jefferson L. Smith
   cost: $22,864
   completed: 1939

RUSTON

Ruston High School, 900 Bearcat Dr.
   architect: J. W. Smith and Assoc.
   contractor: Caldwell Bros. and Hart
   REIs: T. C. Larsen, James A. Marmouget
   cost: $587,320 including project below
   completed: 1940

Ruston High School special education building, originally the home economics cottage
   architect: J. W. Smith and Assoc.
   contractor: M. T. Reed
   REIs: T. C. Larsen, James A. Marmouget
   cost: included in above project
   completed: 1940

waterworks/sewer extension
   engineer: Louis V. Voorhies
   contractors: J. B. McCrary, B. and M. Const. Co.
   REI: P. M. Davis
   cost: $108,235
   completed: 1939

Reese Hall, Louisiana Tech University
    architect: Edward F. Neild Jr.
    contractor: C. E. Andrews
    REI: P. M. Davis
    cost: $2,054,270 including projects below
    completed: 1940

Bogard Hall, Louisiana Tech University
    architect: Edward F. Neild Jr.
    contractor: T. L. James
    REI: P. M. Davis
    cost: included in above project
    completed: 1940

power plant, Louisiana Tech University
    architect: Edward F. Neild Jr.
    contractor: C. E. Andrews
    REI: P. M. Davis
    cost: included in above project
    completed: 1940

Tolliver Hall, Louisiana Tech University
    architect: Edward F. Neild Jr.
    contractor: Gravier and Harper
    REI: P. M. Davis
    cost: included in above project
    completed: 1940

Robinson Hall, Louisiana Tech University
    architect: Edward F. Neild Jr.
    contractor: T. L. James
    REI: P. M. Davis
    cost: included in above project
    completed: 1940

Aswell Hall, Louisiana Tech University
    architect: Edward F. Neild Jr.
    contractor: T. L. James
    REI: P. M. Davis

cost: included in above project
completed: 1940

Howard Auditorium, Louisiana Tech University
architect: Edward F. Neild Jr.
contractor: Nathan Wohlfeld
REI: P. M. Davis
cost: included in above project
completed: 1940

SAMSTOWN

school, Hwy. 69 near junction with Hwy. 404, not in use
architect: William T. Nolan
contractor: L. W. Eaton
REIs: Neville Sattoon, Walter J. Ferguson
cost: $28,986
completed: 1937

SCOTLANDVILLE

A. W. Mumford Stadium, Southern University
architect: William T. Nolan
contractor: Pittman Bros.
REIs: William B. Robert, William P. Cullan, Horace R. Brown
cost: $103,179
completed: 1939

school and dormitory building, State School for Deaf and Blind Negro Children, Southern University campus, burned
architect: William T. Nolan
contractor: E. E. Rabalais and Sons
REI: Horace R. Brown
cost: $73,525
completed: 1938

gym/auditorium, Southern University
architects: William T. Nolan, Ulisse M. Nolan
contractor: L. W. Eaton

REIs: Horace R. Brown, Neville Sattoon, J. G. Welburn, Louis Bryan
cost: $47,705
completed: 1938

Grandison Hall, Southern University
architect: William T. Nolan
contractors: L. W. Eaton, Pittman Bros.
REIs: Horace R. Brown, William B. Robert
cost: $201,262
completed: 1940

freshmen dormitory, Southern University, torn down
architect: William T. Nolan
contractor: L. W. Eaton
REIs: Horace R. Brown, William B. Robert, J. Chris Nelson
cost: $34,264
completed: 1939

Wallace L. Bradford Hall, Southern University, originally a women's dormitory
architect: William T. Nolan
contractor: L. W. Eaton
REIs: William B. Robert, Solomon Finkelstein
cost: $199,963
completed: 1940

SHADY GROVE

North Iberville Elementary-High School, Hwy. 977, originally Shady Grove High School
architects: William T. Nolan, Ulisse M. Nolan
contractor: Pittman Bros.
REIs: Horace R. Brown, Walter J. Ferguson
cost: $114,103
completed: 1938

SHREVEPORT

firehouse, torn down to make way for interstate highway
architect: Henry E. Schwarz

contractor: Maple Const. Co.
REIs: P. M. Davis, Edmund B. Mason
cost: $20,615
completed: 1934

city hall repairs
architect: Clarence W. King
contractor: Werner Co.
REI: Walter J. Ferguson
cost: $46,540
completed: 1935

fire alarm system
engineer: Edward A. Brass
contractor: Glover and Maple
REIs: Miles Hutson, Marcus D. Weeks
cost: $57,077
completed: 1934

Shreveport Chamber of Commerce addition, 400 Edwards St., originally Shreveport Public Library
architects: J. Cheshire Payton, Edward F. Neild Jr.
contractor: Werner Co.
REIs: Marcus D. Weeks, John A. Brown, Frank C. Wilson
cost: $45,612
completed: 1939

maintenance shops, Department of Water and Sewerage, 2139 Greenwood Rd., originally the Farmers' Market
architect: Henry E. Schwarz
contractor: W. Murray Werner
REIs: Edmund B. Mason, F. W. Ferguson, Marcus D. Weeks
cost: $51,762
completed: 1934

firehouse repairs
architect: Henry E. Schwarz
contractor: unknown
REIs: Edmund B. Mason, Marcus D. Weeks

cost: $11,079
completed: 1934

municipal courthouse addition
    architect: Edward F. Neild Jr.
    contractor: Werner Co.
    REIs: Edmund B. Mason, Marcus D. Weeks
    cost: $19,549
    completed: 1934

streets
    engineer: H. E. Barnes
    contractor: Flenniken Const. Co.
    REI: Edward G. Riesbol
    cost: $147,394
    completed: 1935

Municipal Auditorium repairs, 705 Elvis Presley Ave., repairs and building completion by Seymour Van Os
    architect: Samuel Wiener
    contractor: K. C. Wilson
    REI: Walter J. Ferguson
    cost: $38,301
    completed: 1934

park improvements
    architect: Edward F. Neild Jr.
    contractor: McMichael Const. Co.
    REI: William B. Robert
    cost: $84,541
    completed: 1935

police radio system
    engineer: Edward A. Brass
    contractor: John F. Maple
    REIs: Miles Hutson, Marcus D. Weeks
    cost: $7,063
    completed: 1935

incinerator, torn down 1974
   architect: Jones, Roessle, Olschner, and Wiener
   contractor: McMichael Const. Co.
   REIs: Marcus D. Weeks, Walter J. Ferguson
   cost: $185,841
   completed: 1937

Booker T. Washington High School, torn down
   architect: J. Cheshire Peyton
   contractor: Werner Const. Co.
   REIs: John A. Brown, Marcus D. Weeks
   cost: $59,523
   completed: 1939

Linwood School, Linwood Ave. and 70th St.
   architect: Edward F. Neild Jr.
   contractor: Delaney and Tatum
   REIs: Edmund B. Mason, Marcus D. Weeks, P. M. Davis
   cost: $94,376
   completed: 1935

A. C. Steere Elementary School addition, 4009 Youree Dr.
   architect: Henry E. Schwarz
   contractor: Glassell General Const.
   REIs: John A. Brown, Marcus D. Weeks
   cost: $37,225
   completed: 1939

Alexander Learning Center auditorium, Coty St. and Herndon Ave., originally Alexander Elementary School
   architect: Jones, Roessle, Olschner, and Wiener
   contractor: A. J. Lerasseur
   REI: Marcus D. Weeks
   cost: $27,021
   completed: 1939

Central Elementary School auditorium, 1627 Weinstock St., originally Central Colored School
   architect: Edward F. Neild Jr.
   contractor: F. D. Welch

REI: Marcus D. Weeks
cost: $17,350
completed: 1938

Line Ave. Elementary School auditorium, torn down to make way for community college building
architect: Henry E. Schwarz
contractor: McMichael Const. Co.
REI: Marcus D. Weeks
cost: $35,351
completed: 1939

Laurel Street Early Child Development Center auditorium, 1730 Laurel St., originally Parkview Elementary School
architect: J. P. Annan and Son
contractor: McMichael Const. Co.
REI: Marcus D. Weeks
cost: $24,175
completed: 1937

George F. Hendrix Elementary School auditorium, 700 Pierce, closed, up for lease, originally Allendale School
architect: William B. Wiener
contractor: McMichael Const. Co.
REIs: John A. Brown, Marcus D. Weeks, Frank L. Wilson
cost: $27,423
completed: 1939

Queensborough Elementary School auditorium, 270 Catherine St.
architect: Seymour Van Os
contractor: F. D. Welch
REI: Marcus D. Weeks
cost: $39,387
completed: 1938

Fairfield Elementary School auditorium
architect: Edward F. Neild Jr.
contractor: McMichael Const. Co.
REI: Marcus D. Weeks

cost: $27,987
completed: 1937

State Exhibition Building
    architect: Neild, Somdal, and Neild
    contractor: A. J. Rife
    REI: Marcus D. Weeks
    cost: $553,247
    completed: 1938

SIMMESPORT

Avoyelles Correction Center gym/auditorium, originally Simmesport school
    architect: William T. Nolan
    contractor: E. E. Rabalais and Sons
    REIs: Arthur A. Defraites, William B. Robert
    cost: $25,776
    completed: 1939

SIMPSON

Simpson High School, 4262 Hwy. 8
    architect: Herman J. Duncan
    contractor: T. Miller and Sons
    REI: William B. Robert
    cost: $90,001
    completed: 1938

SLIDELL

Slidell High School addition
    architect: Sam Stone Jr.
    contractor: Reiman Const. Co.
    REIs: Albert G. Garrett, Charles D. Evans
    cost: $4,140
    completed: 1939

SPRINGHILL

Springhill Junior High School, W. Church St., originally an elementary school
  architect: Edward F. Neild Jr.
  contractor: O. L. Crigler
  REIs: Marcus D. Weeks, H. W. Hundley, James A. Marmouget
  cost: $88,191 including project below
  completed: 1939

Springhill Junior High School gymnasium, N. Arkansas St., originally an elementary school
  architect: Edward F. Neild Jr.
  contractor: O. L. Crigler
  REIs: Marcus D. Weeks, H. W. Hundley, James A. Marmouget
  cost: included in above project
  completed: 1939

ST. GABRIEL

East Iberville Elementary gym/auditorium, 3285 Hwy. 75
  architect: William T. Nolan
  contractors: Joe E. Anzalone, E. E. Rabalais and Sons
  REIs: J. G. Wilburn, Horace R. Brown, L. J. Bryan
  cost: $20,693
  completed: 1938

ST. JOSEPH

Tensas Parish courthouse repairs
  architect: J. W. Smith and Assoc.
  contractor: A. G. McBride
  REI: Albert G. Garrett
  cost: $15,262
  completed: 1934

St. Joseph Community Center, Levee Rd. and Hancock St.
  architect: J. W. Smith and Assoc.
  contractor: Burnside and McDonald

REI: Clyde V. Downing
cost: $14,321
completed: 1939

filtration plant
engineer: A. D. Evans
contractor: Salley and Ellis
REI: Fred L. Hargett
cost: $6,675
completed: 1937

ST. MARTINVILLE

disposal plant
engineer: Louis J. Voorhies
contractor: Mick Mitchell and Sons
REI: J. J. Krebs
cost: $133,833
completed: 1939

STERLINGTON

A. L. Smith Elementary School gymnasium, Old Sterlington Rd.
architect: H. H. Land
contractor: Salley and Ellis
REIs: George T. Littlefield, P. M. Davis
cost: $36,098
completed: 1939

SULPHUR

sanitary sewer
architect: Louis V. Voorhies
contractor: J. B. McCrary
REI: Charles D. Evans
cost: $134,997
completed: 1939

SUNSET

waterworks
   architect: J. B. McCrary
   contractor: Littrell Contracting Co.
   REIs: Clyde V. Downing, Allen D. McCord
   cost: $30,497
   completed: 1937

TALLULAH

Tallulah High School gym/auditorium, 600 Bayou Dr.
   architect: J. W. Smith and Assoc.
   contractor: J. A. Harper
   REIs: Edward J. Kelly, Clyde V. Downing
   cost: $99,654 including project below
   completed: 1939

Tallulah High School repairs, 600 Bayou Dr.
   architect: J. W. Smith and Assoc.
   contractor: J. A. Harper
   REIs: Edward J. Kelly, Clyde V. Downing
   cost: included in above project
   completed: 1939

Madison Parish courthouse
   architect: D. Curtis Smith
   contractor: M. T. Reed
   REIs: Clyde V. Downing, Edgar J. Kelly, George T. Littlefield
   cost: $134,790 including project below
   completed: 1939

Madison Parish jail
   architect: D. Curtis Smith
   contractor: M. T. Reed
   REIs: Clyde V. Downing, Edgar J. Kelly, George T. Littlefield
   cost: included in above project
   completed: 1939

THIBODAUX

storm drains
  engineer: J. B. McCrary
  contractor: Sullivan, Long, and Hagerty
  REI: Archie Douglass
  cost: $225,706
  completed: 1939

power improvement
  engineer: J. B. McCrary
  contractor: Transamerica Const. Co.
  REIs: Archie Douglass, William Myhan
  cost: $83,800
  completed: 1939

Thibodaux Elementary School, 7th St. and Goode, originally Thibodaux High School
  architect: Favrot and Livaudais
  contractor: E. E. Rabalais and Sons
  REI: Albert G. Garrett
  cost: $73,360
  completed: 1935

TICKFAW

school addition, closed
  architect: Favrot and Reed
  contractor: G. L. Whitaker and Son
  REIs: Horace R. Brown, Jefferson L. Smith
  cost: $19,646
  completed: 1939

VIVIAN

Vivian Elementary and Middle School addition, 100 W. Kentucky Ave.
  architect: Edward F. Neild Jr.

contractors: Ashton Glassell, General Const. Co.
REIs: Marcus D. Weeks, Fred L. Hargett
cost: $35,369
completed: 1937

paving
    engineer: Jones, Roessle, Olschner, and Wiener
    contractor: A. C. Campbell
    REI: John A. Brown
    cost: $40,193
    completed: 1939

WELSH

Welsh High School home economics cottage, Sarah St. and Nicholsnow, privately owned
    architect: William R. Burk
    contractor: T. Miller and Sons
    REIs: Dick A. Hunt, Allen D. McCord
    cost: $15,594
    completed: 1939

sanitary sewer
    engineer James M. Fourmy
    contractors: Pittman Bros., Mike Mitchell and Sons
    REIs: Dick A. Hunt, Ralph A. Allor
    cost: $129,600
    completed: 1939

Olde Time School Apartments, Sarah St. and Hudspeth, originally Welsh High School gymnasium
    architect: William R. Burk
    contractor: Pittman Bros
    REIs: Allen D. McCord, Dick A. Hunt
    cost: $37,399
    completed: 1939

WHITE CASTLE

White Castle High School gym/auditorium, Bowie St., leased by city
   architects: William T. Nolan, Ulisse M. Nolan
   contractors: Joe E. Anzalone, E. E. Rabalais and Sons
   REI: Horace R. Brown
   cost: $44,504
   completed: 1938

WINNFIELD

Louisiana Technical College, Huey P. Long Campus, 304 S. Jones St., originally Huey P. Long Trade School
   architect: J. W. Smith and Assoc.
   contractor: Tudor and Ratcliff
   REIs: Stephen P. Cooley, S. Logan McConnell
   cost: $98,505
   completed: 1939

WINNSBORO

Winnsboro Elementary School, 1310 Warren St., originally Winnsboro High School
   architect: John W. Baker
   contractor: C. H. Treadwell
   REI: Clyde V. Downing
   cost: $147,513
   completed: 1939

Winnsboro Elementary School gymnasium, 1310 Warren St., originally Winnsboro High School
   architects: Neild, Somdal, and Neild; John W. Baker
   contractor: C. H. Treadwell
   REI: P. R. Alford
   cost: $161,205 including project below
   completed: 1938

Winnsboro Elementary School addition, 1310 Warren St., originally Winnsboro High School
    architects: Neild, Somdal, and Neild; John W. Baker
    contractor: C. H. Treadwell
    REI: P. R. Alford
    cost: included in above project
    completed: 1938

waterworks/sewer addition
    engineer: Swanson-McGraw
    contractor: Littrell Const. Co.
    REI: P. R. Alford
    cost: $60,158
    completed: 1938

WISNER

waterworks
    engineer: Swanson-McGraw
    contractor: McKechin and McKechin
    REIs: A. H. Shaw, P. R. Alford
    cost: $45,643
    completed: 1938

ZACHERY

gas distributor
    engineer: Huey and Gage
    contractor: Apex Const. Co.
    REIs: Fred L. Hargett, Clyde V. Downing, Walter J. Ferguson
    cost: $16,949
    completed: 1936

NOTES

INTRODUCTION

1. William E. Leuchtenburg, *Franklin D. Roosevelt and the New Deal: 1932–1940* (New York: Harper and Row, 1963), 2–3; Arthur M. Schlesinger Jr., *The Crisis of the Old Order, 1919–1933* (Boston: Houghton Mifflin, 1957), 3–4.
2. Leuchtenburg, *Roosevelt and the New Deal*, 10–12; James MacGregor Burns, *Roosevelt: The Lion and the Fox* (New York: Harcourt, Brace, 1956), 153–155.
3. Arthur W. Macmahon, John D. Millett, and Gladys Ogden, *The Administration of Federal Work Relief* (1941; reprint, New York: DeCapo Press, 1971), 74; Robert E. Sherwood, *Roosevelt and Hopkins: An Intimate Portrait* (New York: Harper and Bros., 1948), 71.
4. The term was borrowed from the military. It meant fixed installations like base camps, airstrips, and ports. David C. Perry, "Introduction," in David C. Perry, ed., *Building the Public City: The Politics, Governance, and Finance of Public Infrastructure* (Thousands Oaks, Calif.: Sage, 1995), 6.
5. For descriptions and photographs of just some (a sample of almost 700) of these projects, see C. W. Short and R. Stanley-Brown, *Public Buildings: A Survey of Architecture Constructed by Federal and Other Public Bodies between the Years 1933 and 1939 with the Assistance of the Public Works Administration* (Washington, D.C.: Government Printing Office, 1939).
6. Harold M. Mayer and Richard C. Wade, *Chicago, Growth of a Metropolis* (Chicago: University of Chicago Press, 1969), 364.
7. David L. Carlton and Peter A. Coclanis, eds., *Confronting Southern Poverty in the Great Depression: The Report on Economic Conditions of the South with Related Documents* (Boston: Bedford/St. Martin's, 1996), 42.

1. HOW TO RESPOND TO A GREAT DEPRESSION

1. Burns, *Roosevelt*, 334.
2. Raymond Moley, *After Seven Years* (New York: Harper and Bros., 1939), 369–370.
3. "Address at Oglethorpe University, May 22, 1932," in Samuel I. Rosenman, ed., *The Public Papers and Addresses of Franklin D. Roosevelt* (New York: Random House, 1938–1950), 1:646–647.
4. Daniel T. Rogers, *Atlantic Crossings: Social Politics in a Progressive Age* (Cambridge, Mass.: Harvard University Press, 1998), 330–343.

5. Mary Hoffschwelle, *Rebuilding the Rural Southern Community: Reformers, Schools, and Homes in Tennessee, 1900–1930* (Knoxville: University of Tennessee Press, 1998), 146; Carlton and Coclanis, *Confronting Southern Poverty*, 4.

6. Hoffschwelle, *Rebuilding the Rural Southern Community*, 67–88.

7. Emergency Relief and Reconstruction Act of 1933, Public Law 302, *U.S. Statutes at Large* 47 (1933): 709; William J. Barber, *From New Era to New Deal: Herbert Hoover, the Economists, and America Economic Policy, 1921–1933* (New York: Cambridge University Press, 1985), 1–2, 7–8, 13–19, 177–178; Udo Sautter, *Three Cheers for the Unemployed* (New York: Cambridge University Press, 1991), 272, 308–322; J. Kerwin Williams, *Grants in Aid under the Public Works Administration* (1939; reprint, New York: AMS Press, 1968), 33; James Stuart Olson, *Herbert Hoover and the Reconstruction Finance Corporation, 1931–1933* (Ames: Iowa State University Press, 1977), 77–79; Arthur Gayner, *Public Works in Prosperity and Depression* (New York: National Bureau of Economic Research, 1935), 88.

8. Benjamin Kleinberg, *Urban America in Transformation: Perspectives on Urban Policy and Development* (Thousand Oaks, Calif.: Sage, 1995), 95–97; John James Wallis and Wallace E. Oates, "The Impact of the New Deal on American Federalism," in Michael D. Bordo, Claudia Goldin, and Eugene N. White, eds., *The Defining Moment: The Great Depression and the American Economy in the Twentieth Century* (Chicago: University of Chicago Press, 1998), 170.

9. Arthur W. MacMahon, John D. Millett, and Gladys Ogden, *The Administration of Federal Work Relief* (Chicago: Public Administration Service, 1941), 69.

10. Burns, *Roosevelt*, 371.

11. John A. Salmond, *The Civilian Conservation Corps, 1933–1942: A New Deal Case Study* (Durham, N.C.: Duke University Press, 1967). Testimonials to this "life-changing" experience are legion. The following three books provide a good sample: Perry H. Merrill, *Roosevelt's Forest Army: A History of the Civilian Conservation Corps* (Montpelier, Vt.: Perry H. Merrill, 1981); E. Kay Kiefer and Paul F. Fellows, *Hobnail Boots and Khaki Suits* (Chicago: Adams Press, 1983); Reed L. Engle, *Everything Was Wonderful: A Pictoral History of the Civilian Conservation Corps in Shenandoah National Park* (Luray, Va.: Shenandoah Natural History Association, 1999).

12. Sherwood, *Roosevelt and Hopkins*, 52. See also George McJimsey, *Harry Hopkins: Ally of the Poor and Defender of Democracy* (Cambridge, Mass.: Harvard University Press, 1987); Donald S. Howard, *The WPA and Federal Relief Policy* (New York: Russell Sage Foundation, 1943).

13. Michael V. Namorato, *Rexford G. Tugwell: A Biography* (New York: Praeger, 1988); Diane Ghirardo, *Building New Communities: New Deal America and Fascist Italy* (Princeton, N.J.: Princeton University Press, 1989); Edward C. Banfield, *Government Project* (Glencoe, Ill: Free Press, 1951); Brian Q. Cannon, *Remaking the Agrarian Dream: New Deal Rural Resettlement in the Mountain West* (Albuquerque: University of New Mexico Press, 1996); Cathy D. Knepper, *Greenbelt, Maryland: A Living Legacy of the New Deal* (Baltimore: Johns Hopkins University Press, 2001); Lester M. Salamon, "The Time Dimension in Policy Evaluation: The Case of the New Deal Land-Reform Experiments," *Public Policy* 27, no. 2 (Spring 1979): 129–183.

14. C. Herman Pritchett, *The Tennessee Valley Authority: A Study in Public Administration* (Chapel Hill: University of North Carolina Press, 1943); David E. Lilienthal, *TVA: Democracy on the March* (New York: Pocket Books, 1945); Edwin C. Hargrove and Paul K. Conkin, eds., *TVA: Fifty Years of Grass-Roots Bureaucracy* (Urbana: University of Illinois Press, 1983).

15. James S. Olson, *Saving Capitalism: The Reconstruction Finance Corporation and the New Deal, 1933–1940* (Princeton, N.J.: Princeton University Press, 1988), 221–227; Dewey W. Grantham, *The South in Modern America: A Region at Odds* (New York: HarperPerenniel, 1995), 165.

16. Jordan A. Schwarz, *The New Dealers: Power Politics in the Age of Roosevelt* (New York: Alfred A. Knopf, 1993), xii; Hargrove and Conkin, *TVA*.

17. Williams, *Grants in Aid*, 122–123.

18. Public Works Administration, *America Builds: The Record of the PWA* (Washington, D.C.: Government Printing Office, 1939); Lois Craig and the staff of the Federal Architecture Project, *The Federal Presence: Architecture, Politics, and Symbols in United States Government Building* (Cambridge, Mass.: MIT Press, 1978), 281.

19. Roger Biles, *The South and the New Deal* (Lexington: University of Kentucky Press, 1994), 15.

20. David L. Carlton and Peter A. Coclanis, *The South, the Nation, and the World: Perspectives on Southern Economic Development* (Charlottesville: University of Virginia Press, 2003), 10, 141, 148.

21. Carlton and Coclanis, *Perspectives on Southern Economic Development*, 7–9, 168–170; Numan V. Bartley, "The Era of the New Deal as a Turning Point in Southern History," in James C. Cobb and Michael V. Namorato, eds., *The New Deal and the South* (Jackson: University Press of Mississippi, 1984), 140; Carlton and Coclanis, *Confronting Southern Poverty*, 8, 35.

22. Agricultural Adjustment Act, Public Law 10, *U.S. Statutes at Large* 48 (1934): 31,

23. Stanley Baldwin, *Poverty and Politics: The Rise and Decline of the Farm Security Administration* (Chapel Hill: University of North Carolina Press, 1968), 48–52, 130–131, 158; Leuchtenburg, *Roosevelt and the New Deal*, 137; Greta DeJong, *A Different Day: African-American Struggles for Justice in Rural Louisiana, 1900–1970* (Chapel Hill: University of North Carolina Press, 2002), 96–97.

24. George Brown Tindall, *The Emergence of the New South: 1913–1945* (Baton Rouge: Louisiana State University Press, 1967), 594–599; Grantham, *South in Modern America*, 166.

25. Carlton and Coclanis, *Confronting Southern Poverty*, 33, 50, 59.

26. Carlton and Coclanis, *Confronting Southern Poverty*, 10, 16, 30–31, 42; Tindall, *Emergence of the New South*, 598–599.

27. William Boyd, "The Forest Is the Future: Industrial Forestry and the Southern Pulp and Paper Complex," in Philip Scranton, ed., *The Second Wave: Southern Industrialization from the 1940s to the 1970s* (Athens: University of Georgia Press, 2001), 168–218.

28. Harold L. Ickes, *Back to Work: The Story of PWA* (New York: Macmillan, 1935), 80–89.

2. HAROLD ICKES GOES TO WORK

1. Harold Ickes, *The Autobiography of a Curmudgeon* (New York: Reynal and Hitchcock, 1943).

2. At 852 pages, not counting notes, T. H. Watkins's *Righteous Pilgrim: The Life and Times of Harold L. Ickes, 1874–1952* (New York: Henry Holt, 1990) is the most thorough and comprehensive biography of Ickes. Jeanne Nienaber Clarke's *Roosevelt's Warrior: Harold L. Ickes and the New Deal* (Baltimore: Johns Hopkins University Press, 1996) is also useful. Linda J. Lear's *Harold L. Ickes: Aggressive Progressive, 1874–1933* (New York: Garland, 1980) concentrates on Ickes's pre–New Deal life. Graham White and John Maze attempt to put Ickes's stormy private life together with his public career in *Harold Ickes of the New Deal* (Cambridge, Mass.: Harvard University Press, 1985). The result is a Freudian psychoanalysis viewing Ickes's political commitments through a lens of Oedipal fears of castration.

3. Watkins, *Righteous Pilgrim*, 103, 108–109; Ickes, *Curmudgeon*, 118–144.

4. Watkins, *Righteous Pilgrim*, 95–98; Jane Addams, *Twenty Years at Hull House* (1910; reprint, New York: New American Library, 1961), 285–287. Addams's brief account does not mention Ickes or how the incident was resolved. Perhaps she never knew or was embarrassed by Ickes's blackmail.

5. Watkins, *Righteous Pilgrim*, 104–105.

6. Watkins, *Righteous Pilgrim*, 199–205.

7. Ickes, *Curmudgeon*, 157–164.

8. Watkins, *Righteous Pilgrim*, 126–135, 211–213.

9. Watkins, *Righteous Pilgrim*, 258; Ickes, *Curmudgeon*, 191, 260.

10. Ickes, *Curmudgeon*, 263.

11. Ickes, *Curmudgeon*, 265–270; Watkins, *Righteous Pilgrim*, 274–280; Moley, *After Seven Years*, 127.

12. Clarke, *Roosevelt's Warrior*, 182; Watkins, *Righteous Pilgrim*, 643–649; Harvard Sitkoff, *A New Deal for Blacks The Emergence of Civil Rights as a National Issue*, vol. 1, *The Depression Decade* (New York: Oxford University Press, 1978), 68–69.

13. Jonathan Dembo, "The Curmudgeon: Harold Ickes," in Katie Louchheim, ed., *The Making of the New Deal: The Insiders Speak* (Cambridge, Mass.: Harvard University Press, 1983), 247.

14. The National Association of Civilian Conservation Corps Alumni has a headquarters and a museum at Jefferson Barracks in St. Louis.

15. National Industrial Recovery Act, Public Law 67, *U.S. Statutes at Large* 48 (1934): 195.

16. Ickes, *Back to Work*, 12–13.

17. Thomas Ferguson, "Industrial Conflict and the Coming of the New Deal: The Triumph of Multinational Liberalism in America," in Steve Fraser and Gary Gerstle, eds., *The Rise and Fall of the New Deal Order, 1930–1980* (Princeton, N.J.: Princeton University Press, 1989), 18.

18. Kenneth Feingold and Theda Skocpol, *State and Party in America's New Deal* (Madison: University of Wisconsin Press, 1995).

19. Robert D. Leighninger Jr., "Work Relief," in Paul H. Stuart and John M. Herrick, eds., *Encyclopedia of Social Welfare History in North America* (Thousand Oaks, Calif.: Sage, 2005), 450–453; MacMahon, Millett, and Ogden, *Administration of Federal Work Relief*, 21.

20. Ickes, *Back to Work*, 56.

21. Laurence S. Knappen, *Revenue Bonds and the Investor* (New York: Prentice-Hall, 1939), 175–176; Williams, *Grants in Aid*, 41, 111–112. Williams's book is an essential source of information on the organization and operation of the PWA. Unfortunately, there has been no comprehensive study of this agency since it first appeared in 1939. Jack F. Isakoff, "The Public Works Administration" (Ph.D. diss., University of Illinois, 1937), is also useful, but concludes in 1937 before the last big spending program.

22. Ickes, *Back to Work*, 27–30.

23. Williams, *Grants in Aid*, 104–105, 133.

24. Williams, *Grants in Aid*, 105.

25. Ickes, *Back to Work*, 34–35.

26. Ickes, *Back to Work*, 41–45.

27. Moley, *After Seven Years*, 190; Ickes, *Back to Work*, 44; Watkins, *Righteous Pilgrim*, 115–116, 206–208, 371.

28. I've read hundreds of project files in eight geographically dispersed states and have yet to find a woman in this position.

29. Davis to A. W. George Jr., State Engineering Inspector, July 9, 1937, Reel 5643, Docket #1023, Microfilm Records of Non-Federal Projects, 1933–1947, Records of the Public Works Administration, Record Group 135, National Archives II, College Park, Md. (hereafter cited as PWA Microfilm).

30. Investigation document 12502, Reel 2611, Docket #La.3068, PWA Microfilm.

31. Peter Tamboro, Memorandum Report, February 4, 1938, 6, Reel 5902, Docket #1042, PWA Microfilm.

32. Watkins, *Righteous Pilgrim*, 115–117. Glavis was later accused of being overzealous in some of his investigative activities, which included wiretaps on telephones within the Interior Department. Ickes became disenchanted with Glavis and was relieved when the president recommended Glavis for a position with Senator Hugo Black to investigate campaign funding. Watkins, *Righteous Pilgrim*, 432–437.

33. Williams, *Grants in Aid*, 105–106.

34. Ickes, *Back to Work*, 19, 66.

35. Ickes, *Back to Work*, 68.

36. The chief architect of the station was Roland Wank, who would soon be hired to design the dams of the Tennessee Valley Authority, widely praised as fine examples of modernist architecture and engineering. Talbott Hamlin, "Architecture of the TVA," *Pencil Points* 20 (November 1939): 721–722; Kenneth Reid, "Design in TVA Structures," *Pencil Points* 20 (November 1939): 691; Lewis Mumford, "The Architecture of Power," *New Yorker*, July 7, 1941, 60.

37. Williams, *Grants in Aid*, 60; Watkins, *Righteous Pilgrim*, 352; Burns, *Roosevelt*, 192. Separating the PWA from the control of the National Recovery Administration deprived the latter of some leverage in persuading industries to adopt production codes.

Keeping them together, however, might have doomed the PWA to extinction along with the NRA.

38. Williams, *Grants in Aid*, 160–161.

39. Arthur Goldschmidt, in Louchheim, *Making of the New Deal*, 248–249.

40. Williams, *Grants in Aid*, 96 n.83, 260–261; Isakoff, "Public Works Administration," 107.

41. Bonnie Fox Schwartz, *The Civil Works Administration, 1933–1934: The Business of Emergency Employment in the New Deal* (Princeton, N.J.: Princeton University Press, 1984); Forrest A. Walker, *The Civil Works Administration: An Experiment in Federal Work Relief* (New York: Garland Press, 1979); MacMahon, Millett, and Ogden, *Administration of Federal Work Relief*, 18.

42. Emergency Relief Appropriations Act of 1935, Public Resolution 11, *U.S. Statutes at Large* 49 (1936): 115.

43. Williams, *Grants in Aid*, 137, n.70.

44. "Cumulative Supplement for Report No. 5, Status of Completed Non-Federal Allotted Projects, September 13, 1939," Box 1, Records of the Public Works Administration, Record Group 135, National Archives II.

45. Gale Radford, *Modern Housing for America: Policy Struggles in the New Deal Era* (Chicago: University of Chicago Press, 1996), 85–109; Michael W. Straus and Talbot Wegg, *Housing Comes of Age* (New York: Oxford University Press, 1938).

46. Paul K. Conkin, *Tomorrow a New World: The New Deal Community Programs* (Ithaca, N.Y.: Cornell University Press, 1959); Russell Lord and Paul H. Johnstone, eds., *A Place on Earth: A Critical Appraisal of Subsistence Homesteads* (Washington, D.C.: Bureau of Agricultural Economics, USDA, 1942).

47. Leuchtenburg, *Roosevelt and the New Deal*, 70–71; *Wall Street Journal*, January 5 and 27, 1934; *Business Week*, January 20, 1934, 3; *Business Week*, February 10, 1934, 3; *Business Week*, February 24, 1934, 3; Alan Brinkley, *The End of Reform: New Deal Liberalism in Recession and War* (New York: Vintage, 1995) 28, 73; Theodore Rosenof, *Economics in the Long Run: New Deal Theorists and Their Legacies, 1933–1993* (Chapel Hill: University of North Carolina Press, 1997), 9, 49–50; Kenneth Roose, *The Economics of Recession and Revival* (New Haven, Conn.: Yale University Press, 1954), 5, 9, 173–178, 241.

3. HUEY LONG VERSUS THE PWA

1. T. Harry Williams, *Huey Long* (New York: Bantam, 1970), 862; Robert E. Snyder, "Huey Long and the Presidential Election of 1936," *Louisiana History* 16 (1975): 117–143; James A. Farley, *Behind the Ballots: The Personal History of a Politician* (New York: Harcourt, Brace, 1938), 250; Raymond Moley, *The First New Deal* (New York: Harcourt, Brace and World, 1966), 372.

2. Williams, *Huey Long*, 35–36, 47–53, 55, 79–81; Alan Brinkley, *Voices of Protest: Huey Long, Father Coughlin and the Great Depression* (New York: Vintage, 1983), 13

3. Glen Jeansonne, *Messiah of the Masses: Huey P. Long and the Great Depression*

(New York: HarperCollins, 1993), 23; Brinkley, *Voices of Protest*, 14; Williams, *Huey Long*, 2.

4. Williams, *Huey Long*, 257–293, Brinkley, *Voices of Protest*, 17–24; Jeansonne, *Messiah of the Masses*, 59–60.

5. Williams, *Huey Long*, 3, 287, 295, 318–327; Brinkley, *Voices of Protest*, 20–21, 24, 30; Jeansonne, *Messiah of the Masses*, 68–69.

6. Anthony J. Badger, "Huey Long and the New Deal," in Stephen W. Baskerville and Ralph Willet, eds., *Nothing Else to Fear: New Perspectives on America in the Thirties* (Manchester: Manchester University Press, 1985), 88.

7. Williams, *Huey Long*, 353–358; Jeansonne, *Messiah of the Masses*, 91; Brinkley, *Voices of Protest*, 27–28.

8. Williams, *Huey Long*, 121, 726–728; Badger, "Huey Long," 81; Brinkley, *Voices of Protest*, 105–106, 114–116.

9. Badger, "Huey Long," 83–84; Will Alexander, *Memoir No. 185*, Columbia Oral History Collection, vol. 3, 521, quoted in Snyder, "Huey Long," 140–141.

10. Quoted in Betty Marie Field, "The Politics of the New Deal in Louisiana, 1933–1939" (Ph.D. diss., Tulane University, 1973), 39.

11. Jeansonne, *Messiah of the Masses*, 5; Williams, *Huey Long*, 200; Garry Boulard, *Huey Long Invades New Orleans: The Siege of a City, 1934–1936* (Gretna, La.: Pelican Press, 1998), 39–41.

12. Williams, *Huey Long*, 449; Boulard, *Huey Long Invades New Orleans*, 34, 37, 232 n.17.

13. Brinkley, *Voices of Protest*, 24, 26.

14. Williams, *Huey Long*, 506–509, 703; Jeansonne, *Messiah of the Masses*, 136; Badger, "Huey Long," 86.

15. Biles, *South and the New Deal*, 129–131; Lyle Dorsett, *Franklin D. Roosevelt and the Big City Bosses* (Port Washington, N.Y.: Kennikat Press, 1977).

16. Badger, "Huey Long," 83; Field, "Politics of the New Deal," 43.

17. Field, "Politics of the New Deal," 8–11; Badger, "Huey Long," 85.

18. Farley, *Behind the Ballots*, 240–242; Williams, *Huey Long*, 669.

19. Hodding Carter, "Kingfish to Crawfish," *New Republic*, January 24, 1934, 303.

20. Badger, "Huey Long," 85–86; Field, "Politics of the New Deal," 18, 114–115; Williams, *Huey Long*, 495, 636.

21. Harold Ickes, *The Secret Diary of Harold L. Ickes: The First Thousand Days, 1933–1936* (New York: Simon and Schuster, 1953), 284.

22. List of All Allotted Non-Federal Projects, All Programs, by State and Docket, as of May 30, 1942, 65–66, Federal Works Agency, Public Works Administration, Record Group 135, National Archives II (hereafter cited as Final Status Report).

23. Reels 2606–2617, Docket #La.3068, PWA Microfilm.

24. Williams, *Huey Long*, 695–697.

25. Report #1, Index to Status of Non-Federal Projects, September 13, 1939, 34, Records of the Public Works Administration, Records Group 135, National Archives II (hereafter cited as Status Report #1), Final Status Report, 65.

26. Williams, *Huey Long*, 697.

27. Status Report #1, 34.
28. Status Report #1, 34.
29. Fleming to Henry, March 15, 1934; Henry to Fleming, March 21, 1934, Reel 8406, Docket #La.3908, PWA Microfilm.
30. Field, "Politics of the New Deal," 117.
31. Field, "Politics of the New Deal," 147.
32. Reel 4902, Docket #La.9251, PWA Microfilm.
33. "Long Takes Charge, Give Up Pay Bed Plan for Charity," *New Orleans Item Tribune*, June 21, 1934; Long to Ickes, August 11, 1935, Reel 8462, Docket #La.4529, PWA Microfilm.
34. Carter, "Kingfish to Crawfish," 303.
35. "Quota of PWA Funds Exhausted, Ickes Informs State's Solons," *New Orleans Times-Picayune*, September 29, 1934.
36. Williams, *Huey Long*, 752–754.
37. Field, "Politics of the New Deal," 132–137.
38. Snyder, "Huey Long," 139–140; "Long Acts to Rule Relief Bill Funds," *New York Times*, April 15, 1935.
39. John Robert Moore, "The New Deal in Louisiana," in John Braeman, Robert H. Bremner, and David Brody, *The New Deal*, vol. 2, *The State and Local Levels* (Columbus: Ohio State University Press, 1975), 147–148.
40. "Ickes Threatens Recall of PWA Louisiana Loans," *New Orleans Times-Picayune*, April 17, 1935; "Ickes Scores Long," *New York Times*, April 17, 1935; "Long Excoriates President's Aides," *New York Times*, April 23, 1935.
41. Ickes, *Secret Diary*, 346.
42. Ickes, *Secret Diary*, 400–401.
43. Williams, *Huey Long*, 892–896.
44. Williams, *Huey Long*, 902–903; Field, "Politics of the New Deal," 156–157.
45. Williams, *Huey Long*, 903; William Ivy Hair, *The Kingfish and His Kingdom* (Baton Rouge: Louisiana State University Press, 1991), 317.
46. Turner W. Battle to Ickes, "Subcommittee on the Status of States Under Quota," September 29, 1933, Correspondence Relating to Federal Projects, 1934–1941, Box 5, Records of the Public Works Administration, Record Group 135, National Archives II.
47. Williams, *Grants in Aid*, 48, 104, 113–119. Williams always places the word "quota" in quotation marks, a further indication that it never attained official status.
48. Field, "Politics of the New Deal," 113.

4. THE SECOND LOUISIANA PURCHASE

1. Field, "Politics of the New Deal," 232–254.
2. Badger, "Huey Long," 87.
3. Harnett Kane, *Louisiana Hayride: The American Rehearsal for Dictatorship, 1928–1940* (1941; reprint, Gretna, La.: Pelican Press, 1971), 181–183.

4. Field, "Politics of the New Deal," 288–290.

5. Kane, *Louisiana Hayride*, 201; Fields, "Politics of the New Deal," 304–307, 343.

6. Kane, *Louisiana Hayride*, 185; Field, "Politics of the New Deal," 309. Fair Park, the site of the centennial, was created with the aid of PWA money. Most of its buildings, including a PWA-built museum, are still standing and in use.

7. "'Second Louisiana Purchase' Scored by Dakota Solon," *New Orleans Times-Picayune*, June 21, 1939; Kane, *Louisiana Hayride*, 251.

8. Farley, *Behind the Ballots*, 252; Kane, *Louisiana Hayride*, 184; Brinkley, *End of Reform*, 15–16.

9. In per capita terms, Louisiana did somewhat better than other southern states in overall New Deal spending: $369.80 compared with $358.18 for Mississippi, $309.43 for Alabama, and $272.69 for Georgia. It lagged behind Arkansas at $396.12. The willingness of states to accept New Deal programs and put up local matches is an important influence in this. Don C. Reading, "New Deal Activity and the States, 1933 to 1939," *Journal of Economic History* 33, no. 4 (December 1973): table 1; see also Gavin Wright, "The Political Economy of New Deal Spending: An Econometric Analysis," *Review of Economics and Statistics* 56, no. 1 (February 1974): 30–38. These analyses attempt to cover all New Deal programs, not just the PWA.

10. Emergency Relief Appropriations Act of 1935, 115; Williams, *Grants in Aid*, 51–52.

11. Williams, *Grants in Aid*, 52–58.

12. Williams, *Grants in Aid*, 150.

13. List of all Allotted Non-Federal Projects, All Projects by State and Docket, as of May 30, 1942, 65–66, Final Status Report.

14. First Deficiency Appropriations Act of 1936, Public Law 739, *U.S. Statutes at Large* 49 (1936): 1597; Charles Coates to Horatio Hackett, December 18, 1936, Reel 5843, Docket #1026, PWA Microfilm. LSU did not meet the deadline because the companies manufacturing the special equipment could not deliver it fast enough. But extension of the life of the PWA saved the project.

15. Final Status Report, 66.

16. Brinkley, *End of Reform*, 19–20, 23–24.

17. Richard Hofstadter, *The American Political Tradition* (New York: Vintage, 1954), 324–325; Burns, *Roosevelt*, 320–323.

18. Rosenof, *Economics in the Long Run*, 9; Burns, *Roosevelt*, 331; Brinkley, *End of Reform*, 24–28.

19. Brinkley, *End of Reform*, 26–28, 31–42, 48–49, 56–57; Clarke, *Roosevelt's Warrior*, 249–251.

20. Burns, *Roosevelt*, 335–336.

21. William T. Foster and Waddill Catchings, *The Road to Plenty* (Boston: Houghton Mifflin, 1928); Brinkley, *End of Reform*, 75–77, 82.

22. Rosenof, *Economics in the Long Run*, 58–63.

23. Brinkley, *Voices of Protest*, 74. According to Moley, the tax on surplus corporate profits proposed by Roosevelt in 1935 was an attempt to "steal Long's thunder" (Moley, *After Seven Years*, 305, 308–310). See also Robert E. Snyder, "Huey Long and the Presidential Election of 1936," *Louisiana History* 16 (1975): 117–143.

24. Williams, *Grants in Aid*, 142.

25. "Lake Providence Beats PWA Limit by Use of Plane," *New Orleans Times-Picayune*, October 1, 1938.

26. Biles, *South and the New Deal*, 137–143.

27. "The President Presents Plan No. 1 to Carry Out the Provisions of the Reorganization Act, 25 April 1939," in. Rosenman, *Public Papers and Addresses of Franklin D. Roosevelt*, 8:245–271; Williams, *Grants in Aid*, 285–287; Jason Scott Smith, "Public Works and the Postwar World: The Legacies of New Deal Public Works Programs, 1943–1956," paper presented at the Policy History Conference, St. Louis, 2002, 8. See also Jason Scott Smith, *Building New Deal Liberalism: The Political Economy of Public Works, 1933–1956* (New York: Cambridge University Press, 2005).

5. SCANDAL

1. Drew Pearson and Robert S. Allen, "WPA Corruption in Louisiana Charged," *Shreveport Journal*, June 17, 1939.

2. Williams, *Huey Long*, 862.

3. Interviews with Lynn Johnson, Summerfield Caldwell's granddaughter, and Liza Jo Stelly, his niece, conducted by Robert Leighninger, February 7, 2000, T. Harry Williams Oral History Center, Louisiana State University; interview with Roe J. Cangelosi, James A. Whitty, George L. Schwalb, and Walter B. Calhoun, LSU employees in the 1930s, conducted by Quinn M. Coco, summer 1978, Hill Memorial Library, Louisiana State University; see also Kane, *Louisiana Hayride*, 230–232, 281, 307, 452.

4. "Parish Indicts Hart, Smith, Leon Weiss in Double-Move Case," *New Orleans Times-Picayune*, September 27, 1939; "Caldwell, Hart Indicted in Plot to Defraud U.S.," *New Orleans Times-Picayune*, September 30, 1939; "New Indictment of Hart, Leche, 13 More," *New Orleans Times-Picayune*, October 1, 1939; "Two More Dips of LSU Funds Charged to Trio in Indictment," *New Orleans Times-Picayune*, October 7, 1939; Kane, *Louisiana Hayride*, 353.

5. Harnett T. Kane, "WPA Cracks Down on Two State Aids," *New Orleans Item Tribune*, July 16, 1939; Kane, *Louisiana Hayride*, 212, 272–288, 299–305, 384–385.

6. Williams, *Grants in Aid*, 202–206, 153 n.110. The PWA could, however, take action in cases where fraudulent information was given to them in applications or reports, as was the case in the Geology Building.

7. Investigation of Alleged Excess Hours Irregularities on the Part of T. Miller and Sons, General Contractors, February 25, 1939, Special Agent George Wolf, Reel 5969, Docket #1150, PWA Microfilm.

8. Investigation of Alleged Underpayment of Wages by Pittman Bros. Construction Co., General Contractor, B-4, August 18, 1939, by Special Agent J. Roy Orr, Reel 5828, Docket #1119, PWA Microfilm.

9. Investigation of Alleged Misclassification of Israel Fradieu by T. B. Merrill, Plumbing, Heating, and Electrical Contractor under M. T. Reed Construction Co.

General Contractor, March 15, 1940, Special Agent Jeremiah Tempone, Reel 5968, Docket #1145, PWA Microfilm.

10. Investigation of Alleged Misclassification and Wage Underpayment on the Part of James McDaniel and Son, General Contractors, January 5, 1940, Special Agents Doyle H. Willis and Michael J. Sherry, Reel 5849, Docket #1219, PWA Microfilm.

11. Investigation of Alleged Misclassification and Wage Underpayment on the Part of Gravier and Harper, General Contractor, October 7, 1939, Special Agent Doyle H. Willis, Reel 5804, Docket #1157, PWA Microfilm.

12. Investigation of Alleged Discrimination in the Employment of Labor and Irregularities Concerning Financial Interests of James A. Sewell, Board Member in Materials Purchased by Humble and Humble, Contractors for Use on Contract #8, Martin High School, Ward B., November 29, 1939, Special Agent Paul C. Gerhart Jr., Reel 5827, Docket #1242, PWA Microfilm.

13. Alleged Use of Foreign Labor by Nile Yearwood, General Contractor, September 9, 1937, Special Agent James J. McLaughlin, Reel 5844, Docket #1029, PWA Microfilm.

14. Jacqueline Jones, *Labor of Love, Labor of Sorrow: Black Women, Work, and the Family from Slavery to the Present* (New York: Basic Books, 1985); Christopher G. Wye, "The New Deal and the Negro Community: Toward a Broader Conceptualization," in Melvyn Dubofsky, ed., *The New Deal: Conflicting Interpretations and Shifting Perspectives* (New York: Garland, 1992), 247–269; Sitkoff, *New Deal for Blacks*, 47.

15. H. A. Gray, Director of Inspections Division, to Louis M. Glavis, Director of Investigations Division, June 21, 1935, Reel 3710, Docket #4531, PWA Microfilm.

16. Reel 6021, Docket #1179, PWA Microfilm. Ickes's nondiscrimination policies worked in places outside the South. His system of requiring the percentage of black workers on a project to reflect their proportion of the population became a model for fair employment practices in other agencies. Sitkoff, *New Deal for Blacks*, 68–69, 331.

17. Special Agent C. L. Willis, Memorandum Report, February 25, 1938, 2–3, Reel 5791, Docket #1081, PWA Microfilm.

18. Alleged Use of Inferior Materials in the Construction of Schools at Hanna and Martin on the Part of J. J. and W. J. Hardy and Humble and Humble, General Contractors, October 15, 1940, Special Agent P. O. Roberts, Reel 5828, Docket #1242, PWA Microfilm.

19. Investigation of Alleged Suppression of Competitive Bidding, "Kick-Back," and Employment Irregularities on the part of Salley and Ellis, General Contractor, December 3, 1937, Reel 5843, Docket #1027, PWA Microfilm.

20. Reels 4813–4814, Docket #9353, PWA Microfilm; Investigation of Alleged Excess Hours and Falsification of Payrolls on the Part of R. P. Farnsworth and Co., General Contractor, October 31, 1939, Special Agent O. J. Van Valin, Reel 5607, Docket #1019, PWA Microfilm.

21. Investigation of Alleged "Kick-Backs," and Injury to an Employee Due to Defective Steps in Connection with the Work of A. J. Rife Construction Co., General Contractor, June 23, 1938, Special Agent Michael J. Sherry, Reel 7551, Docket #1049, PWA Microfilm.

22. Investigation of Alleged Wage Underpayment to William Day on the Part of Independence Lumber Co., General Contractor, October 7, 1938, Reel 5786, Docket #1068, PWA Microfilm.

23. Inspection of the Construction Work of Caldwell Bros. and Hart, General Contractors, and Investigation of Construction, Change Order, and Completion Irregularities, March 5, 1940, Special Agent S. C. Gibson, Exhibits 19 and 20, Reel 4902, Docket #La.9251, PWA Microfilm.

24. Kane, *Louisiana Hayride*, 350.

25. Investigation of Alleged Fraudulent Change Order Request (1-1-1) Submitted by Caldwell Bros. and Hart, General Contractors, October 7, 1939, Special Agents C. L. Willis and A. A. Benevento (hereafter cited as Change Order Investigation) Exhibit 8 and 8a, Reel 5804, Docket #1162, PWA Microfilm.

26. Alexander Allaire, PWA Regional Engineer to G. H. Butler, Director, Investigations Division, May 31, 1939, Change Order Investigation, Exhibit 3.

27. Change Order Investigation, Exhibit 50.

28. Statement by F. N. Palmer, Pittsburgh Plate Glass, August 17, 1939, Change Order Investigation, Exhibit 28; Statement by H. J. Bremerman, National Sash and Door, August 19, 1939, Change Order Investigation; Memorandum of Special Agent C. L. Willis, November 20, 1939, Reel 5804, Docket #1162, PWA Microfilm.

29. Hebert to Weiss, Dreyfous, and Seiferth, September 21, 1939, Change Order Investigation, Exhibit 20.

30. Statement of Von Osthoff, October 31, 1939, Exhibit 21, Inspection of Construction Work by Caldwell Bros. and Hart, General Contractors, and of Supervision by Weiss, Dreyfous, and Seiferth, Architects, and Investigation of Irregularities Disclosed, November 28, 1939, Special Agent C. L. Willis; Hebert to Vel Stephens, Acting Regional Director, PWA, December 13, 1939, Reel 5804, Docket #1162, PWA Microfilm.

31. Hebert to J. J. Madigan, Executive Officer, PWA, January 17, 1941, Reel 5804, Docket #1162, PWA Microfilm.

6. SCHOOLS

1. Louis W. Rapeer, ed., *The Consolidated Rural School* (Chicago: Scribner's, 1920); National Commission on School District Reorganization, *Your School District* (Washington, D.C.: National Education Association of the United States, 1948).

2. Peter G. Filene, *Him/Her/Self* (Baltimore: Johns Hopkins University Press, 1986), 45.

3. Hoffschwelle, *Rebuilding the Rural Southern Community*.

4. Reel 3839, Docket #4635, Record Group 135, PWA Microfilm.

5. Fred L. Hargett, Report to the Director, Inspections Division, July 7, 1937, Reel 5958, Docket #1008, PWA Microfilm.

6. Bulger, Memo from the Director of the PWA Engineering Division, July 26, 1937, Reel 5960, Docket #1030, PWA Microfilm.

7. Fred L. Hargett, Special Report, July 18, 1937, Reel 5787, Docket #1077, PWA microfilm.
8. Whitney to L. L. Kilgore, December 20, 1938, Reel 5831, Docket #1317, PWA Microfilm.
9. Donald E. Devore and Joseph Logsdon, *Crescent City Schools: Public Education in New Orleans, 1841–1991* (Lafayette: University of Southwest Louisiana, 1991), 91, 179; Robert Meyer Jr., *Names Over New Orleans Public Schools* (New Orleans: Namesake Press, 1975), 144–152.
10. Jones to Hackett, April 10, 1937, Reel 5959, Docket #1011, PWA Microfilm; Reel 5939, Docket #1119, PWA Microfilm.
11. Drawings of architect J. Cheshire Peyton, Reel 5862, Docket #1168, PWA Microfilm.
12. Reel 5787, Docket #1077, PWA Microfilm.
13. Reels 5827–5828, Docket #1242, PWA Microfilm.
14. Reel 5953–5954, Docket #1132, PWA Microfilm.
15. Audit, November 13, 1937, Reel 5959, Docket #1010, PWA Microfilm.
16. Memo, April 23, 1934, Reel 2606, Docket #La.3068, PWA Microfilm.
17. Reel 5969, Docket #1149, PWA Microfilm; Reel 5845, Docket #1109 and #1110, PWA Microfilm; Reel 5807, Docket #1019, PWA Microfilm.

7. UNIVERSITIES

1. Thomas F. Ruffin, "The Greater University," *LSU Magazine*, 70 (Spring 1994): 24–28, 42.
2. Williams, *Huey Long*, 526–540, 545–546.
3. Because the other regional universities have also undergone a series of name changes, all will be referred to by location in subsequent references. That, at least so far, has not changed.
4. Regional Director George Bull to Asst. Administrator H. A. Gray, "Description of Southeastern Louisiana College," August 2 and 16, 1938, Reel 5874, Docket #1210, PWA Microfilm.
5. "Picturing Woeful Events," pamphlet supporting application, Reel 5858, Docket #1251, PWA Microfilm.
6. "LSU Finances," *New Orleans States*, August 23, 1934.
7. Harris to Bull, July 27, 1938, Reel 5952, Docket #1067, PWA Microfilm. This letter is in the files of the Deaf and Blind School project. The Southern University gym/auditorium is on Reel 5951, Docket #1057, PWA Microfilm. The school for deaf and blind students is on Reel 5952, Docket #1067, PWA Microfilm.
8. Reel 5844, Docket #1106, PWA Microfilm.
9. Reels 5968–5969, Docket #1146, PWA Microfilm; Reel 5969, Docket #1147, PWA Microfilm.
10. L. W. McCarley of Brooks, Mays, and Co., in "Memorandum Report" by Spe-

cial Agent Gilbert B. Carter, February 5, 1940, 4, Reel 5804, Docket #1156, PWA Microfilm.

11. Reels 8415–8416, Docket #1160, PWA Microfilm; Reel 6486, Docket #1161, PWA Microfilm; Tugwell to Bull, July 23, 1938, Reel 8415, Docket #1160, PWA Microfilm.

12. Reel 5804, Docket #1162, PWA Microfilm.

13. Mildred B. Gallot, "Grambling State University: A History, 1901–1977" (Ph.D. diss., Louisiana State University, 1982), 41; *Monroe Star News*, July 30, 1939, in Gallot, "Grambling State University," 88; Reel 6021, Docket #1181, PWA Microfilm.

14. Gallot, "Grambling State University," 46.

15. Overton to Grey, September 19, 1938, Reel 5858, Docket #1251, PWA Microfilm.

16. Bull to Gray, "Description of Southeastern Louisiana College," 2, Reel 5974, Docket #1210, PWA Microfilm.

17. Reel 5829, Docket #1211, PWA Microfilm.

18. Reel 5857, Docket #1204, PWA Microfilm.

19. Reel 5849, Docket #1263, PWA Microfilm.

20. Reel 5829, Docket #1215, PWA Microfilm; Reel 5849, Docket #1220, #1229, #1222, PWA Microfilm.

21. Albert A. Fredericks, *Summary Report*, Northwestern State University Archives.

22. "$3,692,025 Spent for LSU Works on WPA Program." *New Orleans Times-Picayune*, July 7, 1939.

8. COURTHOUSES

1. Carl A. Brasseaux, "Louisiana's Parishes and Courthouses," in Carl A. Brasseaux, Glenn R. Conrad, and R. Warren Robinson, *The Courthouses of Louisiana*, 2nd ed. (Lafayette: Center for Louisiana Studies, 1997), xv–xvi, 181–182. This book provides a compact, parish-by-parish history of courthouse building and rebuilding. Unfortunately for those interested in the New Deal, it frequently attributes PWA projects to the WPA, and sometimes vice-versa, or omits the contributions of both agencies.

2. R. Warren Robinson, "Louisiana Courthouse Architecture," in Brasseaux, Conrad, and Robinson, *Courthouses of Louisiana*, xx.

3. Reels 4030–4031, Docket #La.4927, PWA Microfilm; Reel 6051, Docket #1022, PWA Microfilm.

4. Le Corbusier, *Towards a Modern Architecture* (1927; reprint, New York: Praeger, 1960), 210; Gwendolyn Wright, *Building the Dream: A Social History of Housing in America* (Cambridge, Mass.: MIT Press, 1981), 241.

5. An interesting and important example is Paul Phillipe Cret, "Ten Years of Modernism," *Architectural Forum* 59, no. 2 (August 1933): 91–94; see also Talbot F. Hamlin, "A Contemporary American Style: Some Notes on Its Qualities and Dangers," *Pencil Points* 19 (February 1938): 99–106. Cret, a faculty member of the Ecole des Beaux Arts in Paris, was brought in to teach at the University of Pennsylvania. He is one of the

fathers of PWA moderne through the design of many influential public buildings, including the Folger Shakespeare Library in Washington, D.C.

6. David Gebhard, *Robert Stacy-Judd: Maya Architecture and the Creation of a New Style* (Santa Barbara, Calif.: Capra Press, 1993), 71; David Gebhard, *Romanza: The California Architecture of Frank Lloyd Wright* (San Francisco: Chronicle Books, 1988), 13.

7. James Howard Kunstler, "Home from Nowhere," *Atlantic Monthly*, September 1996, 43–66.

8. Hamlin, "Contemporary American Style," 101.

9. Reel 5933, Docket #1104, PWA Microfilm; Index to Status of Non-Federal Projects, Report No. 1, September 13, 1939, Records of the Public Works Administration, Record Group 135, Box 1, National Archives II.

10. Reel 5825, Docket #1054, PWA Microfilm.

11. Quoted in C. Vann Woodward, *The Strange Career of Jim Crow*, 2nd rev. ed. (New York: Oxford University Press, 1966), 12, 40–43.

12. Woodward, *Strange Career of Jim Crow*, 54–55, 77–81; Grantham, *South in Modern America*, 14–16.

13. Woodward, *Strange Career of Jim Crow*, 82–86, 116–118; Grantham, *South in Modern America*, 16–22.

14. Woodward, *Strange Career of Jim Crow*, 118, 127, 134.

9. THE U.S. MARINE HOSPITAL AT CARVILLE AND OTHER FEDERAL PROJECTS

1. In fact, the PWA seems to have had a hand in a prodigious amount of naval construction, including the carriers *Enterprise*, *Ranger*, and *Yorktown*; seven heavy cruisers; four light cruisers; five submarines; and thirty-two destroyers. "Vessels Under Construction," April 10, 1934, Navy Department, Bureau of Construction, Repairs, and Engineering; Correspondence Relating to Federal Projects (hereafter cited as Federal Project Correspondence), Box 3, Record of the Public Works Administration, Record Group 135, National Archives II.

2. "Federal Projects," November 30, 1936, Box 4, Federal Project Correspondence.

3. Daniel C. Roper, Secretary of Commerce, to Ickes, May 16, 1934, Box 5, Federal Project Correspondence; Transcript, "Meeting of the Special Board for Public Works, Executive Session-Confidential, Vol. LXXXIII, Thursday, June 7, 1934," 4, Box 3, Federal Project Correspondence; Bonnie Fox Schwartz, *The Civil Works Administration, 1933–1934: The Business of Emergency Employment in the New Deal* (Princeton, N.J.: Princeton University Press, 1984), 234.

4. L. Walker Evans, "Preliminary Inventory of the Records of the Public Works Administration (Record Group 135)," Civil Records Research Room, National Archives II, 22.

5. "Federal and Non-Federal Projects Approved during the Period from September 1 to September 8 Inclusive," October 2, 1933, Box Y1379, Publications of the U.S. Gov-

ernment, Record Group 287, National Archives II. This is the second of fourteen reports. The first is dated July 18, 1933. The rest span the weeks from October 1 to December 1. If not otherwise attributed, information on Louisiana federal projects comes from these reports.

6. George R. Bienfang, "History of Barksdale Field," unpublished ms., 1937, Hill Memorial Library, Louisiana State University.

7. "Construction of Projects Appropriated for by Congress but Curtailed or Stopped Due to Budgetary Restrictions," Federal Project Correspondence, Box 5, lists most of the Barksdale components as 75 to 99 percent completed. The NCO quarters is listed as 46 percent completed, and the officers' quarters is 39 percent finished. C. W. Short, *Survey of the Architecture of Completed Projects of the Public Works Administration, 1939* [microform] (Alexandria, Va.: Chadwick-Healey, 1986), fiche 10.

8. Don Kermath, Frederick J. Cushlow, Eleanor L. Esser, Lisa M. Puryear, James A. Gorski, Kimesia C. Isbell, Victoria McCleary, Irene J. Cohen, and Charles L. Sejud, "The Barksdale Air Force Base Historic District" (N.p.: U.S. Army Corps of Engineers, 1995).

9. Lynn M. Alperin, *History of the Gulf Intracoastal Waterway* (Washington, D.C.: Government Printing Office, 1983), 16; L. W. Robert, Asst. Sect'y. of Treasury, to Ickes, August 10, 1933, Box 5, Federal Project Correspondence.

10. Box 1, Federal Project Correspondence.

11. Rear Admiral L. C. Cowell, U.S. Coast Guard, to Administrator, Federal Works Agency, March 29, 1940, Other Records Relating to Federal Projects, 1933–1939, Box 4, Records of the Public Works Administration, Record Group 135, National Archives II.

12. Report of Thomas A. MacDonald, Chief, Bureau of Public Roads, January 1, 1935, 47, Box 4, Federal Project Correspondence.

13. Patrick Feeny, *The Fight against Leprosy* (London: Elek Books, 1964), 130–135.

14. Feeny, *Fight against Leprosy*, 22–26.

15. Stanley Stein and Lawrence G. Blochman, *Alone No More* (New York: Funk and Wagnalls, 1963).

16. Betty Martin, with Evelyn Wells, *Miracle at Carville* (New York: Doubleday, 1950); Betty Martin, with Evelyn Wells, *No One Must Ever Know* (New York: Doubleday, 1959), 231.

17. Short and Stanley-Brown, *Public Buildings*, 389.

18. Stein, *Alone No More*, 171.

19. Feeny, *Fight against Leprosy*, 63–67, 141–144; Stein, *Alone No More*, 215–225.

20. Only 3 percent of the population is susceptible to the disease. Those infected are contagious only in the early stages, and only those in very close contact are at risk. Nonetheless, there are places in the world where contagion is still a concern. World Health Organization, *A Guide to Leprosy Control* (Geneva: WHO, 1980); American Medical Association, *Home Medical Encyclopedia* (New York: Random House, 1989), 634–635.

10. THE NEW ORLEANS CHARITY HOSPITAL

1. John Salvaggio, *New Orleans Charity Hospital: Story of Physicians, Politics, and Poverty* (Baton Rouge: Louisiana State University Press, 1992), 118; Merlin Kennedy, "Patients Sleep on Floor, Two to a Bed in Charity Hospital," *New Orleans Times-Picayune*, June 21, 1934.

2. Opposition of Orleans Parish Medical Society to Application for Loan from the Federal Emergency Administration for Public Works made by Charity Hospital at New Orleans, Louisiana through the Advisory Board of the State of Louisiana, November, 1933 (hereafter cited as Opposition I), 5–6, Reel 8461, Docket #La.4529, Microfilm Records of Non-Federal Projects, 1933–1947, Record Group 135, National Archives II (hereafter cited as Hospital Docket).

3. Salvaggio, *New Orleans Charity Hospital*, 126.

4. Alfred Danziger, Brief Submitted to the Federal Emergency Administration for Public Works through the Advisory Board of the State of Louisiana by the Board of Administrators of Charity Hospital at New Orleans in Furtherance of Its Application for a Loan to Be Used in Erecting and Equipping a New State Hospital, November 25, 1933 (hereafter cited as Brief), Reel 8461, Hospital Docket.

5. Carey Brown, Acting Chair, PWA Board of Review, to Danziger, May 17, 1934, Reel 8461, Hospital Docket.

6. Opposition of Orleans Parish Medical Society to Application for Loan from the Federal Emergency Administration for Public Works made by Charity Hospital at New Orleans, Louisiana through the Advisory Board of the State of Louisiana, May 11, 1934, Additional Data in Support of Contentions Advanced in Opponents' Brief of November 1933 (hereafter cited as Opposition II), Reel 8461, Hospital Docket.

7. Herman Deutch, "Long Takes Charge; Gives Up Pay Bed Plan for Charity," *New Orleans Item-Tribune*, June 21, 1934, Reel 8461, Hospital Docket.

8. Huey P. Long to Harold Ickes, August 11, 1934, Reel 8462, Hospital Docket.

9. Recommendations of the State Medicine and Legislative Committee Adopted by the Orleans Parish Medical Society at a Special Meeting Held August 6, 1934, Reel 8461, Hospital Docket.

10. Brief, Reel 8461, Hospital Docket.

11. PWA State Engineer Orloff Henry to Col. H. M. Waite, PWA Deputy Administrator, August 8, 1934, Reel 8461, Hospital Docket.

12. Henry to Waite, August 8, 1934; Lester M. Marx, Supplemental Report, August 23, 1934, Reel 8461, Hospital Docket.

13. Boulard, *Huey Long Invades New Orleans*, 168.

14. Delos Smith to Horatio Hackett, June 27, 1935; Hackett to Smith, July 5, 1935, Reel 8462, Hospital Docket.

15. "Holds Charity Hospital Tax Is Legal," *New Orleans States*, March 22, 1935.

16. Henry to Arthur J. Bulger, Director, PWA Engineering Division, August 16, 1937; Weiss to Bulger, May 3, 1938; Bulger to Weiss, May 12, 1938, Reel 8462, Hospital Docket.

17. Henry to Hackett, August 30, 1937, Reel 8462, Hospital Docket.

18. Marx, Report, May 14, 1937, 3, Reel 8462, Hospital Docket,

19. Harry M. Brown to Arthur Bulger, Director of the Engineering Division of PWA, February 10, 1939, Reel 8462, Hospital Docket.

20. Karl Terzaghi, "Final Report on the Settlement of the Charity Hospital Building in New Orleans, Louisiana," December 21, 1939, 2, 4; Hardy Cross, "Final Report on the Safety of the Superstructure of the Charity Hospital of Louisiana," July 12, 1939, Reel 8462, Hospital Docket; Frederick F. Wenderoth, PWA Engineer Examiner, Memo, December 12, 1939, Reel 8462, Hospital Docket; Salvaggio, *New Orleans Charity Hospital*, 142–143.

21. Fowler to Bulger, July 14, 1939; Bulger to Fowler, July 18, 1939; Perrilliat to PWA, February 25, 1939, Reel 8462, Hospital Docket.

22. Enrique Alferez in Salvaggio, *New Orleans' Charity Hospital*, 332–333; Kane, *Louisiana Hayride*, 206.

23. J. W. A. Richardson, assistant REI, pointed out to Mason that Monte Hart had used old conduit instead of new in an electrical installation. Mason said it was not a concern of the PWA as long as current was provided. Exhibit 83, July 7, 1939, Investigation of Alleged Graft and Change Order Irregularities, January 20, 1940, Reel 8465 (hereafter cited as Graft Investigation), Hospital Docket. Special Agent Gilbert Carter found Mason's records incomplete and his actions prior to the investigation lax. Carter, Memo, November 27, 1939, Exhibit 56, Graft Investigation. Regional Director George Bull, however, defended Mason's performance. Bull to Director, Engineering Division, January 25, 1940, Reel 8465, Hospital Docket.

24. W. Harold Skelly, PWA Examiner-Reviewer, to B. W. Thornton, Advisory Board on Contract Awards, January 4, 1940, Reel 8465, Hospital Docket.

25. Graft Investigation, Summary, 4, 6.

26. Gilbert Carter, Inspection of the Construction of Superstructure and Investigation of Alleged Irregularities, Except as to Change Orders, February 9, 1940, Reel 8465, Hospital Docket.

27. Stella O'Conner, "The Charity Hospital of Louisiana at New Orleans: An Administrative and Financial History, 1736–1941," *Louisiana Historical Quarterly* 31, no. 1 (January 1948): 5–109.

28. Salvaggio, *New Orleans' Charity Hospital*, 137.

29. Douglas L. Smith, *The New Deal in the Urban South* (Baton Rouge: Louisiana State University Press, 1988), 114.

30. Adam Nossiter, "Dispute Over Historic Hospital for the Poor Pits Doctors against the State," *New York Times*, December 17, 2005.

11. THE FRENCH MARKET

1. Robert Tittler, *Architecture and Power: The Town Hall and the English Urban Community, 1500–1640* (New York: Oxford University Press, 1991).

2. Title II, National Industrial Recovery Act, Public Law 67, *U.S. Statutes at Large* 48 (1934): 195.

3. H. L. Abbott, Engineering Division, Report on Loan Application, 5/13/35, Reel 7866, Docket #La.5914, Microfilm Records of Non-Federal Projects, 1933–1947, Records of the Public Works Administration, Record Group 135, National Archives II (hereafter cited as Market Docket).

4. Marta McBride Glaicki, "Outline of Architectural History" (New Orleans: Vieux Carre Commission, 1979); "French Market, New Orleans" (New Orleans: French Market, n.d.). These two pamphlets are the basis of the brief history of French Market buildings that follows.

5. Smith to Walmsley, December 6, 1933; "Housewives Pay 'Famine' Prices for Vegetables as Farmers Destroy Produce," *New Orleans Times-Picayune*, April 3, 1934; Smith to PWA, December 31, 1937, Reel 7867, Market Docket.

6. Architects' drawings, "French Market, New Orleans"; "French Market, Gallatin Street, Showing Farmers Market," February 6, 1934, Reel 7866, Market Docket. The drawings appear not to be Stone's; the initials on the bottom are H.G.M.

7. Emile V. Stier and James B. Kerling, *A Treatise on the Famous French Market of New Orleans* (New Orleans: French Market, 1938), 13, 41. This can be found in Hill Memorial Library, Louisiana State University. There is also a microfilm copy on Reel 7867, Market Docket.

8. Reuter to Roosevelt, March 21, 1938, Reel 7867, Market Docket.

9. Ickes to Reuter, March 16, 1938, Reel 7867, Market Docket.

12. THE SHREVEPORT INCINERATOR

1. Charles C. Phillips, "An Attractive Incinerator?" *Louisiana Architect* 4 (June 1965): 6–7.

2. Blueprints, Document 109, Reel 2606, Docket #La.3068, Microfilm Records of Non-Federal Projects, 1933–1947, Records of the Public Works Administration, Record Group 135, National Archives II (hereafter cited as Shreveport Docket). This Shreveport Docket, the city's first, subsumes eleven separate projects and runs for twelve reels of microfilm. There was a later attempt to give the projects separate numbers, but this was not followed in organizing the documents. Perhaps to mitigate this confusion, a document numbering system was used that does not appear in other dockets.

3. C. E. Olschner to Michael Straus, March 9, 1937, Document 1436, Reel 2607, Shreveport Docket; Olschner to John M. Ford, Shreveport Commissioner of Accounts and Finance, January 16, 1935, Document 3955, Reel 2608, Shreveport Docket.

4. Karen Kingsley, *Modernism in Louisiana: A Decade of Progress 1930–1940* (New Orleans: School of Architecture, Tulane University, 1984), 2.

5. Ford to Jones H. Aldersholt, Project Auditor, December 5, 1935, Document 8031, Reel 2609, Shreveport Docket; C. E. Olschner, "The Design of Municipal Incinerators," *American City* 50 (October 1935): 47–49.

6. Wiener to Hodges, February 18, 1939, Louisiana State University at Shreveport Archives. I am grateful to Karen Kingsley, Tulane University, for finding this.

7. Olschner, "Design of Municipal Incinerators," 47; Marcus D. Weeks, "Modern Municipal Incinerator," *Manufacturers Record* 93 (October 1935): 25, 58.

8. J. E. O'Leary to C. McDonough, PWA Director of Engineering, September 13, 1934, Document 2972; A. C. Felton Jr. to Incinerator Division, PWA, October 17, 1934, Documents 2879, 2607, Shreveport Docket.

9. Phillips, "Attractive Incinerator?" 6.

10. "Municipal Incinerator," *Architectural Forum* 63 (November 1935): 482–488; Lewis Mumford, "The Sky Line: The Golden Age in the West and South," *New Yorker*, April 30, 1938, 50.

11. Weeks, "Modern Municipal Incinerator," 25.

13. SUGAR

1. C. W. Steward, "A Brief Description of the Audubon Sugar School," unpublished ms., 1956?, Hill Memorial Library, Louisiana State University.

2. C. E Coates and A. G. Keller, "The Production of Direct Consumption Sugar in Louisiana and Its Possibilities for the Permanent Relief of Unemployment," Reel 5843, Docket #1029, Microfilm Records of Non-Federal Projects, 1933–1947, Records of the Public Works Administration, Record Group 135, National Archives II (hereafter cited as Sugar Docket).

3. Coates and Keller, "Production of Direct Consumption Sugar," 13.

4. Coates and Keller, "Production of Direct Consumption Sugar," 21–25.

5. Resolution of the Executive Committee of the American Sugar Cane League, May 29, 1935; Paul Hebert, LSU, to George Bull, PWA Regional Director, March 29, 1938, Reel 5843, Sugar Docket.

6. Andrews to Hopkins, July 13, 1936; Long to Hopkins, June 1, 1936; Fernandez to Graham, May 29, 1936; Overton to Ickes, July 14, 1936; Sandlin to Ickes, May 18, 1936; Sanders to Ickes, May 19, 1936, Reel 5843, Sugar Docket.

7. Col. Horatio Hackett, Asst. Administrator, PWA, to Overton, December 14, 1936; Coates to Hackett, December 18, 1936, Reel 5843, Docket #1026, PWA Microfilm.

8. Hebert, in George L. Kelly, PWA Engineer/Investigator, Memorandum Report, February 25, 1938, Reel 5843, Docket #1026, PWA Microfilm.

9. R. Charles Hodson Jr., "U.S. Sugar Policy since the 1930s," in Center for Louisiana Studies, *Green Fields: Two Hundred Years of Louisiana Sugar* (Lafayette: University of Southwestern Louisiana, 1980), 134–137.

14. THE NEW ORLEANS SEWER AND WATER PROJECT

1. David C. Perry, "Building the City through the Back Door: The Politics of Debt, Law, and Public Infrastructure," in Perry, *Building the Public City*, 203–214; Gail Rad-

ford, "From Municipal Socialism to Public Authorities: Institutional Factors in the Shaping of American Public Enterprise," *Journal of American History* 90, no. 3 (December 2003): 872; Alberta M. Sbragia, *Debt Wish: Entrepreneurial Cities, U.S. Federalism, and Economic Development* (Pittsburgh: University of Pittsburgh Press, 1996), 59–79.

2. David C. Perry, "Building the Public City: An Introduction," in Perry, *Building the Public City*, 5, table 1.1.

3. List of All Allotted Non-Federal Projects, All Programs, by State and Docket, as of May 30, 1942, 65–68, Federal Works Agency, Public Works Administration, Record Group 135, National Archives II.

4. Short and Stanley-Brown, *Public Buildings*, 445–447, 449, 455, 460, 465.

5. Reel 4801, Box 402, Record Group 135, Docket #9341, PWA Microfilm.

6. Welsh, Reels 5630–5631, Box 488, Docket #1273, PWA Microfilm; New Roads, Reel 5113, Box 511, Docket #1142, PWA Microfilm; Jackson, Reel 4811, Box 403, Docket #9203, PWA Microfilm; St. Joseph, Reels 3921–3922, Box 328, Docket #4887, PWA Microfilm; Logansport, Reel 8043, Box 672, Docket #6073, PWA Microfilm; Independence, Reels 4460–4461, Box 373, Docket #6387, PWA Microfilm; Sunset, Reel 4588, Box 384, Docket #6702, PWA Microfilm; Ringold, Reel 4897, Box 410, Docket #8801, PWA Microfilm.

7. Metarie, Reels 5856–5857, Box 490, Docket #1203, PWA Microfilm.

8. Pierce F. Lewis, *New Orleans: The Making of an Urban Landscape* (Cambridge, Mass.: Ballinger, 1976), 17–30.

9. Lewis, *New Orleans*, 9.

10. Craig E. Colten, *An Unnatural Metropolis: Wresting New Orleans from Nature* (Baton Rouge: Louisiana State University Press, 2005), 38–40.

11. Colten, *Unnatural Metropolis*, 83–90.

12. Gus Llambias, Special Counsel to the Sewerage and Water Board, to PWA, April 16, 1934, Reel 3528, Box 295, Docket #4284, PWA Microfilm (hereafter cited as New Orleans Docket); "Sewerage and Water Board Has Made Enviable Record," *New Orleans States*, December 6, 1934; Orloff Henry, PWA State Engineer, to Arthur J. Bulger, Director of Engineering Division, PWA, October 29, 1936, Reel 3538, New Orleans Docket.

13. Lewis, *New Orleans*, 61–62; Colten, *Unnatural Metropolis*, 92–93.

14. Lewis, *New Orleans*, 62; James Gill, "Pols Evacuate En Masse to Holland," *New Orleans Times-Picayune*, January 13, 2006.

15. Colten, *Unnatural Metropolis*, 94, 100.

16. George G. Earl, "Status as to Sewerage, Water, and Main Drainage Improvements for New Orleans," March 16, 1927, Reel 3528, New Orleans Docket.

17. Emergency Relief and Reconstruction Act of 1933, 709.

18. Williams, *Grants in Aid*, 232–236; Barber, *From New Era to New Deal*, 177–178; Olson, *Herbert Hoover*, 77.

19. Llambias to PWA, April 16, 1933, Reel 3532, New Orleans Docket.

20. "Sixty-ninth Semi-Annual Report of the Sewerage and Water Board of New Orleans," 8, 14, Reel 3528, New Orleans Docket.

21. Field, "Politics of the New Deal," 132.

22. Field, "Politics of the New Deal," 134–135.

23. "Two Court Attacks Opened on State Act Establishing New Sewerage Board Here," *New Orleans Times-Picayune*, December 6, 1934.

24. Gaston Porterie to Alfred Theard, General Superintendent, Sewerage and Water Board, October 2, 1935; Edward H. Foley, PWA General Counsel, to Ickes, October 18, 1935, Reel 3528, New Orleans Docket; Field, "Politics of the New Deal," 246.

25. Colten, *Unnatural Metropolis*, 100–101. Colten gives the credit to the WPA, not the PWA. It is quite possible that WPA workers were involved as well. Walter K. Grant, Municipal Engineer to Bryson Valles, General Supervisor, Sewerage and Water Board, Reel 3528, New Orleans Docket.

26. A. B. Wood, Mechanical Engineer, to Theard, October 8, 1936; Wood to Henry, November 5, 1936; Robert D. Maestri, Mayor, to Sewerage and Water Board, September 1, 1936, Reel 3528, New Orleans Docket.

27. Wood to Henry, November 5, 1936; Henry to Arthur J. Bulger, Director, Engineering Division, PWA, November 20, 1936, Reel 3528, New Orleans Docket.

28. Charles F. Holman, PWA Special Agent, "Investigation to Determine Whether Labor Unions Were Responsible for Burning of Dredge Boat Used on PWA Docket 4285, New Orleans, Louisiana," September 5, 1935, Reel 3532; C. L. Crowell, REI, to A. W. George, PWA State Engineer/Inspector, November 12, 1935, Reel 3529; Crowell to George, November 21, 1945, Reel 3528; Felix O. Cox, PWA Special Agent, "Investigation to Determine the Means by Which Copies of Correspondence Emanating from the Office of C. L. Crowell, Chief REI, PWA, New Orleans, Louisiana Were Obtained by H. B. Banister, Labor Union Agent," January 29, 1936, Reel 3532, New Orleans Docket.

29. J. E. Fitzmorris, Gen. Taylor St. Property Owners Assn., to A. G. Moffatt, July 1, 1937; Weiss and Weiss, Attorneys for Bethany Evangelical Church, to Sewerage and Water Board, April 1, 1939, Reel 3529, New Orleans Docket.

30. Christopher Drew and Andrew C. Revkin, "Design Flaws Seen in Orleans Food Walls," *New York Times*, September 21, 2005; Alan Levin, "Shortcuts Alleged in Building Levees," *USA Today*, November 3, 2005; Alan Levin and Pete Eisler, "Many Decisions Led to Failed Levees, *USA Today*, November 3, 2005; Nicholai Ouroussoff, "How the City Sank," *New York Times*, October 9, 2005.

15. BEYOND THE BAYOUS

1. The PWA did not originate the ferry, but it added three new boats to the fleet at a cost of almost $3 million. Short and Stanley-Brown, *Public Buildings*, 600.

2. "PWA Has Changed Face of U.S.," *Life*, April 1, 1940, 62.

3. "No Vote against School Bond Issue," *Bunkie Record*, August 18, 1938.

4. "PWA Has Changed Face of U.S.," 62.

5. Watkins, *Righteous Pilgrim*, 378–379.

INDEX

Page numbers in **bold** indicate illustrations.

A. J. Rife Construction Company, 159–60
Abbeville, 57
Addams, Jane, 12, 13, 272n4
African Americans, xv, 4, 13–14, 36, 53, 103; and higher education, 94, 96–97; Ickes's actions in behalf of, 15–16; and Jim Crow laws, 122–23; job discrimination against, 61, 64; and public schools, 77, 85–88
Agricultural Adjustment Act, 10, 49
Agricultural Adjustment Administration, 165
Aldrich, W. R., 175
Alex Box Stadium, xx, 103
Alexandria, 35; L. S. Rugg Elementary school, **79**; swimming pool, 53, 60. *See also* Rapides Parish Courthouse
Alexandria Town Talk, 121–22
Alferez, Enrique, 145–46, **146**, 147
Alfred P. Tureaud Elementary School, 89, **89**
Alice in Wonderland, 24
Allaire, Alexander, 144
Allen, Oscar K. "O.K.," 29, 30, 37, 139
Allen, Robert, 56, 67
Alumni Hall, 93
American City, 159
American Sugar Cane League, 163
Amite, 64–65
Amos and Andy, 29
Andrews, W. G., 184
Annie Boyd Hall, 65
Arizona, 181

Army Corps of Engineers, 54, 131
art deco, xxi, **xxiv**, xxv, 119, 181; courthouses, 110–14, **114**, 116, **116**, **117**, **119**; public school buildings, 49, 78–80, **83**, 88, **88**; university buildings, 95, **97**, 100, **100**, 101
Atkinson Hall, xx
Audubon Sugar School, 162, 184
Avoca ferry, 53, **54**

Baker, John A., **73**, **80**
Bannister, H. D., 174
Barksdale Field, 130–31
Baron and Roberts, **78**, **79**
Barre, Vermont, xxii
Barton, Vermont, xxii
Bastrop, 131
Baton Rouge, xviii–xxi, 34, 36, 37, 41, 57, 61; Capitol Annex, **xxiii**, 49; Police Department (Louisiana State School for the Deaf), 84, **84**; Public Library (Capitol Area United Way), **xix**
Bayou St. John, 170
Bell City, 78
Berle, Adolph, 51
Bernice, 48
Bethany Evangelical Church, 175
Biedenharn Hall, **97**
"big government," 184
Blair, A. Farnell, 22
Blanco, Gov. Katherine Babineaux, 171
Bodman and Murrell, **xxiv**, 83
Bogard Hall, 99
Bois Courier, Bayou, 131

291

INDEX

Bond and Tax Board, 38, 46, 141, 173
Bonita, 78
Bossier City High School, xxix, 71, 78, 86–87
Bradford Hall, **105**
Brass, Edward, 22
Broussard, Edmund, 32
Broussard Hall, **102**
Brown, Harry M., 144
Brown, REI Horace R., 65, 66
Brezner, Barnet, 67
Building "G," 57
Bulber Auditorium, **95**
Bulger, Arthur J., 77
Bull, George, 96
Bunkie, 183
Burdick, Rep. Usher, 46
Burk, William R., **39, 75**
Burns, H. E., 159–60

Cabot, Vermont, xxii
Caddo Parish, 85
Café du Monde, 155
Calcasieu Parish, 94, 167, **168**
Calcasieu River, 167
Caldwell, George, 56, 57–58
Caldwell, Summerfield "Summa," 57, 67
Caldwell, Tom, 57
Caldwell, Vernon, 57
Caldwell Brothers and Hart, 57, 58, 65, 67
Caldwell Parish Courthouse, 61, **115**
Camelia, lighthouse tenders in, 131
Cameron Parish Courthouse, 21, 49, 109, **109**, 113, 116
Campbell Hall, **101**
Canal Street, 176
canning, 75
Capitol Annex, xx, **xxiii**, 49
Carlin, Bayou, 131
Carmody, John, 54
Carter, Special Agent Gilbert B., 147
Carter, Hodding, 33, 35, 36
Carville (Gillis Long Hansen's Disease Center), 133–37, **135**, **136**

Catchings, Waddill, 52
Chalmette battlefield, 132
Charity Hospital, 138–48, **142, 143, 144**
Chicago, Illinois, xxiv–xxv; Ashland Ave. Bridge, xxiv; Cook County Hospital, xxiv; DuSable High School, xxiv; Lake Michigan shoreline, xxiv; Outer Drive Bridge, xxiv, xxv; sewage system, 167
Christy, Edgar A., **81, 88**
"chronological connectivity," 117–18
Citadel, 180
Civil Works Administration (CWA), 6, 25, 27, 54, 93, 130, 172
Civilian Conservation Corps (CCC), xxii, 5–6, 11, 16, 25, 26, 45, 181, 270n11
Clayton, 78
Clinton, 87
Coates, Charles E., 163, 164
Collier, John, 13
colonialization of the Southern economy, 10
Columbia, **115**
Como Park Zoo, xxi
Concordia Parish, 109
Corondelet Canal, 170
Country Life Movement, 4, 74
Coushatta, 86, **86**
Covington, 48, 87
Cross, Hardy, 144
Crowell, REI C. L., 174
Crutcher, Joseph H., 46
Cyr, Paul, 30

Dallas, Texas, 181
Danziger, Alfred, 139–40
Davis, P. M., 21–22
Dear, Cleveland, 32, 45
"dee ducts," 145
Desoto Parish, 72, 75, 76
Drainage Commission, 171
Drew, Harmon, 34
Duncan, Herman J., **109**

Earl, George G., 171
Early, Harry J., 32, 38, 46

East Carroll Parish, 110
East Point, 86
Eccles, Marriner, 52
Ellender, Allen, 139
Emergency Relief and Construction Act, 5, 172
Emergency Relief Appropriations Act of 1935, 25, 38
Employment Stabilization Act of 1931, 129
Evangeline Hall, 94

Fall, Albert, 21
Farley, James, 28, 32–33, 46
Farm Security Administration, 6, 11, 26, 30, 32
Farnsworth and Company, 126
Favrot and Reed, **xix**, **84**
Fechner, Robert, 6, 8
Federal Emergency Relief Administration, 6
Federal Housing Administration, 8, 111, 157
federalism: cooperative, 5, 123; dual, 5
Fernandez, J. O., 164
Fleming, Major General Philip B., 36, 54
Ford, John M., 159
Fort Knox, Kentucky, Gold Depository, 180
Fort Necessity High School, **73**
Fort Pulaski, Georgia, 180
Fort Worth, Texas, 181
Foster, Rufus, 32
Foster, William, 52
Fowler, Charles, 145
Francis T. Nicholls Vocational School, 71, 78, **81**
Franklinton, 48, 72, 76, 78, **80**
Frederick Douglass High School, 71, 78, **81**
Fredericks Auditorium, 102, **103**
French Market, 149–56, **149**, **150**, **152**, **153**; as produce market, 151, 153–54; as "tourist destination," 154–55
French Market Corporation, 151, 152, 155

Gillis Intermediary School, 59
Gillis Long Hansen's Disease Center, 133–37, **135**, **136**
Glavis, Louis, 22, 273n32
Grace King Hall, 94
Grambling University, xxviii, 96–97, 103; Long-Jones Hall, **98**
Grand Bayou, 86
Grandison Hall, **106**
"greco-deco," xxv, 111, 112, 114
Greenwood, 72
Grosjean, Alice Lee, 30
Groz, L. A., **xix**

Hackberry Bayou, 131
Hackett, Col. Horatio, 85, 141
Hall Summit, 86
Hamlin, Talbot, 119
Hammond, xxv, 35, 65. *See also* Southeastern Louisiana University
Hanna, 62, **63**, 86
Hansen, Alvin, 52
Hansen, Dr. Gerhard Henrik Armauer, 136
Hargett, Fred L., 76–77
Hart, Monte, 56, 58, 65, 67
Harvey, 151
Hathaway, 60, 78, 85
Hebert, Paul, 67–68, 164
Henry, Orloff, 33, 36, 140, 142
Hodges, L. A., 159
home economics, xxvii, 4, 25, 74–76, **75**, **76**, 77, 81, 86
Hoover, Herbert, 4, 26, 35, 50; and Ickes, 15; and public works, 5, 18, 129–30, 172
Hoover (Boulder) Dam, 8, 150, 181
Hopkins, Harry, xviii, 4, 8, 25, 32, 38, 46, 164
Houma, 131; Terrebonne High School, 71, **79**; Terrebonne Parish Courthouse, 112, **113**, **114**
Houston, Texas, 181
Howell, Roland B., 33
Hill, Lister, 9

Himes Hall, xx, **xxi**, 95
Hudgens, Robert W. "Pete," 30
Huey P. Long Bridge, 35–36, **38**
Hunter, 76
Hurricane Audrey, 109
Hurricane Katrina, xxix, 81, 88, 142, **142**, **143**, 148, 153, 155, 171, 176
Hurricane Rita, 109, **109**
Hutson, Miles, 22

Iberia Parish Courthouse, 112–13, **115**
Ickes, Harold L., xviii, xxvi; early career, 12–13; and French Market, 155; and Herbert Hoover, 15; and Richard Leche, 46; and Huey Long, 30, 33, 36–42, 173; and planning, 8; and public investment, v, 11; PWA Administrator, appointed as, 23–24; racial discrimination, action against, 16, 61, 279n16; and recession of 1937, 51; and Franklin Roosevelt, 15; and Theodore Roosevelt, 14–15; scandal, fear of, xxvii, 20–22, 24, 68; Special Board for Public Works, chairs, 18; and WPA, 25–26
Independence, 168
Indian Camp Plantation, 134
infrastructure, xix, 27, 110, 137, 167, 176, 269n4; cultural, xviii, **xix**, **xx**, xxvi, xxvii, 71–108; and economic development in the South, 9–11, 165; physical, xviii, xxvi, xxviii, 4, 72, 129–80

Jackson, 168
Jackson, E. N., 56, 67
Jackson Parish Courthouse, 113–14, **118**
Jeanerette, 61, 131
Jennings, 23, **75**, 77, 85, 87
Jim Crow laws, 122–23
Johnson, Gen. Hugh, 23–24
Johnson, Lyndon, 9
Johnson's Bayou, 131
Jones, E. W., 85
Jones, Jesse, 8

Jones, Roessle, Olschner, and Wiener, 86, 157, 158–61, **158**
Jonesboro, 113–14, **118**

Kane, Harnett, 46–47, 65–66
Kansas City, 181
Kaufmann Hall, **96**
Keller, Arthur G., 163, 164
Kelly, 48, 78
Key West Overseas Highway, 180
Keynes, John Maynard, 3, 52
Kinder High School, 25

Lafayette. *See* University of Louisiana at Lafayette
Lafayette City Hall (French Cultural Center), **xix**
Lafourche, 72
LaGuardia Airport, 150
Lake Borgne, 170
Lake Charles, 167, **168**. *See also* McNeese State University
Lake Pontchartrain, 57, 155, 170
Lake Providence, 45, 53, 76–77, 85. *See also* East Carroll Parish
Lamoille River, Vermont, xxii
Land, H. H., **64**
Leche, Richard, xxvii, 45–46, 58, 86–87, 142, 145–46
leprosy, 133–34, 284n20
Liddieville, 76–77
"lighted highway," 131
Lighthouses, Bureau of, 131
Lilienthal, David, 7
Lincoln Parish, 96–97
Link, Theodore C., 92
Logansport, 168
London Ave. drainage canal, 171, 174
Long, Huey P., xxvi–xxvii, xxix, xxx, 9, 93; Bond and Tax Board, use of, 38, 39–40, 93; Charity Hospital project, support for, 36, 39; "dee ducts," use of, 145; early career, 28–29; and Ickes, 30, 33, 39, 42; LSU, interest in, 92; and New Orleans

sewer project, 37; and Old Regulars, xxx, 31–32, 37, 40, 141, 172, 174; PWA projects, possible use against, 34–37, 40–41, 47, 141; and Franklin Roosevelt, 28, 30, 32–33, 36–38, 53; Share Our Wealth Plan, 53; on James Monroe Smith, 58
Long, Rose, 164
Long-Jones Hall, **98**
Lorio, Dr. Clarence, 56
Louise Garig Hall, 65
Louisiana National Guard, 41, 137, 140
Louisiana Polytechnic Institute. *See* Louisiana Tech University
"Louisiana scandals," 59; 65–68
Louisiana State Exposition Building, 49, **49**, **50**, 63
Louisiana State School for Deaf and Blind Negro Children, 94
Louisiana State School for the Deaf, 84, **84**
Louisiana State University (LSU), xviii, xxvii, 36, 39–40, 46, 56–59, 92–94, 137, 139, 148; Alex Box Stadium, xx, 103; Alumni Hall (School of Journalism), 93; Annie Boyd Hall, 65; Atkinson Hall, xx; Evangeline Hall, 94; Faculty Club, **xxii**, 95; Geology Building, xx, 59, 65–68, 95–96; Grace King Hall, 94; Himes Hall, xx, **xxi**, 95; Louise Garig Hall, 65, 94; Medical Center, 58, 101; Nicholson Hall, 104; Panhellenion, 57, 104; Parker Coliseum, xx, 6, **7**, 25, 104; Student Health Center, xx, 103; Sugar Factory, xx, xxviii, xxix, 47–48, 49, 162–65, **165**; Tiger Stadium, xx, 103; university lakes, xviii, 104; women's dormitories, xx, 49, 65, **66**, 94
Louisiana Tech University (Louisiana Polytechnic Institute), 58, 93, 97–99, 100, 102, 104
Luce, Henry, 183

Magnolia, lighthouse tenders in, 131
Maple, John, 22

Marie C. Courvent Elementary School, 89, **89**
Marthaville, 60
Martin, 78, 86
Marx, Lester, 140, 143
Mason, REI Edmund B., 61, 144, 145
Maurepas, **39**, 72
Maurice, 61, 131
Mayan architecture, **109**, 116, **118**
McClimans Hall, 99, **99**
McDonough, John C., 85
McLachlan, Mrs. James, 56, 57
McNaspy Stadium, 105
McNeese State University, 94, 103; Bulber Auditorium, **95**; Kaufmann Hall, **96**
Mead Hall, 99
Mermantau, **78**
Metarie, 56, 168
Minden, 34–35
Minnesota, University of, xxii
Minnesota State Fair Grounds, xxi
Miserie, Lake, 131
modernism, 100, 102, 110–13, **115**, 119, 157–58, 160, 273n36
Moley, Raymond, 3, 15, 21, 28, 277n23
Monroe, 62, **64**, 74. *See also* University of Louisiana at Monroe
Monticello, 77, 78
Mooringsport, 63, **169**
Morgan, A. E., 6–7
Morgan, Harcourt, 7
Morgan City, 54
Morgenthau, Henry, 51, 132
Morning Call, 151, 154, 155
Mt. Mansfield, Vermont, xxii
Museum of Modern Art, xxix, 157
Mumford, Lewis, 157, 160
Myers, W. R., 63–64

Napoleonville Colored School, 87
Natatorium, **104**
Natchitoches, 60, 76; fish hatchery, 131; high school, 71, 78, **82**; Natchitoches

Parish Courthouse, 116, **119**. *See also* Northwestern State University
National Association for the Advancement of Colored People (NAACP), 13
National Industrial Recovery Act (NIRA), 16–17, 20, 49
National Recovery Administration, 16, 23, 273n37
Neild, Edward F., Jr., 102, **103**, **121**
Neild, Somdal, and Neild, **xxiii**, **49**, **50**
Netherlands, xxix, 110, 111, 157, 159, 171
New Basin Canal, 172
"New Canal," 170
New Orleans, xxviii, xxix, xxx, 26, 33, 48, 57, 63, 133; airmail beacon lights to, 131; Huey P. Long Bridge, 35–36, **38**; Intercoastal Waterway to, 131; Jim Crow Laws in, 122–23; lighthouses serving, 131; and Old Regulars, 31–32, 37, 40–41; schools, 71, 78, 84–85, 88, **88**
New Orleans States, 56, 93
New Roads, 168
New York City, 159, 167, 171, 180
New York Museum of Modern Art, 157
New Yorker, 157
Nicholls, Gov. Francis T., 122
Nicholson Hall, 104
Nolan, William T., **63**, **73**, **82**, **86**, 103, **105**, **106**
Nolan, Ulisse, **73**, 103, **105**, **106**
Northwestern State University, 94, 102, **102**, 103, **103**, 104–5, **104**; Fredericks Auditorium, 102, **103**; Natatorium, **104**; Varnado Hall, 102

Oglethorpe University, 3
Okaloosa, 74
Old Regulars, xxx, 31–32, 37, 40–41, 141, 172, 174
Olschner, Clarence, 158–60
O'Malley, Clint, 35
Orange Bowl, 180
Oregon, 182
Orleans Parish Medical Society, 138–40
Overton, Sen. John, 32, 98, 164

Panhellenion, 57
Parker, John, 32
Parker Coliseum, xx, 6, **7**, 25, 104
Pearson, Drew, 56, 67
Pepper, Claude, 9
Perkins, Frances, 19, 23–24, 46
Perrier, Theodore L., **118**
Perrilliat, Claiborne, 145
Peterman, Frank, 38, 46
Petite Anse, Bayou, 131
pilaster, 112–16, **115**, **116**
Plaquemine, 131, **132**
"pork," 182–83
Port Allen Middle School, xxi, **xxiv**, 49, 78, 80
Pottle Music Building, 100, **100**
Poydras St., 170
Progressives, 4, 13–15, 32, 74
Public Health Service, 134–35
public jobs, 17, 27; vs. direct relief, 17; vs. work relief, 17–18
Public Roads, Bureau of, xxix, 18, 132
Public Works Administration (PWA): defaults on loans, 48; Engineering Division, 8, 19, 22, 24; federal projects, 18, 19, 54, 129–37; Finance Division, 8, 19, 22, 24, 36, 93, 172; freeze, 40–42, **43–44**, 45, 47, 93, 173; FWA, subsumed under, 53–54; Housing Division, 26; Investigations Division, xxviii, 22, 24, 59–65, 164; Legal Division, 8, 19, 22, 24, 172; Huey Long, possible use of projects against, 34–37, 40–42, 47, 141; and "Louisiana scandals," 59, 65–68; NIRA, created by, 16; non-federal projects, 18–20, 22–23, 24; in other states, xxi–xxii, xxiv–xxv, 167, 180–83; policies, 20–23, 41, 59; political appointments in, 33; post offices, 131–32, **132**; racial bias in projects, 85–88; racial discrimination, action against, 16, 61; revolving fund, 48, 51; slowness of, 24, 184; structure, xxvii, 8, 19–20, 26, 59, 93; Subsistence Homesteads Division, 26;

WPA, confusion with, xviii, 61, 164, 282n1, 290n25; WPA, projects transferred to, xxv, 26, 53, 94; WPA, relationship to, 6, 25–26; WWII, contribution to, 129, 130–31
Pumping Station # 21, **175**
PWA Moderne, xxi, xxv, xxviii, 111–20, 282n5

Rapides Parish Courthouse, 116–17, **120**, 121–22, **121**
Rayne, 78
Reconstruction Finance Corporation (RFC), 5, 8, 11, 18, 35, 38, 172, 181
Red River Parish, 61, 62, 86, **86**, 87
relief, direct, "the dole," xxiv, 17, 40, 163, 183. *See also* work relief
"Report on Economic Conditions of the South" (1938), xxviii, 9, 10, 123
Resettlement Administration, 6, 11, 26, 30, 32
Reuter, J. Richard, 155
Rife Construction Company. *See* A. J. Rife Construction Company
Righton, Edward, 33, 36, 37
Ringgold, 168
River Walk, San Antonio, Texas, 150
Road to Plenty, 52
Robert, Lawrence, 20, 21
Roosevelt, Franklin D., xvii, 182; administrative style, 5, 23; and the CCC, 5–6; and court-packing, 49–50; and the CWA, 25; and economic development, xxviii; economic orthodoxy of, 3, 50–51; and Harold Ickes, 15–16; and Richard Leche, 45–46; and Huey Long, 28, 30–33, 36, 38, 40, 52–53, 110; and the NIRA, 16–17; and the recession of 1937, 51, 53
Rosenwald, Julius, 4
Rugg Elementary School, **79**
Ruston High School, 71, **76**, 78, 80, **83**

San Francisco, California, 23, 157, 167, 181
Sanders, J. Y., Jr., 164

Sanders, J. Y., Sr., 32, 35
Sandlin, John, 32, 45, 164
Saussy, Dr. Juliette, 148
Sawyer, Col. Donald, 18
Scotlandville. *See* Southern University
Seattle, Washington, 182
Secret Diary of Harold L. Ickes, 33, 39, 40
Seekers Springs Ministry Retreat Center, 74
"self-liquidating" public works, 18, 23, 172
Seventeenth Street drainage canal, 171
Sewerage and Water Board, 33, 37, 170–71, 172
Shady Grove, **82**
Share Our Wealth Plan, 53
Shreveport, 22, 34, 45, 130, 151; Municipal Auditorium, **34**; parks, 87; schools, 48, 72, 76, 85
Shreveport incinerator, xxix, 157–61
Shreveport Journal, 56
Simpson, 78
Skyline Drive, xxii
Smith, D. Curtis, 114, **118**
Smith, Delos, 141
Smith, Gerald L. K., 45
Smith, J. W., **xx**, **83**, 95, **97**, **115**, **119**
Smith, James Monroe, 40, 56, 58–59, 67
Smith, Mrs. A. V., 153–54
Smoky Mountain Parkway, xxii
Southeastern Louisiana University, 93, 99–100, 102, 103; Campbell Hall, **101**; McClimans Hall, **99**; Pottle Music Building, **100**
Southern University, xxviii, 94, 102–3; Bradford Hall, **105**; Grandison Hall, **106**
Special Board of Public Works, 18–24, 41
Squire, George L., 164
St. Bernard Parish, 113, **116**, **117**
St. Helena Parish, xxv, 109
St. Joseph, 168
St. Joseph Community Center, **xx**
St. Landry Parish Courthouse, 114, **118**
St. Louis, Missouri, 181

Stein, Stanley, 134
Stone, Frank, 154
Stone, Sam, Jr., **149, 150, 152, 153**, 154, **154**
Straus, Michael, 158
Sugar Act of 1934, 164
Sugar Factory, xx, xxviii, xxix, 47–48, 49, 162–65, **165**
Sunset, 168

Talmadge, Eugene, 9, 45
Tangipahoa Parish, 110
Teapot Dome, 21
Tennessee Valley Authority, 6–7, 8, 158
Terrebonne High School, 71, **79**
Terrebonne Parish, 26
Terrebonne Parish Courthouse, 49, 112, **113, 114**
Terzagji, Karl, 144
Tigre, Bayou, 131
Time, 28
Times-Picayune, 145, 154
Town, A. Hays, 112–13, **115**
Treasury Department, xxix, 8, 18, 20, 51, 129, 131–32, 134
Triborough Bridge, 150
Tugwell, A. P., 36, 96–97
Tugwell, Rexford, 6, 8, 19, 46, 51
Tulane University, 28, 31, 145

underconsumption, 11, 52–53; in the Southern economy, 10
University of Louisiana at Lafayette, xxv, 100–1; Campbell Hall, **101**, 102, **102**, 104–5; Pottle Music Building, **100**
University of Louisiana at Monroe, 94–95, 103; Biedenharn, 95, **97**
U.S.S. Yorktown, 129

Van Os, Seymour, 34
Varnado Hall, 102

Vernon Parish, 108
Vidalia, 132, **133**

Waite, Col. Henry, 23
Walmsley, T. Semmes, 31, 35–36, 153, 172
Weeks, REI Marcus D., 64, 160
Weiss, Leon, 56, 58, 66, 68, 144, 145, 147
Weiss, Dreyfous, and Seiferth, 67, 68, 92, 94, 99, 101, 141, 142; Charity Hospital, **142, 144, 146**; Natchitoches High School, **82**; St. Bernard Parish Courthouse, **116, 117**; university buildings, **xxi, xxii**, 66, **95, 96, 99, 100, 101, 102, 104**
Welsh, 168
Westwego, 151
White Castle, **73**
Whitney, John M., 77
Wiener, Samuel, xxix, **34**, 86, **158**, 158–60
Willis, Special Agent Doyle H., 60, 68
Winnsboro, 76, 78
Wogan and Bernard, **79, 113, 114**
Wood, A. Baldwin, 171, 176
work relief, 3, 17–18, 19, 25, 31, 36, 46, 52
Works Progress Administration (WPA), 11, 40, 45–46, 48, 65, 103, 150; courthouses built by, xxvi, 109; FWA, subsumed under, 53–54; Long's work programs, compared with, 29; and "Louisiana scandals," xxvii, 24, 56–57, 67; at LSU, xviii–xx, **7**, 25, 57, 103–4, 164; neutrality attempted by, 32; political appointments to, 38, 46; projects in other states, xxii, xxiv; PWA, confusion with, xviii, 61, 164, 282n1, 290n25; PWA, relations with, 6, 25–26; PWA projects transferred to, xxv, 26, 53, 94; and racial discrimination, 61; Strawberry Stadium built by, xxv, 99, 103; and Sugar Factory, 163–64; and war preparation, 26; as work relief, 17–18
Wright, Frank Lloyd, 100, **101**, 116